MICHAEL DOBBS

FIRST LADY

Also by Michael Dobbs and published by Headline

Churchill's Triumph

Other novels by Michael Dobbs

Winston Churchill Series
Winston's War
Never Surrender
Churchill's Hour

Tom Goodfellowe series
Goodfellowe MP
The Buddha of Brewer Street
Whispers of Betrayal

Francis Urquhart series
House of Cards
To Play The King
The Final Cut

Other Titles
Wall Games
Last Man to Die
The Touch of Innocents

MICHAEL DOBBS

FIRST LADY

headline

First published in 2006
by HEADLINE PUBLISHING GROUP

1

Cataloguing in Publication Data is available from the British Library

0 7553 2683 0 (hardback ISBN-10)
9 780 7553 2683 9 (hardback ISBN-13)
0 7553 2684 9 (trade paperback ISBN-10)
9 780 7533 2684 6 (trade paperback ISBN-13)

Typeset in Hoefler by Avon DataSet Ltd,
Bidford on Avon, Warwickshire

Printed and bound in Great Britain by
Clays Ltd, St Ives plc

Headline's policy is to use papers that are natural, renewable and
recyclable products and made from wood grown in sustainable forests.
The logging and manufacturing processes are expected to conform
to the environmental regulations of the country of origin.

HEADLINE PUBLISHING GROUP
A division of Hachette Livre UK Ltd.
338 Euston Road
London NW1 3BH

www.headline.co.uk
www.hodderheadline.com

To Nonie.

'Nothing can seem foul to those that win.'

– *William Shakespeare, I Henry IV.*

Part One

One

NIGHT. THE WITCHING HOUR. That time when the air grows thick and men are prone to stumble in the darkness. And it is those with their heads in the clouds who somehow stumble hardest of all.

It seemed a night in Westminster like any other, one that began in ways so commonplace that it gave no clue as to the rare follies that were to follow. As the world of Westminster started to move into stand-by mode, its offices emptied and its hostelries and watering-holes began to fill.

A distraught parliamentary researcher stood on Westminster Bridge, gazing at the reflection of the moon in the turbid waters of the Thames. She was contemplating bringing all her miseries to an end, but the waters at low tide are no more than six feet deep and this muddy pond seemed in no way fitting for the profound depths of her despair. So, instead, she turned and walked back to the Red Lion, hoping that by now her prayers had been answered and her unfaithful lover had met an unnatural and exquisitely painful death.

Her route took her past Portcullis House, the clumsy bronze and glass parliamentary office building that glowers across the street from Big Ben. In the subway beneath, a homeless man was trying to find comfort from the night by lying on a bed of corrugated cardboard. He wasn't supposed to be there; in fact, according to those crowding the bars directly above his head, he wasn't supposed to exist. Homelessness was 'no longer an issue', in the words of the Minister. But, nevertheless, here he was, as good as calling the

Minister a liar. A young police constable ordered him on, and when he was slow in responding, the officer encouraged him with the toe of his polished boot. Not a kicking, nothing brutal, little more than an idle nudge designed to get him on his way. No malice intended. Like clearing up litter. But the tramp's liver, swollen from years of abuse, had dropped beneath his ribcage, just at the point where the boot struck. In its fragile state the liver began to bleed, and since his body chemistry was all screwed up the blood wouldn't clot. He would soon be in a police cell, warm, at least, but by the time the duty surgeon had arrived, three hours after he had been summoned, the tramp was dead. They never did discover his name, and his former wife and two rapacious kids back home in Colchester never found out what had happened to him. Not that they cared.

Yet it was what was about to happen in the room gazing out from a red-brick building on the North Bank, across from the slowly turning wheel of the London Eye, that was to transform the life of Virginia Edge. Ginny herself wasn't there: she was putting the children to bed in her home eighty miles away, yet her world was about to be wrenched from its foundations. The room in the red-brick building was part of the complex that had once been known as New Scotland Yard when it housed the head-quarters of the Metropolitan Police, but had since been renamed after its architect, Norman Shaw, and was now encompassed in the ever-extending sprawl of offices that stretched out from the main parliament building. Here, beneath the shadow of Big Ben, the Leader of the Opposition has his official rooms. During the day they bustled but, with the coming of night, the frenzy had begun to fade and slowly grow quiet. A time for reflection and relaxation.

Colin Penrith enjoyed these moments as much as any in his overcrowded life. He was a widower, his home full of silence and ghosts, and these moments at the ebb tide of evening, when his staff had been dismissed and the telephone ceased its insistent ringing, were precious, to be shared only with those closest to him.

The affair he had been conducting with one of his colleagues wasn't particularly sordid by Westminster standards: he had no ties and she was married to a distant and rather dull husband who laid no claim to virtue himself, so it seemed harmless enough, usually little more than a few disturbed cushions and a spilled glass of wine in a room lit only by the street-lamps of the Embankment. It was a casual but not infrequent arrangement that suited them both, a tangling of minds and bodies that neither laid claim to their hearts nor got mixed up with their other responsibilities. And sometimes, afterwards, as this evening, they would sit and say little, sharing the warmth of each other's body, their attention focused on nothing more demanding than the gentle blinking of the Eye from the other side of the river, until the tolling of the thirteen-ton bell of Big Ben dragged them back to the moment. She rose.

'Another drink, darling?'

She crossed to the cupboard where he hid the bottles. From outside came the sound of a police siren racing through the night. Another security alarm, but there were so many in these ever-watchful days that no one any longer took much notice. Anyway, they were safe here, tucked away behind the fortress of barricades and scanners that had been thrown round the Palace of Westminster. No one had been killed here since Airey Neave, the Member of Parliament whose car had been blown up by Irish terrorists almost thirty years before. Come to think of it, the car had exploded on the ramp to the underground car park, right across from where they were . . .

'Colin?' She turned, glasses in hand.

He was sitting slumped on the sofa, his palm pressed to his forehead. 'Something's happened,' he said, gazing at her, his eyes watery, troubled. 'It's gone wrong.'

'What's gone wrong?' she asked. But he didn't answer. Slowly, like an old tree, he toppled sideways. 'Colin?' She rushed to his side. He didn't respond, even when she shook him. 'Colin, darling, wake up.' But he wouldn't. Nothing but silence. And shallow, laboured breathing.

'Dear God,' she whispered, wiping his brow, which was covered with cold sweat. Something dreadful had happened – a seizure, a heart-attack, a stroke? She was no doctor, but didn't need to be to know he was in the gravest danger. She rushed to the phone, then paused. If she summoned help right now she might as well call a firing squad. To be discovered *in flagrante* here would be the end of everything for him, not to speak of her own inevitable discomfort. She knew Colin well enough to understand he'd risk dancing with the devil rather than be condemned for the rest of his days to languish as the butt of every low-life comedian's jokes. And already she could see the photo calls that would be required of her, the last image the world would remember of her before they spat her out: leaning over the garden gate in front of a thousand smirking photographers, clutching her husband's hand while the children clung tearfully to her skirts. No, not that, anything but that.

Still he didn't move. Hurriedly she gathered up her clothes, then took a moment to inspect her hair and repair her makeup by lamplight. She was almost out of the door when she stopped, returning to fold his clothes neatly, placing them on the back of a chair; it might just persuade those who found the *corpus erecti* that he was guilty of nothing more than stretching out for a sleep.

'Sorry, my love,' she whispered, bending down to kiss his forehead.

Then she was gone.

Three minutes later, from an anonymous phone in a distant part of the palace, she summoned help for Colin. She didn't leave her name.

Bad news spreads on the wings of eagles. By midnight, half the world knew that Colin Penrith, the Leader of Her Majesty's Loyal Opposition, had suffered a massive stroke. By morning the rest of the world would know it, too.

At the same time as poor Colin Penrith was taking a huge stride along the pathway towards political immortality, another event was taking place nearby whose roots would also gradually become entangled with Ginny Edge's life. Ajok Arob was a cleaner, about as far down the food-chain in Westminster as it is possible to be. She was a Dinka from the Sudd area of the Sudan, tall, slim, chocolate dark, with a characteristic fan tattoo on her forehead, and proud, like most of her kind. That was their problem, the Dinka, their pride. The Sudd was part of the floodplain of the White Nile, fly-bitten and dust-blown in summer but ideal for cattle grazing, and the combination of rich pasture and perceived arrogance had made Ajok's people a constant target for others in the cauldron of tribal venom that was the Sudd. Hadn't mattered so much when they'd fought with little more than spears, and in any case the Dinka were no slouches in a fight, but spears had made way for AK-47s that could fire six hundred rounds a minute and kill from a distance of a mile.

Way back in an earlier life, just as the huge African sun began to set, strange men had come to Ajok's village. Baggara Arabs, from the north. She had been washing her two youngest boys, Chol and Mijok, in the river so had been hidden from the first assault; from her hiding-place in the reeds she had watched as they had forced the men in the village into the meeting hut, every man they could find, and put a torch to it. Some tried to run from the flames but had no chance: you can't outrun a Kalashnikov in bare feet. The rest could do no more than scream as they died. And as soon as the piteous cries began to fade, the raiders set upon the women and children. This was a part of the world where in many tribes the word for 'black' and 'slave' is identical, where children lived shackled, and young women were habitually raped and recycled. What was left of Ajok's village was burned, completely, until there was nothing but blackened scars on the earthen floor.

At last the dawn came. When Ajok felt it was safe to bring her children out from the reeds, she found no trace of her old life. Everything was gone. She stumbled upon the body of her husband, Acai, cut to pieces – he had been one of those who had tried to run. Of her eldest child, Jaklek, there was no sign.

There was nothing left for her in this world. She still had a few cows the raiders had failed to steal: she sold them, and with the money started upon the long journey that took her, first by foot and then upon the exposed roof of an old, straining steamboat, to the scruffy regional capital of Juba. Third class. Two young children, and another she discovered she was carrying, although it would soon be lost. Then onward to Khartoum. A lone woman in a world run by the laws of Sharia and of men, which was filled with dust, hunger and suspicion. A world she was determined to leave.

Things move slowly in the Sudan, especially for a single woman. It took her more than a year to find her way, in the guise of a student nurse, from the endless floodplains of the Sudd to Passport Control at Heathrow. There she claimed asylum. It was almost another year before that claim was accepted, long years during which the life of a proud, contented wife of a man of some substance in a village in the south of Sudan was exchanged for that of a common cleaner and a cold council flat in Camden.

She always spoke slowly in her new language. She had keen, cautious eyes and made few friends in a workforce that was in a constant state of flux. The pay was pathetic, barely above the minimum wage, but it was regular, and if the work was mind-numbing it was, to Ajok, a blessing. Helped seal wounds.

Her bosses liked Ajok. She was reliable, hard-working, been around now longer than most. Never grumbled, not like a lot of the others, kept herself to herself and got on with things. If she seemed by nature a little on the quiet side, that was her business. No one took the time to get past those sad eyes. It was enough that they could rely on her, or thought they could.

That was, until the moment they asked her to clean the Prayer Room – the small and unpretentious little room on the ministerial corridor where the Ministers held their 'prayers' or private discussions. Security was paramount: no scattered papers were left here, no idly discarded notes, no wastepaper bin or tell-tale doodles, only bare walls and one small window, with little more than a collection of chairs set round a polished metal table. But, even here, teacups made rings and scratched brows left dust, so Ajok was asked to clean. And she refused. Because she knew this was where they gathered to discuss the new troubles in Iraq.

Bloody Iraq. So many lives lost, so many reputations torched. Now they were at it again. In spite of the biblical floods of reassurance that had flowed across the country, it was bubbling up once more. Suicide bombs. Wrecked pipelines. Leaders who couldn't lead, power stations that had no power and priests who honoured no god. Now someone had kidnapped the Prime Minister's wife from her hospital bed. Well, bugger Baghdad. So far as the Defence Ministers in London were concerned, they were glad to be out of it – well, almost out of it. Eighteen hundred British troops were still there, designated 'technical advisers' and 'engineers' to make it sound as if the mucky job of warring was done and the only thing that mattered any longer was renewal and reconstruction. But it was proving difficult to reconstruct a country that was still knee-deep in flaming oil. Damn them. Their ingratitude seemed endless, and in recent weeks clouds of thick, malevolent dust had begun sweeping across the desert once more, engaging the attention of those in the Ministry of Defence who met in the Prayer Room. Now they wanted it cleaned. A civil servant was standing by, waiting to lock up. He was glancing impatiently at his watch, wanting to be elsewhere. But Ajok said no.

'What is matter with you, Ajok?' her supervisor, a Cypriot, asked in his fractured English.

But she would say nothing, just stared at the floor.

'Come on, girl,' the Cypriot encouraged, but she pushed her squeaky cleaning trolley out into the corridor and refused to go back. He began tugging in irritation at the crucifix that hung round his neck. 'Ajok, we're short-staffed again. I has no time for this.'

Ajok moved not a muscle. She had seen enough of what men could do to her world; she would not help them destroy it further.

The civil servant appeared at the door. 'What is she doing?' he asked, as if Ajok had no right to respond for herself. Just like the government agent she remembered in Khartoum. She had queued in intolerable heat for days, part of a meandering stream of humanity that had shuffled slowly around the old colonial façade of the Interior Ministry, interrupted five times a day by the call to prayer and for even longer by the unexplained departures from their posts of those in charge. She had been with her male cousin. He was the one who would give the family's formal permission for her to leave: in the Sudan only men can give permission, women are left to do as they are told. After many hours, at last they had come to a small window in the wall of a fly-infested room, where they had found a small, bored-looking man who picked his nose, pretending not to notice them. When eventually he raised his eyes, he scowled. 'What does she want? Why does she want to leave? Where is she going?' she remembered the man from the Ministry had demanded. He had refused to address Ajok directly, treating her like livestock. That was a world she thought she had escaped, left behind, but here, in the old colonial capital of Westminster, the habits died hard.

'What is she doing?' the civil servant repeated, growing irritated, impatient to be gone.

So was the Cypriot. 'Ajok, what the hell? Clean the bloody office. Please.'

'No, thank you,' she replied softly.

'Now, Ajok.'

Slowly, with lowered eyes, she shook her head. 'This is not fair.'

'Then, *skila*, you slings your hook and don't bother you coming back. I never wants to see your black arse in here again. Y'hear that? Never!'

And with that he summoned the security guards. They came scurrying, as though she had just committed murder. They took away her security pass and wouldn't allow her to speak to her workmates. They marched her like a prisoner towards her locker, which they ransacked as though expecting to find cocaine or uncut diamonds. Her pockets and bag were searched. Only then did they allow her to take her coat and leave.

Ajok Arob had been followed around by so much suffering in her life. She had grown accustomed to it. Yet, as she gathered up her belongings and walked back out into the dull-lit night in search of a bus home, she hadn't any idea how much more was still to come.

Damn. Ginny Edge had been spotted.

'Bus?' Maggie Andrews enquired pointedly, as Ginny stepped off the number thirty-six and straight into her clutches.

'Just down from the constituency. And taxis are like husbands. Never around when you want one,' Ginny replied, struggling with her overnight bag. 'Didn't want to be late.'

'No, not today. Not today of all days,' Maggie agreed.

They were both making their way to the monthly gathering of the Other Half Club, a lunch date for the partners of those Members of Parliament who had risen to the often less than dizzying heights of the Shadow Cabinet, the Opposition's Front-Bench team. It wasn't always well attended, but today it would be. A packed house.

'A pity about Colin,' Maggie continued, taking Ginny's arm in conspiratorial fashion as they started down the street. 'Such a terrible, exquisite pity.' And she giggled.

Her attitude took Ginny aback – but so much about Westminster took her aback. 'It's a sailing pond,' her husband, Dominic, had reassured her. 'You just have to wait for the right breeze.' But it was a pond where pike ate the minnows and piranhas took their turn to feast upon the survivors of any capsize. Ginny had made the trip to Westminster from her home in the constituency for no other reason than her sense of duty, but she was good at that. Duty. It was a habit that had been bred and frequently beaten into her from the moment she had first drawn breath, thirty-eight years ago, at her parents' home on the moors outside Catterick, on a night when thick January snowdrifts carried on an east wind had prevented her mother making it to the hospital.

She'd been something of a camp follower ever since. Her father had been an ambitious and, in his own view, outrageously under-promoted officer in the East Dorsets, so Ginny had spent the first sixteen years of her life dragging her toys and schoolbooks behind her everywhere from Germany to Cyprus and Salisbury Plain, then back once more to Catterick. It had done great things for her organisational abilities but bugger-all for her emotional develop-ment. She'd spent more time with books than with boys, so when she'd met Dominic at university in Nottingham and he had smiled back at her from the other side of the Greenpeace stall at a Freshers' Fair, she had thrown herself into their relationship in a manner that had left him breathless, with or without his trousers. She was studying English, he law, and only the differing syllabus enabled her to hide from him the fact that she had the better brain.

She went into publishing, he went into a leading firm of London solicitors, but he really wanted politics and she wanted children so, once again, her sense of duty had come to the fore. Dominic came first. He became the lawyer and parliamentary candidate while Ginny devoted herself to raising their two children, at the same time embarking upon the novel that had always burned a path inside her. Yet, slowly, and as so often, under the pressure of children and his career, the literary flame began to flicker and die. It was never fully extinguished but, as the years of children had rolled by, the pages of the manuscript had sat in the corner of her office-cum-ironing room, staring at her, morose, accusing, unfinished. They had long since ceased to be friends.

Now Jemma was ten and Ben eight; perhaps their growing independence might allow her time to stir a few embers and get her own personal, selfish things back on course. Except little Ben had been throwing up all night and was now at home in Northamptonshire with a raging temperature in the care of her cleaner, while Jemma had protested all the way to school that it was her turn to be sick and why couldn't she stay at home instead?

Home. Once it had been the only place where Ginny felt truly comfortable, after the door to their cottage had been slammed shut, locking out the outside world, but even at home she was starting to feel – hunted. That was the word that kept coming into her head. As though, wherever she was nowadays, life was stalking her, crowding her out. The children, the constituency, everyone wanted some part of her. And Dominic's new job as party chairman meant they all saw less of each other. Added to that, there was somehow never enough money on a politician's salary to do things properly. Which was why, today, she had arrived from the railway station by bus.

Sensing her discomfort, Maggie Andrews tried to reassure her – or was she simply taking advantage? It was so difficult to tell.

'You haven't worked it out yet, have you?' Maggie said, as they walked up St George's Drive in a gentle early-summer breeze.

'Worked out what?'

'That you and Dom are never going to make it in Westminster on the back of a bendy-bus.'

'I thought it was good for the image,' Ginny replied defensively, as the wheels of her overnight bag dragged in disagreement across the stones of the broken pavement.

'It's all very well Dom putting himself about as a man of the people, but trust me. He needs to be married to a queen.'

'I'm afraid we don't stretch to a tiara and gilded coach.'

'Not even a taxi, it seems. You must learn how to make things work for you.'

'Like . . .'

'You could start with the spouse's travel allowance.'

Ginny stopped, looking perplexed. 'But how? We're only allowed – what is it? – fifteen trips a year from the constituency to London. I like to watch Dominic speaking in the House, be with him when he has official dinners, that sort of thing. The allowance barely gets me past Easter.'

'But that's why it's so unfair,' Maggie replied, leading on once more, her heels making sharp clicking noises as she walked. 'The other lot' – she meant the Government – 'swan around in their ministerial cars with their sanctimonious noses stuck up each other's backsides while we're left to stumble around on . . . well, buses. Don't do buses, Ginny. It does no favours to the rest of us. Seems like you're trying to make a point.'

'The point is I'm—'

'Anyway, it's easier if you go by car. You just have to be a little creative.'

'Sitting on the M1 in a five-year-old Nissan with a split exhaust at forty p a mile somehow seems to squeeze all the creativity out of me.'

'Then share the trip. Dozens of us come up and down the M1.'

'At the risk of sounding completely anti-social, how would sharing the trip help?'

'So you can double up on the allowance. Use one car, but both put in a claim.'

Ginny wrinkled her nose. 'Isn't that just a touch – unethical?'

'Oh dear, I was forgetting. I've heard your Dominic's one of those devout creatures who spends a lot of time on his knees. Wouldn't he approve?'

'I'm not sure that I would approve,' she replied archly. 'Let alone the Fees Office if they heard we were operating a scam.'

'Not a scam, dear. No, not that at all. Why, the Fees Office turns a deliberate blind eye to it all. Practically Bolsheviks, the lot of them. Know that those with all the money have no trouble with these irritating details, so are perfectly happy for the rest of us to . . . well, even life out a bit. I've known three, even four, share a car. Doesn't cost the taxpayer a penny extra, just sort of spreads it around a little further. The greater good, and all that. Unless, of course, you prefer to ride a bike, in which case you can claim twenty p a mile . . .'

'I'll think about it,' Ginny replied, knowing that she wouldn't and grateful that they had almost reached their destination. She felt as if she'd just been groped.

The Other Half Club – known by them all as the Better Half Club – was one of those institutions that sometimes ebbed, and sometimes flowed, depending on the state of agitation of the political pond, but since Tina Saunders had taken charge its popularity had increased considerably. She had organised a private room at Marrakech, a Moroccan mostly veggie restaurant off Warwick Way in Pimlico, and the charge for the lunches was almost embarrassingly small, although no one showed much interest in enquiring how they could get two courses plus as much wine and filter coffee as they wanted for less than a tenner. It was simply one of the things that Tina did. She was a powerhouse of the Westminster social scene, the bubbling wife of the party's deputy leader, Jack Saunders, and she seemed capable of arranging almost anything. Her personality was expansive and sometimes explosive, always seeming to be on the point of bursting forth through straining seams, which came as a considerable relief in party circles since her husband was, in many people's view, dispiritingly wet. She was in her fifties, twenty years older than some of the other club members, but the age gap seemed only to egg her on. She had no children left at home, no silly distractions, and seemed to have time for everything.

If Tina was the most effervescent member of the group, Maggie Andrews (Culture, Media and Sport) was the most outspoken and Lisa Pound (Trade and Industry) the most intellectual, while Ron (Pink's and Ralph Lauren) was always the most immaculate. He was the gay partner of the Environment spokesman and the only regular male member of the club. Ginny qualified merely as the newest. Dominic had been appointed but three months previously, much to the surprise of many; both he and his wife were generally regarded as *nouveau* and not yet *arrivé*.

Even before they had settled down to their *chourba* soup and *tagine Berbere* there was only one topic of conversation. Tina introduced it. 'Poor bloody Colin,' she declared in a loud Yorkshire accent, before sipping her sauvignon and drawing back to let it all take place.

'It happened in the office. While he was working his heart out.'

15

'On the job.'

'So sad. He's given his life to the party.'

'No, not *that* job, you idiot.'

'You mean . . . ? No! Was he really?'

'I first met him twenty years ago. Blackpool. Conference. You should have seen him then. Best damned proselytiser I ever knew.'

'Weren't the two of you an item for a while?'

'But I thought he was happily married.'

'Oh, he was. His wife Debs was very understanding. And often away. That's why he was so abominably happy.'

'The key to a happy political marriage. Distance.'

'And discretion.'

'Westminster rules!' And they laughed.

Ginny took little part in this increasingly undignified conversation. She was distracted with thoughts of Ben and, in any case, she'd met Colin only a handful of times. She rather liked him. 'He's not even dead,' she heard herself whisper but, of course, by Westminster rules, he already was.

By the time the soup had been drained and the *tagine* had arrived, the conversation around the starched white tablecloth had broken into smaller groups, which allowed for a far greater margin of indiscretion. At one stage Ron raised his head from the gaggle at the other end of the table to declare in a voice of mock horror that he was the only one present who seemed not to have slept with Colin. Perhaps he wasn't far wrong. And while they gossiped they began to position themselves – and their menfolk – for the battle that was to come, when the fallen standard would be picked up and once more raised high. A compliment here, a slight there, particularly against those who weren't present, an alliance forged as an opponent was hunted down. Ginny noticed that Tina, having kick-started the discussion, had taken no further part and was sitting back like a mother hen, occasionally preening her feathers, listening intently, making detailed mental notes of the scratching and barging that were taking place around her.

Ginny took a break to freshen up and get away from it all. Anyway, she wanted to check up on Ben. This wasn't her scene, among these predatory, atavistic women. It rankled with her that as they discussed the runners and riders in the forthcoming Leadership Stakes, dissecting everyone from hot favourite to hopeless outsider, no one mentioned Dominic. That was, perhaps, inevitable. Dom was too young, too recently in post, she knew that, but still it hurt that they – what? Underestimated him? Took him for granted? Thought he wasn't good enough? Whatever the reason, it left Ginny dissatisfied. OK, so he was a man who behind the highly polished and carefully practised exterior showed moments of private hesitation. It wasn't a sin. If he harboured doubts, it was only because he so fervently wanted to do well for everyone. He sometimes found it difficult to reconcile his deep moral and religious beliefs with the practices of politics, but at least that made him human, and so very different from her father, a man who thought he had the answer to all problems and, when he discovered he didn't, simply tried to kick the crap out of everything. Dom wasn't like that. He was gentle, some said too much so for the harsh world of Westminster, but a brilliant speaker, had a great chin, and in less than six years in Parliament he'd already become chairman of the party and one day might go very far.

If she had any qualms about her role as camp follower, Ginny hid them well away. That had been part of the deal from the start, from the very first time she'd thought she was pregnant and they'd discussed getting married. Dom wanted a life in politics and she wanted a life with him, so . . . It had seemed such a small sacrifice. She hadn't reckoned without the lost weekends, the cancelled holidays, the disrupted family dinners, the times she'd watched a school play or prize-giving on her own with an empty, accusing seat beside her. Yet in all the discussion over cracked-wheat bread and couscous that had gathered pace around the table, his name hadn't been mentioned, not once. So, feeling out of place, and more than a little out of sorts, she hid for a while in a cubicle in the ladies' washroom.

It was while she was there, secure behind her locked door, that she heard Maggie Andrews and Penny Madden come in. Penny was the wife of the Treasury spokesman and had enjoyed her lunch – but, then, she always did. Over the years, it had done her no favours. She was small and blonde, still attractive for a woman in her mid-forties, but the strength of her genes was increasingly being overwhelmed by her appetites. The looks that had entranced many men in her twenties, and had still been the cause of much surreptitious fluttering in the dovecotes of Westminster a decade later, were now starting to fade. The lusts that continued to burn in her eyes were now directed towards power rather than physical pleasures, which had the advantage of putting less strain on her marriage. She wanted to be the wife of the most influential man in the country and, after a few drinks, it showed.

And Ginny heard it all.

'I get the impression Lisa thinks her husband should stand. Poor thing,' Penny said, staring intently into the mirror, struggling to focus without her glasses.

'Ridiculous. The man's about as exciting as a mucky afternoon in Margate.'

'She's been going on about how loyal he's been to her.'

'Precisely.'

'And what about your Derrick? Might he throw his hat into the ring?' Penny tapped away distractedly at the flapping skin that in the last few months had begun to appear beneath her chin, trying to make the question sound like an idle enquiry, but the booze had already won the battle with discretion.

Maggie looked up and paused, intent on giving her answer a measure of authority. 'I've burned all his hats.'

'No ambition? Really?'

'Penny, we've known each other long enough. My husband's a dickhead who couldn't organise a Sunday-school picnic, let alone a Cabinet meeting. I know that, you know it, the rest of the world knows it, apart from him and his besotted mother. I've no intention of allowing myself to be humiliated. When the time comes I'd be very happy for him to be the Minister for Fine Food and Running Water, and after he's screwed up on that I could even live with him being shunted off to one of those rather nice little earners they have at the Commission in Brussels. I have a comfortable life. I enjoy it. All I ask is that Derrick is kept busy enough for me to be able to get on with it.'

'So . . . not Derrick. Then who? Who do you think?' The pink eyes were alert.

'Iain, of course.'

'My Iain?' She tried to feign surprise.

'Your husband would be my choice, and he'll be Derrick's choice, too. I'll make sure of that.'

'You really think . . . ?'

'Of course.'

'But . . .'

'What?'

A protracted sigh. 'Oh dear. We've got no money, you see. I don't think we can afford it.'

'Penny, you can't afford *not* to do it.'

'How on earth is that?'

'You have that rare and beautiful opportunity which is given to so few of us – to become the Leader's wife. The Prime Minister's wife, perhaps. And that's the only job truly worth having around here, the only way you can nail down your future for what's left of eternity while the rest of us get left to scratch around for a free holiday here or a handout there, hoping someone will come along with a share tip or a loan car that won't cause a ripple in the Members' Register.' She brushed a strand of wayward hair from her temples. As she did so, Penny couldn't fail to notice the glittering watch that slid up Maggie's forearm. She thought she'd recently seen something similar in a glossy magazine on the wrist of the latest Russian tennis star.

'Government. That's what it's all about, Penny. And pray to all the gods it'll be our turn soon. When did you last see a Cabinet minister who had to pay his own way – even pay his own mortgage, in some cases? Ministerial office is the checkout counter of all desires. A villa in Tuscany for as long as you want, an upgrade on the flight there and back, not even a bar bill to pick up. When you're in government, all of a sudden you have friends everywhere you turn, and in exchange for an inside track or a recommendation for the honours list you've got people throwing themselves down in every puddle to make sure you don't get your hand-stitched shoes wet, or draping a towel for you over some exclusive bit of beach front in Barbados. Oh, it doesn't last, of course, unless you work at it.'

'Meaning?'

'Well, you smile upon them in office in the expectation that they'll smile upon you – or your wife's PR company or your son's design consultancy or whatever – when you're out and back on the street.'

'Some sort of secret deal, you mean?'

'No, no, nothing so sordid. Nothing written, nothing even openly discussed, not if they're sensible. You don't need a contract, just a meeting of minds.'

'I've always wondered . . .'

'Have you ever stumbled across a former Defence minister who was short of the odd million, or a Treasury mogul who starved? Get yourself into government, stay out of the clutches of senility and the *News of the World*, and you're made.'

'And the watch?'

Maggie smiled. 'From a German media mogul who, I suspect, might one day want to buy a few radio licences here.'

'But we're not in government, Maggie – may never be. He must know there's nothing you can do.'

'Not now, of course. That's why it's only a bit of bling, a trinket – a token of what might be, as and when. Something to remember him by, just in case Derrick makes it to a seat at the Cabinet table. Oh, don't worry, I didn't accept it as a corrupt gift. I insisted on paying him for it, even got a receipt somewhere. Not the size of a Mandelson mortgage, I grant you, but it cost me almost a hundred pounds.'

'Really?' Penny couldn't stop her fingers from reaching out to touch, desperate to see if the embedded diamonds were authentic. 'It's beautiful. And all I ever seem to get is the odd free theatre ticket.'

'Try it on,' Maggie offered, laughing as Penny blushed like a schoolgirl accepting her first cigarette.

'Oh, I couldn't.'

'Course you can. Borrow it for a while. It's OK. I've got another.'

So their minds met. No one had been corrupted, it was little more than a moment of gentle seduction, a baring of ambitions. And, all the while, Ginny sat in her cubicle as still as a startled mouse, praying that a suitable moment to interrupt might present itself. She was just about to take a deep breath and cough loudly when she heard Dominic's name mentioned.

'Do you think he'll get involved? Help out? A few whispers here, a little arm-twisting there,' Penny was asking.

'Party machine's supposed to be neutral, of course, but it never is. Usually a right little nest of vipers.'

'You don't think . . . ? No, of course not. Silly. But . . . He couldn't be thinking of getting involved himself, could he?'

'Dominic Edge?' Maggie let out a shriek of laughter. 'I can assure you, Penny, that he won't. Can't. Couldn't possibly.'

'Too new, too inexperienced?'

'Too damned distracted.'

'By what?'

'By *who*.' A pause to straighten her collar. 'A young tart named Julia Summers. Works in the press department. Likes the late shift, apparently.'

'You sure? Oh, how delicious!'

'Derrick, dear Derrick . . .' She shook her head in despair. 'Derrick found them in Edge's parliamentary office the other week. Stumbled in drunk, forgot to knock, caught them red-handed. Well, wet-lipped, to be forensically accurate.'

'Dominic Edge? But I thought he was . . . so saintly. Holier than thou.'

'Not an obvious suspect, I grant you. Little wonder he keeps his confessor so busy.'

'As you say, not the best time to come out fighting. Particularly with his trousers tangled round his ankles!'

There were peals of laughter before Ginny heard their voices dying in the distance. And something inside her died with them.

Her world had stopped. Everything had changed. There was no gravity, no place, no meaning left. It was as though the seas had shrunk back from the shore, the sun had been smothered and Ginny snatched up by a roaring wind that filled her head with madness and whirled her round and round before tossing her casually aside. She found herself falling through a void where once her life had been. Yet somehow she was still alive, still breathing, her heart racing, feeling her blood force its tortured path through every vein in her body. And she was back in the cubicle. Her mind turned a chaos of images: of Dom, of her father, of someone called Julia, of cruel, cackling women. Then she saw her mother's tears, and felt her own, burning down her face. Every part of her felt as if she were on fire. She sat, alone, in misery, until she knew she couldn't hide any longer. She would have to do it, unlock the bloody door of this wretched cubicle, and from somewhere find the courage to step out onto the ashes of what had been, until that moment, her life.

Two

OMINIC EDGE WAS, BY most standards, an exceptionally promising politician. Lawyer, Member of Parliament by his early thirties, he had sandy hair, rugged good looks, a broken nose that suggested some glorious past on the playing-fields of England, and a way with words that made him a natural beneath the television lights. If it also made him a target for some of the predatory women who are attracted to power and who prowl the corridors of Westminster, it was a temptation that, up to now, he had been able to resist. His rise through the ranks had been as startling as it had been swift, his reputation made by one speech shortly before the resignation of the previous Prime Minister. It is rare that an unknown backbencher is given the opportunity to confront the Prime Minister, and many around him thought the Speaker had made a mistake when his name had been called yet Dominic had grasped his chance with the appetite of an alligator.

Prime Ministers usually die by fractions, and in public. There comes a tipping point that marks, if not the end, then the beginning of the end when the process of decay becomes irreversible. Many thought that Dom's speech had marked that point, the moment when they realised that the Prime Minister was capable of being savaged by a man whose name he didn't even know.

'Mr Speaker, through his trials and tribulations, most of which have been self-inflicted, the Prime Minister has constantly sought to carve out his place in history. He has even, we are told, in private likened himself to Winston Churchill. Well, we on this side of the

House believe we know our Winston. And I can tell him, he is no Churchill.'

Stirred by their whips, the Government's backbenchers had begun a defiant baying of support for their master accompanied by much waving of arms and Order Papers in an attempt to howl down this impostor, but Dom had been up to his task.

'Oh, listen to them cheer,' he had declared, delighted, pointing individually to his opponents, 'whipped like dogs in a kennel. But they would be just as noisy were they waiting to see him hanged. And they will.'

His own side loved this. More MPs began to drift into the Chamber as word got out that some pup was nipping at the PM's ankles. The growing bustle had spurred Dom onwards.

'He is no Churchill. Rather, he reminds me more of the hapless Neville Chamberlain, in command of his ship of fools, blinded by his own self-belief, unable to hear the mutterings of disillusion that swirl around him or understand the evidence of his own folly. We have begged him, beseeched him to reconsider, to believe from the bowels of the Christ whom he so often quotes that he may be mistaken. But he listens to no one. Not those in front of him, nor those on the benches behind.'

That was true, they all knew it. After many years in office the Prime Minister had dispensed with so many colleagues and disappointed so many more that even his own side had grown cold.

'I tell the Prime Minister that weeds and nettles have sprung up in his shadow, and the briars of discontent grow ever closer round him.'

By now the government benches were silent.

'He has sat there so long – too long for any of the good he has done, parading his conscience like the inquisitors of old. I do not say – I dare not say – that his conscience is a bad conscience, that he is insincere—'

Voices of disagreement were raised amongst his own colleagues who sat around him.

'The Prime Minister may be sincere – yes, he may be, he may be,' Dom insisted, turning to silence the protests. 'But if he is, if he is . . .' a pause while they hung on his every word '. . . he's simply too much of a saint to continue any longer in his great office.'

Laughter rippled around the Chamber, and wasn't confined to the Opposition benches. The Prime Minister had withstood many things in his long years of office, but had never learned to deal with mockery. The anger was clear for them all to see in loud red marks on his cheeks.

'So go. Have done with it, sir. In the name of God, go. And let us all rest in peace.'

He had sat down to the most sustained cheers many could remember in that place, leaving the scribblers in the press gallery frantic to choose which of the feast of soundbites they would use to decorate their columns.

It was perhaps all too easy for Dom to mock the Prime Minister about his moral uncertainties for, deep down, he shared many of them. He hid them, of course, buried deep, but they were there none the less, growling away inside. In Opposition it didn't matter so much, he could dine with the Devil and share it with no one other than his confessor, but he slept with the fear that one day his words of derision might come back to haunt him.

Yet tomorrow could take care of itself. His task today was to survive.

Trust is like a crystal vase, carefully fashioned over time, exquisitely beautiful yet inherently fragile – something that, once broken, can never be put back together again. That was perhaps why Ginny decided to use the wedding present given to them by her brother-in-law to hurl at Dom as soon as he walked in the room. He entered entirely unsuspecting, not ready for the cry, the hurled missile, the explosion of glass and the huge hole it left in the wall.

'What the—'

'You lying, two-faced, duplicitous bastard! You total and utter shit!' she screamed. That, and much more. Even when he held her arms to stop her hitting him, the cursing continued. He shook her, violently, trying to quell the onslaught. 'What the hell's going on?' he demanded.

'Julia Summers – that's what's going on!'

And she watched the colour drain from his cheeks as though his throat had been slit.

She pulled away, could no longer look at him. He could find no words. He stepped towards her, his feet crunching on the broken glass, but she turned with a picture frame in her hand, ready to hurl it after the vase. It was their wedding photo.

'Don't!' he pleaded.

'You pig!'

He fell to his knees, head bowed, hands clasped, rocking back and forth. 'I'm so sorry, so sorry.' He was weeping. There was glass in his knee. She slapped him as she passed. She grabbed blindly at a bottle and poured a drink, downed it, then poured another.

'It was only a momentary . . . A moment of madness. Please forgive me.'

'A moment? *One* moment?'

'A few weeks,' he sobbed. 'Never serious.'

She didn't know what she despised most: his infidelity or his grovelling. Yet as much as she scorned him she was even more terrified by the decision she had to make, and the knowledge that whatever was said in the next few minutes would mark them for the rest of their lives. How should she react? Forgive him? Swallow her humiliation? It was what her mother would have done – had done countless times as she waited for Ginny's father to come home smelling of whisky and another woman. At least Dominic would have showered first.

'Please forgive me,' he whispered.

'Why the hell should I?' Her hand was trembling, spilling the drink. It was whisky, her father's drink.

'Because if you don't you'll destroy me.'

'Destroy your career, you mean. Mr Morality cheating on his

wife and kids. Just think of the headlines.' But even as she spat out
the words, she knew she had no appetite for the scorn that would
be heaped upon them both. He would be denounced as the cheat,
she branded for ever as the hapless and hopeless wife. So what
would she do? Press him for every sordid detail of times, places,
orgasms, orifices and changes of underwear, demanding to know if
his slut was a better shag than she was, then get her revenge by
selling the story to one tabloid while watching helplessly as her
good name was trashed in the others? Or should she do the quiet
thing, simply leave him, slink silently away into the shadows, let
him get on with it and leave her children with nothing but a
memory for a father?

She remembered how Maggie and Penny had treated it so
lightly, as if it were of no consequence, yet she couldn't do that. She
wanted to rage at the world because Dom had been screwing
around, couldn't control himself, was no better than some beast in
a farmyard. But, in one of those dark places buried deep inside, she
knew she should have expected something like it; in fact, hadn't she
been brought up to expect precisely that? She'd tried so hard to
idolise Dom, praying he would be better than the rest, and different
from her father, but in the end he wasn't. He was just a bloody
man. She'd been living a dream and should have known it couldn't
last. Some day she'd have to wake up. But what hurt even more
than the pain of being shaken from her dreams was the sense of
burning shame she had felt in that cubicle as the two women toyed
with her private life, then threw it away like a used tissue. And that
was only the start of it. There would be more, so very much more
humiliation, as her neighbours mocked from behind every curtain
and mothers whispered at the school gates, while little children
pointed at her in the supermarket, if ever they knew.

No, whatever she was to do, she would do it quietly. Which
meant . . . she had to keep him. Keep this odious, grovelling
wretch who was bleeding all over her carpet. Not for him but for
her own sake, and for the sake of her children.

She remembered the other things that Maggie and Penny had chattered about. Security. Using the system to fiddle a few pounds here and more shekels there. She didn't want to go that way: she was better than that. Yet now more than ever she needed some measure of security, in case – well, in case Dominic couldn't keep his prick in his pocket and went off in search of pastures fresh. An abandoned wife, two fatherless kids, all those weekend visits, with Jemma and Ben being passed back and forth like a parcel at a party game. No, there had to be another way. Maybe she should screw around, using all those nights when Dom was away, get her own taste of those forbidden fruits, but she knew she wouldn't. That would only give him an excuse, make her no better than all those other silly, scavenging tarts. She had a better idea. She was going to keep her family together, no matter what it took.

'I'll give her up. Never see her again,' he was snivelling.

'You dump her now and she'll run straight off to a tabloid.'

'She wouldn't do that, she's a—'

'Good girl?' Her mockery slashed at him like a razor.

'Then what the hell should I do, Ginny?'

She didn't reply.

'It's over between me and her. That side of it. No more. I want to spend . . . more time . . . with the family.'

She burst into bitter, scornful laughter. 'I scarcely care what you do any longer. Except one thing. You will do whatever it takes to keep her quiet.'

'What?'

'I will not be humiliated because of you. Neither will I have the children made laughing stocks at school.'

'And . . . us? You and me?'

'We're going to make a few changes around here.'

' "We"? I like the sound of that.'

She stared at him, eyes of ice. 'Oh, Dom, I really wouldn't count on it.'

★

Ajok did not rush the decision about what she must do next. The Dinka did not rush. Unlike the English. They were strange folk, these English, always rushing yet to no apparent purpose. Certainly they lived in solid houses rather than in reed huts, but only to protect themselves from the clinging damp. They earned so much more yet somehow always complained of their debts; drove fast motor-cars, and spent most of their day sitting in queues in search of somewhere to park.

She did not dislike these people, but she had no great affection for them either. Even after all these years she knew only a few. So many barriers. So much reserve. The people here lived like children, always squabbling, distracted and in discord. She remembered the chaos and confusion she had found in the crowds when she had first arrived at Heathrow, how the pushing and the noise had left her feeling dizzy for months. Yet, among all the crowds, there was no one. It was as if everyone were invisible, or at least empty, hollowed-out humans with nothing inside. They rushed past her in the streets with vacant eyes and downturned faces as if they were ashamed of themselves.

In her village in the Sudd there was a community, or had been, before the Arabs arrived. Everyone knew the business of the other, and helped with it. They lived with the cycle of the days and the seasons, and they shared the tranquillity that settled on their village with the coming of evening when they would sit and talk around the fire or sing songs to their children, teaching them of the old ways of the Dinka. In London there was no tranquillity, and nothing she could find that resembled roots.

> *'My husband has left me,*
> *When did I not hate him?*
> *How can a marriage spoil?*
> *I will keep his cattle and his children,*
> *We must not starve.*
> *What shall I do with today?*

Shall I go to drink coffee?
What shall I do with tomorrow?
Shall I go to drink tea?
What shall I do with tomorrow?
I am bewildered with what has happened to me.
I have not understood.
But I must survive.'

As she sang one of the songs of her village, she heard her younger child, Mijok, coughing in the night. It had been several days now. He would need medicine. A new coat. That would cost money. They must survive.

The following day Ajok went in search of the man who might yet save her life, the trade-union representative in the Ministry. She found him in his office – a wooden-panelled booth in the Admiral Lord Nelson, a small pub buried at the end of a cul-de-sac in the middle of Whitehall, just far enough away from the main thoroughfares to discourage tourists.

Patrick Creasey was seated at an old polished table scouring newspapers, making marks against a number of horses' names and scrawling figures in the margin. Beside his right hand a pint of dark beer with a huge creamy top was making damp circles on the table. He looked up, offered a broad, friendly smile; he recognised her, so slender, with her distinctive face tattoos and exceptional height, without being able to recall her name. When she gave it to him, he checked it against a list he kept in a folder.

'So, not here for a social chat, then, are we?' he enquired, beckoning her to take a stool.

'They have thrown me out, Mr Creasey. Given me the sack. Four days ago. I would have come earlier, but my son is sick,' she explained, in her slow, deliberate way.

'And why would they be doing that, then, to a fine girl such as yourself?'

'I would not clean the room from which they make war.'

'And why was that?'

'It is wrong what they do in there. All the fighting.'

'I agree. And, what's more important, so does your union. Terrible what's been going on out there, so it is. Terrible.'

'But I need work, Mr Creasey. Need the money. For my children. For clothes. For heating.'

Slowly he took the top off his pint, then some more, and started scribbling in a little notebook he kept in his shirt pocket along with five pens, all of different colours. 'You wait to hear from me. That's what you do. Be a couple of days, till I find out what those blockheads have been up to and extract their brains from their rear ends for them. We'll sort it for you. Don't you go worrying about a thing now, little lady. Everything'll be all right. You just wait and see.'

'Thank you, Mr Creasey. Is there anything I can do?'

'Well, that's very good of you, I'm sure. Another glass of this black stuff would be fine, seeing as you're offering. Help me get on with my work, so it will.'

She had brought with her money for her bus fare, no more. And with it, Ajok bought him his drink, then set off on the long walk home.

Pat Creasey was as good as his word, or part of it. Early the following week he got back to her. Trouble was, he hadn't sorted it. The men from the Ministry were unwilling to take Ajok back, accusing her of gross misconduct in refusing what they said was their entirely reasonable request for her to do the job for which she was paid. Apparently they thought she was a political, someone who was working to undermine the policy of the government that paid her. Ridiculous, of course, Pat Creasey said. So the union would pursue it. Put pressure on them. Get her an apology and her job back. Even told Ajok the union would take the matter to something called an employment tribunal, if necessary. That might require a little time, though, he said.

So Ajok began to take in washing, just to keep herself going.

★

During most of that long, rainless summer, Ginny refused to allow Dom back into her bed. He'd been sleeping on the sofa, trying to joke that he was like Bill Clinton, telling the kids he was suffering from a bad back. It was August before she relented. She had her needs, too, and Dom was the simplest, safest answer.

It was taking even longer for Colin to do the decent thing and die. While he lingered, life seemed to come to a standstill for his colleagues as they waited for the inevitable. No one wanted to be the first to break cover and declare a leadership contest while the life-support machine was still plugged in. Anyway, it was the idle months of summer. But as Colin's life slipped away, so it seemed did the life of the party, except for Jack Saunders, the deputy leader. He had the perfect excuse to run round the constituencies, rallying the faithful, reassuring them. And he was good at that. Jack of all trades and master of none, the perfect deputy, with Tina at his side to prompt and guide him. He had just the right measure of seriousness for a wake, while Tina had the effervescence to help them all enjoy it.

The only other noticeable player during those long days of August was Dom in his role as chairman. The leading members of the party encouraged him, in contrast to their growing resentment of Jack Saunders. Dominic Edge was 'safe', not a threat to their interests or ambitions. He could appear on the news or give a front-page interview without them feeling he was parking his tank on their lawn. But Dom also made a point of being at home a lot, playing with the kids, trying to be the indispensable father, and when he wasn't at home he offered detailed explanations of his whereabouts to Ginny, leaving her as little room as possible for suspicion. To give him his due, he was trying hard. And Ginny began to appear at his side much more. Smiling. Holding his hand as if she wanted never to let him go. They made, it was widely agreed, the perfect political family.

Until Ginny burst into tears over lunch.

Tina had invited her – all but insisted, suggesting she'd be passing nearby on her way down from Yorkshire and would love to see her. Didn't make much sense, it seemed a hell of a detour on what was a long drive, but Tina had already booked a table for two in the best pub restaurant for miles. Her treat. She knew her eating places, did Tina.

It was so hot that they sat outside in the shade of a twisted yew. Tina's dress was suitably low cut for the weather, and she was wearing black nail varnish, which was chipped. From somewhere near at hand they could hear the monotonous whirring of a combine harvester, while on the table a sparrow came to inspect the remnants of their meal, seared scallops washed down with a bottle of pinot grigio, of which Tina drank the major part. It wasn't until the dishes had been taken away that she came to the point. 'What d'you hear about the lunatics who want to take over the asylum?'

'Very little. They seem to be keeping their heads low.'

'Not for much longer.' A pause. 'You know we've decided that Jack should run.'

'No, I didn't.'

'You must have noticed. It's all too painfully obvious, if you ask me. Any more cream teas around the constituencies and we'll explode like a supernova. Or do they implode? Never quite sure.'

'I think they do a bit of both. A lot of both, actually.'

'Anyway, we're going to run. And we'd like your help.'

'But you know Dom can't. He's chairman, got to remain neutral, above the fray.'

'Phooey.' It was a favourite word, delivered with Yorkshire relish. 'He can't be neutral. He's a politician, for heaven's sake.' She stared suspiciously at the wine bottle, now empty, then summoned a young waiter and ordered reinforcements.

When two large glasses arrived Ginny pushed hers carefully, but not too obtrusively, to one side. 'Dom's not going to put his own name forward, if that's what you're thinking.'

'But that's what makes him so perfect, Ginny. Think about him and Jack together. They make a perfect double act. Youth and experience. Craggy good looks and academic earnestness. One a deep thinker, the other the talented orator. And your Dom has a full head of hair.'

'I don't understand. A double act?'

'Look, Jack's late fifties. This is his last chance – but with luck and a little help like yours, I think he can make it. And it's his most attractive selling point – being too old to hang about for long. Four, five years – six at the outside – and he's gone. Jack's only got one election in him, Ginny. Then it could be Dom's turn.'

'You mean—'

'I want Dom's support for Jack in this campaign. Oh, it's got to be delicately done because he's chairman, I know that, but –' she rolled more wine round her mouth '– nothing too delicate. At Party Headquarters you gather all sorts of useful little nuggets from around the country, who's moving from one camp to another, or one bed to another. That sort of thing could be vital.'

'There's no way Dom could endorse Jack.'

'Doesn't have to. Just let them be seen around together. A team effort. People will get the message without a word being spoken. If Jack's elected he gives Dom whatever job he wants, then throws his own weight behind him when the time comes.' She wiped her glowing face with her napkin and moved deeper into the shade. 'Think about it, Ginny. Dom could be prime minister in a few years' time. You could be this country's First Lady. Have everything you want.'

'It can't be as easy as that.'

'Get real, woman! Course it bloody is,' Tina spluttered. When she'd had a drink her self-restraint wobbled; after a skinful it often toppled entirely. 'A guaranteed pay cheque for the rest of your lives, no matter how much of a cock-up he makes. You'll never have to buy another car or plane ticket. Even if he makes a complete idiot of himself he writes a book about it. Then he becomes a director of some enormous conglomerate, gets paid a hundred thou' just to fly to Milwaukee or Monterey for lunch. And as for you . . . Jesus, with a figure like yours, every fashion house and jewellery designer in Christendom'll be parked outside your door demanding you wear their stuff and paying you for the pleasure of it.' She was panting, her chest heaving. 'I just hope I make it while my cleavage is still in the contest.' She flapped at the scavenging sparrow, then reached for Ginny's hand. 'Look, I don't mean to sound grasping, but get to Number Ten and it's all laid out on a plate for you. And think of the children. The best schools and universities, the juiciest job opportunities, every door thrown open to them. And you never having to worry that one day the ungrateful brats are going to move you into a cheap retirement home as an economy measure. Getting to Downing Street will be the means to satisfy your every need – well, except the one, perhaps. Politicians are rubbish in the bedroom, in my experience. Give all they've got in the office.' Her eyes clouded. 'You know, I used to be beautiful once, had men falling over themselves for me. Now I practically have to beg.' She drank once more, but this time from Ginny's untouched glass.

It was at this point that the tears began to tumble down Ginny's cheeks.

She hadn't shed tears in front of anyone else since she had learned of Julia Summers. In the days after her dreams and illusions had been left in pieces on the floor, she had been surprised to discover an unexpected feeling of liberation. She owed nothing to anyone. She was free to do as she liked, obligated to no one, apart from the children. For the first time in her life there was no father, no teacher, no tutor, no sermonising priest or sanctimonious husband whom she couldn't look straight in the eye and mock. Suddenly her life was her own. This realisation had startled her, inspired her, even exhilarated her, but then, day by day, it had come slowly to terrify her. She was free, but her bed was cold and her life empty. It was all routine, with neither shape nor substance, apart from the children. And one day they would grow beyond a mother's reach and she would be left with nothing but the memories of their laughter. There had to be something more, something for herself. But what?

'Oh, my dear,' Tina gurgled, spotting the tears, 'have I gone and said something silly? I'm always doing that, you know.'

Ginny shook her head and wiped her eyes.

'What is it? Husband? Children? Money? Oh, it's always men, isn't it? Even for a beautiful woman like you – perhaps especially for a woman like you. Oh, bloody men!'

'No, nothing like that. It's just that . . . politics seems such an unfeminine business at times, always choosing sides, looking for conflicts. Even within the same party we have to decide who we're going to support, and who we're going to let down.'

'Someone else asked you already?' Tina demanded, her eyebrow arched until it disappeared beneath her fringe.

'Not yet. But of course they will. I heard some of the girls talking the other day . . .'

'Who? What was said?'

'Just Maggie and Penny discussing Iain's plans.'

'Iain Madden's going to stand? Well, of course he'll bloody well stand!' she spat dismissively, answering her own question. 'A man who's filled a thousand columns in Hansard without offering an inch of sense. And Maggie and Derrick will be supporting him?'

Ginny nodded. 'I'm sure that's what she said.'

'May she catch crabs!' Her fist banged down on the table, causing the sparrow to flutter away in alarm. 'She promised me. Gave me her worthless word.'

'Oh dear, I didn't mean to—'

'Don't you worry about a thing. I'll put Maggie Andrews back in her box, too right I will!' She drained the last drop of wine. 'Anyway, doesn't matter a damn. Derrick's such a dickhead. Carries no weight.'

Ginny nodded. At least on that point Maggie and Tina were agreed.

'So what about us?' Tina asked pointedly.

'Isn't it really something for Jack and Dom to discuss?'

'Phooey! If we left politics up to the men there'd be nothing but pestilence and starvation. No, they need our guiding hand. Jack'll do what I tell him. And, if you don't mind me saying, Dom needs taking in hand a bit, too.'

Ginny caught her breath. Was Tina trying to tell her something? Did she know? Perhaps the whole of Westminster knew, her life reduced to a crumb of common gossip. Once more she felt as if she had been scraped out inside. Tina was prattling on, but Ginny was no longer listening. She was so desperately tired of others telling her what she was supposed to do. She had to make up her own mind.

'So, what do you think?' Tina was saying, almost slurring her words. 'If you want, it could be yours, Ginny. Yours and mine. So – are we a team?'

Ginny stared at the other woman. A deep flush that had started its life between Tina's ample breasts had risen until it entirely consumed her face. It wasn't just the wine: there was real passion here, a resolve that might yet change the world – Ginny's world.

'Well?'

Slowly, Ginny began to nod.

'And Dominic?'

'I don't think you'll have to worry about Dominic.'

'Good girl!' Tina exploded with delight. Suddenly she was rummaging in her handbag until she found a tube of mints. She piled several into her mouth – 'In case I meet PC Plod,' she explained, fanning herself. 'Wouldn't want him getting the wrong idea.' Then she laughed. 'Now we've got to get this show on the road, my darling.'

'I suppose so.'

'And the first thing we have to do is organise ourselves a funeral . . .'

★

Colin Penrith died as the first brittle breezes of autumn were scattering leaves across roads and pavements like swarms of marauding rats. He was a widower and had neither children nor close relatives and died a lonely man, if not entirely alone. There had been much speculation about the nature of his final words, but most were agreed that he hadn't had his mother on his mind. His first cousin was closest in the thin Penrith bloodline, but they hadn't spoken since a quarrel over the miners' strike, nearly twenty-five years earlier, had turned to beer-spilling violence. He had no intention of attending the funeral, and was more than happy for the arrangements to be taken off his hands. And so it fell to the party hierarchy to handle what would inevitably be the biggest outpouring of manufactured regrets since . . . well, since Maggie Thatcher had left her fingernails embedded in the carpet of Downing Street on her way out.

So the party took over the job of burying poor Colin, and the responsibility for the task inevitably fell to the deputy leader and chairman – or, given that they were exceedingly busy men, to their wives. And what a grand occasion they made of it, that late September afternoon. Two high-stepping black stallions with dark plumes sprouting from their heads drew the hearse and its plain coffin towards the cathedral at Wells. The Shadow Cabinet walked behind, wives (and Ron) by their side, with Jack and Dominic at their head. An early-autumn sun shone in welcome upon the magnificent west front of the cathedral, its hundreds of heroic stone figures standing tall in welcome.

Inside, the aisles were filled with mourners and every detail had been cared for, thanks to a committee of wives set up by Tina. One had chosen the flowers, another the choral music, a third was responsible for inviting the necessary local dignitaries and a fourth and fifth were to ensure that a suitably large gaggle of glitterati and television celebrities turned up. To a woman, the members of the committee had been keen to help: many of them were burying not only Colin that afternoon but, alongside him, some precious and very private memories.

And Maggie took charge of the media arrangements. Volunteered. In her capacity as wife of the spokesman for Culture, Media and Sport. 'It's not really something for the children in the press office at Party HQ,' she had explained. 'This has got to be a grown-up affair.' And she had performed magnificently. A splendid turnout. Scribblers of every kind and colour filed dutifully into the cathedral like a conclave of cardinals, heads bowed, thinking great thoughts, with the images captured by – oh – so many cameras. Maggie had even placed a good number of black and Asian faces in their path – what she called the 'ethnic footprint'. This was not to be an occasion for the squeamish. The ordinary people of Wells were there, too, from curiosity, along with a good number of late-season tourists.

After the service, Colin was to be buried more privately. No great fuss. At a spot in his own back garden, *circa* thirty acres complete with lakes and Victorian follies located deep in his beloved Mendip Hills where, if it wasn't raining, he might see all the way to the great tor of Glastonbury. Only the members of the Shadow Cabinet in attendance, plus a few distant cousins, along with a couple of media representatives 'for the record'.

As the mourners filed in through the great west door they were greeted by a brass band with the enchanting strains of Elgar's 'Nimrod', an arrangement that was reckoned to be both classic and classless. And as the coffin appeared at the door, with the rays of the afternoon sun crowding in behind it, a single trumpeter in a small gallery set high near the roof poured out the sound of the Last Post.

Dom read the lesson – oh, how beautifully his voice reached out to them, with its exhortation to trust in their faith and a peroration about the resurrection of the dead that gave even those with the most marginal majorities renewed hope.

And, after they had all sung 'I Vow to Thee, My Country', Jack gave the eulogy. This was, he declared, the spot where they had buried kings of Wessex. Yet, as many were later to observe, no king of Wessex had ever had such a fine send-off. As the coffin left for its private burial, a lone piper played it on its way. Not that Colin had a drop of Scottish blood in him, but he had been an old sentimentalist and a by-election was due in Dundee.

Only two things spoilt the occasion. One was the treatment of Derrick and Maggie. Most of their colleagues seemed anxious to avoid them, and in spite of their efforts to ensure the success of the day they were left to trail along behind, forlorn and forgotten at the back of the procession. It was unfortunate that the photographer Maggie had chosen to capture the private burial was from *Hello!* magazine, and a matter of deep regret that she had taken a fee for it. Not a huge fee, it was only a funeral after all, but enough of a complicating factor to have made the splash in the most recent *Sunday Times*. Only after forty-eight hours of monastic silence, almost unique on Maggie's part, had she declared that this fee was, of course, intended for one of Colin's favourite charities. So Maggie and Derrick walked alone.

It was not until they were standing by the graveside that Ginny was able to press Tina about the matter. She'd tried earlier, but Tina had offered nothing more than a Delphic smile. 'Come on, tell,' Ginny insisted. 'It was you, wasn't it? Told the press.'

'Guilty as charged,' Tina whispered.

'But how did you know?'

'I didn't. Not for certain. But Maggie has the stickiest fingers in town. Notorious. Can't even settle a lunch bill without breaking into sweat. And when I heard she'd dragged *Hello!* into the picture . . . Well, two and two with Maggie usually makes at least five hundred quid.'

They paused: four black-suited undertakers were preparing to lower the coffin into its grave. Heads were bowed, words were muttered, breasts marked with the sign of the cross. Out of the corner of her eye, Ginny saw Tina smiling.

The second and far less palatable shadow cast across the funeral appeared in the *Record* the following day. The front page of the sensationalist tabloid showed the coffin being unloaded from the hearse, with Dom, Jack and other leading members of the party standing dutifully behind it. Above their heads, the paper ran the headline: 'Waiting To Be Buried'. For most readers, who would be skimming through to the more salacious pictures inside, the image might have seemed entirely respectable, a tribute to a fallen leader, but those who kept their noses close to the trough knew that it had a far more insidious and collective meaning. The weeks while Colin had lingered on life-support had not been helpful. While the Opposition remained rudderless, the Prime Minister had said all the right things about his ailing rival, then set about using the breathing space to cleanse his stables and remorselessly wash out every bit of bad news he could find. His popularity had soared. What he couldn't explain away as his attempt to be honest and entirely open, he blamed four-square on his predecessor. Meanwhile the summer sun shone, the Opposition mourned and nobody else seemed to give a damn. At this rate whoever took over as Leader of the Opposition had about as much chance as a beggar outside Buckingham Palace, and the *Record* was enjoying rubbing their noses in it.

Still, since Maggie had insisted on being responsible for the media coverage, they were able to blame this on her, too. It really hadn't been her day.

Dominic Edge had a reasonable suspicion that he'd got away with it. This wasn't to suggest he felt no remorse, for indeed he did, but man is a complicated machine and other parts of him would never forget those stolen moments of passion. And who was to know what was yet to come? The summer had taken him away from Julia, given him time to sort things out with Ginny, get their life back on an even keel. But the seasons were changing, the nights slowly drawing in. Soon would come that moment of reckoning when once more he would be face to face with Julia and . . . And what? His emotions swirled erratically inside. He loved Ginny, of course, and the kids, yet he so lusted after Julia that he found himself getting aroused in a traffic jam on the M25 and dreaming impossible, dangerous dreams. But they were only dreams.

And what had Ginny said? That he shouldn't dump Julia for fear she would run off and sell her story to some seedy tabloid? But then . . . what? Surely Ginny hadn't meant he should carry on. Yet Ginny was changing. Strange things were happening. She'd always been extraordinarily competent and thorough; it was why she'd got a better-class degree than he had, Dom thought. Devoted mother, couldn't fault her there. And if their sex life had become a little stale, his affair seemed to have thrown fuel on to the embers. She had grown altogether tougher. Decisive. No more deferring to him. She knew what she wanted. No bad thing. Took a lot of weight off his shoulders. And if she could forgive him for his affair, there was little reason to dwell on it, or even discuss it with his priest. An entirely private matter. Almost forgotten. Apparently forgiven. Yup, he seemed to have got away with it.

It was one evening in late September, as he was clearing away the remnants of their dinner in their undersized kitchen, with the children sleeping soundly upstairs after one of their special days with Dad, that he realised it wasn't going to be quite that easy.

'Who do you think's going to be Leader?' she asked, putting the kettle on the stove.

'Difficult to say. Depends how they perform at Conference.' The annual gathering of the party faithful was imminent. In the circumstances, it would inevitably turn into a prizefight between the contenders, and interest in the three incestuous days away at the seaside had rarely been so high.

'Iain?'

'Damaged goods. Derrick was supposed to be his campaign manager, and when Maggie crawled away she dragged Derrick behind her.'

'Hazel?'

'Well, a woman.'

'George?'

'Too nice. Too keen to see the other man's point of view.'

'And Jack?'

'Too . . .' He paused to collect his thoughts, his hands covered with soap suds. 'It's not so much that he's too old, because he's not – not quite, at least. He's just so bloody earnest. Too intellectual. Scares some people.'

'Too clever by half.'

'Something like that,' he replied, handing her a pan to dry.

'So – who?'

'We'll have to wait and see. Someone will either make a huge success at the conference or, more likely, a total balls-up. Either way, things will become much clearer.'

'So who will you support?'

'Me?' He shook his head. 'No one. Not my job.'

'Of course it's your job. To give a lead.'

'But—'

'There are no bloody buts, Dom. If you want to be the Leader in the future, you've got to start taking a few risks now.'

'You really want me to be Leader?'

'I want you to become Prime Minister. I insist on it.'

'Never realised you were so committed.'

'It's the thing that has kept our marriage intact.'

He winced. Said nothing. Tried to bury his thoughts in the soapy water.

'Will Julia be at the conference?'

He scrubbed the pan he was cleaning until it shone like silver. 'I . . . suppose so.'

Of course she would; they both knew it.

'Don't worry, Dom. I know you'll be too busy for nonsense. Anyway, I shall be there.'

'Watching me.'

'No, Dom. Helping you. This is your conference. I want you to take full advantage.'

'I'm not sure I follow you.'

'There's no leader. Everyone doing his or her own thing. A huge, gaping vacuum. Your chance to fill it.'

'How?'

'A great speech. Careful organisation. And making sure that Jack comes out smelling of roses.'

'Jack. Why Jack?'

'Because he's older than the others. He won't last for ever. A few years. And then it can be your turn.'

'I can't support him publicly,' Dom replied, his voice gaining an exasperated edge.

'No, but you can make sure the wind blows in his direction. See he gets good coverage, a couple of high-profile interviews. You can do that, can't you?'

'Yes, but—'

'And how will you choose the speakers' slots?'

'By ballot. It's got to be fair, seen to be fair, what with everyone gearing up for a leadership race.'

'Who's responsible for organising the ballot?'

'I am.'

'Well, I tell you what, Dominic, in order to ensure the most scrupulous fair play, I want you to announce that the ballot will be drawn, in front of any members of the media who want to attend, by your wife. I'd like that. You can do that, can't you?'

'I suppose so,' he replied, cautiously, his voice now soaked in suspicion.

'Excellent. Oh, and another thing. I've kept the following weekend free in your diary. Don't fill it. You'll be busy.'

'Doing what?'

'Moving home.'

'*What?*'

'We're all moving to London. There, I knew you'd be pleased.'

'Ginny, stop this nonsense. We can't all squeeze into my little garret.'

'Of course not. But I've made other arrangements. We've just agreed to take a house in Pimlico. Plenty of room for us all. Good entertaining space. Even a little garden at the back. And only five minutes for you from door to door. You'll love it.'

Dom threw his cloth into the sink, sending up a spray of suds. 'Have you gone completely bloody mad? Pimlico? We can't possibly afford it.'

'But it appears we can, Dom. In fact, it's all agreed. Removal vans booked. Mail redirected.' She handed him a mug of tea. Bromide. 'The house belongs to one of the big estates and we're taking it on a very short lease: A year at a time. No security, sadly, which is why it's so cheap, but that's politics for you. Except that the chairman of the property company in question is one of the party's big, big contributors. He's also a bit of a lech, and after he spent a long lunch last week staring at the buttons on my blouse, he also agreed that the lease will be renewed.'

'For how long, for God's sake?'

'For as long as he remains one of the party's biggest contributors. Which, I suppose, means for as long as you remain nice to him. As I said, that's politics for you.'

He slumped defiantly into a chair. 'This is crazy! What about the kids' schooling? No, this is ridiculous! I'm not having Jemmy and Ben dragged through some inner-city swamp.'

'They've already been accepted at St Xavier's. It's one of the best church schools in London. Catholic to its core. Thought you'd like that.'

'But there must be a huge waiting list for it. How the hell . . .'

'One of the governors is a very understanding member of the House of Lords. I'm told they're keen to have such a well-known and upright Christian father as you send his children there. They see all sorts of advantages.'

'You can't do this, Ginny.'

'But I have. You see, Dominic,' she always used his full name when she was being formal with him, 'you have a great future ahead of you. Party Leader. Prime Minister, even. It's just that you don't realise yet how ambitious you are or how successful you're going to be. So I will be in London, right by your side, to help you.'

'To spy on me,' he retorted angrily.

'To help you avoid some of the more obvious pitfalls in the way of a political career.'

He buried his head in his hands. 'Is this how you mean to punish me?'

'Why, I thought you'd be delighted, Dominic. It seems so much better than any of the alternatives.'

He rose to his feet slowly, his eyes red, his tea untouched. 'This is because of her, isn't it? You don't trust me.'

'What matters more than *my* trust is the trust of other people.'

He stared at her in disbelief, hoping to see some sign that this had all been a joke. Then he turned and walked forlornly towards the door. As he did so, a mug flashed past his ear and shattered against the wall.

'What the hell was that for?' he shouted, as he turned in alarm.

She smiled. 'Nothing, darling. I'm just keeping my eye in.'

And already she was packing, preparing for her new life. She had to discard so many memories, so many hopes. And there were demons, gnawing away at her, telling her it was all her fault. Had she been too distracted, perhaps, by the children, by the daily grind of a politician's wife, even by her ambitions for her book? She was a fine-looking woman, still with her cheekbones and her figure – something the kids hadn't yet taken away from her. Size ten and, yes, they still turned in the street to look.

Yet while she hadn't neglected Dom directly, perhaps she had done so by neglecting herself. Too many comfortable old clothes. Too many cancelled hair appointments. Too much poured into the kids, not enough into herself or her manuscript, until she had reached the point where she knew more about Coldplay and Chelsea Football Club than she could remember about Prokofiev or Proust. That made Ginny a dull girl. And on the few occasions she had managed to get to her novel, she knew her writing was loose and unfocused. A life of too many adjectives. And too many split ends.

But that still didn't excuse what the bastard had done.

It was a moment of metamorphosis, a rite of passage. Perhaps it would matter only to her, but if it didn't matter to her it would never matter to anyone. She had spent the afternoon raking leaves that had fallen in the back garden, wanting to leave behind her a house of which she could be proud. Neat and tidy, everything she had been trained to do and everything her life had ceased to be. She piled the leaves into a tiny mountain of decay at the end of the garden near the crooked apple trees, then set it alight with a twist of paper and a single match. Soon the bonfire of leaves began to glow from within and to send up wisps of smoke into the early-autumn sky. Only when it was well alight, and she knew it would remain so, did she go back into the house to fetch her manuscript. She knelt beside the fire. Almost reverentially she placed the stack of paper, so much effort, so much emotion, so many years, into its heart. An old life. Done with. Over. A gentle change of wind carried the smoke into her eyes. But no tears, not until later, after she had taken care of the children and was once more alone in her bed.

Three

C ONFERENCE. NOT BY CHANCE does it fall immediately before the word 'confession' in most dictionaries for there is, so often, so much to own up to. Yet that isn't the purpose of the annual gathering of the political clan. Conference-goers are not penitents on bended knee come to apologise for past mistakes but advocates eager to make more. Yet, sadly for those keener folk who wallow in the hothouse atmosphere of windswept beachfronts and overheated hotels, Conference (usually a proper noun) has changed. The rest of the world no longer hangs on its every word, and the media nowadays refuses to flock. Conferences have grown smaller, more clinical. What once may have been a boiling cauldron of intrigue has been reduced to the status of an electric kettle, to be switched on and off at will. It's cheaper that way, and in the Brave New World of impoverished political parties shorn of their trade-union funds and huge corporate handouts, cheap matters.

There's even a rule – PCDC. Party Conference Doesn't Count. It used to apply to the many personal indiscretions committed during this time spent away from home, and episodes of inebriation, infidelity and gross ineptitude were rarely referred to in the press; after all, it was so often the minions of the media that led the way. But perhaps it was the wicked bomb at the Grand Hotel in Brighton, more than twenty years earlier, that had changed things. Being woken up in the middle of the night to find half the Cabinet milling outside your bedroom door, or being dragged from the rubble in front of television cameras to be asked, 'Was anyone else in there with you, Harry?' puts a hell of a dampener on things. So, very gradually, these occasions became briefer and ever less ambitious. PCDC.

Except, of course, when Conference was turned into a race for the leadership and the ritual slaughter of the innocents.

It got off to a nervous start. Those involved arrived at Torquay in the middle of an autumn storm with all sorts of foul things being swept across the Channel from France. A tall Scots pine that had stood for decades on the front lawn of the headquarters hotel was torn from its roots and fell across the Volvo from which Jack and Tina Saunders had only just emerged. 'Blown Away', the *Record* roared dismissively, although its initial attempt had simply said: 'Missed!'

Dom and Ginny had arrived the previous day; the arrangements were, after all, Dom's responsibility as party chairman and there were always loose ends. The first thing they discovered as they walked into their suite was a huge bouquet of flowers emblazoned with greetings from Jack and Tina. A little note revealed that Jack wished to share his luck. Wasn't every conference he won the finest speaking slot.

The room was overheated and stuffy; Ginny immediately set about opening windows and creating draughts as a member of the hotel staff brought in an ice bucket out of which was poking a bottle of champagne It was the finest vintage. 'With the compliments of Mrs Hazel Basham,' the functionary announced, 'to wish you well in your first conference as chairman.'

'Ah, our first bribe,' Ginny declared cheerfully. Hazel Basham was the party's shadow minister for Home Affairs and had just declared her intention to run for Leader. 'Wonder what will be next.'

They had only moments to wait. At the door, red in cheek, knocking hesitantly, stood Ed Goodthorpe, Education spokesman and another leadership contender. Big, bluff man with receding hair combed strategically in every direction.

'Come to complain about your speaking slot, Ed?' Ginny enquired. 'My fault entirely. I've got such silly fingers.'

'No, no, it's . . .' A short silence. He stepped across the threshold and closed the door. 'I wonder whether I might have an entirely *private* word?'

'Of course, Ed,' Dom replied.

He came forward, hands clasped. 'Er, would you mind, Ginny? Boys' business.'

Somehow she conjured up a smile. 'I'll go and unpack.' She disappeared into the bedroom.

'Want your advice. And help, Dom,' Goodthorpe began, his tone full of artificial bluster as he perched awkwardly on the arm of a chair. 'Been a bit clumsy. You see, years ago, when I was first asked to be in *Who's Who* . . . Well, you know what it's like. They send you a form with all these damn-fool questions about where you were conceived and what your hobbies are and . . .' the slightest hesitation '. . . where you went to school. All bloody nonsense, but you try to play the game, you know how it is.' A bead of sweat had crept out just below his hairline, even though he was sitting directly in one of Ginny's draughts. 'Anyway, I did it in a rush. Got my secretary to fill in most of it. Not bothered much to check it since.' The flickering of his eye screamed that he was lying. 'And it seems I've left the impression that I got a good degree from Oxford.'

A silence.

'And didn't you?'

'I was at Oxford, for sure. But the poly. Not the university. Did a course in business studies.' He tried to laugh. 'Self-made man, me. Always have been. Proud of it. Not born within spitting distance of any silver spoon.'

'It was a course, you said, Ed. Did you get a degree?'

'Too impatient to meet the challenge of the outside world, I was. Always have been. So . . . not a degree, exactly. A very good diploma.' His eyes fell on the bottle of champagne with the look of a man laid out in the desert, but Dom didn't move.

'A typographical error?'

'Nothing more.'

'And?'

'The wretched thing is, some little shit from our campaigning department's found out about it. Ron Smith, or Don Smith, or some such name. Called me up with all sort of fool questions.'

'Threatening?'

'Not exactly. But I'd be damn grateful if you could have a word. Tell him about the ways of the world. Persuade him to forget it. Either nail his balls to the mast or offer him some thoroughly deserved promotion, whatever you think best. Leave it to you. But let's keep it from the media. Don't want any distractions at a time like this, do we?'

'I could see unfortunate consequences. Particularly for an Education spokesman.'

'I'd be eternally grateful, Dom. Eternally. Capital E.'

'Of course.'

Goodthorpe sprang to his feet as though a catch had been unleashed. 'You know, this leadership campaign's going well for me, Dom. Bit of an outsider, I know, like the Lone Ranger. But between you and me, old friend, I've got several new endorsements up my sleeve to announce after the conference. "Hi-Yo Silver away", and all that.'

'Congratulations.'

'Oh, I know you've got to play the bloody virgin on this one, Dom, but afterwards, if it's anything to do with me, I'd love to have you on my team. Goes without saying, eh, Ke-Mo Sah-Bee?'

Ah, the inducement. Dom had been waiting for it. 'As you say, Ed, it goes without saying.'

A trifle awkwardly, Goodthorpe grabbed Dom's hand and wrung it. 'Just love this teamwork,' he muttered, making for the door. Then a last thought. He turned. 'It's not – d'you think? – a resigning matter.'

'Ed, there's no one to hand any resignation to. You're fine.'

For the first time, as he closed the door behind him, Goodthorpe's smile was genuine. His footsteps were still fading down the corridor when Ginny emerged from the bedroom. It was clear she had heard every word.

'Bloody fool.' Dom snorted. 'To think he could get away with it.'

'Men always do.'

Dom made a mental note to give himself a good kicking later. Perhaps then he'd stop digging his own grave. 'What do you think I should do?'

'Humour him. Do as he asks. That would be the decent thing.'

'Let him off? Forgive him?'

'Forgiveness is for gods, Dom.'

'Then he's safe. No exposure.'

She spent some time rearranging the flowers before she replied. 'I have a feeling, with subtlety like that, Mr Goodthorpe will end up exposing himself.'

In the ensuing hours their hotel suite came to resemble a *souk* with, it seemed, half the world knocking on their door, hauling their wares and ambitions behind them. A kaleidoscope of faces passed through, smiling, frowning, some blank with awe, others burning with ambition. And they all came in search of Dominic. While he dispensed wisdom, Ginny dispensed wine and kept the windows open just wide enough that they neither boiled nor froze. She was quiet, so very warming to the eye yet invisible when the moment required, and devastatingly effective. She knew about entertaining and what some people expected of a hostess; her years spent watching her mother in the officers' mess had seen to that. People came with their cares and usually left with a smile, remarking on what a good team Ginny and Dom made.

Yet there were others who insisted on trying to be part of that team, claiming ownership of Dom. Party officials, agents, press officers, researchers, advisers. Even an advertising man. Peddling their wares. To all of them Ginny smiled and served. One of these itinerant market traders made a particular impression, if only because of his ability to ignore her completely. He was Archie Blackstone, the party's chief press officer, a Scot with a prominent scar on his chin and a brow so dark it would have made a turnip weep. He had manners to match. The fractured veins on his cheeks told of a lifetime spent in battle with some type of bottle or other, yet when Ginny offered him a glass he dismissed it with a curt wave, not even raising his eyes in thanks. Ah, the sinner come to repentance, Ginny surmised. In his politics, too. Dom had told her that at university Archie Blackstone had been an active Marxist who had long since forsaken the creed but who still carried with him many of his old Stalinist habits. A committed man, difficult to please, but tireless in his toiling for the party, with attitudes as hard as poor old Colin Penrith's arteries.

Archie seemed to be everywhere, know everyone, see everything. Not much got past him. He was there the following day, loitering in the hospitality room, just as Dom was preparing to march out on to the platform of the conference hall and open the proceedings. The speech had been written and rehearsed, then well trailed, and the air was rippling with anticipation. The tension — and the heat — was rising. This was Dom's first major speech to the massed ranks of party faithful. His eyes were flickering, his fingers agitated, he was sipping too much coffee, wrapped up in a world of worries. Archie, seeing the signs, was trying to distract him with small-talk, but Dom was evidently not listening. He interrupted the Scot in mid-flow. 'Archie, could you give us a moment alone, please?' he said.

Archie scowled at Ginny, then walked away with evident reluctance.

'Do you have my compact, Ginny?' Dom asked. She fished in her handbag and brought it out, a shiny silver disc full of face powder. 'I'll never get used to using these things,' he complained, as he stared at himself in the small mirror and flapped in vain at his face.

'Here, let me,' she said, taking the compact. Suddenly they were very close.

As she dabbed away at the pinpricks of moisture that were already appearing on his face, he took her hand, stilled it. 'Do you love me, Ginny?'

'This is scarcely the time or place . . .'

'Can't think of any better. It's more important than anything. Do you? Still love me?'

She took a step back, studied him. 'We did that, remember. Didn't work too well.'

'But . . . can't we still try? I'd like to.'

'Perhaps.'

'When?'

'When it stops hurting.'

From the auditorium on the other side of the wall came the buzz of expectation as the last of the crowd moved into their seats.

'I'm so very sorry, Ginny. I'd do anything. Give this all up if it could save our marriage. I can change, you know.'

She saw in his face the blush of remorse and in his eyes the flicker of fear. She also spotted his first grey hair. A special moment, a reminder of how time moved on and waited for no one. 'Thank you,' she replied, 'but it's me who has to change.'

An assistant was walking towards them, waving a sheaf of papers, but a look from Dom warned her away.

'You've been a fool, Dom, but so have I. I should've expected something would happen. You're a man, an imperfect creature of habit, and we all know what men's habits have been ever since you crawled out from your caves. So I'm angry with myself. For painting this silly, simplistic picture of what our life together was going to be about. I should have known better, been more grown-up. Stupid of me. And I don't normally do stupid. So, you see, it's me who's got to change.'

'Change?'

'Look at things a different way.'

'Such as?'

'It's about means and ends. You are still the means in my life, Dom. It's simply that the end has changed.'

'How?'

'Very simple. It's what you men might call the Get Lost Option.'

'What?'

'The Get Lost Option. Being in a position to tell the world to get lost and not giving a damn. Not relying on anyone else.'

'Even me?'

'Reliability is scarcely your hottest asset right now.'

He blanched.

'But don't worry. This should bring us closer together, Dom. You want to be Prime Minister. It's the most important thing in your professional life. And I want that, too. Very much. So I've decided we must work on it together. Save our marriage while we save your career. Be like the Clintons.'

'You've got political ambition?'

'No, I've got two kids. And I want to make sure they're taken care of no matter what. No matter what,' she repeated, with feeling.

'They're my kids, too, Ginny.'

'Of course.'

'I'd never let them down,' he replied heatedly.

'Any more than you'd let me down, Dom?'

'Are you still trying to punish me?'

'Punish you? I want you to become Prime Minister. Doesn't sound like much of a punishment to me.'

Archie was back, and others, at the door, waiting to escort them into the auditorium.

'What the hell is it you really want, Ginny?'

She gave his face another dab of powder. 'I want you – to go out there – reach deep into their underwear – and give them the time of their lives. You can do that, can't you?'

'Christ, you've changed.'

'There,' she said, with a final dab. 'We're in agreement already.'

★

The speech was, as the press later reported, a minor triumph. A mixture of eulogy for the old and incitement to the new. Kennedyesque, as some referred to it, although all the more obvious Kennedy clichés with which the first draft was littered had long been thrown out. As Ginny had bidden, the faithful were touched, and they responded.

Afterwards, keen to catch the tide, Dom had been hauled off to various television studios by Archie while Ginny was left to her own devices. Sitting under television lights for more than an hour and whittling your face into a smile can wilt even the most fragrant flowers, and she was keen to grab a few moments alone. When she returned to the hotel, all was still. The whirlwind of people that had passed through their suite had vanished, and she relished the freedom. Her clothes were uncomfortable, sticky, and she threw them off impatiently as she made her way to the bedroom. She ran the shower and stood beneath it until every trace of the last few hours had been washed away.

She towelled her hair as she walked back into the sitting room to retrieve her clothes. Suddenly, as she hummed a favourite tune, she realised she was no longer alone.

A man was staring at her. A young, dark face. Asian. Male. With round white eyes. And the only thing that stopped Ginny screaming in fright was the far more profound look of terror that had already laid siege to the young man.

He was well dressed, suited, an unlikely molester. He was carrying a bundle of papers that was slowly fluttering to the carpet. Then she recognised him. He was one of hundreds that had passed through her life in the last few chaotic hours. An aide.

'I . . . I knocked . . . It was open . . .' he gasped, his body twisting so that he could point to the door while his eyes remained fixed like a rabbit's on her body. His jaw kept sagging, and suddenly his knees buckled as though he were going to faint.

Then he fled, leaving his papers scattered among her clothes on the floor.

Ginny stepped back into the bedroom, locked the door, and sat on the bed next to a box of chocolates – another small gift. She popped one into her mouth and settled back on the pillow. The encounter after the shower was yet another of the multiplying moments that showed Ginny how she was losing control of her life. She seemed to have no hiding-place, not in her home, not in her bed, not even here in the shower. No use complaining: it was part of the game. Get on with it. Just make sure the game was worthwhile. She popped another chocolate into her mouth and fell into a fitful sleep.

If she was losing control of her life, at least she had the consolation of some influence over her evening when Archie dragged Dom off to a *Newsnight* interview. Strange man, Archie. Still hadn't spoken to her directly. Either very shy or very focused or simply bloody rude. Either way, she had the feeling they were going to come into conflict somewhere down the line. In fact, the way he seemed to be laying claim to ownership of Dom, she might have to insist on it.

A dutiful wife would have stayed in and watched the *Newsnight* interview, but she had decided that she no longer did dutiful so she went for a walk. Fresh air. Clear the mind. Refresh the soul.

A security cordon had been thrown round the hotel and conference area, but it was full of people she might know who would insist on talking to her. She wanted to be alone, so she passed beyond the cordon and wandered aimlessly for a while through the streets of Torquay. She shunned the crowded bars and pubs around the old harbour and instead headed towards the rising moon. Soon the bustle of the marina was little more than an echo across the water, and she followed a path that led across open ground towards the silhouette of Torre Abbey, not, perhaps, the wisest walk for a lone woman at night, but the isolation appealed to her.

She began to think she might have made a mistake when, from up ahead, came a cry and the sounds of a disturbance. She could hear someone running towards her, and others were in pursuit. She looked around. There was nowhere to hide but a few scattered trees. She was making for them when a figure grew out of the darkness, stumbling in its haste and all but knocking her over.

It was the boy from the bathroom. Once more his eyes were filled with bewilderment and fear. He was panting, exhausted, and she stretched out an arm to stop him falling. He was too breathless to speak but his pursuers were drawing nearer in the darkness. As they did so, she could hear their shouts. They were angry, threatening, inciting each other and exchanging all sorts of foulness about 'the bloody little queer' and 'that stinking Paki poofter'. In her arms, the young man seemed to sag still further, his eyes now flooding with terror. She had no time to ask questions or debate the issues, only to remember the description her father had once given, when in his cups, about what he and his fellow officers had done to two squaddies who'd been caught together. They'd set their body hair on fire with cigarette lighters, then kicked out the flames with their boots. And they had been proud of what they had done. The memory made her tremble, almost as violently as was her new companion. She pulled him towards the trees; they gave them no proper cover but, as the hunters came into view, she threw her arms around the young man and kissed him.

The pursuers slowed, peering through the darkness, laughed crudely at what they thought they saw. Then they hurried on their way.

For a while the young man was too breathless to speak. She let him collect his wits before she spoke. 'I think you owe us both a drink.'

So they settled themselves in a harbour-side pub clad in plastic and jukeboxes, and he bought them both a glass of wine. Only then did he speak, with his eyes fixed firmly upon the table. 'I'm Bobby Khan.'

'It seems as though our paths are destined to cross, Mr Khan. I think you know who I am.'

'I'm so terribly sorry about earlier. About everything.'

'You offended me. Doesn't do much for a girl's esteem when a man sees her naked and screams in terror. But I guess that's not your main area of expertise.'

There was a lightness in her voice and a gentleness in her tone that encouraged him to raise his eyes and engage her for the first time. 'Thank you,' he whispered, through lips that she could see had been split. 'I seem to end up shocking you every time we meet.'

She shook her head. 'Not entirely. There was something in your eyes – something missing – when you saw me coming out of the bathroom. Not quite what I expected. Call it feminine instinct, if you like.'

'I . . . I don't usually go cruising,' he spluttered, as though anxious to unburden himself. 'It's just that . . . it gets unbearable for a gay Muslim guy at times, and when you're far away from home . . .'

'You're not married,' she asked tentatively.

His eyes flared with resentment. 'I'm not a hypocrite, Mrs Edge. But if my family ever found out . . .' His head sank once more.

'They will. Eventually. Probably guessed already. Like I did.'

'They must never know. The disgrace would kill my mother. And my father would kill me. Yes, kill me! He came to this country, nothing but a poor tailor from a village near Mirpur, dragging all the old beliefs and prejudices behind him. He is very proud, a self-made businessman, gives a shedload of money to the party, yet in so many ways he is still stuck in his village in Kashmir. That's why he has such high hopes for me. Wants me to become an MP. The first Asian Prime Minister!' He laughed in self-contempt. 'Wants me to take over the world when he doesn't even know what my world is.'

'Is it so wrong for him to have high hopes for you?'

'For himself! He wants to brag to his friends about his important son. Start a dynasty. Except—'

'The dynasty thing's a pain for a guy who drives in reverse.'

'Something like that.' He dived into his drink. Warm. White. Disgusting. He couldn't even do that right. Then he slumped into sullen silence.

When she spoke again, her voice was low, but it couldn't disguise the silent shame. 'I was never what my father wanted, either.'

'You?'

'I was supposed to be the son my father never had. Climb all the mountains he'd tripped up on. Make a mark. Make sure his name was never forgotten. But all he got was me.'

'Even so, he's got to be very proud of you.'

'That's sweet. But ridiculous. We haven't spoken in years.'

'So sad. But in some ways I envy you. Being able to live your own life.'

'Doesn't always work that way for a woman, Bobby.' She used his name, and spoke with such wistfulness that, for a moment, he forgot his own sorrows. Then she dragged herself back from the world into which she had slipped and stared at him across the smeary table. 'What do you do in the party?'

'A researcher.'

'Of what?'

'Just about everything. They kick me from one department to the next, like I've got some awful disease.'

'The skin thing?'

'The money thing. They know my old man bought me my job. They resent it. Call me the Curry King.' He swallowed more of his wine, trying to wash away a bitter taste with stale chardonnay. 'But you want to know something, Mrs Edge? I know more about the party than anyone else you're ever likely to meet on a dark night.'

'Or in my bathroom. Except my husband, of course.'

For the first time, he smiled, split lip and all. It was infectious. And through the noise of a blaring jukebox she made one of those instantaneous, instinctive decisions she was coming to discover she rather enjoyed. 'I'd like us to become friends, Bobby.'

'Why?'

'Oh, many reasons. Because I need someone like you. Because you bloody well owe me. And because I like you. We've a lot in common. Both outsiders in this game. Butterflies tangled in the same net.'

'Friends? You want to go to the cinema or something?'

She laughed. 'I was thinking more that you might help me swim through this pool of venom they call a political party.'

'But you have your husband.'

'As you have your father. And I suspect that some of the help I want might fall outside your formal job description. That's why I would like to share – as friends.'

'Share what, exactly?'

'Well, in the first place, everything you know about Archie Blackstone. Then there's a girl called Julia Summers. You can talk to me as you walk me back to the hotel.'

He stared at her, uncertain what he was getting into but, whatever it was, it had to be better than being beaten up on the beach. 'OK.'

They rose to their feet, their chairs scraping on the bare wooden floor.

'But one thing, Mrs Edge.'

'Ginny, for God's sake. Friends, remember.'

'One thing, *Ginny*. As a friend. It may be a spectator sport for me but I still have an eye for the game. And I just thought you'd like to know. You have a fantastic body.'

'Why, thank you, Bobby. If you carry on displaying judgement like that, I think we're going to be very considerable friends.'

Conference was a swirling tidal pool into which all kinds of life were washed. The following morning the pool overflowed into Ginny's suite. When she came out from her bedroom she discovered the sitting room filled with party aides – headed by Archie – who occupied every conceivable chair, window-seat and squatting place. She decided to take her breakfast in the dining room, hoping she might get lucky and find a few moments for herself. Yet as she came down the long staircase and past the reception desk, she couldn't avoid noticing the fuss. A man of around thirty in an expensive but crumpled Italian suit and with professionally distressed hair was making it known that he was unhappy. He wanted a larger room, overlooking the sea, and, no, he didn't wish to wait. Not a man of great patience. His accent sounded as if it came from the mid-Atlantic during the hurricane season, and Ginny suspected it was manufactured. So, she knew, was the fuss. A man who wanted to be – insisted on being – noticed. Suddenly he turned from harassing the receptionist and smiled. 'Hello, Mrs E.'

'I'm sorry, have we met?'

'No, but I know who you are. It's my job.' He stuck out a hand. 'Max Morgan. I edit the *Record*.' Ah, that daily paper whose front page passed itself off as the defender of all British virtues while the pages inside took turns at degrading women and defrocking priests. Hugely controversial. And highly profitable.

'The man who published that really nasty front page about Colin's funeral.'

'Yes, that was a mistake,' he admitted. 'The readers weren't interested in him, dead or alive. Circulation dropped fifty thousand that day.'

'As a friend of Colin's I found it offensive.'

'Course you did. Wouldn't expect anything else.'

She found his bluntness disarming. 'I suppose, as Dom's wife, I'm expected to be friendly,' she began.

'Why? You don't know me. And I'm not a friend of yours.'

'I imagine it's rather difficult being the friend of an editor.'

'But it's amazing how many people like your husband form a long queue at my door and apply for the job.'

'Are you trying to be offensive, Mr Morgan?'

'I'm a journalist. What do you expect?' Yet the words were

delivered with such unbridled enthusiasm and self-mockery that, in spite of herself, she found she was smiling.

'I'm not sure what to expect of journalists nowadays.'

'Then come to lunch with me and learn.'

'I don't think that would be such a good idea, Mr Morgan. People will think I'm selling out to you.'

'Then I'll let you pay your own whack. Can't say fairer than that. See you at Moby Nick's. Fish restaurant just round the corner. Shall we say . . . twelve thirty? By the way, like the new hair.' Then he saw someone across the far side of the room and was gone.

'Rude bastard,' she muttered to herself. Lunch with him would be about as much fun as a smear test. But, as she went in search of fresh grapefruit, she reflected on the fact that he had noticed her new hair. Toni & Guy would be gratified, yet Dom hadn't said a word, hadn't noticed, too distracted.

It was only much later that morning, and after yet another glance in the mirror, that she resolved to go. What had she to lose, after all? Wouldn't do to poison the well for Dom. Yet no sooner had she made up her mind than she grew agitated. She was being foolish. He was taking her for a ride; she would even have to pay for herself. It would be yet another of those unexpected expenses and editors didn't lunch cheap. Maybe just a prawn salad. And he could pay for the wine.

She had no need to worry. When she turned up a deliberate fifteen minutes late she discovered that Moby Nick's served little other than fish and chips. It would do more damage to her diet than her bank account. He was sitting at a window table, his mobile phone clamped to his ear, and lassoed her with his smile as she came over but didn't put down the phone. He listened for another minute or more before saying simply, 'No.' Then he cut the phone dead. 'Bloody lawyers,' was all he offered by way of explanation and apology. 'And I've already ordered for both of us. Knew you'd be in a hurry, and it all tastes pretty much the same. Deep fried.'

'How considerate.'

'Me? Nah,' he said, shaking his head. 'I'm in a hurry, too.'

He was deliberately trying to provoke her, get some reaction that would give him the upper hand. Everything seemed to be a game with him. She decided to play by her own rules. 'Do you enjoy being disliked, Mr Morgan, or is it something you've just grown used to?'

'I might ask the same of your husband and his party.'

'Do you take anything seriously?'

'Let's see. There's my Arsenal season ticket and my Maserati.' He was counting off on his fingers. 'That's about it.'

'I always suspected you of having absolutely no judgement.'

'And yet you came to lunch.'

She wasn't doing very well here, she realised. Still a lot to learn.

Suddenly his tone softened. 'Come on, Mrs E, let's enjoy this. I'm only kidding. I've got plenty of time. Hope you have, too.'

'We'll see.' For the first time she had an opportunity to study him up close. The crumpled nature of his clothes was, she decided, calculated. The Common Man image. But his eyes were bright, his skin smooth, the dental work expensive, and somewhere beneath the folds of wool and silk she suspected she would find a public-school education and a pretty rugged physique. He probably spent more time in the gym than in a pub. And, unlike so many editors, not a speck of dandruff.

'Don't get me wrong,' he was saying, 'I'm only brutal about politicians on a professional basis. Nothing personal in it. And you have to admit I'm pretty even-handed about it most of the time.'

'But if you dislike them all, why bother coming here?'

'Oh, to look. To listen. To see who runs off with the hotel towels. To throw around a lot of champagne and see how they react.'

'Incitement?'

'Not necessary.'

'Invention, then.'

'God, you mean David Mellor didn't really play for Chelsea?'

'You judge so harshly.'

'A man who cheats on his wife deserves everything he gets, don't you agree?'

'Unless he's your proprietor, of course.'

'Ouch. You fight dirty. You ever want a job, little lady, you let me know.'

She shook her head. 'I've got a job, thank you. So why did you invite me to lunch, Mr Morgan? Apart from wanting to offer me employment.'

'Three reasons, I guess. First, I was hungry. Second, there's a leadership election, so I thought I might ply you with chips and see if you coughed up any juicy insights.'

'They're all saints.'

'Saints? Trouble with sainthood is that you usually have to get yourself martyred first.'

She couldn't help laughing. 'I think if you want insight, Mr Morgan, you should talk to someone like Archie Blackstone. He knows much more than I do.'

'I'm sure he does. But he only gives what he wants to give. One of the toughest damned press men I know. They cut that one out of solid rock.' Morgan's tone implied that he meant it. 'When old Colin got caught with his pants down, Archie managed to persuade the world for a while that he died giving his all to the nation. Hell of a spin, that was.'

The wine arrived. He whistled as he studied the bottle. 'Jesus, this had better be good. Costs a fortune. Got a name that only my royal correspondent could pronounce.' He noticed her flinch. 'And I hope you'll allow me to make it my treat, Mrs E. It's been a while since anyone gave me such a good run for my money.'

'Your proprietor's money,' she reminded him.

'I think, Mrs E, that I'm going to have to watch you.' There was a twinkle in his eye that had a distinctly masculine edge. Ginny was surprised by how good it felt to be appreciated. He was amusing, uncouth, entirely lacking in pomposity, overflowing with testosterone and exceedingly dangerous.

'So what about politics, Mrs E?' he asked, as two slabs of fish arrived that fell over the edge of the plates.

'Oh, I don't know much about politics, Mr Morgan, except that yours are all upside-down, slavishly supporting this silly government.'

'This government's got more pricks in it than my old dad's dartboard,' he declared, conducting with his fork.

'Yet you support it.'

'For the moment.'

'You might change?'

'It's possible. Depends on many things. Like who wins this leadership race of yours. I mean, there's Jack Saunders, but he's—'

'Old?'

'I was just thinking dull. Listening to Jack is like sitting in the front row of a lecture on flower-arranging. Now Tina, there's a fun woman.' He chuckled. 'Unlike Hazel Basham, who's about as much fun as a visit to the dentist. Frightful creature. You think that any moment she's going to leap on you and rip out a couple of teeth. I once timed how long she could talk without a single prompt from me. Twenty-three minutes. Twenty-three! Enough to make the balls of an armadillo ache. And old Goodthorpe – hell, he's got the attention span of a flight of starlings. Talking political philosophy with him is about as dangerous as walking through a farmyard in sandals. Never know what you're going to step in next. And who else is there?'

'There's Charlie Malthouse,' she replied, perhaps a shade too quickly.

'Charles Redvers Stanley Malthouse, you mean? Couldn't fit him in a decent headline now, could you? Name's too bloody long. And too many ancestors.'

'Iain Madden.'

He rolled his eyes as though it were his last moment on the planet.

'And George Pascal, of course.'

'Too French. The English may put up with a Scotsman – or even a Welshman at a pinch – but never a ruddy foreigner.'

'We'll just have to wait and see, I suppose.'

'But I don't. I don't wait, I make things happen. In my job you get to play God. Create thunder, hurl huge bolts of lightning, then rearrange the world. Decide who should be the next leader and see if we can squeeze it in between the tits and the footie.'

She wasn't sure if he was laughing at her.

'And I hear your hubby did himself a power of good yesterday. Excellent speech. A man to watch.'

'I agree.'

'Tough game, politics. Remorseless. Rotten at times.'

'Bit like being a mum.'

'I wouldn't know. Divorced. No kids, thank goodness.'

'Then you don't know what you're missing.'

He held up his hands in mock surrender. 'Fair enough. And if there's anything else you think I'm missing, at any time, just call me, will you? Use me.'

'Use you?'

'Of course. It's the game. Politicians lie to us and we lie about them. Everyone uses each other. But you . . .' he leaned back in his chair, studying her – studying all of her '. . . you, I suspect, aren't into that game. You strike me as cutting a straight furrow. Which means if there's anything you ever want my help with, I'll always be happy to hear from you.'

'Thank you, Mr Morgan. Was that the third reason you wanted to have lunch with me?'

'Not exactly. It's just that when I saw you coming down the stairs this morning, I fancied you something rotten. Couldn't resist.' He was wearing that broad boyish smile once more. He shrugged his shoulders as though in apology. 'Hell, I didn't get where I am today without being pretty damned irresponsible.'

She tried very hard to prevent herself, but once more she laughed. 'Mr Morgan—'

'Call me Max. I can't go round propositioning a woman who calls me Mr Morgan. Slap me, throw your mushy peas at me, pour your wine over me, but for heaven's sake call me Max.'

'Max, I would rather sleep with a goat.'

'Funny,' he said, tucking into his haddock, 'that's what half the girls in my newsroom tell me.' He chewed thoughtfully. 'Thank God for the other half.'

Her instincts about Archie Blackstone were correct. He was going to be trouble. She was walking up the broad stairway of the hotel to her room when she saw him waiting for her at the top.

'I heard you've been having lunch with Max Morgan,' he said gruffly.

'Spies?' she asked flippantly.

'Not necessary when you're sat in a window-seat.'

'I'll remember to choose one of those smoke-filled back rooms next time.' She went to move past him but he stood resolutely in her way.

'What did you think you were doing, Mrs Edge, meeting with an editor, particularly one like that, without telling me first?'

'Sorry, Archie, I had no idea I was supposed to get permission in order to have lunch.'

'Always, when it comes to the press. Only wise thing to do.'

'Can I send you the bill, too?' Her flippancy failed to mask the sarcasm.

'This isn't a game, Mrs Edge. You've no idea how those bastards will try to roast you. So what did he want? What did you tell him?'

'He wanted lunch. I told him I wanted the fried haddock.'

His look would have soured a mother's milk. 'Might I suggest,' he continued, in a tone that would not have been out of place at a bank raid, 'that, in order to avoid any embarrassment to your husband or the party, you ask for a little guidance before launching yourself into the unknown? There are sharks out there, and this is no time for games.'

'I'm not sure I want to play games.'

'Good. That's settled, then. Glad there's been no misunder-standing, Mrs Edge.'

She was gathering herself to lose her temper, but as he spoke, the tiny crenellations in his cheeks seemed to merge into the heavy flock wallpaper behind his head. It made him seem much less threatening, almost pathetic. And this was but a minor skirmish in the war that lay ahead.

'You can call me any time you want, day or night,' he was saying.

She was about to try to defuse the atmosphere by suggesting that he could call her Ginny, but changed her mind. Mrs Edge was fine, so far as he was concerned. She remembered her father's old military maxim. Never get too close to the enemy.

Hazel Basham had many disadvantages for a politician. She was a woman, of course, which didn't help, and what was worse she had far too many ideas. Prolific brain functions don't make for an easy ride through the murky waters of Westminster: they unsettle your sleep and distract your attention from the vital task of guarding your back, but Mrs Basham chose to ignore the realities and insisted on sharing her thoughts with everyone. She was petite, which didn't show up on television but which in crowded company gave the impression of a terrier, always snapping at the ankles. She also had a figure that was the doom of good intentions, not that many good intentions are left loitering around after dark at Conference.

These political gatherings often have an extraordinary effect on the inmates. Those who spend the day preaching and pontificating seem to undergo a metamorphosis as soon as the sun sinks beyond the sea; they relax, they drink, they mix adrenaline and emotion, often with devastating results. And so . . . PCDC. Party Conference Doesn't Count. By the morning everything is forgotten, and what is forgotten doesn't need forgiving.

Hazel Basham was not a hypocrite, so far as politicians go. She wasn't given much to moralising or preaching family values. Indeed, one profile in the *Guardian* had compared her to Lucrezia Borgia, a description she took as a compliment and posted on her website. Better a politician of any reputation than no reputation at all. But her politics showed no such tolerance. She was tough and determined, and very much wanted to be leader. Her brief was Home Affairs, but when she made her speech on the first day of the conference, she strayed far and widely. Most women are not naturally gifted as orators, their rising passion often ending in an undignified screech that plays into the hands of mocking male sketch-writers, but Hazel had got it just about right. She'd struck all the right notes, bashing away at criminals, then the media in general and the government in particular, before moving on to the curse of homelessness and the liberating virtues of patriotism before casting some pretty hefty stones in the direction of foreigners. She had finished with a peroration along the lines of Britain brave, Britain free, Britain under closed-circuit television and Britain under me. In short, she was in danger of becoming the darling of the conference.

When she had taken her standing ovation she was perspiring slightly, but that only served to enhance her image as a resolute fighter. The adulation and interviews that followed only helped inflate the magic of the moment, and by the time late evening came she had gone way beyond party policy and all but guaranteed every household a CCTV system of its own. She failed completely to notice that she hadn't eaten dinner, and was content to ride the flood of excitement that greeted her at every turned corner. When, finally, she sat in the corner of the bar at the headquarters hotel and the director of the party's advertising agency offered her a bottle of Pol Roger, *cuvée* Winston Churchill, very cold, it was the first moment of the day she had felt able to relax.

It's a feature of fiction that it can rarely be stretched far enough to capture the stupidities of real life. People don't always act in their best interests: often they do things that make no sense at all and that seem absolutely revolting in the cold light of day, particularly when it comes wrapped in the front pages of the morning's newspapers. Perhaps it's arrogance, swallowing your own hype, on coming to believe that because you spend so much time looking down the lens of a television camera you are somehow on a different and more elevated plane from others. Sometimes it's simply a combination of innocence and inexperience, and all the time it's a failure to remember that politics are acted out on a stage in a way that demands the suspension of disbelief and any sense of moderation, and is an act that can't be transported into real life without terrible consequence. Wars have been started for less.

So, after the second bottle of Pol Roger had been ordered and consumed, it was silly of Hazel to accept the ad exec's suggestion that he see her to her door, and folly to allow him beyond it. But her husband was in a different part of the world, as usual, and there was no way she was going to be able to sleep with all that adrenaline pumping through her body. The heady mix of sweat and success was getting to her. Anyway, it's what happens on these occasions. Didn't matter.

PCDC.

Four

OM THREW HER OUT of their suite early the following morning. 'Got a big donor who wants to see me. Asian. Think he's going to wave another cheque at us but wants to give it anonymously. They always do. I've offered him breakfast. Here. Hope you don't mind, darling.'

There had been a time when she wouldn't have minded. She did now, felt excluded, but this wasn't one to fight him on. Anyhow, she didn't fancy breakfast. She decided to go for a swim.

The hotel pool was almost empty. As she came out of the changing room she noticed Bobby at the far end, with two other men, splashing each other, filling the place with noise. One she recognised as a journalist on *The Times*. When they saw her they grew quiet, exchanged a few words, then the other two climbed out, leaving Bobby on his own. He swam towards her. He was an excellent swimmer, had the body for it.

'I'm beginning to get a complex,' she said, as his head broke the surface by her feet. 'Every time I take my clothes off, men start running away.'

'Don't take it personally.' He smiled, water cascading from his nut-brown face. 'Those two wouldn't be interested in your body even if you came with a million pounds pinned to it.'

'Unlike my husband. Would you believe it? I've been pushed away from my own breakfast table in favour of some filthy rotten money man.'

'Ah, that would be my father.'

'What?'

'My father. The filthy rotten money man.'

'Oh, shit,' she stammered. 'I apologise.'

'Not necessary.' He laughed, enjoying the upper hand.

She slipped into the pool beside him, her body breaking out in excitement as it made contact with the water. 'Will you be seeing him while he's here, your father?'

'Not unless he's brought his bathing trunks with him. That's why I'm here. Hiding.'

'Hiding? From your father?'

'From all his questions. About my friends. About why I've not brought a girl home in almost two years. That's one of the reasons he sent me to Westminster in the first place. Thinks I'm too shy. Wants me to go forth and sin. If only he knew. He's heard a lot about the women of Westminster. He's hoping some of them will lead me astray.' He laughed again, but this time the sound was empty, without humour.

'You can't hide it for ever, Bobby.'

'Can't I? Westminster's a good place for hiding things. Most people there seems to be hiding something or other.'

'Are you serious? Everything comes out into the open nowadays.'

'Coming out into the open has got several Ministers the sack,' he joked drily.

'Didn't mean it like that.'

'Of course you didn't. I was just making a point. It doesn't pay to be gay.'

She searched the pool, looking for the counter-argument. 'But surely you could—'

'Ginny, you have to understand, you're the only straight person I've ever dared talk to about this.'

'The only one?'

He did a cartwheel in the water; he was so lithe. 'Well, there was a party whip I once confided in. Nice fellow, old, very understanding. Actually, too bloody understanding. He invited me back to his place to talk about it, filled me with drink, then tried to seduce me.'

'Seriously? The bastard. Who was it?'

Bobby smiled and drew a finger across his lips to indicate his silence.

Ginny persisted: 'He's not still a whip, is he?'

'No. Not any more. He got himself promoted. He's in the Shadow Cabinet. But he'll never make leader, of course. Too many skeletons.'

'Wow. I never realised . . .'

'There's a lot of it about, as they say, even in Westminster. What – one in ten?'

'If there's so much of it around, why do you go off in the night looking for it in places like this, risking everything? Is it the thrill? The danger?'

'No. The CCTV. If I want to meet someone new at Conference, it has to be outside the security cordon. Haven't you noticed we've got cameras everywhere around this place? I don't fancy my private life being turned into a low-grade video for the entertainment of my colleagues.'

'No cameras in the bedrooms.'

'But in the bedroom corridors.'

She was still puzzled as they set out to swim a leisurely length. 'Sorry, but I don't understand. You have friends, like the two this morning.'

'Just friends, Ginny. I won't get too close to them, to anyone. The greatest risk I have is falling in love.'

'That's a risk we all have to take,' she replied, gasping, as she struggled to keep her chin above water.

'It would mean that my homosexuality would be out in the open. And my life would be ruined.'

'Not as bad as that.'

'Far worse. You've no idea what such things are like in a traditional

Kashmiri family. Our culture, our religion. The traditional punishment is to be buried alive.'

'Stupid prejudice.'

'Which almost everyone carries.'

'Not me.'

'Really? Ginny, would you have forgiven your husband if he'd been having an affair with another man?'

'You know about that? Damn,' she snapped, spitting out water. 'Does *everyone* know?'

'I told you, I know as much about what goes on as anyone. But, if it's of any comfort to you, more than most.'

'You're an interesting fellow, Bobby.'

Suddenly he stopped in the middle of the pool and held her arm, not harshly, but firmly. Ginny's feet could only just touch the bottom. She was struggling. He was standing in front of her, almost violently serious, but racked with passion rather than aggression. 'And you still haven't answered my question.' It clearly mattered to him, and not only what she thought but also how she answered. She knew she was being tested.

'Would it have made a difference?' She was spluttering, her head only just above the water, their bodies brushing against each other. 'Yes, it would have made a difference. Don't ask me why. Instinct.'

'Instinct is very important. It's what we are. It's just that I have different instincts.'

'What the hell? I'm not sure I've forgiven him anyway.'

'Thank you for being honest with me, Ginny.'

'You keep me here much longer, and either I'm going to drown or I'll ruin your reputation.'

He snapped out of his mood and pulled her towards shallower water. Whatever test it had been, she thought she had passed, and their trust was driven deeper. As she climbed out of the pool, he followed, and she couldn't help noticing the deftly toned body, glistening darkly as it dried. It was the sort of body that would drive even a nun to distraction. A body meant for women. And she knew that his parents, no matter how wilfully blind, must at least suspect.

'Does it really matter so much what your father thinks, Bobby?' she asked, as she towelled her hair dry.

'Very much. I love him.'

'But what if you had an outstanding success, one that many people knew about? Let's say, a senior adviser to the Prime Minister.'

He laughed. 'Not very likely, given that I work for you lot.'

It was her turn to grasp his arm. 'But, Bobby, think. What if we came to power, and I helped ensure that you got a very senior post? In Downing Street. Your own office. All the trappings. Weekends at Chequers. Who knows, maybe even some sort of gong at the end of it? Wouldn't he have to accept who you are?'

He considered the matter for a moment. 'It might give me a fighting chance,' he conceded.

'Then let's do it.'

'Do what?'

'The Downing Street thing.'

'I like the sound of that. Just tell me what to do.'

'First reassure me that you're not one of those . . . you know, gossipy types.'

'You mean a Missy Telltale? A querulous old queen?'

'Something like that. We have to be able to trust each other.'

Once more he drew his finger across his lips to indicate his silence and discretion.

'Then the first thing we have to do is to make sure Jack Saunders wins this leadership race. He's our man, Bobby. The rest . . .' It was her turn to draw a finger, but slowly across her throat.

He took his time to respond. 'OK.'

'Anything we can do to help, Bobby. This could turn into one hell of a catfight. Tears, tantrums, just a little bit of treachery.' She held the tip of her index finger and thumb close together to show how little she meant, then slowly drew them wider.

'I think I can deal with that.'

'It might ruin your reputation.'

'Occupational hazard.'

'For all politicians.'

'And poofs.'

She paused, suddenly less confident. 'Tell me, Bobby, is she here? Julia?' It was a question she'd tried to avoid ever since she had arrived in this place, not knowing whether she was strong enough to deal with the answer.

'Yes,' he said.

With exaggerated care, she wiped water from her arms. 'Seems we've both got a lot of unfinished business to take care of.'

At the same time, in a different world, Ajok sat on board a bus that would, stop by patient stop, squeeze its way through the heavy traffic and take her to the headquarters of her trade union in Battersea. She had never been there before but Pat Creasey had given her instructions and he was waiting to meet her on the steps, already filling out a little form to reimburse her bus fare.

'A very good morning to you, Ajok. It's grand that you could come.'

'I find I have a lot of time at the moment, Mr Creasey.' Her eyes were ringed with sadness.

'Now, let's be having none of that. We'll go and find a cup of tea for us both, and then we'll dig out Mr Messenger.'

Mr Messenger turned out to be a middle-aged man with a long, mournful face, as if a lifetime of disappointment had dragged down the corners of his mouth. He sniffled a lot, too. Not good breeding stock, she decided, judging him in the manner that all Dinka women do when confronted with any man older than themselves. He occupied a stuffy, overheated office yet he wore a thick sweater with a handkerchief tucked up the sleeve for ready access. Pat Creasey introduced him as the union's Rights and Reconciliation Officer. 'Hello,' he said, in a voice that sounded like a cracked bell.

He motioned for them to sit down. Meanwhile, he shuffled through the extraordinary pile of paper that littered his desk and overflowed on to the surrounding cabinets and floor. It was some time before he found what he was looking for. 'Here it is.' He waved a sheet of paper in apparent triumph, but victory was not to last. His face fell once more. 'I'm afraid . . . Well, you'd better look at it.'

He handed the sheet to Ajok, who read it with Pat looking over her shoulder. 'I do not understand,' she whispered.

'It's from the Treasury Solicitors.' Messenger sniffed.

The single page had an imposing stamp at its top. Words such as 'reject', 'refusal', 'dismissal' and 'denied' leaped out at her. 'I do not understand,' she repeated.

'It means they're refusing to re-employ you, Ajok,' Creasey said, his natural enthusiasm waning.

'But this,' she pointed to a section of the letter, 'says that I was abusive.'

'They're saying you swore at them,' Messenger interpreted.

'It was he who swore at me. The supervisor.'

'He denies it. And the office clerk supports him. Obstructive and abusive, they say. It's their word against yours, I'm afraid.'

Ajok stared at the sheet of paper. Official. Stamped. And she remembered Khartoum. Another office, except she wasn't allowed any further than the threshold, and that only after a wait of five hours. She had needed a passport to leave the country, yet she had no husband and without a husband she had no true identity, only a value that was usually measured in head of cattle. It was the Dinka way. And the official had been foul, intent on humiliating her. 'What do you want? Why are you here? What have you done that you are so eager to leave our country?' He had accused her of selfishness and lack of honour, of dressing inappropriately, Dinka rather than Sharia, as if she could afford anything different, and he as good as told her she was some sort of troublemaker. Then he had left for prayers and had not returned that day. The following day the abuse had continued. Where was her husband? Had anyone in her family ever been in trouble? What, never? Not possible. She must be lying . . . He had waved a stamp at her and told her that she could not leave without his stamp, and he was not satisfied she deserved it. He had stamped an empty sheet of paper, taunting, but would not stamp hers; now, in her memory, it had appeared much like the stamp at the top of this new letter. And he had left once more for prayers, pushing her out of his way. When he returned, two hours later, it had begun all over again. She had pleaded. He had eventually suggested sex. She had refused. Then he had left for prayers once more.

It was while he was gone that she had stolen into his office and stamped the form herself. A terrible risk, but by that point she had had so little to lose. And now, it seemed, those same evil forces had caught up with her, were punishing her, for some new invented offence.

'I showed it to our own solicitor,' Messenger was saying. 'She's not optimistic. Not with two of them saying you were out of order.'

'But they would, wouldn't they?' Creasey protested. 'Bastards.'

Messenger simply shrugged and wiped his nose.

Ajok was still staring at the letter. She read the final section three times, as though refusing to comprehend. 'They are saying I am lying.'

'That's about the sum of it,' Creasey agreed.

'So, what do we do?' Messenger said. 'It's got to go to the employment tribunal now. Could be a complete waste of time.'

'I have so much time, thanks to them,' Ajok replied.

'Even so. No point in flogging a dead horse.'

'We could call their bluff,' Creasey suggested. 'Send in our own solicitor to the tribunal. Get them under oath.'

'Which could waste not only time but money,' Messenger replied.

'What might you be thinking, Ajok?' Creasey asked.

'I am thinking . . .' She was thinking of Khartoum. Of blind, stupid officials. Of men lying, taking advantage, for no better reason than that she was a woman. Of fighting back against them, not in the expectation of victory but simply because she had nothing much to lose. 'I want to fight,' she whispered.

'I dunno,' Messenger muttered.

'Come on, Messie – for God's sake, give the girl a chance,' Creasey urged.

'But the cost . . .'

'So turn down your feckin' heating. This is a trade union, not a sauna. Come on, man, she's paid her dues. Payback time.'

Messenger pointed to the letter. 'It seems such an uphill fight, Pat.'

'Thought that's what we were about.'

A strained silence. A sniff. Another sniff. 'Oh, I suppose so. Very well.'

Ginny had declared Conference to be a catfight, but Dom had very different ideas. He and his headquarters staff had worked tirelessly and spent a significant proportion of their scarce party funds to make sure this gathering was not only a fitting tribute to their fallen leader but, much more importantly, a launch-pad for whoever emerged as the successor. The deadline for final nominations was approaching, and all of the announced contenders had been given their moment in the spotlight. Everything had been planned like a military exercise; nothing was allowed to go astray. Archie had made sure of that. Plenty of touches for the media. The pamphlets in the hall had been printed on recycled paper, the cars used for official transport were gas-fuelled and zero-carbon, and they'd even recycled a number of B-list celebrities for the occasion. In a world in which political parties struggle constantly to reinvent and relaunch themselves, this seemed an opportunity sent from heaven.

Until the Government muscled in on the act. On the last day of the conference, as the tide of faithful began to flood and swirl around every corner of the hall, rumour spread of a major announcement to be made later that day. Soon Archie could be heard ranting and throwing chairs around in a back room. The Government was sending more troops back to Iraq. Raising the stakes. Nothing the conference could do to wipe that off the front pages. A pre-emptive strike, a cheap political trick, yet there was no point in complaining because . . . well, because Iraq was too important to play silly party games with, wasn't it?

And Jack Saunders hadn't helped. He'd been given the final speaking slot, an empty space to be filled with whatever mixture of dignified ambition and unbridled emotion he chose, yet when it came, it was less than it should have been, like a gentle summer breeze creeping through woodland that caused a few passing ripples yet had no lasting impact. It had left the faithful feeling like thwarted lovers who had expected and hoped for so much more. It left Dom wondering if Jack's heart was truly in the fight, or whether it had simply been Tina's idea. Jack got his standing ovation, of course, but a sense of unfulfilment was left hanging over the gathering, so that when Dom strode on to the spotlit stage that filled the centre of the hall to deliver the formal farewell, he knew there was both need and opportunity. To lift their spirits and his reputation. But he had no script for this. It was a moment of chance for which he hadn't prepared. He paused, uncertain. They waited, sensed his doubt, grew silent. He stiffened, then began.

'Friends.' His arms rose in salute to them all. 'For we are all friends who are gathered here . . .'

At times he sounded like a preacher so many of them remembered from their childhood, someone familiar, which made them reach out and embrace him. He was strong on his Bible. He compared the five contenders to the prophets, the Government to an Old Testament pestilence and poor old Colin to John the Baptist, the herald of greater times to come. 'And I say from my heart, from the foundations of my soul, that there has never been a better time to be among us.'

He had an actor's talent for the dramatic pause. As they waited for his next words, his eyes wandered to the crowded galleries as though searching the heavens. His hands rose slowly above his head, outstretched, palms forward as though showing stigmata, and trembling with scarcely restrained passion, like an ancient Messiah. 'A curtain is rising on the horizon. A curtain of opportunity. A new day dawning for us all. A day that will be filled with sunlight and success.'

They were shouting their agreement.

'And I tell you. No, I instruct and I demand of you, one and all. Go forth from this place and take with you our message. Go back to your constituencies. Spread the word. And prepare for victory!'

It was nonsense, of course. The Government was ten points ahead in the polls and coasting against an Opposition that had recently lost its leader and had long since lost any sense of direction. Colin had been a fine chap, dear fellow, of course he was, but too fine by half for the world of politics. Yet it was what they wanted to hear. As Dom's chin slumped down to his chest like that of an exhausted conductor and his last note faded away, they leaped up and screamed. They stamped their feet. They applauded until their hands were sore. Music was played, flags were waved, and Ginny joined him from her seat in the front row of the audience. They kissed, hugged, held hands, returned the waves of the crowd.

Ginny had never faced such circumstances. She was blinded by the lights, could see nothing but blurred faces, was deafened by the noise. But she felt the power, so intense it might carry people off and, indeed, often did. The atmosphere of adulation was so thick and sweet she could taste it. Dom, beside her, was surrounded by a masculine aura of sweat and success that touched her deep inside. It was a feeling that was almost sexual.

Then she realised that Julia was somewhere out there among

that sea of faces. Sharing in the moment. Just as she had shared other special moments. And now the other party dignitaries and their wives were joining them on the stage: Ed, Hazel, Jim, George, Jack – and Tina, giggling, whispering in another wife's ear, as she always seemed to do. And there were cameras everywhere, moving round them, capturing everything. And out in the front row she caught a glimpse of a dark, middle-aged face, probably Bobby's father's. And once more she came back to Julia. Bitch Julia. Sweat. Emotion. Stupidity. Tongues. Mistakes. Stimulation. Dom. Still more mistakes.

And, as the cameras closed in on her, Ginny was suddenly overflowing with ideas.

Five

HE CAME STRIDING TOWARDS HER, looking elegant.
'Nice threads. Bobby.'
'Should be,' he said, sitting down at the metal-topped table beside Ginny. 'My father owns four clothing factories with another two in the pipeline.'

'Ah, that's why he's so generous to us.'

Bobby shook his head and smiled. 'He's even more generous to the Prime Minister. What he does for us is simply insurance. Just in case of disaster. "Never stick all your pins in the same lapel," he says. That's why he likes to keep what he does so quiet.'

She clapped in appreciation. The sound reached out across the expanse of the atrium. They were sitting in the main gathering place of Portcullis House, the parliamentary office building that squatted uneasily on the river by Westminster Bridge. It was a clean, antiseptic place, with sweeping steel struts that supported a glass roof above the echoing central courtyard, and on to this large open space pitched bustling restaurants and coffee-shops. These people may no longer rule an empire, but they knew how to eat. At one end a huge portrait of three party leaders glared down upon them, except time had already moved on and they were no longer leaders: Blair, Kennedy, Hague, every one of them gone, blown away by bitterness, booze and premature baldness, leaving their qualities as leaders to be scratched over by no one but historians. There were other portraits, too, dotted around the wall spaces that looked down upon the great courtyard. Cabinet ministers, opposition spokesmen, senior backbenchers. All contemporary, all commissioned at considerable cost to the public purse, and extraordinarily self-indulgent. No sense of history, this place.

Ginny and Bobby were seated at one of the many tables, beneath a towering olive tree. He sipped *latte;* she made do with herbal tea. From all sides came the buzz of conspiracy. This place had no majesty, unlike the dark, wood-clad corners of the Palace of Westminster it was meant to relieve, but its very informality encouraged free exchange.

'How did you enjoy your moment in the spotlight?' Bobby asked.

'I found it . . . exhilarating. Also very dangerous. You can understand why some people are tempted to trade their mothers for a moment like that. It's a little as though you're standing on top of a barricade surrounded by the faces of a wild-eyed mob about to start a revolution.' She paused. 'Actually, come to think of it, it's exactly like that. Could cause all sorts of trouble.'

He noticed the trace of a faint smile crossing her face.

'Thing is, Bobby, there were cameras everywhere – it was a stage, for goodness' sake, it was all an act, but . . . It's astonishing how quickly you come to forget about the cameras. For a moment, as the heat and the excitement cling to you, you even think they're applauding out of passion rather than mere politeness, and you find yourself being lifted quite off the plane of normal mortals.'

'And why is that trouble?'

'Because you begin to think you're special. Different. You forget it's an act, you forget the cameras – and that's when I remembered something you'd said.'

'In the middle of all that you remembered me? I'm flattered,' he responded drily, and sipped his *latte.*

'Shut up and listen, you dark-faced fool.'

'Oh, please don't beat me, Memsahib,' he mocked.

It had come to that. They felt comfortable enough with each other to trade insults. And secrets.

'You talked about the security cameras, Bobby. Remember?'

'Everywhere. And scanners, mesh fences, dogs, armed police. Anything to keep the public away from us.'

'Who was responsible for those cameras last week?'

'At Conference? Well, outside the headquarters hotel and conference centre they're largely run by the police.'

'And inside the hotel?'

'That's up to the hotel itself.'

'Do you have any contacts there?'

His eyes narrowed in suspicion. 'What are you getting at?'

'I wondered whether we might be able to have a look at the tapes, or whatever they record it all on nowadays.'

'What for? There must be hundreds of hours of the stuff.'

'We can narrow it down. Just the bedroom corridors. Between the hours of, say, midnight and six in the morning.'

'But with five floors that's . . . hundreds of hours.'

'Then let's hope there's a fast forward.'

'And what are you hoping to find precisely?'

'Precisely? I don't know. Generally people who in all that heat and excitement might have forgotten the cameras were there.'

'Nasty.'

'So is discovering that your husband's shagging a younger woman.'

They were interrupted by an overweight politician waving at them from a distance.

'Who was that?' she asked.

'One of your husband's deputy chairmen. One of the most sincerely insensitive men I have ever known.'

'Never met him.'

'He thinks he's God. But have you ever seen a painting of God with his belly sagging below his balls?'

'You seem not to like him.'

'And neither should you. He's disloyal and wants your

husband's job. Thinks he'll get it, too, under a new leader. Thinks your husband is over-promoted and under-age and hasn't long to last.'

'Seems I have a lot to learn, Bobby. But I'm a keen student.'

'And your thirst for knowledge has taken a surprising turn. So what will you do with these tapes – if you find anything?'

'I don't know. Depends on what we find. But in this place information is power and, like it or not, we're in the power game, Bobby. Not a place for the squeamish.'

His brow furrowed, dark wrinkles of concern on an otherwise flawless face.

'What's troubling you, Bobby? Be honest.'

'It's just that . . .'

'Scruples?'

'Not quite. I'm trying to remember the name of the assistant manager of the hotel. The one who saw my busted lip and took pity on me.' It was his turn to smile. 'You see, there was no need for me to go cruising, after all.'

You could see it in their eyes. Uncertainty. Fear. Fate had dealt an unkind hand to these would-be leaders of the Opposition and they didn't know how to play it. British troops were in trouble once more in Iraq. Our boys under threat. So you support them, it's what you have to do. And you supported the policies that sent them there, too. You didn't have to do that, but it was so much safer, better than getting yourself accused of being unpatriotic or playing politics with British lives. So, first one, then the rest in a scramble came out to support the Government's policy. They had not only lost their leader they had also lost their sense of direction. Quite forgotten how to oppose.

'Why do we come here, for goodness' sake?' Ginny muttered, sipping at another of the endless cups of tea.

'Oh, to gossip. To bitch. Nothing to do with goodness. I mean, just look at her,' Tina said, waving a glass of champagne in the direction of Geri Hobley, the wife of the Transport spokesman. 'Is that a hairstyle or roadkill she's wearing?'

'Ah, the Hobleys are spoken for elsewhere, are they?'

'Backing Charlie Malthouse apparently.' Tina sniffed.

They were standing at the entrance to a marquee that had somehow been squeezed into the back patio garden of a house in central Islington that belonged to Eddie Blane, a vintage car salesman and one of the party's Treasury spokesmen in the Lords. He was known as Ever-Ready Eddie because of his penchant for trying to sell an old crock even while standing at the Dispatch Box in the middle of a debate. He was on his third marriage and his fifth child, the youngest of whom, Alex, was celebrating his eighth birthday. The turnout had been unusually good, encouraged not only by the vintage champagne he served so freely but also by memories among the children of the extraordinary goodie-bags handed out for Alex's seventh: they had included raffle tickets and the prizes had stretched from cinema tickets to a trip to Disneyland Paris. The competition among the kids in Islington was intense, and Alex's dad was usually ahead of the game. Some parents might content themselves with a little face-painting and party games, but Alex's friends were greeted at the front door by a circus fire-eater and serenaded at the back by a karaoke party. Meanwhile the mothers mingled, and made their plans.

'How are the children enjoying their new school?' Tina asked. 'A little different from Northamptonshire.'

'Too much incense and too many nuns, according to Ben. He's turning into something of an agnostic. I'm not sure Dom will approve, if ever he finds out. And Jemma's missing her friends, of course, but I took her to the theatre this week. She fell in love with it. And Ben has become a football hooligan. I'm trying to wean him off his passion for Chelsea and get him interested in Queens Park Rangers. It'll save a fortune in the long run.'

'Oh, phooey. You and me, we'll be fine, you'll see. Promise. Let's just get through this leadership nonsense and the world will be our oyster. Talking of oysters, have you seen the pearls on—'

The exchange came to an abrupt halt as Ginny's mobile trilled. She apologised and reached into her bag; Tina blew her a kiss and went off in search of another glass.

'Hello?' Ginny said, squeezing herself out of the way beside the rain butt.

'Mrs E, how the devil are you?'

'Max?' she said, in some surprise. 'Hadn't realised I'd given you my phone number.'

'You didn't.' He was laughing.

'How can I help?' she asked, sounding diffident.

'Been thinking of you,' he said, pausing to allow the thought to gather a little innuendo. 'You were talking to me about how difficult it was to be a mum at times. Said it was a bit like politics. And you've just moved to London. So I thought – what about you writing something for the *Record* about the life of a young political mum? The move to London. Kids around the House of Commons. Down-to-earth stuff, something that the girl in the street can relate to.'

'Women read your newspaper?'

'We've got a blinder of a recipe page. You ought to try it some time. But that's what I like about you, Ginny – well, one of the things. You've got a tongue on you, you have, so use it. In a column. Try it out.'

'Now, why would I want to do that?'

'Because it would be good for the image. Help people get to know you. They're going to get to know you, one way or another, Mrs E. Better you get to them before some wretched red-top newspaper like mine invents something really outrageous about you.'

'What would they make of me, for heaven's sake?'

'Well, it's usually shrew or sex kitten, depending on whether you or your husband gets caught with their knickers down first.'

She shielded the phone, afraid that others might overhear.

Evidently he took the silence as encouragement. 'Look, Ginny, I don't often do this, but take a bit of good advice. Set your own image before someone does it for you. You're married to politics so everybody out there thinks they own a bit of you. Better they get to see what you want them to see, rather than leaving it to the imagination of people like me.'

More silence.

'Oh, God, and I suppose I'll have to pay you for it.'

'How much?'

'Let's say . . . a pound a word. And a thousand words.'

'Let's say two pounds a word.'

'OK, but only if we publish.'

'You will.'

'Then let me have it by five tomorrow evening.'

And the connection died, leaving Ginny staring in curiosity at the phone.

'Bad news?' Tina had returned with her glass.

'I'm not sure,' Ginny replied. 'It was Max Morgan.'

'Max? You know Max?'

'Not very well.'

'Sup with a long spoon with that one, Ginny. You didn't tell him anything, did you? They'll twist it all round like a bit of old washing.'

'Didn't say a thing, really. But I was wondering whether I should have told him about Ed Goodthorpe.'

'Ed? What about Ed?'

'You don't know?' Ginny almost giggled. 'I thought you would have heard.'

'Heard what? Heard what?' Tina demanded, almost exploding with interest. She grabbed Ginny's arm to draw her near.

'Well, it's about his entry in *Who's Who*.' And she set about unfolding the travails of the hapless Goodthorpe. 'But in the end,' she concluded, 'I thought it would be unfair to spread a story like that. Even though he's been so ridiculously stupid.'

Tina had difficulty in replying. There was a strange glow in her eye that had burned through the gentle haze of alcohol, and a slight but definite sag to her lower lip. 'You are so right, Ginny,' she gasped. 'Why, if Jack had done something like that, I'd kill him. Even before those swine in the press did.'

'You're not going to tell them?'

'No,' Tina protested, then giggled. 'Not yet, at least. I think there may be another little bombshell that's going to go bang before that one.'

'Meaning?'

'My darling, I'm sworn to secrecy. Absolutely sworn. You understand, don't you? But just let me say that although George Pascal might have got off to a strong start in the leadership race his finish is likely to be positively explosive.' She tapped her forefinger on the tip of her nose in conspiratorial fashion. 'Not a word to anyone. Our little secret, just between the two of us. We make a terrific team, don't we?' With that, she raised her head, squeezed the loose skin beneath her chin, then braced her shoulders in the manner of a soldier about to do battle before moving off in search of the enemy. Ginny watched her go, sipping her tea, not noticing that it was stone cold.

What Tina had meant was revealed in terrible detail on the front pages of the following Sunday's press, along with many pages inside. George Pascal had a daughter, and a wife; in that there was nothing special. Not even in the fact that his teenage daughter had developed a drug problem. It happens, even for those who have a life at Westminster. And, like many young people who have to feed a drug habit, George Pascal's daughter had turned to prostitution. A beautiful, intelligent, much-loved life that had ended up on the streets. And in the newspapers. A journalist had propositioned, had paid and had photographed, and where the *News of the World* led, the others were quick to follow. They all fed on the carcass of Félice Pascal.

It was not her father's fault; they all agreed on that. Privately, quietly, and over several years, he had devoted enormous energy and very large sums of money to trying to break his daughter's habit. He'd even sought the advice of a handful of colleagues he trusted. But he had failed, and was the first to admit it when the jackals had approached. And failure was a ruinous start to a leadership campaign. By lunchtime he had announced his withdrawal. Tina had struck – for surely this was her work. After all, Jack had been one of those trusted colleagues. One down, and the race hadn't yet formally started.

All through that Sunday, as the newspapers lay disembowelled across her kitchen table, Ginny struggled with her feelings. There was deep sorrow, of course, and anger at the ruthlessness of the hunting pack, but also, it had to be said, a touch of excitement at the progress of this bloody race. Then came tingling guilt that she should ever feel that way. But as the day drew on her dominant emotion was an overwhelming and insistent pulse of fear. She knew the Pascals, not well, but well enough. They were decent people. Hadn't deserved this, or to see their child wrenched from them. No mother deserved that, yet it could happen to anyone. Which meant it might even happen to her. To Jemma. And all a mother's private terrors accumulated within her.

They went to Mass that evening – not for the benefit of the cameras or the image, or even because they had promised St Xavier's, but because this was what they were accustomed to do. It settled Dom, the incense, the hushed tones and dark corners. 'God's smoke-filled back room', he called it. And Ginny had always been happy to go along in support, even when they had first met at university, although she wasn't a Catholic or much of a believer of any sort. She was a practical woman. Would sort things out herself. But she did it anyway, for him. As Dom took the rites, she sat in her pew and stared around her new church, with its flickering candles, its sweet, intoxicating atmosphere, its stones worn away by the passage of so many feet. From the dark and dusty corners she imagined she could hear weeping; perhaps it was the Pascals, come to hide after their lives had been ripped apart, innocents plunged into Purgatory. Then her eyes fixed upon the confessional box. She wondered what might have been said in it – what Dom might have said in it – and tried to pick up echoes. But, of course, he wouldn't have told the priest about Julia. Felt too much shame. At least, in that, Dom didn't match her father.

She found no comfort as they walked home. The weather was blustery, on edge, and so were her emotions as she thought about the Pascals, and how being a family in politics made everything so much worse. Elaine Pascal had wanted no more for her family, for her daughter, than Ginny did, and yet . . . Her fears tugged at her on their way home, until a squall of rain burst upon them and they squeezed into a shop doorway. Suddenly they were very close, crowding together under a battered umbrella, and Ginny was swept back more than fifteen years to another shop doorway they had shared one night in Nottingham. They'd known each other only a week and had been walking back from a law-school thrash through the maze of alleys and side-streets that make up the old Lace Market. It had begun to rain hard, cats, dogs and the rest of the farmyard, so they'd taken shelter in the doorway, where they had fallen into another world, and then upon each other. Afterwards Dom had made a tally of how many statutes, decrees, directives, rules and assorted regulations they'd broken. It had been their first time. A moment neither would ever forget.

Now, as the storm tugged at their umbrella and splashed rain across their faces, once more he placed a protective arm round her. She didn't resist. 'You remembering what I'm remembering?' he asked.

'Of course.'

'Always knew you'd get me into trouble.'

'I plan to get you into much deeper trouble, Dom.'

He chuckled and touched her breast.

'No, not that, you gorilla. Too much work to do.'

'Such as?'

'The Leadership.'

'Ah, the dreaded green-eyed monster.'

'Some are born to it. Others achieve it. But some have it snatched from under their nose.'

'I thought we were sorted. With Jack.'

'Tina put that muck about the Pascals in the newspapers today.'

'You sure?'

Her eyes gave him his answer.

'Bugger,' he breathed. The wind tugged at the umbrella. Rain was attacking his collar. 'Does that make a difference for you?'

'Totally. I'm a great believer in people getting what they deserve. And Tina deserves something specially unpleasant for that.'

'Then if not Jack – who?'

'You.'

'One day, maybe, but what about this time round?'

'You,' she repeated, more firmly.

He muttered something, but so softly that the wind snatched it.

'What's the matter, Dom?'

'It's way too soon. I'm too . . .'

'What? Too lacking in ability? Or ambition?'

'Hell, Ginny, I was lucky to get the chairman's job. Colin was my patron. Now he's dead. If I get this wrong, back a loser, my career could get buried along with him.'

'You're not a loser, Dom.'

'But—'

'All these bloody buts, Dom,' she snapped.

'It's not that simple.'

'You want it? Or don't you?'

'Of course, but . . .'

She groaned. That word again. 'I intend to see you as leader whether you've got the balls for it or not.'

He laughed. 'Look, lighten up, Ginny. We can think about it in the morning, not in the middle of a scene from *The Tempest*. Talking of balls, why don't we get back home and—'

'Our campaign starts tomorrow. A little article I've written. For the *Record*.'

'Archie'll go ballistic.'

'Hope so.'

'But' – that horrid, corrupting little word again – 'why didn't you tell me?'

'Because you'd have asked Archie and he'd have – gone ballistic.'

'What does it say about the bloody leadership, Ginny?' he demanded, suddenly anxious.

'Absolutely nothing. Not a word. Not even a whisper. It's mostly about bottled water.'

'Thank God.'

'And it earned me as much in a couple of hours as you get in two weeks.'

'You kidding? Mmmm, sounds like cause to celebrate.' With the tip of his finger he tracked a raindrop that was creeping down her forehead. 'So, why don't we open a bottle and—'

'No, Dominic. I don't want to distract you.'

'From what?'

'All that thinking you've got to do in the morning.'

He sighed. 'Damn it, Ginny, why can't you be like other women and simply get a headache?'

The article, when it fell on to doormats in the morning, was teased on the front page with a strap line: 'Cutting Edge'. Not a bad start for an image-making operation. It stretched over two inside pages and was accompanied by some rather splendid shots of Ginny relaxing on her bed surrounded by half-emptied boxes in her new house. She wrote of a simple approach to life:

> My happiness is based on three Fs. Family, Friendships and a generous helping of Forgetfulness. Well, politicians aren't

perfect, we all know that, and if you marry one you have to ride the rough with the smooth. Which is why, at times, you need to forget about all sorts of things. The dinner that was fed to the dog. The telephone that rings in the middle of the night. The kid's bike he's neglected to fix. The mornings he goes off before breakfast and the nights he never comes home. You also have to forget about the bar-mop hostess who decides to make a power lunge for your husband while he's helping clear up the dishes in her kitchen. It happens, not every week, but you have to be able to deal with it. And forget it.

It wasn't Tolstoy, not even classic Ginny Edge, but the article had humour, perspective and passion, all of which rubbed off on her.

And there are other dangers with the drinking that goes on in Westminster. Not just with the alcohol, even with the water. You find a politician drinking water and it will be from a bottle. Not sensible tap water but water out of a ridiculous glass or plastic container for which someone – rarely the politician – will be paying up to five pounds a splash at some Westminster restaurants. Can you believe it? That's more expensive than petrol, more than a bottle of decent wine. And there are other costs, too. Producing those bottles of water chews up vast amounts of energy. Transporting them costs even more. The empties create mountains of toxic waste. The irony of it is that half of all the water we buy in bottles comes out of the tap in the first place. So do you want to save yourself a fortune – and help save the planet into the bargain? If you must serve water in a fancy bottle, fill it with water from the tap. No one will notice the difference. I know, I've been doing it for years. And so, I suspect, have many restaurants.

Not everyone, however, was happy.

It was seven thirty in the morning when Archie Blackstone telephoned.

'Oh dear,' Ginny yawned, 'you're angry. Dom said you might be.'

He bawled. He shouted. She whispered. And while he poured instructions down the phone to her, she brushed a piece of stray cotton from her blouse, then rattled around with a kettle and a cup to let him know she had more important things on her mind.

'We've got to be a team, Mrs Edge, playing the same game. And this sort of uncontrolled article comes back to bite you. Pictures in your bedroom. What were you thinking of? You're dangling your private life out there as bait. You'll land your husband in the shite – the entire party in the shite,' he told her, pausing to see whether his warnings had made any impact.

Julia. He was threatening her with Julia. And perhaps he had a point. She hadn't thought that one through.

'I'll be sure to remember everything you've said, Archie,' she responded coldly. 'When I do the next one.'

'There's to be another?'

'Didn't I tell you? The *Record* loved it. Already commissioned a follow-up. There, I knew you'd be happy,' she said.

Then she pressed a button and cut him off. If only she could get rid of the ghost of Julia Summers as easily.

Life had not shown its kindest face to Ajok. Her state benefit should have been increased to compensate for her lack of wages, but there had been a problem. Something wrong with the new computer system. Cost millions, yet couldn't cough up a few pence. Apparently her increased benefit had been paid to an altogether different claimant and, until the confusion was sorted, they couldn't let her have more. Not that anyone was accusing her of fraud, of course, but she had to understand how careful they must be with taxpayers' money. Far more careful, it seemed, than those who had ordered the new computer system.

And Mijok, her younger son, needed new football boots. It

didn't seem an unreasonable request: he was making such good progress that they wanted him to play in the first team but he couldn't do that in bare feet, this wasn't the Sudd, yet there was so little money. She tried to take in more washing to fill the gap, but most people had their own machines and only wanted her help with the impossible jobs, and would complain about the results afterwards.

Then Pat Creasey called. Asked her to come and see him. He had news. She decided to save the bus fare once more, and walked. With every step, she grew steadily more homesick. She was not ungrateful: this new country had given her much – a dry apartment, a television, telephone, even a washing-machine, which amounted to riches beyond her wildest dreams. Yet still she yearned for the old days in the Sudd. This place could never be home. She remembered how, as a small girl, she would watch ants marching in great columns through the dust, and how even pouring water on them or beating them with sticks did nothing to stop their mindless progress. This city and its people reminded her of the ants. An accident, an old lady knocked over, lying very still, her bag of shopping spread across the road, surrounded by much commotion, but still the ants marched on, heedless. They were a strange tribe, these British, nothing like the one her mother and father had heard about from the missionaries, with its royal splendours, its empire, and its quiet if sometimes ruthless sense of order that stretched into so many corners of the world. They were scarcely a tribe at all – none that would be recognised in the Sudan. No ties seemed to bind them together. These people shared nothing. The doctor was a Punjabi, the street-cleaner outside her door was from the Ukraine, the woman in the benefit office had an accent thicker than Ajok's own, while the voice on the end of the telephone at her local council was unintelligible. And there was nothing down the street that spoke to her of England, not the convenience store or the coffee-shops or the eating places. Only the charity shops had faces that were clearly English with the sort of accent she had been taught at her ESOL language classes. It was strange, so confusing. What did it all mean? What did *they* all mean? To Ajok, this seemed to be a tribe of many tribes, yet of none. Oh, how willingly she would go back to the Sudd, if only she could, except that the Sudd, as she remembered it, no longer existed – she had seen that on television. And there were the children. There was nothing left back home for them. So Ajok walked on.

When, at last, she came to the Admiral Lord Nelson, Pat Creasey was waiting for her at his usual table. 'Ajok, welcome to you. Come, just be sitting yourself down here. I have news for you.' The union man was smiling.

Tentatively, Ajok took the hard wooden seat. Creasey was waving a piece of paper at her, pushing it across the sticky table. It had the same stamp on it, from the Treasury Solicitors.

'They want to settle,' Creasey said. 'Offering compensation. No acceptance of responsibility, of course.'

'If they do not accept responsibility, why would they try to settle?' Ajok asked slowly, trying to read the letter.

'To get rid of it all. If we take them to the Employment Tribunal they'll have to pay out one hell of a lot more than they're offering, simply in costs.'

Her eyes fell down the page to a figure. Eight hundred and fifty pounds. Oh, how much that money would mean to her. How many pairs of boots might that buy, how many school books and bus fares, how many fresh towels, how many adequate meals? 'What do you think I should do, Mr Creasey?'

'Well, it might be more,' Creasey was saying, 'except they're still insisting that you were in the wrong so they've cut the figure in half. We go to the tribunal, we might bump it up a bit. But you might also be getting less, Ajok. The tribunal might decide you were being stubborn, think you're greedy. It all depends. I'm afraid it's a bit of a game.'

'For them. Not for me.'

His voice came back with less enthusiasm. 'The official view of the union is that you should take the money. Old Messie says this'll make things so much simpler. Saves trouble on all sides. That's his view, at least.'

'And your view, Mr Creasey?'

He took a sip of his dark, thick beer. 'Well, personally I've never been one for the simple life, Ajok. I think maybe you could get more, and I know how much that would mean to you.'

'But it is not just the money, Mr Creasey. I want my job back.'

'Then you'll have to be taking them to the tribunal. That's a risk – a real risk, Ajok. And it'll be delaying any money you might get.'

She scanned the letter once more, and its figures. She had never had so much money in her life, not in one go. Then her eye fell to the bottom of the page. A scrawled, indecipherable signature, and a name typed beneath it. Abdul Rahman. Not an English name. An Arab name. It could even be Baggaran.

In her village they had their own way of settling disputes. The elders would gather together in the shade of the large acacia tree and the chief would lead the discussion. All those with a grievance would come and explain their feelings, and the elders would decide. It was not always a simple issue of right and wrong but often a complicated matter of battered feelings and Dinka pride, and passions would grow as heated as the midday sun, yet at the end the elders would decree that a bull should be given to one claimant or a cow to another, and everyone would accept the judgement of the elders for they represented the accumulated wisdom of generations stretching back to their mythical forefathers. It was the only way to keep their honour, to carry on living with each other, and to stop them settling their disputes with a spear. So it was done in daylight, in public, face to face, not after dark behind some mud hut or in a drinking-hole. No, there could be no settlement through a piece of paper that insisted on telling lies about her. Ajok wanted to defend her honour. She wanted her moment beneath the village tree.

'I will not accept this, Mr Creasey.'

'You sure?' But as he gazed into her dark eyes and the gentle but insistent fires that burned within, he knew he needed no answer. He drained the rest of his pint.

'Good on you, girl. I'll tell Messie.'

Six

THEY EMERGED THROUGH A big metal door on to a mews street in the backwaters of north Soho. Bobby was laden like a Himalayan sherpa. 'I'll have the other stuff sent over, Memsahib,' he muttered to Ginny.

'Don't complain, Bobby. It was your idea.'

Which was true. He had caught her bemoaning the state of her wardrobe, which had suddenly come to seem about as glamorous as an old duster drawer. 'I need something to go with my new haircut,' she had said. So he had arranged it. Through his father. After all, it was their trade. And a couple of days later they had visited a little design shop just beyond the rumble of traffic from Oxford Street, and had spent a couple of glorious hours in admiration of La Belle Ginny, as he put it.

At first she had felt awkward, but he had explained that almost everything there was of little commercial value. It was last-season Soho, he explained, but still funky enough to blow off their toupees in Westminster. So she had asked for something for outdoors, something cool, something that wouldn't make her backside look too big if she were caught bending down.

'You're up to something,' he had accused her.

But all he got for a reply was a smile and a request for something in pale blue. To match her eyes. And Bobby had such a deft touch; soon they were experimenting, giggling, sharing, with Bobby helping her through her moments of indecision, shaking his head or clapping with approval, suggesting one dress was too tight, that another showed too much tit and that she should remember she was a respectable mother of two. She'd taken the dress, anyhow.

They reached her car, just as a parking warden was sticking a ticket to her screen.

'What are you doing?' she protested. 'We've got another five minutes at least.'

The warden said nothing but, with an unpleasant pucker on his lips, indicated her rear wheel. It was almost a foot over the permitted parking space. Then he turned his back and sauntered off.

'Black bastard,' Bobby said, as they watched him walk away.

'You can't say that!'

'I can. I most certainly can. It's you who can't call him a black bastard.'

'An outcast in my own country,' she muttered, peeling the ticket off the windscreen.

'Better than being an outcast in your own family,' he replied. His eyes were mournful, the joy of the morning already turning cold.

'Problems?'

'My father's got the idea into his head that I should get married. Even talking about helping arrange the details for me. You know, just the minor stuff, like who, when and where.'

'That still happens?'

'You can take the Paki out of Pakistan but . . .'

'Oh, bugger.'

'Precisely.'

They drove off in silence. Their route took them round Trafalgar Square and through the heart of Whitehall, a turbulent journey, and not solely because of the crush of cars around them. In truth, Ginny wasn't the smoothest of drivers. As they reached Downing Street, they came to a halt under the weight of traffic. Opposite them stood the black metal gates and the armed policemen. It seemed forbidding, deliberately hostile.

'You know anything about websites?' she asked.

'Downloading stuff, you mean?'

'No, building them. I've got an idea for my next article in the *Record*. Set up my own website. Something green, eco-friendly, family-based. Save the planet and your marriage. Girly stuff, mostly. Call it Future Friends, or something like that.'

'Sounds like a dating agency.'

'Well, in a way it might be,' she responded, riding over the sarcasm. 'Not too much input, haven't got time, but maybe a weekly blog from me, almost like a newspaper column. With links to all sorts of other useful sites. And some means of checking who's visiting. Build up a database. Might be useful.'

'For what?'

'You can't start a revolution with barricades in the street nowadays. Health and Safety won't allow it.'

'You think you're going to break into Downing Street with a website?'

'Bobby, I don't know. I really don't. But if it helps . . .'

'You totally committed?'

'Whatever it takes.'

'And your husband?'

'He's not yet sure, but I'm reviewing his options.' Then a pause. 'God, does that make me sound awful?'

'Right now I'm not sure I know what's right and what's wrong.'

Confusion was swirling in his eyes, and exhaustion, too, as if he were an old man. Ginny also thought she saw a flicker of fear. 'We'll get there, you and me. And when we do, all things become possible.' She placed her hand on his, squeezing it in comfort. 'You're a friend, Bobby. I may ask many things of you along the way. I want you to let me know if ever I abuse that friendship.'

They sat staring at each other, holding hands in the heavy traffic, almost like lovers. Then the moment was broken as the cars were moving once more, leaving Downing Street behind.

'Well, now you come to mention it, Ginny, driving me around in this Dinky Toy isn't doing much for my image. This car's a mobile dustbin,' he complained light-heartedly, scratching away at a sweet-wrapper that had got itself fixed firmly to his shoe. There seemed to be something like an old banana skin lurking down there, too.

'It's a kiddies' car. Fresh from the school run. What do you expect?' she responded, as she crashed through the gears all the way round Parliament Square. Suddenly a beaten-up Vauxhall came out of nowhere and almost took off her front wing. She banged at her horn. 'Black bastard!' she cried, then clamped a hand to her mouth in embarrassment.

'I think you've got that wrong, Ginny,' Bobby corrected. 'He may be black but he's not a bastard – at least, not in the sense that it was his fault. You just ran a red light.'

'Did I? Oh, God. I got carried away. Didn't know when to stop.' She bit her lip. 'But I think that may be my trouble, Bobby. I'm not sure I know any longer when to stop.'

She launched her website in her next article for the *Record*.

I remember when I first became a mother. At times I felt so alone, so inadequate. Being a mum is tough – perhaps the toughest job in the world. In earlier times we had the extended family around us, mothers, aunts and close friends, everyone to help with things. Childbirth. Illness. Education. Bereavement. To share in the happy times and to help us through the awful bits in between. But now the extended family is gone, we're on our own, which is why I've set up a website dedicated to mothers and their families – www.mums-on-top.co.uk – which tries to show you where you can go to get help for so many of these daily problems that drag us down. It doesn't try to give black-and-white answers to all life's questions – I'm not an editor or a politician! – but it does enable me to talk with people about their cares and their hopes, and to

let them know they're not alone. And I've tried hard to
make it a doorway to all sorts of other useful websites on
these vital issues. Sometimes help seems so very far
away. I hope it's only as far as the nearest Internet
connection . . .

And with that, Ginny became a very modern woman. On the
cutting edge of things, as the paper suggested in its promotional
copy. It had taken Bobby and some of his techie friends three
exhausting nights living off little but pizza and Ginny's constant
encouragement to get the website set up, complete with a visitor
counter that started at eighteen thousand hits and clocked up a
tally five times as large as the number of people actually visiting.
Success breeds success – as was shown when, within two weeks, the
Record had offered to pay all the costs involved in maintaining the
site. Within four, Ginny had them paying a handsome sum for
the privilege of advertising their logo on it.

But there was more to the article. It announced that the
following weekend she would be doing something to clear up the
mess that others had left the country in. She would be helping
sweep clean one of those rubbish-strewn lay-bys that pollute our
roads, getting rid of the beer cans and nappy sacks and plastic bags
that seem to breed there, tangled for ever in the hedges. A small
gesture, perhaps, but a chance to fight back, 'to clean up our
future'. And then she was going to seek out a sponsor for the lay-
by – a Boy Scout troop or church congregation or branch of the
Women's Institute, didn't really matter – even a local supermarket,
which might send three or four of its trolley boys to keep it clean.
Only take a few minutes once a fortnight. And put up a little sign
to let passing motorists know who was helping keep their roads
clear and their future bright. And see who dare tip their rubbish
after that!

Inevitably, and entirely intentionally, when Ginny, Dom and the
kids arrived at the lay-by the following Sunday morning, armed

with brooms and rubbish bags and accompanied by the boys of the Bulldog Patrol, 1st St Clement's Scout Troop, they were greeted by a small arsenal of cameras. Ginny looked perfect in pale blue. As the photographers said, it matched her eyes . . .

They arrived back home in less than splendid style. Jemma had thrown up, twice, and Ben had grumbled constantly that he thought hanging out with boys dressed in woggles was dead uncool, while Dom had remained quiet, as though heavy matters were weighing on his mind. He seemed glad to be driving, lost in a world of his own, leaving her to sort out the kids. A man's prerogative. To think great thoughts while the children in the back scream and scream until they're sick.

And almost as soon as they had crossed the threshold, the phone began to ring.

'Ginny, darling, I just had to let you know,' Tina's voice warbled. 'You've got to watch *The Power Game* in half an hour.'

'I could also be getting the children their lunch, shovelling out the car or going to bed with a migraine, Tina.'

'Phooey, stop that. You've really got to watch. Ed Goodthorpe's on. He's going to have a really bad hair day.'

'He's practically bald. He always has a bad hair day.'

'And what's left is likely to be scalped. They've found out about his *Who's Who* entry.'

'How?'

'Oh, don't be so silly, darling. From me, of course. You don't think I'm wicked, do you? But all's fair in love and elections, that's what I say. Oh, it's going to be such fun!'

Fun meant a late lunch. Jemma and Ben were asked if they minded their food being delayed while their parents watched television. Sensing unexpected vulnerability, the children complained sufficiently to extract several benefits from Ginny before disappearing to their bedrooms.

'What's going on?' Dom enquired, as he emerged from his study.

'Lunch is going to be late. But open a bottle, anyhow.' There was something in her tone, a new tone for Ginny, but one he was beginning to recognise, that persuaded him not to argue.

At the BBC studio, Ed Goodthorpe was enjoying himself. His slot on *The Power Game* had arrived as an unexpected pleasure and he had grabbed it. Frankly, he needed the exposure. He knew that his leadership campaign was starting well behind the likes of Jack Saunders and Hazel Basham, he had ground to make up. But anything might happen. That was the nature of these leadership races. And to be one of the front-runners was so often an invitation to disaster. 'The quicker you climb up the tree,' he told the researcher in the Green Room beforehand, 'the sooner they start shooting at your arse.'

When he arrived they had treated him warmly. A drink, makeup, just a little of the first and a whole slapping of the second, given the size of his balding pate and the care with which he had to arrange his hair. Goodthorpe was a decent man, not distracted by too many vices, and dedicated to his job, which was where the ambition came in. When he'd started he'd never thought he'd get this far in the great game, let alone have the chance of taking a huge stride further. Not bad for a lad from the back streets of Burton by the great river Trent who'd started with four O levels and a nasal West Midlands accent that had taken him years to reconstruct. It was one of the tricks of the trade, giving everything that extra little tweak: the accent, the hair, even the teeth. Maybe he'd even take a couple of weeks during the next summer recess to get his eyelids lifted. And he had dressed with considered casualness for a Sunday morning, no tie, button-down collar, just to show he wasn't trying too hard. Informal. Relaxed. In control. That was what he kept telling himself as he waited beneath the lights for the floor manager to count the seconds down. At the very last moment, the makeup girl scurried out to give his forehead another dab of powder. He hoped he wasn't sweating.

And then it began. The red light, the tension in the air, the sudden stiffening in the interviewer's hands, the demonic intensity of the floor manager as she got instructions from the gallery. But all was going smoothly. They'd gone through the leadership bit, with Goodthorpe showing just the right mix of aspiration and modesty, then a discussion of education, and Goodthorpe's conference promise to stiffen up on examinations, if ever he got the chance. 'Driving up, not dumbing down,' had been his rallying cry at Torquay. They even showed a clip of it. And the floor manager was indicating they had only two minutes left.

'So you would like to squeeze the examination system,' the interviewer was saying, 'make sure that exam results mean what they say. "Ensure they're worth the paper they're printed on," I think you told your party conference.'

Goodthorpe nodded.

'Well, in that case I'm forced to ask you about your own examination results. In your entry in *Who's Who* you indicate that you got a degree from Oxford University. But Oxford University has apparently never heard of you, Mr Goodthorpe. We checked. You never went there, never got a degree, isn't that right?'

A camera was being pushed round the studio floor to get a better close-up of the condemned man as they backed him up against the wall. On a screen behind them, an image of the entry suddenly appeared, ringed in red.

'So – forgive me if I put this bluntly – haven't you laid yourself open to charges of hypocrisy? Double standards? Lying, even? You committed yourself to making our children's examinations honest, yet you can't even be honest about your own.'

And as the camera closed in, Goodthorpe began to laugh. Nervously, to be sure, but nevertheless seeming to discover something funny in the moment.

'You find this amusing, Mr Goodthorpe?'

'No, merely your rather ridiculous question.'

'I beg your pardon?'

'Your question is exactly the sort of exaggerated nonsense I'd like to drive out of the system. Delta minus, quite frankly.' He leaned forward, like a man across a pub counter trying to engage the barmaid, just a fraction too affable. 'Look, this silly matter came up some time ago. When I first put in my entry for *Who's Who* I dictated it to a secretary. Never checked it since—'

'Really? In fifteen years?'

'Fact is, I've had better things to do than go around trying to flatter my ego. My record shows that, otherwise you'd never have invited me on to your programme. I've always made it clear that I went to Oxford Poly. Poly, not University – although it was a very fine poly and has become a university in its own right. And I'm proud of that. I've even given them financial support over the years.'

'Yet for so very many years your entry in *Who's Who*—'

It was the interviewer's turn to be interrupted. The Goodthorpe smile had vanished, squeezed into some subterranean hell-hole from which it wouldn't escape for a very considerable time. 'Isn't that just typical of jumped-up media folk who go round preening themselves the whole time? To expect others to spend their time poring over their entry in *Who's Who*. Well, I'll tell you, lad, some of us have got better things to do than disappear up our own egos.' As he grew angry, he grew animated, and the Burton accent broke cover.

'But how can we expect people to trust a man who has been – well, at least you could use the word "clumsy" – clumsy enough to allow a lie to stand for so long?'

'Because people have got more nous than thou, as my old granny used to say. Of course they'll judge me. On my record – it's an excellent one, that's why Conference gave me a standing ovation. And they'll judge me on what I offer for the future, and quite right, too, not on some ridiculous little error in dictation all those years ago. And what does it matter where I was educated? It wasn't my fault I didn't have a rich daddy like yours that could send me to Eton—'

'Harrow.'

'Oh, congratulations, Mr 'Arrow . . . But I'm not one to hold all that privilege against you – millions might, but I don't. I've always said that where you come from shouldn't matter. It's what you can achieve – for yourself, for your family and for your country. That's what matters.' He was leaning so far forward that it looked as though he was about to leap up and walk out, just as the producers had hoped he might.

'It wasn't only one error, was it, Mr Goodthorpe?' the interviewer responded. 'You claimed you got a degree, but you never did.'

'A diploma, that's what I got. And coming from a background like mine, from a little terrace house in Burton with an outside toilet in the shadow of half a dozen breweries and a stonking great Marmite factory, you could be proud o' that. Bet you never had an outside loo at 'Arrow, did you? Probably had some young boy to warm your seat and toast your crumpets for you.'

'That's not the—'

'And you have the brass nerve to talk to me about lying! You lied when you got me on to this programme, didn't you? Wanted to talk about the future, you said. Not a word about this stupid nonsense in *Who's Who*. Got me here under false pretences. Lied to me, so you could look down your nose and have a laugh.' His huge hands gripped the arms of his chair, straining, angry.

Up in the gallery, the producer was bouncing in her seat and shouting. 'Hit him! Hit him!' She didn't much like the interviewer either, and this might yet deliver into her hands one of those most elusive and magical moments of television that would be replayed for decades. A politician thumping someone in front of cameras. Who ever heard of such a thing?

But Goodthorpe refused to co-operate. 'You, young man, are a disgrace. The moral sensitivity of a sack of nutty slack. Crawl back to your parents and learn a few manners, that's my advice. If you have any parents, that is.'

'Mr Goodthorpe—'

But it was too late. The studio manager was counting them out, the titles were rolling and the theme music drowning their last comments. The titles ran long enough for the watching world to see Goodthorpe stand up, rip off his lapel mike and storm away. It would make every front page in the morning.

'Wow, that was enormous,' the producer gasped, when eventually she lifted her head from her control desk. 'A real knee trembler.' Then she frowned. 'But I'm still not entirely sure who just screwed who.'

If it wasn't the most elegant sentence she had ever constructed, she was not alone as many others tripped over their grammar in their rush to judgement.

'God, he just bloody killed himself,' Dom said, pouring himself another glass as they moved into the kitchen, while Ginny began to prepare their lunch.

'Not so sure,' she mused, attacking a bag of potatoes with a knife. 'Never apologise, never admit responsibility, simply attack, attack, attack. Isn't that how modern politics is run? In the circumstances I think he did rather well.'

'But he can't continue, not now that that nonsense with his university has come out into the open. No one will believe it was an oversight.'

'They've started wars on less evidence than that.'

'They're not going to elect someone who goes round calling the interviewer a bastard.'

'That will have done him no harm at all. And, if you get the chance, you should encourage him to stay in the race.'

'Whatever for?'

'To make life easier for you when you announce.'

'Look, Ginny . . .'

'It's a crowded field, Dom. All weak candidates – apart, perhaps, from Jack and Hazel. Crowds mean confusion, and in confusion lies your chance.'

He rolled his glass between his hands, contemplating. 'I'm not sure.'

'Then *be* sure, Dom. At the very least you'll get yourself a name, and a name means everything. Makes you much more difficult to ignore and almost impossible to sack. But if you don't stand, they might still throw you back where you came from, a mere backbencher lost in a big mucky pond, and you'll never be heard of again.'

'They wouldn't do that. I've done a good job.'

She banged a saucepan on the counter. 'You "did" Julia Summers! They all know that. It would give them every excuse they needed.'

They stared at each other across the kitchen, both angry, but her outburst was not what she had intended. She sucked her lip, lowered her head. 'Look, Dom, you have so many talents. You're young, photogenic, an exceptional speaker. A man with the future ahead of him. And you also have a wife who'll back you to the hilt. You have nothing to lose by throwing your hat into the ring, yet you have absolutely everything to lose by staying out.' Her intonation made it sound as if she were talking about much more than his political future. It alarmed him.

'Will you back me, Ginny? No matter what I decide?'

She held his gaze but remained silent.

'It means that much to you?' he whispered, suddenly anxious.

Very slowly she wiped her hands on her apron. 'I didn't put my life aside to watch you make a mess of yours.'

'I didn't . . . realise . . . you felt so strongly.' The words were sticking in his throat. His eyes had begun to melt.

'Don't follow the pack, Dom. Make your own path. Let everyone know where you've been.'

'I – I think . . .' The stumbled word betrayed the insecurities that had haunted him all his life. A suburban boy from a semi-detached family in a semi-detached house, a boy of whom nothing was expected, yet who had done well, the first of the Edges ever to go to university. But something had always dragged him back. A second-class law degree that, in his heart, had made him a second-class lawyer. That was why he had chosen politics. In Westminster, so often, second class doesn't show.

He poured himself another drink. It wasn't so much that he didn't want high office, far from it. He knew – thought, hoped went down on his knees and prayed – he'd make it, but it was a long-term plan. He wasn't by instinct a man of risk. Yet whatever he chose now to do or not to do, he knew some risk was inevitable. Ginny had made that clear. Damned if he did, condemned if he didn't. He was being pushed towards the edge, and he felt the ground crumbling beneath him. He was suffering an acute case of vertigo when his thoughts were interrupted by a ferocious pounding on the front door.

It was Ed Goodthorpe. His eyes were swimming in bewilderment and his hair clamped in all sorts of strange directions round his head. He was sweating through thick makeup. He had clearly come straight from the studio. Without a second thought Dom thrust his glass of wine into the visitor's hand and Goodthorpe started on it straight away. 'Thank you, thank you,' he kept exclaiming, as he stood in their hallway, drowning his sorrows. When he had finished the glass he wiped his mouth. 'What the hell do I do now?'

'We thought you were magnificent,' Dom said.

'What? Really?'

'Really.'

'They'll tear me to pieces in the morning.'

'Some will, some won't. And around ten million people will know you a hell of a lot better than they did this morning.'

'So what should I do, Dom? Have I completely ballsed it up? Tell me. For God's sake be honest.'

'As chairman I'm not allowed an opinion—'

'Yes, yes, but – as a friend. A good friend, Dom. Dammit, but you've been a bloody good friend to me.'

'As a friend I'd say . . .'

Goodthorpe was like a dog, eyes alert, eager, pleading, waiting for his master's command.

'As a friend I'd say hang in there. Keep your nerve. See what tomorrow brings. May not be easy, Ed, but it'll blow over. May even make you a folk hero.'

'They won't leave it alone, though, will they? That –' he searched for the word '– *stupidity* with the degree. I'm buggered. Maybe I should call it a day.'

'If you walk away now, you'll allow that bastard in the studio to win.'

'Never! Never that! Should've thumped the little jerk while I had the chance—'

'So don't talk about your education, get stuck into the disgraceful behaviour of the BBC. A public institution that's got itself a nasty little political agenda. Always good mileage in that.'

'Brilliant! I'll do it! Contrition never carried the day, did it, eh?'

'Stick it to them, Ed.'

'Right up 'em. Too right I will.'

'Great. Er, I'd invite you in but we're about to sit down to family lunch.'

'Of course, yes, of course. So sorry. Got to get back. Bloody pager's vibrating off my belt. But I can deal with them, now I know what to do.' He handed back the empty glass, then folded Dom's hands in his own. 'Give my love to Ginny. Huge hug. I'm so bloody grateful, Dom. So truly bloody grateful. Capital B.' And with that he was gone.

Dom walked slowly back into the kitchen, from where Ginny had been listening to every word. 'You handled that very well, Dom. Such a deft touch. You did the right thing.'

'Did I? Did I really? I dunno, it's just that . . . if that preposterous fool Goodthorpe can be in the race, then almost anyone can.'

'What are you saying?'

'I think I'm saying . . . I'll do it. For you, Ginny.'

The words wrapped her in a blanket of joy. She walked round

the kitchen table to kiss him, fully on the lips, holding him close in a way she hadn't done for months. He didn't mind that she smelt of broccoli and chicken grease, but the unexpected affection almost embarrassed him. He looked into his empty glass. 'Think I need another drink.'

'Make it champagne.'

There was much to celebrate. Including, she thought, the fact that she had decided to page Goodthorpe just before he went on air. To warn him. To prepare him. To give him a chance of fighting back. To keep him alive. So that she might be the one to decide when the time had come to kill him.

Ambition grinds a sharp edge, and it had left Ginny tossing fretfully through many nights. She wanted nothing more than her old life back, but that was like praying for the resurrection of the dead. She had to move on, to face up to her fears, and to confront those responsible for them. She asked Bobby to make the arrangements. At first he'd refused, said she was mad, put up considerable resistance. Even he didn't understand. But a man wouldn't.

A drink at the Cinnamon Club in Great Smith Street, where the old Westminster Library had once ruled in some splendour before its budget had got cut to pieces. In the bar, the tranquil atmosphere of the room's earlier life had been revived with parquet flooring, soft leather sofas and shelves filled with books by the yard. Early evening. Just as the light faded. Candles. Rose petals. Very quiet. Everything just right.

At the last moment Ginny found herself overwhelmed by a tide of panic. What if . . . ? What if . . . ? But she'd gone too far to turn back, she might be lost if she went ahead, but she knew for certain she would never forgive herself if she didn't. She thought of the kids: Ben's toothless, unquestioning smile, Jemma's squeals of delight when Daddy came home. And with that came strength.

Bobby and his guest arrived, settled themselves into a sofa, ordered two glasses of wine, then Bobby looked at his pager and excused himself, leaving his guest alone to gaze at photographs of tiger hunts that hung on the walls. She didn't see Ginny approach, didn't notice anything until Ginny had taken Bobby's seat.

'Hello, Julia.'

The eyes – dark, round, blinking slowly like a kitten, Ginny thought – stared without comprehension. Then the milk of understanding spread slowly across them. 'Mrs Edge.'

'Yes, that's right. Dominic's wife. I've been wanting to meet you for some time.'

Ginny had watched her as she came in – devoured her with a hunter's eyes, and not a little envy. Probably no more than twenty-five, hair that shone and a waist that bore only a little excess flesh. The hemline was too high and the legs perhaps a little too bumpy – oh, in a few years she'd never be able to get away with a skirt like that. A couple of kids and the hips would go, the large breasts would sink and she'd be nothing more than another harassed mother with purple veins and wistful memories. Ginny found herself relishing the thought.

But the skin was close to perfect, the cheekbones high, the lips full and far too free. As they moved, as she spoke, Ginny couldn't help but remember all the moments they had stolen with Dom.

'Would you . . . like a glass of wine?' they asked, faltering, as the eyes searched anxiously for Bobby.

'No, thank you. I don't think you'd want me to stay. It's strange who you stumble over in these dark corners of Westminster. You never can tell when you're going to be spotted.'

Julia didn't reply, simply sipped her wine.

'Do you love my husband, Julia?'

The reply came slowly, but the voice was now resolute. 'No, of course not.'

'So, if you don't want to marry him why have you insisted on trying to ruin him?'

'Mrs Edge, this is a conversation you should have with your husband.'

'Do you ever think of the children? Two of them, Jemma and Ben. They're ten and eight.'

That got a reaction, the passing suggestion of a wince, but still she sipped her wine, her lips – those lips! – clinging close to the rim of the glass as if they needed distraction. Anything other than talking.

'Do you intend to carry on seeing him?'

'I work for him. I can scarcely stop seeing him.'

'Don't be childish. You know exactly what I mean.'

They were interrupted as a waiter, an Indian, came with a tray to place more candles on the table and refresh the Bombay nibbles. There was still no sign of Bobby.

Ginny used the moments to examine Julia – not the body, she'd already done that, but the bitch inside. The personality, like the eyes, not fully formed. Immature. Dangerous, not because she would ever run off with Dom but because she wouldn't be able to come to a grown-up, balanced decision about things. She was a day-to-day girl, shag-to-shag, and let tomorrow take care of itself. A very shallow woman. Superficial. In it for the sex. No wonder the men liked her.

'Wouldn't you find it so much easier if you simply found another job? Away from temptation?'

'But I like my job.'

'You could make life very complicated for yourself, Julia,' Ginny continued, as soon as the waiter was out of earshot. 'A reputation. You know how these things get round in Westminster. So many gossips. So much whispering and pointing of fingers. You'd be branded. Marks that would remain for ever. Ruin your career. I'd make sure of it.'

'Don't threaten me, Mrs Edge. I'm sorry, but you'd never be horrid to me. Because that means – well, it would mean a lot of unfortunate publicity and your children would suffer. Somehow I don't think you would allow that.'

Ah, not so superficial, after all.

The place was filling up. Ginny's heart was pounding, she was shaking inside and she wasn't sure how long she could keep up this act of calm and reason before she lashed out and ruined everything. A voice was screaming in her ear: *Hit the bitch! Hit the bitch!* Soon her hands would be trembling. She had to bring this to a close.

'No, not a threat, Julia. Just a mother's promise.'

She got up, stared down upon the other woman. She'd done what she had come to do. Seen her. Succumbed to destructive curiosity, hoping that by putting form to her nightmares she might make them somehow more containable. It hadn't worked. She had wanted to test how far she might trust Julia Summers in the weeks that lay ahead. And now she thought she knew.

Not an inch.

Many things are gathered together to launch a leadership campaign. Money. Ideas. Energy. Interest. Allies. But not enemies. They gather all by themselves. As Party Chairman, Dom was in an excellent position to assemble several parts of the package. He knew many party donors and could identify a handful who would offer ten thousand each without noticing it and, just as important, without talking about it. He wanted to maintain the element of surprise in the few days left for candidates to declare their names. He was also able to identify those Members of Parliament who hadn't already signed up wholeheartedly to one camp or another and who might form an able backing group when the time came. Once nominations closed, the candidates would have a month of campaigning before the vote. The war would be over by Christmas.

Ginny was left to deal with the more tricky bits. Her first call was on Max Morgan. She asked to see him in his office.

'It's bigger than any politician's,' she exclaimed as she sat down on a sofa, gazing round the expanse of carpet and rain-forest wood.

'More bodies buried under the floorboards, that's why.' He smiled. 'Including those of my predecessors. One day it'll be my turn.' He didn't sit down on the sofa beside her but on a nearby chair. Somehow, in the office, he seemed more formal.

'Are you getting philosophical, Max?'

'No. It's just that in this job you treat every day as your last. And pray that no one in the Royal Family dies on a Saturday and deprives me of the beautiful supplements I've prepared for them all. Could be worth another half a million on circulation.'

'But you spend your life kicking hell out of the prince.'

'And when he's dead we'll be nice to him,' the editor protested. 'Just like all the rest will.'

'In a way that's one of the reasons I wanted to see you. Want to write an article about – well, for want of a better word, about forgiveness. You believe in forgiveness, Max?' She found the answer as she gazed round the room at walls crowded with framed front pages of the *Record* that screamed accusations in all directions.

'Not really,' he confirmed. 'Not of my enemies, or my competitors, and certainly not my ex-wife.'

'I want you to trust me on this one.'

'Well, give me the copy and we'll see. Just don't go all Catholic on me, Ginny. This isn't a place where we hand out papal indulgences.'

'Or seek them, either.'

At that moment the intercom on his vast desk came to life, buzzing like a hornet and flashing its red light. It was his secretary. 'Max, sorry to interrupt, but I've got Mr Charles Malthouse on the line asking for an urgent word.'

'Tell him I'm on the phone to the Vatican or something. Get him to speak to someone on the political desk.' But Ginny was shaking her head vigorously, gesticulating with her hands, urging him to take it. And he loved the way Ginny gesticulated. 'On the other hand – yeah. Put him through. And see who's around. Get them in here, too.'

Seconds later the space round his desk was heaving with journalists, mostly young, armed with an assortment of notebooks and mini-recorders. The desk itself, Ginny noticed, was covered with photographs, marked up in red ink, of a woman she didn't recognise but who had clearly forgotten about the power of a long-distance lens. Then, suddenly, the speakerphone crackled into life.

'Charlie, how are you, mate?' Max bawled.

'Excellent,' a strangely disembodied voice replied. Malthouse was a child of the seventies, a man who, in his search for perpetual youth, still wore his hair too long and his ties too bright and was a genuinely pleasant individual lost in an intellectual world of his own. This made him, in the eyes of the *Record,* a very dangerous man. 'Wanted to call and wish you happy birthday.'

'But that's not till Sunday.'

'Precisely. Didn't want to bother you at the weekend. Thought I'd get in early.'

Max made an obscene gesture with his hand. 'Four bloody days early. That's very thoughtful of you, Charlie. You got any other thoughts, then? Something I might be able to publish?'

'The campaign's going well. Hoping to announce some new supporters any day now.' One of the young women at the desk was silently mocking, shaking her head. 'Bandwagon's starting to roll, Max. Wanted you to know I'd be happy to talk to you – or any of your staff – any time. I'm sure you know that, but I just wanted to make the point directly to you, straight to the horse's mouth.'

'I normally find prodding a stick up the horse's arse gets quicker results, mate.'

'I bow to your greater experience. But I hope we'll always be able to talk – you know, entirely discreetly, confidentially. I'd like to be able to share with you.'

The editor beamed mischievously. 'You tell me it's off the record and nothing goes beyond these four walls, Charlie. Your indiscretions are safe with me. Anything in particular you want to confess?'

'No, no, I meant . . .' A nervous laugh. 'No indiscretions on my part, Max. Too busy for that sort of thing.'

The female journalist was shaking her head once more as the others struggled to suppress their mirth. The front pages on the walls around the room featured defrocked Cabinet Ministers who had shown a remarkable appetite for indiscretion, no matter how busy they had been.

'Tell me, Charlie, do you believe in forgiveness?'

A startled silence at the other end, then 'Why, yes, of course, I mean . . . Compassion is going to be a major plank of my campaign. That . . . and tax reform.' Another silence. 'Why do you ask?'

'Just seems to be the theme of the day somehow.'

'Sounds like excellent advice. I'll bear that in mind. I've got a big speech coming up next Tuesday and—'

'Nice of you to let me know. I'll watch out for it. And you call me any time you want to share, OK?'

'Thanks, Max. Appreciate that. And happy birthday once . . .'

But already Morgan had punched the button on his phone that brought an end to the humiliation. 'It's so dangerous when they're let out on their own,' he declared, much to the merriment of his staff. They were still laughing, too loudly, when they were herded out of the room.

'You treat all politicians like that?' Ginny asked, as the room fell quiet once more.

'I treat everyone like that, except my proprietor and his immediate family.'

'And there was me going to offer you a discreet little deal.'

'I'm listening.'

'But I need to swear you to secrecy for three days.'

'That's possible. Unless I get the story from elsewhere.'

'You won't. Dom is going to put in for the leadership.'

Morgan sucked his teeth. 'Interesting. Scarcely front page. But interesting.'

'He's got money, support, youth. Me.'

'And starts a hell of a long way behind.'

'Leadership elections have become a bit like a wagon rolling along a clifftop with a wheel about to drop off. Never know who's going to get squashed.'

'Could be you, Ginny.'

'That's why I want to offer you a deal.'

'Go on.'

'The most important thing in all this to me, Max, is my family. The children. My marriage. Whatever happens, I don't want that to get squashed.'

'Why should it?'

'Westminster is a dangerous world, for marriages, for reputations. I can't expect you not to print a story, any story, but I'd like to ask you this. If it affects me, if it affects my family, I'd like to know as soon as you know. Not to stop you or anyone else using the story, simply to protect myself and my children. I've seen more than enough of those appalling bloody pictures with a ridiculous man smiling like a waxwork while his wife goes out and serves the jackal pack their tea and cookies.'

'Has Dom been playing away?'

'Seems to me that most of you men do. Prince, priest, politician, particularly press men. You all manage to moralise through the zips in your flies.'

'Glad you're not denying it, Ginny. That would have hurt me, hurt our trust.'

'I'm not confirming anything either. I'm simply trying to protect myself. Just in case.'

'I'd heard whispers,' Morgan said. 'About a young parliamentary arse-nipper. Members of Parliament seem to have so little imagination.'

'You didn't follow it up?'

'No pictures. No proof. You hear rumours all the time. Not all of them can be true. And, to be honest, up to now no one would've given a damn about Dominic Edge. My proprietor's probably never even heard of him. But this leadership thing. You're raising the stakes.'

'Will you help me?'

'In return for what?'

She paused, searching for the words that might convince him. She wasn't sure she would ever find them. 'Trust,' she said eventually. 'In return for our trust.'

'Ah,' he mused, as his words were played back to him. 'But what does that mean, do you think?'

'It means that we help each other. And it means that if ever Dom becomes leader, you get best access, the best inside information.'

'Gossip?'

'Solid, gory details.'

'Sounds a bit . . .' he waved his hand '. . . intangible.'

'That's what trust is all about.'

'Sure you wouldn't prefer some pillow talk? You and me? I'm likely to find that much more persuasive.'

'Have you run out of goats so soon?'

Then the intercom was buzzing again.

'What the bloody hell do you want?' he shouted waspishly.

'It's your mother, Mr Morgan.'

'Aaah.' And the lion became lamb. He turned once more to Ginny. 'My mother comes to have tea with me at three o'clock every Wednesday afternoon. It's a little ritual we have. She likes to make sure I'm getting enough cake and carrots. She brings the cake, which we eat with a cup of tea, and she leaves the carrots for my dinner. It's her grandmother's recipe for a long life.'

'Children are important to a mother, Max.'

He was out of his chair, sweeping the photographs from his desk into a deep drawer. 'OK, Ginny Edge. I'll play along. We trust each other. You keep the articles coming and I'll . . . well, I'll keep you informed. No matter how much it might hurt you.'

'I'm a grown-up girl.'

He turned, smiling roguishly as she hovered, framed in his doorway. 'Oh, yes. You most certainly are.'

Seven

THE ARTICLE, WHEN IT appeared, seemed uncharacteristically elliptical, a long way from the typical tabloid rant.

Have you noticed how bad things are always someone's fault? Someone else's fault? Nowadays we seem unable to forgive, let alone forget. And the blame culture means somebody's got to be hung out to dry. It's ruining us. It's why doctors are afraid to heal, neighbours are reluctant to help, insurance charges are so high and everyone has turned into a litigation lawyer.

Seems to me we all need a little more forgiveness in our lives, and forgiveness starts at home. It's not always fair, perhaps, because we women end up doing much more of the forgiveness thing than men, and political wives have to end up doing more than most. The anniversaries he's forgotten because some secretary hasn't put it in his diary, the school sports day or carol concert missed because he's on duty elsewhere, the hours you've spent waiting alone in a restaurant, the romantic dinner gone cold. And much, much more.

A close friend of mine, another political wife, recently told me that her husband had been 'a total double-dealing jerk'. Actually, her language was much fiercer than that, but you don't need to be a contestant on Mastermind to get the picture. Another woman, of course. You wouldn't believe how much of that goes on at Westminster. So much temptation, so much stress, so many nights away from home, so many separate lives. Throw in a couple of bottles of good wine and it's amazing how those who spend their days making up our rules so often end up spending their nights ignoring every single one of them. The only indulgence you can trust some politicians with nowadays is a choc ice.

Now, my friend's husband is a good man, better than most, in my view, but clearly far from perfect. For a while she was thinking about throwing him out. I asked her what she would get out of ending her marriage and putting her children through the wringer. 'Revenge!' she cried. I spelt out some of the more practical consequences for her. She would end up with more misery than she could imagine, bigger lawyers' fees than she could ever pay, a couple of maladjusted kids and a bed as cold as a nun's cloister. Oh, she would find another man, of course. Eventually. And the sum of it all? She would have swapped one imperfect man for another.

Am I doing our menfolk a disservice? I don't think so.

Anthropologically they may have emerged from the cave, but emotionally they haven't crawled out of their underwear. I'm not suggesting we can simply wash away all the pain and turn a blind eye to their faults. Make him suffer, by all means, share the misery round, pile his plate with humble pie and make sure he doesn't forget next time he's tempted. But there is no point in punishing yourself and your children simply to punish him. Standing by your man is a habit that's gone right out of fashion, but I'm not sure this modern-day rush to judgement has made us any happier.

We do the same with our politicians. One mistake and they're dogmeat. I'm not sure that's made us any better governed. If a politician has never made any mistakes, it's usually because he's never done anything, never achieved anything, never reached for the stars. The best leaders we've ever had – like Winston Churchill and President

Kennedy – made all sorts of mistakes along the way. The point is, the good ones learned the lessons.

So, my advice is always to look for a way out. Revenge is not best supped on your own, least of all in a cold bed. Let a sinner come to repentance, then make him squirm a bit, if necessary, then make him squirm a lot more. But give him – and yourself – another chance.

It would raise eyebrows, the piece, as it would questions about her and Dom, because only the witless would believe it was written about 'a friend'. Yet there were already questions about her and Dom, and she suspected there might be many more. So she would pre-empt them, if she could, with forgiveness.

And as she wrote it, Ginny hoped that one day she might even come to believe it.

Dom began his preparations methodically, as was his fashion. Raised some money, wrung some hands, smuggled out from Party Headquarters as much polling information and experience as he could: he would certainly have to step back from the chairmanship once he announced his ambition. Play must be fair, and be seen to be fair, so it was said.

Meanwhile, Ginny continued with her own preparations. Made sure she had private telephone numbers – direct lines numbers for editors and political columnists. Raised the price plan on her mobile phone. Stocked the freezer with late-night suppers. Bought Dom some new ties. Wondered how the hell she was going to finish the unpacking that was still strewn across the spare bedroom and most of the landing. And treated herself to some new perfume.

She went to visit Father Benedict who ran St Xavier's. Swore him to secrecy. Told him what was about to happen and asked him to make sure the children didn't suffer. No bullying, no teasing. And no cameras. He smiled, his red-apple cheeks lighting up at the prospect of a more famous father, and told her he would pray for them all. Wrapped in his blessings as she left his office, she decided to spend a few moments on her own in the church. It couldn't hurt.

The choir was practising carols for Christmas. As the choir-master waved his hands and the clean cotton sleeves of his surplice flapped, the voices of the young choristers soared like larks in a summer sky. For a moment she was transported back to her own childhood. Her father was nothing of a churchgoer but had insisted she be in the choir, every Thursday evening for practice and twice on Sundays. She remembered her first midnight Mass, the excitement of staying up on Christmas Eve to welcome the new baby Jesus, the dolls in the straw, the first time she had ever been awake past the hour of twelve. That Christmas was also the first time she had seen her father hit her mother, and she had never gone to church again, until Dominic came into her life. She had returned because he had wanted it and she so wanted her life with him to be different – different from the one she had known as a child. A family. United. Loving. And, at times, she thought it still might be. But she was certain of nothing any more, not even her own agnosticism. Her life had become as constant as a Catherine wheel.

She decided it had been a mistake to come. She didn't like this place, with its memories and music, and the cod-morality that kept tugging at her emotions, taking her back, confusing her. She was about to get up and leave when, in the middle of the choir, she saw Ben. He was singing his heart out, his eyes flicking earnestly between the choirmaster and his carol sheet. He hadn't told her about the choir, concerned, perhaps, that it would seem uncool in such a fervent Chelsea fan. He was growing up, making his own decisions, just as he would make his own mistakes. And he was leaving her behind, a little further every day, like a newly launched ship unfurling its sails for the first time, searching its way through the cross-currents as it left home port, heading it knew not where. Suddenly her own life seemed intolerably wretched. She ran from the church before anybody could notice the tears.

Then Bobby called. He sounded exhausted, but excited. He was waiting for her when she arrived home.

'Where's the fire?' she asked, her mood failing to match his excitement.

'On this tape,' he replied, waving a video-cassette.

Ah, the hotel tapes. She'd almost forgotten about them, what with all the other distractions, but Bobby had been working into the small hours for many nights and had finally produced the results. She nestled on Jemma's beanbag, cuddling the teddy bear her mother had given her and that had now been handed down to Jemma, while Bobby turned his attention to the controls. Soon a grainy image was moving across the screen: a man and a woman, walking down a hotel corridor, stopping in front of a door, talking, clinching, going inside. Then an edit to several hours later, the early hours of the morning, when the man could be seen leaving on his own. It was some time later before the woman could be seen leaving, carrying her bags.

'And?' Ginny asked distractedly.

'It's Hazel Basham.'

'Damnably difficult to tell. The images aren't very good.'

'Good enough.'

'And the man – who's he?'

'Not entirely sure – but does it matter? It clearly wasn't her husband. He was asleep in Norfolk at the time. I suspect it was Adrian Boulting.'

The director of the party's advertising agency. 'And why do you think that?'

'Because he paid her hotel bill.' Bobby, his hand shaking with excitement, produced a sheet of paper: a photocopy of Basham's expenditure over three nights at the conference. Room service, bar bills, TV channels, laundry, the lot. It was clearly marked as having been settled by Adrian Boulting. He'd used his agency's credit card. 'He'll probably charge it back to the party on their next invoice,' Bobby mocked. 'I think we've got her – got them both, if we want.

Ironic, isn't it? Stalin's nanny, the woman who wants to smother the country with CCTV cameras, tripped up by her own paranoia.' He didn't like this woman: his passion showed.

Yet Ginny sat on the beanbag, cuddling the teddy bear, staring in silence at the frozen image on the screen.

'There's more on the tape. Others. But I think this is the one,' Bobby said, tentative, sensing something was amiss.

Silence.

'What's wrong, Ginny?'

'I can't, Bobby. Surely you must see that. Glass houses.'

'You mean . . . ?'

'The Edges are not a family in much of a position to launch a campaign about personal morality right now.'

'But no one need know it's you.'

'*I* would know, Bobby. I don't want to be a hypocrite.'

'I thought . . .' He twisted his watch strap in exasperation.

'I thought so, too. But love and leadership can be harsh mistresses.'

'Do you have any idea how long all that took? How many evenings I've wasted?'

'Sorry.'

Bobby's mood was growing heated. 'What's the matter, Ginny? Cold feet?'

'Perhaps. I can scarcely argue principle, can I? Maybe it's simply fear of where we might all find ourselves if the race gets dragged down into nothing more than sexual peccadillo. Hey, that's a long word, wouldn't make much of a headline. But you know what I mean.'

'I thought I knew. I thought we wanted the same things. Now you say you can't be bothered, even though Hazel Basham is a four-star bigot and wouldn't give a second's thought about catching anyone else's fingers in the door.'

'I'm . . . sorry.'

'Yeah. So you said,' he snapped, jumping to his feet. 'And

something else. Whatever it takes. That's what you said. All those hopes you raised, all those broken bloody promises.' His voice sounded as if it were about to crack. 'You also asked me to let you know when you were abusing our friendship.'

She heard the front door slam behind him.

It wasn't planned, but ambition must take its chances.

Tina had called, wanting to come round, brooking no objection. Well, she had to be told at some point. Better, perhaps, that it be done on home ground, Ginny thought. Even as Tina arrived, leaving her car in the roadway like an abandoned wheelie-bin, her presence was overwhelming. Her sweater had taken another plunge, not only in neckline but also in taste. She did so insist on being noticed, no matter what it took.

She skipped and half tripped through the doorway, gushing greetings. Ginny offered tea.

'What? In the middle of a water crisis? Darling, you don't conspire on anything less than champagne. Least, that's what I've been doing.' So Ginny put away the teapot and, with some misgivings, opened a bottle.

'I've been lunching with Maggie Andrews.'

'I thought you were leaving her out in the cold.'

'She's not reliable, of course, but that's what makes her so interesting. No loyalties. Will talk about anyone.' And Tina was off. She was like a furnace, burning inside, and all but impossible to quench. So Ginny poured, and listened to some nonsense about Charlie Malthouse.

'Would you believe it? Apparently one of his former secretaries tried to hang herself from a lamp-post outside his front door.'

'Why?'

'Goodness, it was years ago – although I don't suppose *goodness* had much to do with it,' she chirped, squealing with laughter at her own joke. 'And I doubt it was an industrial dispute either. But who cares? It's up to those mongrels from the media to find out why.'

'You'd leak it to the press?'

'Of course. Why ever not?'

'I was just thinking . . . glass houses.'

'Phooey. All's fair in love and leadership. And don't let anyone suggest we've got no conscience. Why, I argue with mine all the time.' And she was off again, gossiping, sipping, slandering, asking Ginny to extract polling material and research papers from Party Headquarters, not willing to be delayed by any of Ginny's attempted interventions. The girl was on fire.

The onslaught became so intense that Ginny made an excuse and went to the bathroom, where she tried to compose herself, to find the words to tell Tina, but she found only two blank eyes staring back at her with dark smudges underneath. When she returned, the bottle was all but spent.

'Got to fly.' Tina launched herself once more. 'Meeting at home with the caterers. Lunch for the waverers and wobblers. Too many of them, if you ask me. Wish I could ask you, but . . . well, we'll have plenty to celebrate after this silly contest is done. Although I hear mutterings there might be a dark horse about to enter. Who could it be? Got any ideas? Leaving it damned late, whoever it is, with nominations closing tomorrow. Some silly wretch trying to sort out his private life first, I expect. No matter. Can't amount to much.'

'It's Dom.'

A sudden sepulchral hush. Tina knocked over her glass. It was empty. 'What?'

'I've been trying to tell you . . . Dom has decided to stand.'

'Tell me you're joking.'

Silence.

'You two-faced bitch!'

'Tina, I'm so sorry, but—'

'You've been playing me for a fool all this time. And I trusted you, you . . .' For the first time, words failed her. Tina stormed for the door, then stopped just as abruptly. 'He doesn't stand a bloody chance. That little tart of his will do for him. You can't imagine how many bucketloads of sewage are going to be poured over you!'

'Tina, you wouldn't.'

'Just you bloody well watch me!'

'Tina, please!'

But she was through the door, running to her car, fumbling with the keys, dropping them, climbing into the driver's seat, stuffing mints into her mouth, checking her appearance in the mirror, starting the engine. She rolled back and nudged the car behind her, twice, before she managed to pull out into the traffic.

Ginny watched the performance before reaching for her mobile phone.

The police intercepted Tina before she had got even half-way home. She didn't help her case by refusing to stop for some distance, then arguing ferociously with the policemen. 'Do you know who I am?' she demanded, and hadn't they got better things to do with their time? But it didn't seem to make any difference who she was: she might have been married to Napoleon for all they cared, and they still suspected her of being a drunk driver. They insisted she get out of the car. When she declined, one of the officers leaned inside to take her keys, but before he could get to them she had slapped his face and taken off once more. She'd driven almost another quarter of a mile before they caught up with her again, she had pulled into Sainsbury's and pretended to be a shopper.

Then it all became rather untidy. As a crowd of shoppers stared and an enterprising young man took photographs on his mobile phone, Tina was cautioned, told that she didn't have to say anything but it might harm her defence if she didn't mention something which she might later rely on in court. Anything she did say might be given in evidence, the constable said.

This prompted a further outburst of abuse: she threatened him with demotion and castration and things far, far worse, before accusing him of manhandling her and being a Mason. That resulted in another police car being called, and a support van to carry her off in handcuffs. But by the time she arrived at the police station she had run out of wind. She refused to speak, not a word, even when charged with driving under the influence, resisting arrest and assaulting a police officer. Only later, after she had been locked in her cell, and through copious but mainly silent tears, did she say one thing, over and over again. She wanted her husband.

Ginny had tried to call Bobby, but he wasn't answering his phone. Or perhaps he was simply not answering his phone to her. On the third attempt she left a message, saying she was sorry, asking him to call.

She wanted someone to talk to, someone with whom she could share. Instead, she slowly climbed the stairs to peep at the children.

Ben had wrapped himself round his bedclothes in a knot she dared not try to disentangle, as though he were fighting dragons, but Jemma she found sleeping peacefully. She sat down carefully on the bed, brushed a stray lock of hair from her daughter's face, bent to kiss her warm cheek. She had often wondered whether her own mother had done much the same, on that last night, coming in to say goodbye, to whisper silent entreaties as she smoothed the blanket, checking everything was in order, one last time.

Ginny had been eleven, slightly older than Jemma. It was the seventh house of her short life, made home as always by her mother, and made brutal by her father. His career was going awry, in command of his dreary regiment in Gibraltar, about as far from the cannon's mouth as it was possible to be. The regiment had missed out on the Falklands, had faced the bottles and abuse of Northern Ireland, and was now stuck in this little colonial outpost where her father didn't take to the social life, didn't get on with either the governor or his commander, and took out his frustrations on his men. Daily runs up the Rock, tough discipline, constant pressure, he squeezed them ever harder, until the pips began not only to squeak but to scream. Then the paymaster was discovered with his hand in the till. The entire regiment was brought to shame and they all took turns in pointing the finger of blame at her father. He was in command, it was his responsibility. And he, in turn, took it out on his wife. It wasn't so much the beatings, which were occasional and done only when he was in drink, but the constant emotional neglect that ground her down. No matter how hard Ginny's mother had tried, it was never enough. Complaint merged into contempt and depression into despair.

Ginny remembered little more than the confusion, that time when she was woken in the middle of the night with whispers of some sort of accident. She found herself being lifted bodily by one of her father's staff officers past the hastily closed door to her parents' room, with its perplexing crush of people, then placed in the back of a car. After that, she didn't see her father for almost two days. And only later did she hear of pills, and later still of alcohol, and how her mother had died through some dreadful mishap. 'Accidental death' was the verdict recorded. It was only many years later that her mother's sister, in terminal pain and under mood-bending medication, had spluttered the word 'suicide'. When Ginny had asked her father, he had hit her.

Ginny had seen families destroyed, had lived that nightmare, and she had vowed she would never let it happen to her own children, whatever it took. Tina had a family, too, of course, but she had been hell-bent on destroying it all by herself, drowning it in drink. It was bound to have ended this way, in shame. Ginny had done nothing but give the timing a gentle nudge. So why was she crying, hurting so much?

She dried her eyes on the corner of Jemma's duvet, and quietly closed the bedroom door.

The headlines the following morning were not those that Jack Saunders would have wanted on the day the leadership election was formally launched.

'*Law and Disorder*' screamed the *Record,* filling its front page with a photograph of Tina clouting a police officer with her handbag. The quality of the photograph was remarkable, considering it had come from a mobile phone, and other similarly sharp images of Tina's arrest filled pages four, five, six and seven. The other red-top newspapers swam vigorously in the *Record's* wake, several of them pointing out that, with the government having just launched the annual drink-drive crackdown and keen to set an example to others, Tina might easily end up spending Christmas in clink.

Jack had issued a statement that referred to vague and inchoate health problems from which Tina had been suffering and 'bearing bravely for some considerable time', requesting that she be allowed her privacy to continue her recovery. Fat chance. The commentators gave a similar chance to Jack's prospects of winning the leadership race, if he were brazen enough to continue with it, but his statement made no mention of his intentions on that front.

It squeezed the *Record's* exclusive coverage of Dom's expected candidacy way down. A statement would be made before close of nominations at three o'clock that afternoon, the paper suggested, and although it was unexpected and Dom himself was inexperienced, in light of the fate that had befallen Jack Saunders and even Ed Goodthorpe, anything might happen. Would the last Opposition politician left standing please switch out the lights?

By three o'clock, nominations had closed and the story was clearer. There were to be seven candidates – the 'Seven Humbugs of the World', as they were immediately branded by a government minister. Hazel Basham was the only woman and Ken Boston, another last-minute entrant, the only unambiguously gay. He knew he had little chance of success, but put his name forward in the hope that any new leader would find it difficult to sack him. The only unambiguously Scottish candidate was Iain Madden. The rest of the list was made up of Charlie Malthouse, Jack Saunders, and Ed Goodthorpe. And, of course, Dom.

They would have only four weeks to wait before they knew

their fate. Ballot papers would go out to the party's membership that weekend, along with a grovelling letter soliciting donations, to be returned by 15 December, in time for peace to break out for the festive season. And while things had got off to an explosive start, it was clear the affair would now calm down and become more serious. The *Guardian* suggested that in retrospect it might prove fortunate that all the personal indiscretions which seem to snap at the heels of modern leadership elections had been disposed of at the start. Well, they had, hadn't they?

Except no one had told Tina. She had been momentarily distracted, of course, but no sooner had she sobered up and been released from police custody than she began to mete out her retribution, a process interrupted only by her frequent need to consult her lawyers. She was innocent, of course, the victim of a vendetta by her husband's enemies. She regaled everyone she could reach with this, particularly those in the media, not only those she knew but also those who hadn't yet had the pleasure. No amount of argument or instruction from Jack or the lawyers would persuade her to hold fire. She was like an old man-o'-war, wind filling her sails, rigging taut, reeking of rum, manoeuvring right into the heart of enemy ranks and unleashing broadsides in all directions. Goodthorpe, she reminded them, was a fraud, while Ken Boston was a screaming bum bandit, and while the party might subscribe to all sorts of codes about equality and be willing to turn a blind eye, not one of them would be willing to turn their back while Boston was in the room.

No sooner had the smoke from her first fusillade dispersed than she turned towards Madden, dismissing him as a man who had progressed through the ranks solely because he had made a good speech at Party Conference in 1993 and had been trying to repeat it ever since. Then she let fly with stories about Malthouse and his secretary, like grapeshot strafing the deck, before ramming full-sail into Dom's reputation. Unfortunately, once the smoke of battle had cleared, it became apparent that Malthouse's former secretary had long since sailed from the scene and emigrated to Australia, while Julia was nowhere to be found, and without her no one could print a thing.

But that didn't stop Tina. Right up to the moment she fell out of the taxi outside Horseferry Road Magistrates' Court she was telling everyone who would listen. She even tried telling the magistrates until her lawyers jumped in. She was still muttering, even as she was sentenced. Two weeks' imprisonment, as an example to others. At this point she fainted. It was, allegedly, the first time she had been silent since the day of her arrest, which was perhaps why Jack Saunders chose the moment to announce he was quitting the race.

Then there were six.

Almost overnight, as Dom began to bring together an organisation for his campaign, Ginny's world started to overflow with new friends, political friends, some of whom she actively disliked and many of whom she didn't yet know. There were those who treated her with a familiarity that suggested they had known her all her life, while others acted as if she were invisible or her sole purpose was to serve beer and sandwiches. She said little but listened intently, extended greetings to all, biding her time. If Dom was destroyed by the campaign, none of this would matter, but if he was to win, she would have learned whom they could trust and who was merely ballast on their great voyage.

One face she didn't see was Bobby's. He still hadn't called, and when she tried him at Party Headquarters they said he hadn't been at work for several days.

He lived in the top-floor apartment of a tall stuccoed Victorian terrace in fashionable Kensington, not far from the High Street. As she parked her car outside, she reckoned that the rent or mortgage payment would wipe out most of his meagre wage from the party, so clearly Bobby relied on another source of income: presumably his father. There was no lift; the staircase was hung with old advertising prints from the thirties and everything was freshly decorated. Half-way up, a young woman rushed out of a doorway, chatting on her mobile phone and dangling BMW car keys. She raised her eyes in apology – or was it irritation? – as she pushed her way down the stairs, still chattering. Yuppieland.

The door to Bobby's apartment had neither bell nor knocker; she rapped hard with her knuckles. Nothing. She tried again, and only after some time did the door slowly open. The face that stared at her was not that of the Bobby she knew. He hadn't shaved for several days, his shirt was rumpled and his feet were bare, but it was his eyes that particularly caught her attention. The lids were red, angry, rubbed raw with sleeplessness, and the pupils were dull and dead. No sparkle, no hint of welcome or even surprise, and precious little sign of recognition.

'Did you get my messages?' she asked.

He said nothing, simply turned and walked back into the apartment, leaving the door open. He slumped into a black leather sofa; it appeared as if he had scarcely moved from it for a long time. Bowls and mugs were scattered on the stripped wooden floor, and on the low table in front were spread the remains of at least two microwave meals. He was half-way through a bottle of wine. There was an air of hopelessness about the place, the stench of despair, about Bobby in particular, as though he were fifty years older and entirely alone.

'What's going on, Bobby?'

'My apologies. If I'd known I was to receive a royal visit I'd have got the maid to clean.'

She ignored the deliberate attempt at provocation. 'It's me who should apologise. For the other night. Our misunderstanding. I've been worrying about it. About you.'

'No need to worry. Everything's wonderful.'

'I can see.' Instinctively she began to take charge and started clearing some of the dirty crockery.

He jumped up in protest. 'I can do that.'

'Then let's do it together.'

For a moment he seemed to conduct an internal debate on the matter before reluctantly taking up some of the debris. In the kitchen, he hesitated by the sink. As she followed, he let the dishes fall with an ugly crash. 'What's the bloody point?' he said, very angry.

'Of what?'

'Of anything.' He turned to confront her. 'Your ridiculous leadership race. I've seen Archie's betting book – did you know he gambles? Not on horses but on politics. Damned good at it. And his little book says Dom doesn't stand a bloody chance. Even with Jack Saunders out, he's still only fourth. Behind even Malthouse. Way behind Hazel and Iain Madden.'

'So we turn it round.'

'In less than four weeks? How? Oh, Dom may have made one or two pretty speeches, but out there in the real world people scarcely know him, and those who do haven't the slightest idea what he stands for. He's just a cover on another unread book.'

'I have a feeling he's going to get himself much better known.'

'I need a rather more substantial sticking place than your feminine instinct.'

'How about our friendship?'

He glared at her, then stomped back to his sofa and grabbed his drink. As she followed she couldn't help noticing that the apartment was filled with modern furniture and boasted one of the largest flat-screen televisions she had ever seen. His father, once again. Yet one wall was decorated with a beautifully crafted traditional rug, while on another wall, just above the blinking electronic eye of a music system, hung an overly bright piece of calligraphy that Ginny presumed were the words of the Prophet. An uneasy combination of styles, and of lives.

Bobby picked up on her train of thought. 'Yes, my father – all this,' he said, glancing round the room. 'Thinks he owns every part of me, like an ancient caliph.'

'What's happened?'

'Oh, nothing much. Just a minor family misunderstanding.'

'About what?'

'What do you think?'

'Getting married?'

'He has it all arranged. The daughter of one of his business colleagues in Karachi. Plans to fly her over here next month to introduce her. It was all agreed. Whether I like it or not.' He was finding it difficult to breathe, his sentences coming in short angry bursts. 'So I told him I didn't like it. He said it didn't matter, that I had a duty to the family. He was fed up with my prevarication.' Bobby's emotions were in turmoil.

'I'm so sorry, Bobby.'

Suddenly he was at her, his face contorted with fury. 'Not half as bloody sad as he is. Because I told him, you see. I couldn't take it any more. All the deception, the lies. So I told him. I'm gay. A camel-fucker. Goats. And he said he knew, had known for some time. And he was in tears. I'd never seen him cry. But he said I was still to do my duty. Get married. Otherwise I would bring dishonour not only upon myself but upon the entire family.' Bobby was finding it difficult to continue. The memories seemed to have burned away the resistance that was holding him together. He started to tremble.

'What did you say next?'

'Simply that I could not do what he asked.' The voice was quieter now. 'That the greater dishonour would be in living a lie. That he was old, not only in his body but in his beliefs, and the world had moved on from blind obedience.' He paused, flinching under the lash of the memories. 'He said that his world had not moved on. There was wisdom in the old ways, and if I did not follow them it would be as though I were spitting in the face of the Prophet. No son of his would be permitted to do that.' Suddenly Bobby's head came up, fierce and defiant once more. He began to pace, waving his arms as though he were re-enacting the scene. 'I told him I didn't need his permission to live! He was an old fool. What I was, he had made me. Bobby choked before continuing. 'So he said that if he had made me, then he could unmake me. He would cast me out of his world and I would never be part of his family again.'

Ginny gasped, and Bobby stood still.

'I lost my temper. I told him that no father worthy of the name threatened his son in such a way. That I would not be treated like a slave, that he was no better than a pimp and a procurer of women. And . . . he hit me.' His hand came up to his cheek. The eyes that had been filled with fury were now adrift in an ocean of despair, his words coming as a whisper. 'He knocked me to the floor. And when I got up, I told him that if he did not want me in his family, I would save him the bother of kicking me out. Then I left. Walked out on him, walked out on his life, the life that has always been mine. Now, I can never return.'

'I'm sure . . .' Ginny cut herself short. Platitudes were not what he needed, and she had no better words to offer. Instead, she took his hand.

'If I could wave a magic wand and be different, be as he would want me to be, then I would, but I can't. I cannot. Not even for my father.' He was still touching the spot on the side of his face; Ginny could see the faint mark of the bruise. 'He had never hit me before, not once. He loved me, I have always known that, was proud of me, and I love him. But his love is not my love. Now I am alone.'

'I hope not, Bobby,' she whispered, as she held his shaking frame in her arms. 'Not while I'm around.'

She lay awake, restless, worrying. This new life she had chosen – no, that had been inflicted on her – left her days too short and the nights sometimes endless. Dom had returned after midnight, exhausted by his efforts. His campaign had started so late that ever since he'd been playing catch-up, like a long-distance runner who starts a race a full lap behind the others. He'd found premises for his headquarters, backers to pay for it, volunteers to man it and press officers to promote it, an entire team assembled at the gallop.

'But what's it all about, Dom?' she asked, as he, too, rolled over, sleepless.

He grunted, acknowledging that he was awake.

'I hear that Archie Blackstone's running a book and you're fourth favourite. Still, could be worse. A week ago you weren't even on the list.'

'It's a crowded field, Ginny, everyone struggling for breathing space and the media showing bugger-all interest. If I could get a tenth of the coverage that poor old Tina achieved I'd be happy till my dying day.'

'Be careful what you wish, Dom.'

'Meaning?'

She sighed. 'Julia.'

'For pity's sake, will you never—'

'I'm not using her as a stick, Dom, simply pointing out the possibilities. You might yet get more coverage than you could ever wish for, if it's left up to your enemies.'

'Enemies? Do I have enemies now?'

'They swarm round ambition like flies.'

'And all I ever wanted to do is to help, make things better. Sounds so pathetic, I know, but . . .'

'Those who wish to help others must first help themselves. Isn't that the first rule of Westminster?'

'You make it sound so selfish.'

'A politician without power is about as useful as a sweet-wrapper in a running gutter. There has to be a sticking place, some point to it all other than wailing in the wind.'

'I know, I know. At times I feel like the soldiers in Fort Apache surrounded by the bloody Indians. Time to break out.'

'What have you got in mind?'

He didn't reply for a few moments, settling back on his pillow as he gathered his thoughts, watching the patterns made by the street-lights on the bedroom ceiling.

'Nothing too complicated,' he said at last. 'There's not enough time to develop more than a few clear thoughts. But I was thinking, why don't we build it round family and the future? Just like your articles suggested. After all, that barren bitch Hazel doesn't have any kids, and Iain's are all grown-up.'

'Use Jemma and Ben for the campaign?'

'Within limits, of course. But they exist, can't deny that. The most important things in our lives. They've made me what I am as a politician, focused all my thoughts. And it's to their benefit if we succeed. Bit like Mark Thatcher. Got lost in the bloody desert and been living off it ever since.'

'I don't want Ben getting lost in the desert.'

Dom chuckled softly. 'And I don't suppose he ever will with you around, my love.' He reached out, fumbling in the darkness for her hand. 'And talking of deserts,' he said, 'I think the time has come to bring every last one of our troops back from Iraq. Let the Iraqis sort things out for themselves.'

'Breaking ranks?'

'Not just with government, with Hazel and Iain, too. Hazel won't stop till she's driving the bloody tanks herself, while Iain has never done more than plod along behind in the dust. We've suffered too long for the sin of believing what we were told when it started. Time to grow up, face up to it all.'

'It would certainly set you apart. But do people care enough about Iraq? You know what the pollsters say.'

His response betrayed exasperation. 'Ginny, it doesn't matter very much to me whether other people care, or what the wretched focus groups say, or even at the end of the day whether I win or lose. It's what I believe.'

She rolled over, pressed her body against him so that he could feel the warmth of her breath. Then she kissed him, full on his lips.

'What was that for?' he asked.

'You know, Dominic Edge, we might just make a politician of you yet.'

And, for the first time since the affair had come between them, they made full and mutually satisfying love.

Ajok put on her best dress, buttoned up her only coat, and walked to the employment tribunal. It was on a roaring road in the centre of London, a part of town she had never been before called Holborn. The name above the door declared it to be Victory House.

The tribunal room was a bare, dully practical place, set out like a school classroom. The furniture was plain and laminated, the window looked out on to a bare brick wall, allowing no direct light, no sun, no perspective. Recycled air. Jugs of warm, stale water. It seemed designed to anaesthetise, to squeeze out any trace of passion and animation. Suddenly Ajok felt lost, and yearned for the shade of the giant acacia that stood in the middle of the village market place. She wanted the warmth of the breeze as it rustled through the leaves and brushed against her exposed skin, to sense the colours and the rich fragrances that marked out her village and to hear once more the sound of complaining cattle. She felt a very long way from home, and a sense of panic rose in her.

She was asked to sit at a table that bore a label declaring her to be 'Claimant'. No names, all very impersonal. The solicitor provided by the union tried to help her relax, but his efforts were clumsy; he was young and awkward and they had met briefly only once before. He had brought many papers with him in a suitcase on wheels and he spent much time dipping inside, like a grazing steer. Not much of a steer at that, she reckoned, casting her practised eye over him. In her village he would have had his manhood cut off so that he could be fattened up for the cooking pot. Not meant for the long haul, this one.

At another table, marked 'Respondent', sat the Cypriot

supervisor, along with a Treasury solicitor named Omar. Paddy Creasey was there, too, sitting nearby, the good man that he was. This was a place of many accents, truly a Wealth of Nations, even the chairman of the three-man panel had a dark hue about him, but as proceedings got under way, for Ajok it came quickly to resemble a Tower of Babel. Her solicitor and the chairman tried to ensure she understood the meaning of everything, but they were lawyers and their meaning was often as clear as a fishing-hole during a rainstorm.

The chairman was in his fifties, a trained lawyer, with a gentle smile and a handkerchief flopping out of the top pocket of his suit. When the time came for her to read out her witness statement he asked her to swear an oath, but she was neither Christian nor Muslim nor Hindu and she didn't adhere to any of the other religions spelled out on the cards in front of her. She was an animist who worshipped the spirits of her ancestors that inhabited the rocks and the trees, and the tribunal didn't have a form of words for that, so instead she was allowed to make a solemn affirmation that she would tell the truth. Apart from Ajok, there were only two other witnesses and they, too, had to take an oath, in their own ways. Didn't stop them lying.

The main witness on the other side was a tall, narrow-faced man with thinning hair and a cross eye that constantly swivelled behind thick-framed glasses. Another steer for the pot. She had never met him before, but that didn't stop him trying to rip up her life. It seemed he was something called the dismissing officer, and he had a title at the Ministry that sounded like an assistant director of Human Resources. She never did get to know his name but there he was, after swearing the oath on his Bible, whispering with the Cypriot and uttering such shameful untruths. Calling her unreliable. Stating that she was always complaining.

'Mrs Arob's witness statement claims that she was frequently praised for her work. Is that the case?' the chairman asked.

'Not to my knowledge, sir,' Cross Eye replied. 'Quite the

contrary. It's my understanding that her reliability left rather a lot to be desired.' He referred to a sheaf of papers in a dark brown folder. 'In fact, in the week before she was fired, on one night she turned up very late, and on another not at all.'

'But that—' Ajok began, eager to rebut, but she was shushed into silence by her solicitor and got a frown from the chairman for her trouble.

'You'll get your chance to respond,' her solicitor whispered. Yet all she had wanted to do was to explain that little Mijok had been ill, a very high fever, and his needs had had to come first. The Cypriot had known that, hadn't complained at the time, but now . . .

'And I'm told the claimant had constant complaints to make about the equipment,' Cross Eye was continuing.

But only about the old vacuum cleaner that kept breaking down. It broke down for everyone and they took it in turns to grumble about it, the Cypriot most of all. He'd once kicked it half-way down the ministerial corridor after it had blown a fuse. The beating hadn't persuaded it to work any harder. But Cross Eye didn't appear to know about this. Didn't stop him arguing with considerable force that her work had been sloppy, her time-keeping worse and her attitude 'not the sort we would encourage inside the most sensitive corridors of Whitehall'. Surprising how precise he was about everything when this was the first time he had ever laid eyes on her. With every lie, every deceit, Ajok felt as though she were being whipped with humiliation.

Then it was the turn of her own solicitor to question Cross Eye. She sat up; now at last the tribunal would hear the truth. 'It is the case — isn't it? — that Mrs Arob was often commended for her reliability and conscientiousness,' he asked.

'No, sir.'

'Never?'

'No. Not to my knowledge.'

'Yet she was one of your longest-serving employees.'

'Yes, we were very patient.' He sighed.

'But I put it to you that Mrs Arob was one of your better employees. Indeed, one of your stars, which was why she was given the responsibility of cleaning the ministerial corridor.'

'We had to keep moving her around. She'd worked in several areas, but the other cleaners complained about her.'

'Have you any written record of these complaints?'

'Not at all. If we wrote that sort of thing down it would bring everything grinding to a halt. In most cases these matters are best sorted out by a private word, rather than an official complaint. That's what we encourage.'

'So you haven't a shred of evidence in writing.'

'Evidence of what?'

'Mrs Arob's unsuitability.'

'Her constant moving around the building from station to station is evidence of that.'

But – but that had all been the result of her hard work, of her being given more and more responsibility. Now it was being used as evidence to damn her. Everyone around her seemed to remain so polite, so calm, while Ajok was burning up inside. She felt as if she had caught a fever. And it grew still more fierce when the time came for the Cypriot to give his evidence. She had never seen him in a suit before, or a tie, rarely without a cigarette in his hand and a coarse word on his lips. He didn't once look at her, just took his oath to tell the truth and began giving Ajok's confused world a further twist.

'Your witness statement implies that you did not like the claimant,' the chairman said.

'No, sir. She was difficult at times – but I loves all my workers. I tries to get along with them all.'

'Then why didn't you ask someone else to clean the room in question?'

'But we all works so hard, everyone is busy. So much to do. I would do it myself if I had the time, but . . .' His shoulders heaved in a desolate shrug.

'The claimant's witness statement says you were abusive to her, used foul language. Is that correct?'

'No, sir, on my honour!' The Cypriot was instantly excitable. 'I never uses bad language. I am God-fearing man, sir, never is abusive to a woman, never, never.'

'You are sure?'

'On my mother's grave, your honour, your reverend.'

'No need for that. I am not a judge, certainly not a man of the cloth. A simple "sir" will be more than sufficient.'

'Thank you, your . . . sir. But it is upsetting for me to hear these nonsenses. I was brought up good and proper,' he blustered, beating his chest.

'Are you saying – I want you to be very clear about this – that the accusation you were abusive and used bad language is false? A lie, even?'

He took a deep, dramatic breath. 'Sir, I leaves that for you to decide. But it is not true. It is imaginations.'

From the table where he sat, Cross Eye nodded approvingly, like a proud parent at a school play, but the chairman was shaking his head in confusion, clearly bothered. 'I find it very difficult to deal with a case where there is such a clear conflict of evidence,' he said, polishing his spectacles furiously as though it might give him clearer sight. 'My job and that of my colleagues is to decide who in this case has acted unreasonably. Mrs Arob, I would like to return to you, if I may.' He replaced his glasses, ever the kindly tutor. 'Do you understand what has been going on, and what has been said? Forgive my asking, but it is important that you are fully aware of the matters before us.'

'I think so, sir,' she said hesitantly.

'Let me ask you, were you treated differently from the other cleaners?'

'Other cleaners?'

'The English ones, for instance.'

'Most of the cleaners are foreign.'

'The white ones, then.'

'Not really.'

'But you claim in your statement that when your supervisor abused you he referred to your colour.'

'He abused everyone, sir. It is his way.'

This was scarcely helping. So many crossed wires, so much conflicting evidence. The chairman hadn't known a Cypriot who didn't swear and bluster and have a very pronounced view about the superiority of his own culture, but perhaps this one was an exception. He decided to change tack. 'Then would you accept that, possibly, in the circumstances, you acted a little rashly?'

'How, sir?'

'Don't you accept that you put your employers in a difficult position?'

'No, sir. There were other people to clean the room. It would have taken less than five minutes.'

'In addition to compensation you are asking for reinstatement to your job, I see.'

'Yes, sir. I want to work.'

'You want to work in the Ministry.'

'Yes, I do. My old job.'

'So, if you were reinstated, you would happily clean the ministerial floor?'

'The floor, yes. That room, no.'

'I'm sorry to press you, Mrs Arob, but I must make sure. You would still refuse to clean the Ministers' room?'

'Yes, sir.'

'Even after all the bother and problems this has caused?'

She thought about it, then nodded.

'Hmm, I see, I see,' he muttered. 'Might there be other places in the Ministry you would refuse to clean? Places that are directly connected to the war?'

It was at this point that her solicitor intervened: 'Sir, if I may, it's fundamental to my client's case that it is unreasonable to ask her to assist in any way whatsoever with a war that she finds morally repugnant.'

'But where do you draw the line? One might argue that every room, every corridor, every nook and cranny of the Ministry is embroiled in some way with the war.'

'Mrs Arob is not an unreasonable woman, sir, neither is she political.'

'She's a refugee, isn't she? And she clearly has strong views about the war.'

'She is simply someone who has been trying to do her best to fulfil the commitments of her job while steering clear of that which she finds unacceptable.'

'But if we all . . .' The chairman shook his head in confusion, as though to dispel troublesome flies. 'Why this room, Mrs Arob? Why not any other part of the Ministry?'

'I did not want to cause any trouble, sir. But . . . the war,' she responded.

Her solicitor jumped in: 'I repeat, my client is not a political activist with a determined agenda, sir. She is simply an ordinary cleaning lady with standards of decency who wants her job back.'

'You say she is not an activist but this claim is becoming very political.' The chairman sighed. There was a silence for a few moments while he held his hands as though in prayer, grappling with deep thoughts. 'Mrs Arob, one last question, if I may. Can I be clear – if the circumstances repeated themselves, if you were asked to clean that room once more, or any room like it, would you do the same? Refuse to comply?'

'Yes, sir.'

'Then I think we have heard enough.'

The chairman and the two lay members, who had said almost nothing throughout the proceedings, rose and disappeared through a side door. It was after a short break for lunch when they returned. The chairman shuffled his papers, cleared his throat, then said they had found great difficulty in dealing with evidence that was so clearly contradictory. But in the end, he declared, perhaps it didn't matter. Ajok's refusal to clean the room had been a clear breach of her contractual undertakings, and although a margin of flexibility had to be permitted for matters of deep personal conscience, her continuing refusal to obey the instructions of her employers was political, or if it wasn't political it was at very least unreasonable. Either way, it compromised her. Fatally. So they pronounced their decision. Ajok's claim was struck out. She had lost.

The scene whirled in Ajok's confused mind. As the chairman and his panel left by a rear door, Cross Eye and the Cypriot were shaking hands, congratulating their solicitor, while her own solicitor mumbled his regrets and, with downcast eyes, rushed away, dragging his suitcase behind him. Paddy Creasey, too, offered his apologies before departing, explaining that he was due at another tribunal. In an instant, before her mind had had a chance to clear, she was alone. She had come to this place expecting justice yet she hadn't found it. Instead she had been forced to listen to her character being torn apart by people who knew nothing of her. She felt angry, bruised, on the verge of tears, and she ran to the ladies' room to hide her humiliation. Yet, no matter how hard she tried, no matter how many times she splashed her face, she couldn't rinse away shame. Slowly, through her confusion, she became aware of another woman looking at her. Dark, formal suit, with a round face and bobbed hair.

'Are you all right?' the stranger enquired.

Yes, she was fine, thank you, Ajok replied, but it was clearly a lie.

'This place can be so impersonal,' the woman muttered, 'even when you win. And I guess you didn't.'

Ajok found it difficult to deal with the gentleness of her tone. Suddenly her defences were down and the tears were winning. The stranger offered her a paper towel and it wasn't long before Ajok was blurting out her story, of Cross Eye and the Cypriot and the ministerial Prayer Room and the war in Iraq.

'Iraq?' the stranger said, suddenly alert. 'They sacked you because of the war in Iraq?'

Ajok nodded.

The stranger sat silently for a moment, considering what she had been told. 'You know, your case needn't be over yet,' she said, sucking thoughtfully at the end of a thumb. 'I might be able to help. My name is Sophie Gaminara.' She held out her hand to complete the introduction. 'I'm a barrister from the Free Representation Unit – we do *pro bono* work. That's unpaid work for clients like you. It's so we can get experience. And, although it's a million miles from the sort of stuff we normally work on, I'd love to help.'

Ajok's case had been declared political even though she had crossed half the planet in an attempt to flee from the curse of politics. She was a woman who had never voted, who was accustomed to doing what she was told by others, who believed in tradition and an ordered way of doing things, a woman who knew her place. Her place was not here, of course, for here she would always be a dark-faced Dinka who would never quite fit in, but she had accepted that as inevitable and was, indeed, grateful. No other tribe she knew would have taken her in so openly and with so little question. She had no ambitions, other than to find peace for herself and her children, a respite from the troubles that had taken hold of her world. Yet even here, two thousand miles from her home, she could find no hiding-place. Enemies still pursued her, sought her out for punishment, attempting to take away what was rightfully hers, even her dignity. And that would not do. So she thanked the stranger and accepted her offer of help. It had to be better than swallowing the shame. Yet what she didn't know, couldn't possibly have realised, was that this would put her world and that of Westminster on a course destined for collision. The consequences were to be devastating.

Eight

'I'M CALLING. JUST AS you asked me to, Ginny.'

'Max, I don't remember—'

'Julia Summers. She's selling her story.'

Ginny set aside the laundry she was piling into the machine and reached for her mug of coffee. 'What's she saying?' Her voice sounded weak, distant, as though it belonged to someone else.

'An affair. Details of times and places. Sofas, drinks, carpet burns, that sort of thing.'

She'd known this might happen, of course, but the foreknowledge did nothing to still the feeling of infinite emptiness that had opened inside her. The coffee was trembling in her hand, in danger of spilling. She put it down.

'When? When will it appear, Max?'

'Day after tomorrow.'

'You sure?'

'Positive. The lawyers have cleared it and the desk is preparing the front page now.'

'*You?* You are doing this?'

'It's a good story.'

'Please. Max . . .' She stared out of the window across the small urban garden. A cold day, one of the first frosts of winter. A gust of wind rustled through the top of the maple tree. As she watched, its last surviving leaf spiralled forlornly to the ground.

'Come on, Ginny. If we don't do it someone else will. And I'm doing more than I should by telling you. But we had a deal. I'm honouring it.'

'Honour? You dare talk to me of honour?'

'I didn't have to make this call, Ginny. But you're getting a far better deal than you'd ever get from the *Mirror* or the *Sun*. Gives you and Dom time to think about what you'll say. Send the kids to Grandma's, or whatever.'

'It will destroy Dom.'

'Probably.'

'Is there nothing . . . ?'

'Not even your body.'

Her world was spinning furiously, so fast that all the familiar things she knew seemed to be flying off into the darkest reaches of space.

'I'm sorry, for what it's worth,' Max continued. 'Thought Dom had a real chance.'

Yet as her world spun out of control and her thoughts were tossed around in the gale of confusion, something stuck. 'In a way, Max, I'm so glad it's you.'

'Really?'

'I suppose things do have a habit of coming out.'

'Too damned right.'

'Tell me, Max, would you consider swapping the story for a copy of a tape of you and that chambermaid?'

'What bloody chambermaid?'

'You know, the one in the lift at Party Conference.'

'You're delirious.'

'Oh, come on, Max, it's pretty grainy, not exactly up to Spielberg standards, but more than enough lighting to see your face, even if not hers. Well, you wouldn't see her face, not with what she was up to, would you? And you can also see what looks like the fifty-pound note you gave her, although it might have been a twenty. But you're not that cheap, are you, Max?'

'You're bluffing.'

'Seems you overlooked the CCTV cameras. You weren't the only one.' Indeed, even Bobby had overlooked the significance of that little interlude as he was editing the tape. He hadn't recognised Max but, then, Max was an editor, not a celebrity.

'What,' Max asked slowly, 'do you intend to do?'

'Depends.'

'On?'

'You.'

'I can't stop the Julia thing, Ginny. Not even I can do that. Not now.'

'You're the editor.'

'For about another thirty seconds if I tried to pull the story. Too many people know.'

A silence.

'And so bloody what about the lift? I'm a single man. I'd survive. Boost my street cred. Unlike Dom.'

'You'd have an interesting time explaining it to your mother.'

'That's cheap. Don't bring her into it.'

'You bring my kids into it and I'll make you squirm till you disappear up your own arse, Needledick!' she spat, banging the kitchen table with her fist.

'She will still be my mother,' Max replied, doggedly but clearly affected. 'And I still can't stop it. You must realise, Ginny—'

'Shut up, Max. I'm thinking.'

She could hear him breathing anxiously down the phone. It entirely mirrored her own state.

'You've presumably signed her to some sort of exclusive contract, haven't you, Max? Something to stop her talking to others?'

'Of course.'

'Then you do this. Print, if you must. But wait for a week.'

'And give you time to call in the lawyers? Won't work, Ginny. We're watertight.'

'No, Max. We had a deal, remember? I won't try to stop you printing. I just want a few days to prepare our defences.'

'And what will you do with the tape?'

'Nothing. Just play it at a few private parties, perhaps. Maybe invite your mother over. It all depends.'

'On what?'

'On how unnecessarily gruesome you make all this. And whether Dom manages to survive.'

'You think he might really stay in the race?'

'We stayed in Iraq. Anything is possible.'

'Jesus, Ginny, you've got balls of iron.'

'No, I've got a husband and two kids. A woman doesn't need anything more.'

Without thinking she wiped away the drops of water that had spilled on the tabletop, until she realised they were her tears.

Max, meanwhile, was thinking of his mother. Then he thought of the Honours Scrutiny Committee. One day, he knew, his name might go before them. His mother would like that, and so would he, but he'd never heard of them granting a knighthood to a man caught being sucked off in a lift.

He sighed. 'Ginny?'

'Yes, Needledick?'

'I hope we still have a deal.'

Oh, but leadership elections are cruel and unpredictable forms of self-mutilation. Those who wish to stand tall must first survive the onslaught of others who would see them brought low, the sort of levellers who would have done for a Palmerston or a Gladstone and had already done for Blair and his blind men. They were also about to do for Ken Boston.

His main fault was that he had begun his career as a gay-rights campaigner and had never succeeded in leaving that mantle behind. They wouldn't let him. He had made a speech more than fifteen years previously to a private assembly of gay activists in which he had appealed to them never to give in. It wasn't quite 'fight on the beaches, fight in France' stuff, but he was never one to pass by an easy cliché in the height of passion and he had invoked the name of Winston Churchill who, in his darkest hour, had implored those around him to KBO. Keep Buggering On. A tasteless comment, and silly of Ken to try to impress such a name into the cause. He knew he was too lippy, it was a fault, but the meeting had been held in private. There had been no way for him to know that someone had a tape-recorder. Yet even now, almost two decades and several career starts later, people remembered, and many refused to forgive. A leadership contest is a numbers game and the numbers simply didn't stack up for Ken – 'Bottom of the Class', as one tabloid wrote. And plenty of others were writing in a similar vein, hinting that a closet full of lurid revelations was about to pour forth now that Ken had opened the door. They were intent on humiliating him and, as much as Ken enjoyed a little sporadic humiliation, that was strictly for private occasions.

So he gathered the press to his front door and, with the ever-faithful Ron standing in the wings, declared that he had already achieved what he had set out to achieve, namely, to ensure that a gay candidate could enter such a race without either discrimination or dishonour. That would not have been the case twenty years ago, he said. It was a victory, a historic triumph for human rights and political tolerance and, above all, for Ken Boston. He had attained all the main objectives he had set himself in this campaign, simply by standing. In a moment that showed he had still not risen above his weakness for cliché, he announced that he had never intended to set himself up as a Messiah, he was more like John the Baptist, blazing the trail for those who would follow. Which was why he felt it appropriate to quit. He promised fealty to whoever won this great clash of the Titans and declared his confidence in the victory of the entire party at the next election. And, with the broadest smile he could muster and a wave for the benefit of the photographers, he retreated behind his front door, where Ron was already in tears.

It was a vengeful world that overflowed with intolerance. And in little more than a week, seven had become five. Or four, if you discounted the tub of intellectual lard that was Ed Goodthorpe, which almost everybody did.

Yet, as retiring as he had pretended to be, Ken Boston was not a man stripped of ambition. He asked to see Dom, very privately. The following weekend, the second of the campaign and three weekends before the result would be announced, he called on Dom at home.

He nestled into a wicker chair in the conservatory with the mug of coffee Ginny had offered. Even in casual clothes, he managed to seem as if he were in uniform, all Cordings and Oliver Brown. He was never a man to overlook a label. 'Just hoping for a private chat, Dom,' he said. 'Wanted to say how impressed I was by the speech you made the other day. You know, the stuff about the role of the family in protecting the environment. Mirrored my own thoughts entirely.'

Dom smiled, trying to remember for how long Ken had been the party's Environment spokesman without once reaching for that particular mirror.

'I've scribbled out a few additional ideas on the theme,' Ken continued, moving quickly to cover his flank. He reached into his pocket for several sheets of paper. 'Hope these might help. Feel free to use them, if they strike a chord.'

Dom glanced over them. Rather to his surprise, the points were well argued; Ken might have a weakness for cheap lines, but he wasn't a fool. Quitting the race had shown that. 'How very kind of you, Ken. Didn't know anyone had seen the speech. The coverage in the press didn't exactly keep the pulp mills on overtime.'

'I want you to know you have my support, Dom, and those I count as my close political friends. The first thing I wanted to do after quitting the race was see you and let you know that if there's anything I can do to help, it's yours.'

'I'm delighted . . .'

'There are still many things I want to do in politics. My best years lie ahead, so you can count on me, Dom.'

The wicker chair creaked as he leaned forward, his expression earnest, as though offering some valuable confidence. The message hidden in it took only moments to decipher. He wanted preferment. To be part of the play.

'You're not pushing yourself into the most obvious chorus line, Ken. But at last the show's under way.'

'And those others!' Boston dismissed the opposition with a flick of his hand, his cufflink sparkling in the weak winter sunshine. 'Hazel's a vicious bitch,' he spat, suddenly venomous. 'Iain's so bloody wary he won't step outside his front door without a weather forecast, while Goodthorpe – well, really! And Malthouse stammers and gets a weak bladder every time I enter the room.'

His feelings were raw and recent. Perhaps, contrary to his protestations, this wasn't the first visit he had made to the contenders. He felt rejected, shunned, not just politically but personally and deeply. Basham was a homophobe and scarcely bothered to hide it in private, while Madden and Malthouse were too cautious to decide what they were. As for Goodthorpe, nobody cared what he felt about anything.

'I'm considering coming out and making a public declaration of support for you,' Boston said, frowning, sounding awkward now and failing in his struggle to squeeze the pomposity out of the announcement. 'Wanted to know what you felt about that. I know I've been a bit outspoken on gay rights for some but . . .'

'Not a problem for us,' Ginny intervened, reappearing from the kitchen and settling herself into a chair with a mug of tea. 'Is it, Dom?'

'Of course not.'

'Forgive me, I'd wondered,' Boston replied haltingly. 'You know, with your religious views . . .'

'Ginny's right. Not a problem, Ken. I try not to moralise about people's private lives, that's never a safe sanctuary for a politician.

And isn't it superb,' Dom continued, turning to his wife, 'Ken wanting to offer his support?'

'Be part of the team, give the old bandwagon a bit of a push,' Boston confirmed. 'Throughout this race. And, hopefully, afterwards . . .'

'I value loyalty, Ken. And repay it.'

At last the visitor felt able to smile again, rocking back and forth in his creaking chair.

'But I wonder,' Ginny mused, 'if that would be for the best.'

'What? Are you suggesting that my support would be an embarrassment?'

'Don't be silly, Ken,' she replied, leaning over to touch his hand and quell the storm that was about to erupt within him. 'It's just that you men are always so full on about everything, in such a ridiculous hurry. Sometimes it's better to take matters a little more slowly – trust me.' She was smiling, almost teasing. 'I think I might have a better idea. Do you mind if I suggest something?'

If you close your eyes, drown the incessant noise of traffic, ignore the speechifying and rumbles of indignation, muffle the sounds from passing tourboats and skip round the insistent striking of Big Ben, you may be able to catch the whispers of Westminster. These soft, seditious sounds are everywhere, like a great river that at times meanders gently, creating deep pools of discontent as it sifts slowly through the weeds, while at other moments it comes to full flow and rages madly, sweeping all before it. Many have drowned in that river, yet others still insist on trying to swim in it.

Bobby was an excellent swimmer. His private circumstances had led him to be cautious about serving up too many of his own confidences to others, but he was a gifted listener. He was also gregarious, like many of the younger apparatchiks of Westminster, no matter which political master they served. They had the same lifestyles and workplaces, and it wasn't uncommon to see Opposition and Government aides sharing gyms, drinking-holes, eating places and, often, the same beds. So, when Bobby bounced back from his misery, it was inevitable that he would bump into friends from the other side of the political divide. One evening he found himself rubbing elbows with an undersized, Napoleonic figure named Colin at the bar of the Red Lion in Parliament Street as they waited to be served. Colin worked in Downing Street as a policy adviser, a job that kept him away from the coarser end of politics, which he rather regretted. It made him overly anxious to show others how close he was to the centre of power, even if he saw the Prime Minister only once a fortnight and then as part of a group. He tended to be gabby, particularly when up against 'the enemy', and now he found the enemy right by his side.

He smiled in greeting. 'Haven't seen you at the gym lately.'

'Been sweating at the office.'

'Too right. You guys are having a tough time. To lose one leadership contender is, as they say, a touch careless, but to lose two in a week . . .' He chuckled. 'Come on, cheer up. Let me buy you a drink.'

'Thanks. Could be needing it. A Bud.'

'Who you backing?'

'No one, keeping my head low,' Bobby lied. Headquarters employees were supposed to be neutral.

'We're looking forward to it, whoever it is,' Colin said. 'Been too bloody easy over the last couple of months. Ten points ahead in the polls and rising. No fun without someone to kick.'

'You poor things. Perhaps I should be buying you the drink.'

'Next time,' Colin suggested, as he placed his order with the barman. While he waited, he turned once more to Bobby. 'Actually, we're sacrificing chickens in the hope that the gods will be kind and deliver up Hazel to us.'

'Hazel? She's the one who usually does the kicking.'

'Not for much longer, old buddy.' Colin was smiling, very smugly.

'You guys, you're full of it,' Bobby replied dismissively.

'No, seriously. We've got the old bird bang to rights, we have. Can't wait till she's leader and we let her have both barrels. Talk about the dance of the dying swan. It's going to be so-o-o messy. Her feathers'll be floating all over the shop. We're just waiting for the right time.'

'You saying you've got something on her?'

'Better believe it. Tits in a wringer.'

'You've been working too long in Downing Street, my friend. Sounds like you're suffering from a bad attack of wind.'

'It'll be like Guy Fawkes Night all over again. What does it say on the packet? "Light blue touch paper and retire"? Give yourself a laugh. Vote for Hazel and watch her go up in flames.'

'You going to give me a clue as to what you're on about?' Bobby pressed, trying to affect a tone of scepticism as he accepted his drink.

'Couldn't possibly, old buddy, not even to you,' Colin replied, gathering up glasses in both hands and preparing to back away. 'But it'll be big, you mark my words. Oh, Mother. Oh, Mother. Ooooh, Mother!' he repeated, his voice rising like a pantomime dame's as he disappeared into the crush.

It was little more than a passing encounter but it preyed on Bobby's mind, perhaps because so many things had been preying on his mind, and also because that was precisely what Colin had intended. Offering up the tantalising hint, spreading unease, stirring troubled waters. All part of the game. But it bothered Bobby. A pack of half-formed thoughts and ill-bred ideas pursued him through the rest of his evening and all the way home. They were snapping at him even as he climbed the stairs, then followed him past his door. They were still snarling at him at three in the morning as he pounded the keys of his Internet connection, but by then he thought he had them beaten.

'You see, he kept repeating it, mocking me. "Oh, Mother, oh, Mother," that's what he said. And he's a lippy sort of guy, always gives too much for his own good, and it kept banging against the inside of my skull, so I thought – well, maybe it's about Hazel's mother. So I go to *Who's Who,* find out her name and that she's still alive – but pretty old now – and I just wondered where she might live. So then I went through the electoral registers and—'

'I think you'd better come in.'

Bobby had arrived breathless on the doorstep, unshaven and wild-eyed, soon after Ginny had returned from the school run, and he hadn't stopped gabbling from the moment the door opened. She took great pleasure in seeing how he had bounced back from his depression, even if it had left him like a food-mixer with a power surge. Perhaps he was on something other than adrenaline. She pinned him down to the kitchen table, made him eat some toast, and summoned Dom, who arrived in his shirtsleeves.

'It's just that –' Bobby wiped crumbs from his lips, eyes darting back and forth between them, '– she lives in an old people's home near Folkestone. Not in Hazel's constituency, but nearby. And it's had lots of problems, you see. A couple of the old biddies died and the coroner got very shirty, as good as accused the nursing-home of neglect. They're threatening to close it down. Local papers are full of it.' He paused to gulp down his glass of orange juice.

'It seems perhaps unwise of Hazel,' Dom reflected, 'and sad for Hazel's mother, but otherwise I don't see—'

'She owns it,' Bobby interrupted. 'She's got shares in the company that's responsible. She's making money out of her own mother's misery. How do you think that's going to look on the front pages?'

'She couldn't be that stupid,' Dom protested. 'Could she?' The question was met with a deafening silence, but he was not to be deflected. 'I won't go raiding her private life. She's a colleague.'

'She's your rival and she's winning,' Ginny countered. 'You may change your mind when you realise just how dirty this war is going to get, Dominic.'

They stood staring at each other across the kitchen; there was something in her eyes, her tone, that made him cautious. He swallowed the outpouring of righteousness he had been preparing.

'Bobby, you look as though you've spent the night in a spin-dryer,' she said. 'Take a rest for half an hour. There's a bed in the spare room at the top of the stairs – don't mind the packing cases. Have a nap. I'll bring you coffee in a bit.'

'But there's more, there's more,' he exclaimed.

'Bobby, please . . .'

And he, too, caught the edge in her eyes. 'Perhaps you're right. Could do with a rest. Haven't slept for days,' he said, rising slowly from his stool. At the door, he turned, still eager. 'But there is more, you know.'

'Thank you, Bobby,' she said. 'You know how very much we appreciate it.'

She busied herself tidying the kitchen until they heard the door to the spare room close.

'What the hell's this all about, Ginny?'

'It's about you preparing for the worst week of your life.'

'You want to give me a clue?'

She wiped her hands on a towel. 'On Saturday the *Record* will be publishing the details of your affair with Julia.'

His face went through a variety of expressions before settling on blustering anger. 'What? They can't. I'll sue.'

'On what grounds?'

He began to pace up and down the kitchen. 'I'll get a bloody injunction.'

'Julia's helping them. Sold them her story. You'll never stop it. Even if you were granted a temporary injunction, the whole world would know about it and they'd guess why.'

'It's an invasion of my privacy.'

'Not with you standing for the leadership, it's not.'

'But it's so wretchedly unfair!'

'Unfair? It's awkward, it's embarrassing, it's politically explosive, but I'm not sure I see it as unfair.'

Suddenly he stopped pacing. 'Whose bloody side are you on, Ginny?'

'In the matter of the affair between you and Julia, you dare ask me to take sides?'

It was as though she had slapped him. He sank in despair on to a stool, his head bowed. It was some time before he was able to look at her again. His eyes were damp with pain, but also covered with a film of suspicion. 'Saturday, you say. Why Saturday? How do you know all this, Ginny? And how long have you known it?'

'Only long enough to work out what we're going to have to do about it.'

'Which is?'

And she sat down beside him, and held his trembling hand while they talked.

Archie Blackstone's book showed that Dom had made progress. The interviews he'd given on Iraq had set him apart from the other candidates, and those who had taken the time to read his remarks on the environment had been impressed. He'd moved ahead of Charlie Malthouse into third place, but they were both still way behind Hazel, who had made a lot of noise, and Iain, who was regarded as a safe pair of hands. And perhaps that was what the faithful needed, Archie was saying, a safe pair of hands. It had been a pretty disastrous campaign for the party so far, what with all the distractions of Tina and that silly bugger Boston, and somewhere in his water Archie sensed it was about to get worse, for, as the weekend approached, all sorts of rumours were flooding around that one of the remaining candidates had been a total bloody fool.

Ginny sent Jemma and Ben to Dom's parents. The house was about to become a war zone, no place for children. Father Benedict had rolled his eyes in despair when she had told him why they might not be back in class the following week; his decision to welcome a political parent to the school had clearly been a rash one. On their doorstep she had mumbled thanks to her parents-in-law, the words falling uneasily, like the first uncertain trickles of an avalanche, asking them not to tell the children anything, to put off the moment of reckoning. She could see both sorrow and support in their eyes, which should have been a comfort, but why did she feel the whole mess was somehow as much her failure as Dom's?

On the way home, she called at the supermarket to stock up. The house might be under siege for a few days and she doubted she would want to be seen in a supermarket for several weeks, yet as she wheeled the groaning trolley round the aisles she was confronted by the newspaper stand with all its front pages blaring at her, just as on Saturday they would be blaring about her. It was too much. She left the trolley meandering gently under its own momentum and fled.

Meanwhile Dom sat himself down at home with the telephone and began to make any number of calls. The first was to his solicitor, who passed him on to a specialist media lawyer. He, in turn, and at three hundred pounds an hour, told him the best he could hope for was something libellous for which he might later sue, and save a little from the wreckage. Then, at six on Friday evening, Dom phoned his constituency chairman to prepare him for the storm that was to come. After that it was his key supporters, trying to explain, all the while apologising. They struggled to wish him well, yet behind the understanding words he could sense their frantic mind games as they tried to recalculate the odds and decide on which other ship they might seek passage.

Archie came round. Sat in the kitchen but declined coffee as, while Ginny watched, Dom stumbled out his story, squirming with embarrassment. Archie listened as if he'd heard it all before, which, indeed, he had. Then he explained that Headquarters could offer no help. This was personal, he said, and involved a party employee. Dom and Ginny were on their own. Were they staying together?

'Of course,' Dom snapped.

Archie raised an eyebrow but said no more, while Ginny remained propped by the window, feeling as if her stomach were being ripped out.

Archie didn't moralise and displayed no hostility. 'When I was a drunk I did much worse than anything you've got up to,' he told Dom. 'It's a great pity, a very great pity, in my opinion, to see a career like yours go down the pan. There was a moment when I thought you might have made it all the way.'

'Did you?'

'Well, now we'll never know.'

On the doorstep, Dom explained that he was going to make a statement on Sunday morning.

'Too late,' Archie replied. 'A month ago you could have saved it, but it's out of your hands now.'

'What could I have done a month ago?'

'The easiest thing would have been to leave your wife and take up with the girl. Plenty have done that and survived.'

'Politics isn't always about doing the easy thing,' Dom bit back, upset by the other man's bluntness.

'Nor marriage, eh? I wish you luck.' And Archie disappeared.

Dom didn't go directly back into the kitchen. He scrabbled aimlessly through a few papers, trying to find an excuse not to look Ginny in the eye. Eventually he reached for his jacket. 'I think I'll go to church for a while,' he said to her back, as she leaned over the sink.

'OK,' she whispered, almost inaudible.

He left, so he didn't see the uncontrollable shaking of her shoulders that struck her like a fit as she tried to flush out with her tears all the pain she felt inside. She had never realised how much this would hurt. And there was still such a long way to go.

Bobby picked up a copy of the *Record* outside King's Cross station as the first bundles were dropped off by a delivery van. Twenty minutes later, as his taxi pulled into Ginny and Dom's street in Pimlico, he could see the huddle of reporters and cameras that had gathered on the pavement outside their home. He offered up a small prayer of thanks that it was pouring with rain and only marginally above freezing. It kept the pack distracted. He left the taxi at the end of the street and used the small service entrance to the rear of the property, inadvertently kicking over a dustbin in the dark. He didn't stop to clear up: it was going to be one of those messy nights.

They were in the kitchen – why, Ginny screamed inside, had her kitchen become a perpetual battlefield filled with casualties and war councils? Why couldn't it be what it was meant to be, just a bloody kitchen? But this was not the time. No one said a word as Bobby produced his copy of the newspaper from beneath his raincoat and laid it out on the table.

'*Sex on the Sofa*', the headline screamed. 'We bonked to the chimes of Big Ben – every hour, on the hour.' The story offered a virtual travelogue round the Palace of Westminster, suggesting there were few places, apart from the Chamber itself, where the couple hadn't – well, coupled. The double-entendres and cheap gibes piled on top of each other in their frantic attempt to thrill. An assignation in a broom cupboard famous as a hiding-place for a suffragette. A sofa beneath a portrait of Tony Blair, and 'a large leather chair beneath a portrait of Maggie Thatcher – to balance things up'. Even a night-time tryst on the roof terrace, 'looking down upon the voters, wondering if I could help increase the size of his majority'.

It could have been worse. There were only three pages of the stuff, including a prominent photograph of Julia curled up, inevitably, on a leather sofa, and another with her arms round a large and unmistakably phallic model of Big Ben. But there was a surprise in the tail. Julia declared that she intended to continue working for the party: 'Why shouldn't I? Politicians don't resign for having affairs – or starting wars or fiddling their expenses, for that matter. I'm going to carry on!' She knew that was preposterous, in the circumstances, but it might force them to pay her something for the pleasure of getting rid of her.

Meanwhile the *Record* recorded that Dominic Edge had been unavailable for comment.

'But this is mostly make-believe,' he protested, as he leaned over the kitchen table and read it. 'It didn't happen like this. Truly it didn't. This is nonsense. We never . . .' In agitation he pushed the paper across the table to Ginny.

'You really think I'm going to read it?' she muttered coldly. But she would, of course, much later, when no one was looking.

Saturday. A day for the Undead. Not alive, but not yet formally buried, existing in a world of drawn curtains and shrouds, with only the ghouls of the press pack for company. The silence inside the house was oppressive and all but complete, except for the ring-ing of the phone. They let the answering-machine take the calls; mostly from the media. Ginny was at first surprised and then hurt at how few others rang – an aunt in the country, an old schoolfriend, Jemma's godmother, but not a single voice of support from their Westminster friends. It was the silence that surrounds the damned. It got to the point where she would have welcomed any form of contact, even a few words of outrage or an outburst of moral exasperation: at least it would be recognition of their continued existence. But nothing. The world of politics had already spun on, leaving Ginny and Dom on the dark side.

On Sunday morning they dressed in silence. The mechanics of breakfast were automatic and largely skipped. Barely a word was said, until Bobby arrived. They had asked him to drive them to the television studio, knowing they would be distracted, not trusting themselves to manoeuvre their way through the media minefield, remembering how many people in similar positions had wiped out wing mirrors, door trim and even in one case a baby's buggy as they tried to ease their way out of a parking space.

Once outside their front door, Dom and Ginny were all smiles, ignoring the questions of the media 'shouters' about whether he was going to resign or they were planning to divorce, trying to appear as relaxed as if they had nothing more on their minds than a drive in the country. It was important not to let the pack know how much they were hurting inside.

They took Ginny's car, the small red Renault she used for the school run. The back seat was filled with sweet-wrappers and biscuit crumbs, and the windows covered with young fingerprints. As Bobby drove them towards the Embankment and the bridge that would take them to the studio on the South Bank, they were pursued by a posse of cars filled with photographers, driving madly, dangerously, forcing them to brake sharply, trying to provoke, desperate to get the classic shot of the woman in tears or the man with a raised fist or, even better, a finger.

'I'm not sure this is such a good idea, Ginny,' Dom said, through clenched teeth, his knees tight up against the front seat as he pretended to read a newspaper.

'I will not – ever – allow my family to be ripped apart by vermin,' she replied, and would say no more. But her hands were trembling.

There were more rodents waiting outside as they arrived at the ugly glass box on the South Bank of the river that masqueraded as television studios. Inside, the welcome was scarcely any warmer. The receptionist had not been born on these shores, could not spell very well and appeared not to have slept much. 'Who?' she asked twice, through enormous yawns, then gave them two visitors' passes made out in the name of Ejj. Soon they were wafted to a hospitality room strewn with faded chairs and half-digested newspapers. Breakfast came in the form of croissants and pastries, but others had got there first, leaving little but crumbs. Ginny and Dom were reduced to comforting themselves with coffee, served in Styrofoam cups. Then a makeup girl arrived.

'Not necessary, thank you. We did our own,' Ginny told her.

'But . . . the producer likes us to do it,' the flustered assistant announced.

'I know. That's why we did it ourselves,' Ginny replied, turning her back. The programme rarely finished without its measure of blood. This was, of course, no accident. Ginny had noticed the tendency of many guests to appear almost cadaverous, washed-out, as though they had not been able to sleep. Guilt by exhaustion, even before they had entered a plea. So Ginny had decided to take care of her own makeup, and Dom's too. She wanted to look her best while being dragged to the block.

The Heaven and Hellfire Club had become something of an institution. In the hands of its Canadian presenter, Marcus White, it had taken over from the more traditional Sunday-morning chat-shows and introduced an element of righteous venom. It found its roots in the Old Testament rather than the New, and set its view point above Sodom and Gomorrah rather than the gentle shores of Galilee. It painted its moral vision in colours of black and white, which often proved to be the kiss of death for middle-of-the-road politicians. In spite of that, many were nevertheless tempted by the considerable viewing figures and seemed content to be dragged, willingly and repeatedly, to the slaughter.

'This could be a disaster,' Dom murmured, as they were ushered into the studio past a picket line of cameras and floor crew.

'We've got nothing to lose,' she whispered in reply, 'not even our reputations.'

White was seated in an armchair on the other side of a low table on which stood glasses of orange juice and an embossed, leather-bound Bible. He was a tall, ascetic-seeming man in his fifties, with a mane of long silver hair, piercing grey eyes and a permanent tan that made him appear as if he had just wandered in from the desert. He didn't look up or offer any greeting but busied himself with his notes as they were seated opposite him and a sound engineer fussed over the placement of microphones. Dom noticed a folded copy of the *Record* peeking out from beneath the Bible, and almost before he had time to check his tie or clear his throat, the floor manager called for quiet and was counting down.

White smiled for the camera, the one with the red light on; he still hadn't said hello. Then he was mouthing words from the autocue, about scandal, about leadership, about misfortune and hazard and political careers, and about broken commandments. As he spoke, the front page of the previous day's *Record* was flashed on to a large screen.

'So, in the circumstances, I'm both fascinated and delighted to welcome the man in the middle of all this, Dominic Edge. And his wife, Virginia.'

To Ginny, it felt as though her inclusion was almost an after-thought. She was just an addendum, an irrelevance to White, and anyway she hated her full name, Virginia. She hated Marcus White, too. And she needed such passion if she was to find the strength for what was to come.

'And so, Dominic Edge,' White was saying as, for the first time, he turned from the autocue to talk directly with them, 'you are – well, for want of a better description, a common adulterer. Is that right?'

Dom's hands tightened on the arms of his chair. 'I don't know how common I am. But, yes, I'm an adulterer. Sadly. I take no pride in that.'

'"Pride"? A strange word to use. Does anyone take pride in adultery? I would have thought it more a matter for deep and abiding shame.'

Dom nodded, stretched out to find Ginny's hand, squeezed it. 'Yes, I am ashamed. I have done my wife and my family a great hurt, and that fills me with remorse.'

'So, a man who has been shamed. A man who has been caught breaking the Seventh Commandment and who has done terrible wrong to his family.' White's voice was deep and his words were delivered slowly with an evangelist's sense of theatre. 'Not much of a claim for standing as leader of your party, is it?'

'My faults are not why I wish to be leader of my party. I rather hope people will look to my strengths.'

White stirred in his seat, alert. 'Are you saying you intend to carry on?' he asked, his voice dripping with disbelief.

'Yes.'

'My, my, Dominic, that is a surprise. I thought you'd come here to renounce ambition. Come to repentance and come to quit. But strengths, you say?' He picked up the copy of the *Record* from beneath the Bible. 'Doesn't say much about your strengths in here, does it? Although the young lady in question refers to you as her favourite honourable Member. What do you suppose she meant by that?'

Dom was incapable of mustering a reply; he could only squeeze Ginny's hand all the harder.

'Dominic, why in Heaven's name are you continuing with this travesty? Why inflict still more pain and punishment on your wife?'

'I love my wife, Mr White.' There was a catch in his voice. 'I have failed her, certainly, but I believe the best way I can make things up to her is by never forgetting my faults, and by making a success of my career in politics.'

Ginny picked up his thought. 'Many men deal with their private shame by committing themselves to public service, Mr White. It's happened throughout history.'

'Instead of committing themselves to the family?'

'You can leave my family to me,' Dom replied. 'But as far as the leadership campaign is concerned, we had a huge number of calls yesterday encouraging us to continue. The telephone scarcely stopped.'

Well, it wasn't the whole truth. The calls had been from journalists wanting not to encourage but simply to enquire.

'Apparently, Dominic,' White responded, trying to turn the discussion back to the defendant, 'the phone stopped ringing long enough for you to contact us and ask to be on the show this morning . . .' Which, although he didn't know it, was even less of the truth. It hadn't been Dom's idea but Ginny's. She had insisted, against Dom's own judgement, but he hadn't been in much of a position to argue the point with a copy of the *Record* spread across the kitchen table.

'You're hoping to bluster your way through this,' the broadcaster continued, 'and hope that those miserable mortals who have such short memories may be persuaded to forget your shame. But you are no Moses. You are in no position to lead your party to the Promised Land. Surely the only decent thing for you to do now would be to repent and withdraw.'

'I do repent, most humbly and publicly. Yes, a sinner come to repentance. But I won't withdraw. I don't pretend to be perfect, and certainly not a Moses. I've no intention of leading my party and least of all my family through the desert for the next forty years.'

'Are you trying to mock the prophet?'

'Not at all. I'm simply saying that, right now, it's up to ordinary people to cast judgement on me. We'll leave eternal judgement for a little while, if you don't mind. And by the time I come to my Maker, I want to have a very much better record than I do now. A record of service, and unselfishness.'

'A record of infidelity and lies, as it stands.'

'A man who has learned from his mistakes.'

Then Ginny interrupted. 'And when it comes to it, can you name one great leader – a British leader – who didn't have his faults?'

'Me? But I'm Canadian,' White protested.

'Surely if you want to preach you should take the opportunity to get to know your audience. Come on, you must be able to name one or two.'

'Gladstone!' White declared, almost triumphant.

'A well-known moral crusader,' Ginny concurred, 'who crept out at night from Number Ten to go looking for prostitutes. Next?'

'What?'

'Next. Come on, even my ten-year-old can name more than one.'

'Lloyd George, then.'

'Prolific adulterer. Perjurer.'

'And sold peerages,' Dom added. 'Sounds familiar, doesn't it?'

'Didn't stop the old Welsh ram from being one of our greatest Prime Ministers,' Ginny continued. 'But I won't press you any further, Mr White. You are, after all, a foreigner. Yet I think you've helped illustrate things very clearly. Making mistakes has never been a bar to high office. In fact, any decent historian would tell you that it's the process of learning from their mistakes that has often been the key to greatness in these men.'

'Well, if you'll let me turn to the man who is, after all, the focus of this interview—'

'Oh, I'm sorry, but you get us as a team, you see,' Ginny countered. 'At home. And in politics.'

'So you're standing by your man like some country crooner, are you, no matter what he's done?' White was unable to hide his irritation.

'No, you've missed the point. I haven't forgotten the mistake he's made — and neither will he. And, in all honesty, I've had to struggle hard, very hard, to forgive him. But let me tell you something about this forgiveness thing — it's worthwhile. After all, Mr White, the statistics show that the majority of men over their lifetimes will stray from the path of marital righteousness — sixty-eight per cent, I think the latest research shows. You called my husband a common adulterer. Well, it seems most men are.'

'You seek to justify the breaking of Commandments?'

'Of course not! But politicians break Commandments all the time. They worship idols, bear false witness, all sorts of things. Yet since you raise the question, can you tell me — can you place your hand on that Bible — and swear you aren't one of those sixty-eight per cent?'

'This is preposterous. This is not supposed to be an examination of my morals but of your husband's.'

'Fair enough. It's just that, well, you sit in judgement on others so I thought it fair to ask where you stand. I don't see what the problem is. The Bible's right there in front of you. Why won't you swear?'

The producer in the gallery should perhaps have jumped in at this stage and given White some firm direction, but his judgement was clouded. It was excellent television that would make all the newspapers in the morning, which wasn't bad for a semi-religious show. Anyway, he'd always found White a self-important and thoroughly odious moraliser, and he had just learned that the Canadian was trying to get him replaced as producer of the show. Let the bastard squirm on his bed of nails.

White tried once more: 'I'm not going to allow you to turn this show into a game of charades, Mrs Edge,' he said, and for a moment they struggled to talk across each other until the producer barked into White's earpiece that he should let her speak. Unable to deal with stereophonic heckling, he did.

And Ginny was reaching forward, tense, the passion in her body unmistakable, tears welling in her eyes. 'You speak of games, but this isn't a game for me, Mr White. This is my family we're talking about here, and not just for the half-hour of this programme, not just tomorrow or next week, but for the rest of my life. I've been struggling to deal with the consequences of Dom's affair for a long time – he confessed to me, I've even written about it.'

'When was that?'

'In the *Record*. It's on the website – oh, what's it called?' she asked rhetorically, as she dabbed with a handkerchief at the tears. 'www.mums-on-top.co.uk – about the role of forgiveness in keeping the family together. And the family, that's the important thing, isn't it?'

'Are you trying to tell me that your article was about your own husband's infidelity?'

Her expression suggested disbelief, her voice contempt. 'Oh, Mr White, any woman who read it would have known straight away what I was on about. If you didn't understand that, you must be more than just a little dull!' And she was staring across the studio at White, in tears, with accusation, defiance.

It was not until this point that White realised how badly he had lost their encounter. He had brought a wronged woman to tears, had made a fool of himself, had shown how poor he was at taking what he so regularly gave. Trouble was, now every viewer knew it, too. He was holding his earpiece, staring at the camera with an expression suggesting that something inside his head had caught fire and the voice, when it came, sounded cracked and dry. 'Sadly, that's all we have time for this morning.'

White walked straight out of the studio, even while the credits were still rolling. Dom and Ginny were left to sit there, gripping each other's hands, until the sound engineer came to disconnect them. After that, faces and voices seemed to pass them by in a blur.

Moments later they were squeezing through the pack of press hounds still gathered on the pavement and into the back of their car.

'How was it?' Bobby asked warily. He'd stayed with the car throughout the interview.

'Awesome. Just sodding awesome,' Dom answered slowly. 'You know, he came across as a total tosser. Wouldn't even answer questions about his own personal life. As good as admitted to his . . .' He hesitated, still embarrassed to use the word 'adultery' in front of Ginny. 'To his own failings. But how did you know about that, darling? It seemed like one hell of a risk.'

Ginny said nothing. She was trembling once more, her hands shaking uncontrollably as the adrenaline and fear poured out of her. He reached across to still them but this time she pulled away.

'I'd heard all sorts of rumours about White,' Bobby interjected.

'Had you? Hadn't picked up anything at Westminster,' Dom replied.

'No, not on the political circuit. Bumped into one of his production crew in one of the clubs I go to. Not your sort of scene, Dom.

Apparently he's an appalling drunk and a persistent groper. Lots of his female assistants end up asking for a pretty rapid transfer.'

' "And let he who is without sin . . ." ' Dom chuckled, relaxing in triumph.

Suddenly, inside her bag, Ginny's mobile phone was ringing. It seemed to bring her out of her trance.

'Absolutely gut-rippingly fantastic, Mrs E,' Max's voice was saying. 'Amazing performance.'

'It wasn't a performance.' Her voice sounded weak.

Max laughed. 'Best I ever saw! You deserve an Oscar for that one – and more. So I want you to consider two things.'

'I'm listening.'

'Write a regular column for me, Ginny, every week, no matter what the outcome of the leadership thing.'

'And what do you think about that leadership thing, Max? Do we have a chance?'

'Of winning? Not a hope in hell. Of surviving, perhaps doing well enough to save Dom's career? Well, maybe. You just threw him one hell of a lifeline. You're going to be on the front page again tomorrow, and somehow I think you're going to enjoy it rather more than yesterday.'

'And the other thing you want?'

'More advertising on your website. You're going to get a million hits after that little outing. We should make use of it. Both of us.'

'I'll let you know, but before I do anything I want to have a word with Dom.'

'That's fine. Just let me know soonest. Strike while the iron's hot, as you girls say. And, Ginny . . .'

'What?'

'I'm so glad we still have that deal.'

The phone went dead and almost hesitantly she replaced it in her handbag. Beside her, Dom felt an aura of calm settle about him. For the first time in days, he relished being alive. They were crossing Lambeth Bridge. The traffic was light, no posse in pursuit.

To their right the Palace of Westminster was picked out like a Gothic gingerbread castle in the early winter sun, and the winding river was calm on an ebb tide. Dom settled back in his seat, content. 'Who was that?' he asked.

'Max.'

'The bastard. What was he offering?'

'Congratulations.'

'Great! And the word you need to have with me, darling?'

Her handbag closed with a gentle click. She gazed out of the window, at the passers-by, ordinary people, whom she so very much envied. Then she turned slowly back to her husband. Her voice was low, still exhausted, she was crying again, sobbing a little, but every syllable carried above the sound of the wheels across the Tarmac: 'You ever – *ever* – do this to me again, and I promise you, Dom, that I will personally rip off your balls and throw a party while they get fed to the vultures.'

Ajok was feeling homesick. Her adopted homeland had turned on her, so when Sophie Gaminara suggested they meet somewhere outside her office, somewhere Ajok could relax, she suggested the Abbey Community Centre in Belsize Road. It was where refugees from many countries gathered, and Sophie seemed to enjoy it, too.

She was in her late twenties, a pupil in chambers, a lawyer's apprentice, and anxious to break through the log-jam of other aspiring young lawyers who stood in her way. She was kind, attentive, genuinely wanted to help, but made no secret of the fact that she thought Ajok's case could be of help to her, too. It might be just the thing to cause a fuss. It was the objective of all young barristers to generate enough noise that others would take notice, and what created more noise than a damned good war? While they drank coffee and ate roasted peanuts, Sophie told of her excitement. They would appeal Ajok's case on the basis that the war leading to the occupation of Iraq was almost certainly illegal, and that therefore any orders or instructions given to assist with it must by definition be unreasonable. The argument would probably fall flat on its face at an employment appeal tribunal, but there were other options. They could press on to the Court of Appeal, even the European Court of Human Rights.

The issue of the war was a cause for enthusiasm in a young lawyer like Sophie, but it left Ajok unmoved and more than a little sceptical. Could war and wholesale slaughter ever be considered legal? Only if all the lawyers were Baggaran. Yet Sophie's smile was warm, enthusiastic, and what had Ajok to lose? Sophie was offering her services for free, and her presence had persuaded the increasingly dubious Mr Messenger to continue supporting the case.

It was also at the community centre that Ajok found a letter waiting for her. It was from a male relative, a distant one, to be sure, and one she had never met, but in Sudan the extended family was taken seriously. Malith Bulabek was, like Ajok, a refugee. He had recently arrived in Britain and was anxious to find an alternative to the appalling bed-and-breakfast accommodation provided by the local council. Ajok remembered her own time in such lodgings – the damp walls, the constant coughs and colds, the broken lavatory, the petty pilfering and the queues for cooking facilities. It seemed strange to say so, but the mud-floored huts of her village had been cleaner and safer than that, at least until the Arabs had arrived. So, spurred on by the kindness shown by Sophie, Ajok sent a message that the young man might come and lodge with her. No money needed, except what he cost in food and light, until he had got himself properly settled. Anyway, it would be good for the boys to get to know a Dinka man. The Dinka were a community: they looked after each other, and a lodger might help fill their evenings with something more comforting than the agonies of East End soap.

Malith Bulabek turned out to be a polite and excellent companion, and Ajok quickly became glad she had extended the hand of friendship. But, as things turned out, it might have been better had she decided to chop it clean off.

Nine

H AZEL BASHAM WAS A talented woman, handsome rather than beautiful, with a quick mind and eyes so dark they made some suspect she wasn't of entirely British stock. It was an image she sought to dispel by wrapping herself at every turn in the Union flag, although in truth there was probably something of the black Irish in her. And, like most animals bred for the hunt, she had an excellent nose for prey. She was merciless about the Government and had developed a refined line in mockery on those frequent occasions when government backbenchers tried to shout her down. She adopted the role of a headmistress faced by a class of dull, rather stupid pupils, and let them know that they rarely failed to live up to their reputation. Little wonder that the Government wanted to do her down – but not yet. Much better if they held fire until she became Leader of the Opposition and, with less than two weeks to go before the election was completed and the result announced, they were content to wait.

But timing is everything in politics, and Ginny was as good at timing as Hazel was about to be unfortunate in hers.

The first editions of most of the Monday newspapers made copious references to Ginny's performance of the previous day – *The Times* suggesting that she and Dom had pulled his leadership campaign back from the brink and given it an opportunity for redemption, although the *Telegraph* preferred to concentrate its initial attention on Marcus White and what it called 'the strange silence of the mud-slinging moralist'. The *Mirror* however, had an altogether different agenda. Hazel's secret was out, and so were the *Mirror's* knives. The front page left Hazel's reputation in ribbons, and the other tabloid newspapers and television news outlets struggling to catch up.

Hazel owned shares in a company that operated private nursing-homes. Nothing wrong with that, it was all in line with the Government's desire to seek a private solution to the growing problem of finding parking-space for pensioners, and it was only natural that she should have parked her frail old mother in one of the homes in which she had an interest. But, as Bobby had told Ginny, there was much more to it than that. Several of the nursing-homes in Hazel's portfolio were having trouble with their standards, and the one in which her mother lived was the poorest of the lot. They were having the book thrown at them. Reinspec-tions. Warnings. The threat of closure. There were allegations if too few night staff and too many pressure sores. But the *Mirror* had found much more. 'Is This The Meanest Woman in Britain?' its front page screamed, before describing in lurid detail the misery of her mother's life, attended by nurses who often couldn't speak proper English, in a home where several inmates had died in distressing circumstances and where the newspaper's photographers had found dirty bathrooms, mouse-droppings, out-of-date food and, perhaps a little too conveniently, an old syringe cast casually down outside the back door.

It was the sort of story that Hazel couldn't control. There were too many avenues for the pack to investigate. Every recent death was written up as suspicious, every failure for the past many years was reported as though it had happened yesterday, and all of it blamed directly on Hazel's greed. A local pet-shop owner claimed there had been a sudden run on the purchase of rats by people who looked suspiciously like press photographers, but nothing could help Hazel. 'She's the sort of woman we'd always known would happily skin her granny,' one unnamed colleague was reported as declaring, 'but we had no idea she'd sold her mother, too.'

The *Mirror* had been given the story – anonymously, of course, since no one on its news desk had a chance of recognising Bobby's voice – on the explicit understanding that if it didn't use the story by Monday it would be handed to someone else. And the story had legs – long legs. Later that day the *Evening Standard* reported that Hazel had made no mention of her financial interest in the nursing-homes in the Register of Members' Interests, even though she was required by law to do so. Under pressure, she came up with the excuse that she had made no declaration because she received no money from the company; instead, and in lieu, it housed her mother for free. It took no more than minutes to work out that this benefit was probably worth at least twenty-five thousand pounds a year.

The legs grew still longer. By Tuesday she was being asked if she had paid income tax on that benefit, as she was required to do by law. Hazel's office was unable to provide a clear, unqualified answer to this question. Twenty-four hours later, under pressure from the media and several politicians, the Inland Revenue announced that it was to undertake an investigation into Hazel's financial affairs. That was when the Parliamentary Committee on Standards and Privileges announced its own investigation. After all, the rules were clear, and Hazel had voted for them.

Her life had become a nightmare, her name was blackened and her campaign had been consumed within a dark hole of despair.

Yes, timing was everything. By Thursday, which was only a week before the deadline for casting votes, Hazel, who hadn't been seen in public for three days, issued a statement announcing her withdrawal from the contest. She did this, she said, 'in order to allow me the time to deal with these totally inaccurate slurs, and to protect my poor mother from unwarranted media intrusion'. Typical of Hazel, she went down fighting, threatening to sue half of Fleet Street for libel and to report the other half to the Press Complaints Commission for so cruelly trampling upon an old lady's privacy. She also threw a bucket of water at a journalist who was trespassing on her front lawn, then followed up with the bucket itself. 'Basham and Soak 'Em', so it was said.

And, by this time, even well-informed people had to struggle to remember the name of Julia Summers.

They had survived. The children were back at home, the cat was fed and strange, unpredictable things were happening. Their telephone had begun to ring again with messages of congratulation, mostly directed at Ginny, it must be said, for standing up to the media and to 'those bloody men'. She and Dom received a flurry of invitations to appear on daytime chat-shows, which were ostensibly not about politics but he'd spent three weeks of the campaign talking about political matters to little effect so they were delighted with any opportunity to raise their profile in a gentler arena. Ginny called up Adrian, Hazel's very good friend at the advertising agency, and used his experience to screw Max to the floor on the advertising contract for her website. Her new column in the *Record* about helping kids through family crises was widely syndicated. Suddenly their world was moving again. People were listening, paying attention – and paying them good money.

Ironically, it was Tina, fresh out of gaol, who helped push the process along. No sooner was she standing outside the gates of HMP East Sutton Park than she began laying into all the remaining candidates, but Dom in particular. During her long and, post-lunch, increasingly rambling diatribes she denounced Dom and Ginny for having betrayed her, referring to them as Judas and Jezebel. Nothing about Ginny could be trusted, she declared, claiming that even her breasts were false. It was difficult to keep the good woman down.

Then an opinion poll was published. The newspapers hadn't bothered to commission any up to this point as, frankly, few of their readers seemed interested and the cast of candidates had developed the habit of changing so quickly. The Prime Minister, during one of his easier moments at the Dispatch Box, had described the contest as 'not so much a gathering of bandwagons but more like a stock-car race, complete with multiple casualties and wreckage strewn all over the course'. Yet with a week left, the *Telegraph* published a poll that put Dom in clear second place, still well behind Iain Madden but in what had become a two-horse race. And second is sometimes good. There is nothing more tedious to an editor than a foregone conclusion, and nothing more enjoyable than watching a front-runner fall flat on his face, so, regardless of their political inclinations, editors began to take an interest. They resurrected Dom's hard-worked speeches on the environment, contrasted the new boy on the block with the old and decidedly shelf-worn Madden, gave the waters a stir. Even those who didn't accept Dom's position that all British troops should be brought back from Iraq acknowledged that he argued his case with passion, and that his unambiguous stance set him apart from the confusion of the crowd. Iain Madden was many things, intelligent, capable, long-serving, but no one could ever accuse him of being over-loaded with charisma, and he was said to be 'too clever by half', a charge that has always been as good as a garrotte for a British politician.

Dom realised how much his chances had improved when Archie Blackstone turned up once more, seeking him out in his office overlooking the atrium in Portcullis House.

'I got it wrong,' Archie began, in his usual blunt fashion.

'I know.'

'Don't usually do that.'

'I know that, too, Archie.'

'But it needed saying. I apologise.'

'You voiced an honest opinion. I can deal with that.' Dom paused, rolling his pen between his fingers. 'So, what do you think of my chances now?'

'Improving.'

'I look forward to working with you when this is all over.'

'Think you're going to win, do you?'

Dom smiled. 'Who knows? Anything could happen.'

'And in this contest, it usually does.'

So why, oh, why, oh, why, Dom screamed to himself, was she about to blow the whole thing to pieces?

It was Saturday. The last weekend. Voting closed next Thursday with the result announced the following Sunday, 15 December.

Neither Dom nor Ginny had slept. This was their last chance, the final opportunity to give the fickle winds of fortune a gentle nudge. The candidates had been summoned to a rally in the Queen Elizabeth II conference hall, a modern glass and concrete extrusion nestling in the lee of Westminster Abbey, where they would appear in the Churchill Auditorium before the massed ranks of the party faithful, with the whole proceedings broadcast live on the Internet and beamed to other smaller party gatherings in cities around the country. It was advertised as a debate but in effect it was a shoot-out, a place where someone would be gunned down and left for dead. A wisp of dust and it might be mistaken for a scene from a spaghetti western.

It had been agreed that wives should attend, and they were to be given a prominent place, although no one was sure why. To lend the proceedings a more tactile feel, maybe, and to soften its image. Or perhaps it had been a ruse cooked up by the party hierarchy to embarrass Ken Boston, had he reached this stage. But, whatever the reason, Ginny was crucial. None of this would have happened without her, Dom knew that now. There had been so much absurd coincidence and unexpected circumstance thrown into this campaign, more than could have been expected in a dozen leadership contests, and in Dom's eyes this was more than good fortune; perhaps it was one of those things that were meant to be, a touch of destiny, even. But if Destiny had brought him this far, it had been hand in hand with Ginny, every step of the way. She was his talisman, his charm, the one who had brought Providence knocking.

She had played such a vital part in the preparations for this moment, even down to the politics. Dom had become extraordinarily sensitive about his lack of credibility on economic matters. Some commentators, stirred up, no doubt, by his opponents, had said he showed no signs of being able to balance books, sniggering that he couldn't even balance a wife and a mistress properly. And Dom had got himself into a stew, until Ginny had stepped in. She reminded him that he would have only a few minutes to make his mark, that this was scarcely the time to launch some half-baked taxation proposal, that it would smack of desperation and anyway no one would remember a word he said, unless it was something stupid. With four contenders at it the audience would get overloaded with ideas, leaving behind little more than an impression, an enduring image, if you like, of what those men were about. Does he smile, look confident, have a sense of humour, show charisma and charm? Would the men really want to go drinking with him, would the women desire to drag him into the bushes, have his children? It wasn't rocket science but human nature, and if the media wanted a little more meat on the bone, there were other ways of providing it.

So they had laid out a plan. And it had begun so well. The party hierarchy had insisted that the whole affair be conducted with decorum, as a grown-up party should – no banners, no pamphleteering or rowdy demonstrations inside the centre. But as the nine hundred party members had arrived, they were greeted by a scrum of young people dressed up as Santa Claus, elves and reindeer, waving placards and cheering excitedly for Dom. They were having fun, braving the wintry conditions and setting a smile on the faces of the voters as they passed. Harmless enough, unless you were a Madden man. And who was to know that most of them weren't political activists but a group of friends, gathered together on the promise of free drink and thirty quid in cash for a couple of hours' work? It had taken almost a thousand pounds out of Dom's campaign budget, but Ginny had thought it a sound investment. As the party faithful filed into their seats, they were smiling.

They smiled all the more when they saw Dom's video clip. The candidates had all been allowed to prepare a four-minute film that was to be shown by way of a warm-up once the audience was seated and before the entrance of the contestants. Goodthorpe, with campaign floundering and money spent, talked straight to camera. Cheap. And dull. Charlie Malthouse showed a home movie of him with his family, which worked rather well, even though the kids playing in the garden looked frozen. It was Madden who had spent the money, with a glossy package that showed him walking the streets, from his birthplace in an unprepossessing quarter of Dundee, through his constituency in Yorkshire, right up to the gates of Parliament. He walked, he talked, he greeted, he reflected, he looked forward to the future and the whole thing oozed with confidence. If it had a fault, it was perhaps too slick, but no one could make that more than a minor quibble.

Dom's film came last, and it didn't feature Dom at all. It simply showed clips of the 1973 Grand National. A national institution. The greatest steeplechase on earth. A murmur of surprise mixed with anticipation began to rustle through the auditorium. What the hell was he playing at?

The quality of the old TV footage wasn't great, but good enough. Most of those watching had seen it many times before and remembered the emotion, the tension, the history, the crowds gathered beneath overcast skies, the sense of expectation as they waited for the start, then the horses flying, and falling, crumpling beneath the enormous fences, until one horse was way, way out in front. It was the top weight, the favourite, Crisp. The race seemed all but over. By Becher's Brook the second time round he was twenty lengths clear and with only 250 yards to go, as they approached the Elbow, he was still out of sight of the rest. Except one. A stubborn animal who refused to recognise that he was already beaten, and who was struggling hard to make up a little lost ground. And then a little more. The camera angle showed that he still had no chance – he was scarcely more than a dot in the distance – but Crisp was tiring, wandering off the true line, and the crowd was going wild. Steam was rising from both horses, the jockeys whipping them on, the effort immense. And now the chasing horse was no longer a distant dot but had become a mighty beast on the charge.

And many in the auditorium began to cheer. Some might have realised that the commentary had been tampered with, just a little, but no one was in a mood to care.

'And are we seeing a miracle?' the breathless commentator shouted, above the thunder of his own excitement. 'Can Crisp possibly lose it at this late stage? He's tired, he's done too much, he's given his all. And is he going to be caught?'

The shouts of approval in the auditorium were becoming infectious. 'Come on, Rummie!' someone cried.

'This is the most sensational finish to the Grand National I can remember!' The commentator's voice seemed sieved through sandpaper; you could hear him bouncing up and down in his chair. 'They're past the Elbow, less than two hundred yards to run, it's almost over but – I can't believe what I'm seeing. Crisp is going to be caught! *Crisp is going to be caught!*'

And, with the last stride of the race, he was.

It was Red Rum's first crack at the Grand National, his first victory. He was to become the greatest horse in the history of the race. As those in the auditorium cheered as one with the joyous crowd in Liverpool, they couldn't help but be taken up in this little piece of conceit that compared their great enterprise with a horse race. They got the message. The race wasn't over until those behind stopped trying, no matter how far ahead the favourite was. Anything was possible.

As he waited in the wings with the others, Dom felt a surge of anticipation. Before he had even opened his mouth, the audience had been turned into a band of happy buccaneers willing to gamble everything on a horse race. Ginny had been right. The last thing they needed was a lecture on fiscal prudence. Judging by the rictus on his face, Iain Madden had come to that conclusion, too.

Yet that was the moment when Ginny had blown it, only moments before they were all to walk on stage. She had wandered into a corner and was listening to her mobile phone. 'Not the time, not the time!' Dom muttered. What could be more important than the next couple of hours? But here she was, apologetic, a little frantic, telling him that she had to go, couldn't stay with him. Threatening to rip the whole thing to pieces. He told her not to be ridiculous, that he wasn't going to walk out on stage and sit beside an empty bloody chair, but it was all too late. The fanfare had started. The others were marching. And Dom was marching with them. Alone.

Ginny ran as fast as she could to her unkempt car, thanking whoever was listening up there that it was Saturday and the traffic might be moving a little less like cold treacle. She was too anxious, reversing the car sharply until she felt a thud and heard the tinkle of broken glass. She didn't wait to discover whether the glass was hers or that of the other poor so-and-so. Then she was racing up Birdcage Walk, beside the park, swinging round in front of Buckingham Palace. The lights were changing to red but she put her foot down and gambled. A black cab swerved, a driver's hand raised in exasperation, and she felt the flash of the traffic cameras catching it all.

Half-way up Constitution Hill she was scrabbling frantically in her bag for her phone. Her purse spilled, her makeup bag went flying, tipping its contents on to the floor. She didn't have hands-free and her attention careered wildly between the buttons on her phone and the traffic ahead. She tried three times, but Bobby wasn't answering. She speeded up still more. The lights at the great intersection of Hyde Park Corner were in her favour, but still she had to change gear. One hand on the lever, another holding the telephone, little more than an elbow and a knee for the steering-wheel.

More horns blared in protest as she scuttled across the lanes like a shopping trolley. Another camera in its big yellow box was peering at her; the bloody things were everywhere now, but not a policeman in sight. Where were they when you needed them? All stuck behind the Home Secretary's screens or issuing fixed-penalty tickets? So she dialled the emergency services, and fought her way on.

There has to be an element of the actor in all successful politicians. Some take the comic route, a few may even rise to the heights of a great Shakespearean, but all must be able to hide their feelings from the public if they are to survive. As Dom walked out on stage without his wife and talisman, his mind was racing. She hadn't even hinted at the reason for her disappearance, simply rushed off. Was it the kids? What else could it be? Was she hiding terrible news, trying to protect him, keep him calm before his big moment? Yet what chance did he have of that? Inside he was in turmoil, his mind wiped blank. Thank God he'd practised his bloody speech until he could recite it in his sleep. The thing might yet fly on automatic pilot. But there was one thing he couldn't have practised. His excuse for Ginny.

As he blinked in the strong stage lights, he could see little of the audience stretched out in front of him but he could sense their rustling and growing anticipation, then their questioning of the empty seat beside him. He paused, not for dramatic effect but for one final moment of panic. He felt dizzy, as if he had developed a terrible case of vertigo, was teetering, about to fall, needing something to cling to, needing Ginny, but the bloody woman wasn't there . . . Then he smiled, raising his hands in welcome.

'Friends,' he began, 'and fellow fighters! I must first bring you best wishes – and apologies – from Ginny.' What the hell was he going to apologise for? He didn't know, had no idea, yet from somewhere deep inside his political psyche, instinct took over and excuse took shape. 'You all know what family life is like and, as you know, we have a family.' He chuckled to encourage himself. 'Young kids today seem to have lost the capacity for passing by a kitchen table without stumbling and cracking something or other. A spot of boyish bother' – yes, that was it! – 'I suspect not much more than a grazed knee. But I hope you'll understand that, when the call came a few moments ago, she felt her ultimate duty lay with the family. As, indeed, does mine.' And that was about as close as he was going to get to any mention of Julia Summers. 'You know, I think that's why God gave us all two parents. So that our children can give us twice as many headaches. And so that we can be in two places at once, as the Edge family is today. She asks for your patience and begs your forgiveness.'

From the darkness beyond the lights came a prolonged outburst of sympathy that massaged his confidence and revived him. After all, Ginny had helped plot these proceedings with meticulous care, and he still had a couple of surprises up his sleeve. She was here in spirit.

So, pausing only to take a deep breath, he jumped from his cliff, praying that he would miss the jagged rocks that were waiting for him below.

She dumped the car on a double-yellow and ran. When she reached the communal front door to Bobby's apartment block it was firmly shut and looked formidable. She simply pressed every single bell and screamed, repeatedly, 'Emergency. Please let me in!' The anguish in her voice did its work. A buzzer sounded, she heaved open the tall door with a bang and was running up the stairs, past the old advertising prints, using the banister to heave herself up two steps at a time. Behind her, doors opened as the occupants tried to discover the cause of the commotion. Then she was pounding on Bobby's door, screaming at him to open up. But there was nothing.

A door on the other side of the hallway moved a crack and a young woman peered out through her security chain, her face white with alarm.

'It's Bobby,' Ginny cried, breathless. 'I think he's in there. Had an accident.'

The neighbour's brow creased with uncertainty. 'I have a key,' she replied tentatively. 'To water the plants when he's away.'

'Then get it, for God's sake!'

A few moments later they were forcing their way into the apartment.

Madden was a respectable performer, not in the Olivier mould but a man who oozed gravitas. And that was what he gave them. While Dom had given them raw meat, the Treasury spokesman, who was last to speak, presented the faithful with a slab of well-done beef. In truth it was probably a little overcooked for the occasion, but he had nothing to gain by changing his faithful recipe at this stage of the game. It had got him through the last thirty years, it would get him through another thirty minutes. So, safety first. An entirely respectable performance. Until the rats got at it.

As he finished his remarks, the applause was genuine, but from seats surrounding the tables that had been set aside for journalists it was clear that the enthusiasm wasn't as great as it might have been – or, indeed, had been for Dom. There was muttering, shaking of heads. The men from the media sensed a story. After all, 'everybody safe, no casualties' was unlikely to be a message to warm their editors' hearts. And when they turned to ask those behind them what they felt, there was no shortage of volunteers. 'Dull and predictable' was one description. 'Like being nuzzled by a tortoise' came another. It was malicious nonsense, of course, and well rehearsed. Ginny had seen to that. So what if it was unfair about Iain Madden? It was nowhere near as malevolent as the rumours she'd heard his wife helping to spread in the cloakroom at the Marrakech. It was payback time. And the supporters that she and

Dom had deliberately packed round the media benches were doing no more than their job.

Yet it was Ken Boston who stole the after-show commentary. He had suggested to the BBC that they put a camera on him throughout the speeches as a gauge of the audience reaction. They'd agreed. So they had watched him sleep serenely through Goodthorpe, struggle to raise polite applause for Malthouse, and respond to Dom's speech as if he was attached to electrodes. He could be something of a drama queen, could Ken. And he was still fizzing when Iain Madden stepped forward, almost bouncing in his seat with expectation, his hands apart, ready to applaud. But somehow they never connected. As the speech went through its points and paragraphs, his shoulders sagged, his hands fell to his lap and his face became a picture of exotic wretchedness.

Afterwards the press pack surrounded him, eager for a reaction that he was just as keen to give. 'Oh, it won't do, it won't do at all,' he wailed, like a priest in the confessional. 'I came here a firm admirer of Iain's. Still am, in a way. I had intended to make that clear and very public today. But . . .' he pointed to the empty stage behind him from where the speeches had been made '. . . we're never going to win over hearts and minds through a detailed recital of economic theory. We might as well feed them Mogadon!'

The reporters were scribbling furiously. He was always good copy.

'So who are you going to support, Ken?' one asked.

It seemed as if the question had taken him by surprise. He shook his head to gather his thoughts, lowered his eyes as though in prayer, then finally cleared his throat. 'I think the party needs to move forward. We've got to find the courage to reach beyond our traditional supporters to the millions of uncommitted young people who are out there just waiting to be turned on. We need sex appeal, not endless statistics. And that,' he declared, 'requires vision!' He prepared to move on, as though everything necessary had been said.

'But who is that?' the press pack shouted as one.

He looked at them as though they were dullards. 'Why, Dommy Edge, of course.'

They'd had to scavenge no further than five feet from their seats and already the journalists knew they had their stories. It wasn't good enough simply to report that Madden was home and dry. Dull and safe never did anything either for circulation or a reporter's expenses. How much better sport it would be to have a tilt at him, Madden, the Mogadon Man, and better business, too. Keep the country guessing. Squeeze a few more stories out of this election before the flag came down on Thursday.

As they raced to file their copy it was possible to hear poor Iain Madden's campaign slowly deflating, like a balloon left over from a birthday party. Just as Ginny had planned. But, still, there were only five days to go. He could still hold up. Couldn't he?

As the faithful filed out of the conference hall they were greeted once more by the band of enthusiastic Edge supporters, their numbers only slightly diminished by the supply of free drink. No one noticed Santa Claus throwing up on the cobbles round the corner.

Blood. There was blood everywhere. On the floor, on the wall, on the tiled surround and, of course, in the bath. At first Ginny could see nothing else. She wanted to scream, but the neighbour was doing enough of that for both of them. Bobby's head and shoulders were floating above the bathwater. Nearby was the phone on which he had called Ginny, and on the floor a kitchen knife.

She felt certain he was dead – no one could survive losing such vast quantities of blood. But where the hell were the emergency services – the ambulance, the police – that she'd called twenty minutes earlier? She was alone, the neighbour had fled, and tentatively Ginny stepped through a puddle of bathwater and touched Bobby's cheek. To her alarm and delight, his eyes flickered open. She hauled him up in the bath, his body cold and slippery, and held him tight, until she saw the savage gash in his groin. Femoral artery. Still weeping savagely.

'Bobby! Bobby!' she shouted, trying to rouse him. 'Hold on, for God's sake. The ambulance is on its way.'

Slowly, stiffly, he shook his head. 'No help.'

'So why did you call me?'

Little by little the words formed through lips that had turned the strangest blue. 'Because I wanted you to know why.'

His call had not been entirely coherent. Bobby had been fighting to hold back tears and the chatter of those backstage had made it difficult for Ginny to hear clearly, but he had told her that he had gone to Friday prayers at the central London mosque, dressed in the traditional flowing clothes of *shalwar* and *kameez,* desperate to see his father and find some way of atoning. '*Abu* – Father,' he had cried, touching his arm. But his father had denied him, turned his back, walked away, sent a colleague to tell him that he would no longer share either a mosque or his home with his former son. *Former* son. Bobby had repeated the words, sobbing. And on the following morning he had received a hand-delivered letter from his father's solicitor telling him that, from this point, he could expect neither financial nor moral support of any kind. He was to vacate the apartment within a month.

'It . . . is . . . impossible . . . Can't . . . go on,' he had mumbled to Ginny, fighting for every word and in a tone that was unmistakably of a man who had reached breaking-point.

'You won't do anything silly, will you, Bobby?' she had said pathetically.

'Too late,' he had whispered. 'Already done.'

Then the connection had died. And Ginny had run. It hadn't been easy, in that moment, to decide where her duty lay, but she had no time to debate it. It wasn't a matter for argument but impulse, and her instinct drove her on, towards Bobby. She prayed that Dom might come to understand and one day forgive her.

But now there was pounding on the stairway behind her. 'About damned time! Where the bloody hell have you been?' she snapped, as two paramedics appeared.

They ignored her, accustomed to hysteria.

'What have we got here? A bleeder, by the look of things,' one said, gently prising Ginny away from Bobby.

'His name's Bobby,' she whispered, unlocking her arms from round him with immense reluctance.

They began to shout his name, but he was gone, unconscious.

'Can't find a pulse,' the first paramedic said, poking at Bobby's neck.

'Best put him on a drip anyway, stick some Gelofusin in him, if you can find a vein,' his partner replied.

They began working on him, putting pressure on the wound and a tourniquet round his leg, anything to stem the terrible seepage. And, for a while, Ginny's mind was taken over by the confusion of body, blood, blankets, bandages and drips, more blood, and a policeman, politely but insistently asking her questions. Then they were ready to take Bobby away. He seemed utterly lifeless to Ginny but the paramedics were still working hard on him, and as the stretcher squeezed past she asked if she could go in the ambulance with him.

'No problem,' the paramedic said. 'Likely need a little seeing to yourself.'

'I'll try to contact his family,' she said.

Suddenly Bobby's eyes flickered open. 'No,' he whispered. Then he was lost to them once more.

Her senses overflowed. The sound of the siren, the swaying ambulance, the throbbing of the wheels, the pounding of her heart. She wondered if he could still hear anything. 'You fight. You just bloody well fight, you bastard!' she sobbed at him. 'I need you, Bobby Khan. I need you! Who the hell else would I trust in my shower?' Then the doors were opening, other doors closing behind her. She was being swept along beside the stretcher, a confusion of people shouting to each other, reaching for blankets, needles, swabs.

Slowly, she grew aware that the panic was subsiding. Bobby was in a bed, wrapped up tightly, his face partly covered by an oxygen mask, being transfused with blood, and hooked up to a monitor giving his vital readings. They'd had a little problem with the pulse oximeter that was attached to his finger: it didn't take kindly to death-cold fingers. But at last all seemed to be stabilised, moving forward, even. Only then did Ginny agree to leave his side so that the medical staff could take a look at her, make sure she wasn't hiding any injury, give her a little something for shock. A cup of tea works wonders.

She returned, only to find renewed panic beside Bobby's bed. Someone mentioned renal failure, kidneys packed up, trauma, oxygen levels low, fluid leaking into the lungs, and another drip was being hoisted beside him, adrenaline, and a tube being inserted down his windpipe to help him breathe through a ventilator.

Throughout it all, as the horror overwhelmed her, one part of her brain kept working, sufficiently well, at least, that she could call her neighbours to ensure the children were cared for. She tried to call Dom, too, but got only his answering service. She started leaving him a message, trying to explain, but couldn't find the words so she told him she was sorry and would be late home. And that she loved him.

There came a time when she had to leave Bobby. There was no point in staying, his condition had stabilised and others needed her now: Dom, the children. She whispered in his ear, squeezed his hand, then slipped away from his bedside.

When she got back to her car, in the full darkness of night, she found it had been clamped, a polythene-clad letter of accusation stuck fast to the windscreen and a yellow boot of imprisonment snagging its wheel. Somehow it didn't seem to matter much right now. It could have been worse. Astonishingly her purse and her mobile were still there, jammed into the footwell on the passenger side. Any number of messages were waiting for her.

She hailed a taxi.

'Blimey, love,' the cabbie cried, as he pulled over, 'what the hell happened to you?'

And for the first time, under the street-lights, she discovered that her dress was smeared with the most terrible dark stains, which made her look as though she had been hugging a sack of coal. Sodium light does that to blood, turns it black, like soot.

And as soon as she had settled into the back seat, her phone started ringing.

'Is that Mother Teresa?'

'What the hell do you want, Max? I'm really in no mood—'

'I can imagine. From what I hear you've had quite a day.'

'What is it that you've heard?'

'Fleeing from your husband's side, just as he was about to make his big speech, to save a friend who tried to kill himself.'

'Where did you get all that?'

'Come on, girl. You know we've got half the Met and most of the chief constables on our payroll. Nothing goes on without us finding out.'

'Or inventing it.'

'Precisely.'

'Max, I could really do without this right now.'

'Oh, no, you can't. The Edges are the family of the moment. Dom's the headline news tomorrow – not on our front page, you understand, it's far too serious for that, but on several others. Now, you would have made our front page, except it's too late. So it'll be the splash on Monday.'

'I'm not sure, Max.'

'You don't have to be. I am. Anyway, it's a news story, Ginny. The others will have it, too. And can you imagine what that's going to do to Dom's campaign? Discovering he's married to Mother Teresa is one hell of a coup, particularly after all the Julia crap. And think, you'll get at least a dozen columns out of it. I'll be practically bankrupt.' He was laughing. 'What's more, we're going to be uncharacteristically sensitive and not ask too many nasty questions about why this young man is so important in your life.'

'It's simply that he's a friend, Max.' She sighed, feeling the last resources of energy draining from her. 'A friend. That's all. I had to help. There was nobody else, you see . . .'

'Great quote, Ginny.'

'Go poach your bollocks, Max,' she whispered, and cut the connection.

As she sat in the taxi on the way home, she realised how wrong things had gone. Revenge. It had been about revenge. But it should be supped with a long spoon, and perhaps sometimes supped not at all. Now she had lost control. This was no longer merely a political game, getting back at their enemies. She had started a process that had taken over her life and now it had taken over her friends' lives, too. She had become just another player in this game, whether she liked it or not, and it was the dirtiest game on the planet.

The voters continued to be bombarded, until the very last minute. A contest that had been made up of jail sentences, academic fraud, adultery and the fleecing of elderly people had not been good for the nerves, so the majority of party members had put off the day of judgement until it could be avoided no longer.

Which was unfortunate for Iain Madden. He was a level sort of man, level-headed, level-paced, a moderate fellow who avoided extremes and was altogether – well, a leveller. But with its reputation lying in pieces on the field and their poll ratings in flight, the party needed reviving, not levelling. On that final Saturday morning, the faithful had been all but certain to ask Madden to take command. By Sunday, he had been branded Mogadon Man and a chisel of doubt had been driven deep into their hearts. And by the time Monday morning crept upon them, when most of them would seal and post their votes, the Edges came riding through the mists of confusion like characters in a soap opera, which was, of course, what the media had made of them.

Thursday, when the deadline for voting expired, found Archie Blackstone in a foul mood. Early in the contest he'd placed a substantial amount of money on Madden at good odds in the belief that it was a two-horse race and that party supporters wouldn't, at the end of the day, vote for a woman, any woman, least of all a flesh-eater like Hazel Basham. Now Archie panicked, which was unusual for him. Once again it had become a two-horse race but with a new contender, so just before midday, when the bookies stopped accepting any further bets, he placed a similar amount of money on Dom, at very low odds. Just in case. It wasn't a show of confidence, more an act of desperation. If Dom won, Archie would cover most of his losses.

The following morning over breakfast, Ginny told Dom she would like Bobby to come and stay with them for a few days once he left hospital, until he got himself sorted out. Dom refused. So Ginny burst into tears, and kept crying until he changed his mind, because she knew right now he couldn't deal with anyone, least of all a photographer, seeing his wife in tears. The next day, Saturday, walking very tenderly as his wound began to heal, Bobby was discharged from hospital. That evening, with the children and Bobby at the table, Ginny cooked Dom his favourite meal.

Iain and Penny Madden were creatures of habit and would normally have gone to their country home near their constituency for the weekend, but instead they stayed in London to wait for the result.

That was where, on Sunday, they heard he'd lost by just under three thousand votes.

It was around that time that Ajok received her own surprising news. It came from Sophie Gaminara. The Treasury Solicitors had been in contact again. No, not another letter filled with lies and threats, but an offer to settle the case once and for all. They'd offered more compensation, raised it to twelve hundred and fifty pounds. They clearly had little appetite for carrying on.

'We've unsettled them, Ajok. I think they're a little nervous about anything to do with Iraq right now. They hate loose ends, want to tie everything up tight. That includes you.'

Ajok considered what she had been told. 'Will they give me my job back, Miss Gaminara?' she asked quietly.

'No, Ajok, I'm afraid they will never do that, not voluntarily.'

She thought some more. 'Will they take back all those wicked things they said about me? Get the Cypriot to swallow his lies?'

'Not that, either. They only make this offer on the basis that you will ask them for nothing else.'

'I am used to being bought, Miss Gaminara. All women in my village are bought, by the families of our husbands. It is our custom. But this . . . It is like they are trying to buy my soul.'

'I'm not sure it's quite that, Ajok. It would allow you to get on with your life. I'm sure you'd find the money useful, and no one will think any the worse of you.'

But she, Ajok, would. Any Dinka would, letting such a grievance go unanswered. 'Do I have a choice?'

'Of course you do. Mr Messenger at the union is rather keen for you to accept, but I think Paddy can talk him round. And I'll still be here to help, if you want me.'

'I have run half-way round the world with my children to escape from bullies, Miss Gaminara. I'm tired of it all. If you will permit me, it is time for me to stop running.'

'You'll be taking on the British government. It will not be easy.'

'What have I got to lose? They have already taken my good name, and I have so little else.' She paused. In her mind she was rubbing ashes on the back of her favourite cow, an old Dinka ritual that summoned up the spirits of the dead, to give her courage. It reassured her. 'I would like to fight,' she said.

Part Two

Ten

THE PRIME MINISTER. THE Right Honourable Alfred Danderson. The man who made all the rest feel as if they were stumbling around in the foothills.

The gravely voiced Prime Minister was in his early fifties, a man born just as the ageing workhorse Churchill had at last been put out to grass, and who was now showing the greyness at his temples that suggested he had been a long time at the helm. He had grown up with the knowledge that his father should have been Prime Minister. Danderson Senior had been an East Anglian Puritan in the Cromwellian mould and he had even told the young Freddie of his ambition, but he had been a sickly man and died young. The son inherited his lost father's ambition, but somewhere along the road, the Fenland fog seemed to have entered his soul, and he grew to be as forgiving as a November night. He had no appetite for the shadows and gentle mists that surround most men's politics; his passions were dark, often impenetrable, swept along by a strong, moralising tide. Not even a decade spent hemmed in by the ramparts of government had done much to grind down his almost obsessive enthusiasm for office. He refused to drown in the detail of ministerial red boxes; instead he had learned when to ignore them, when to rise above them and, most of all when to throw them; he was not renowned for elasticity of temper. And if ugly detail raised its head, he had an entire machine to tell him about it and to guard his flank. That was why he was Prime Minister and those that served him got fat salaries for their long hours and frequent bruises.

If Freddie Danderson had a blind spot, it was his inflexible sense of political morality. It was so fierce that anyone who didn't fit neatly into its framework was disbelieved and quickly discarded. Those who opposed him were not only wrong but often wicked and therefore could be dispatched with formidable ruthlessness. Ends justify means, and the sense of his own righteous mission enabled him to turn his back on old but argumentative friends with barely a flicker of regret. He could dismiss rising crime figures as nothing more than statistical quirks and believe what he was saying because he knew – was absolutely convinced – that, under his guiding hand, the country was moving forward. He could grant to his growing army of state inquisitors – his 'guard dogs of democracy', as he called them – new powers that made civil libertarians squirm with dismay, and dismiss their doubts by arguing that only those with things to hide had anything to fear. 'Let them lie sleepless, knowing that we are looking for them . . .' he thundered. And he tried to be blind to the wretchedness of what was going on in Iraq on the ground that, if that blighted country's inhabitants refused to accept what had been done for them, then they could expect no better. It was becoming an increasingly difficult line to sell, but he comforted himself with the ultimate fallback. He could always blame Blair.

Yes, they all agreed, that was his blind spot, his sense of moral infallibility – that, and his wife.

Lauren Danderson was small and dark, with lips like a postbox that complained every time it was opened. She was exceedingly chippy, carrying with her all the scars of an unfortunate upbringing in Birmingham. She'd known two stepfathers – 'Three too many,' as she sometimes said – and some very poor schools, and had failed to leave behind the insecurities they had bred. That was one of the reasons she had found herself attracted to Freddie in the first place: his sense of certainty. It had never been much of a physical thing between them; he preferred to have his hands round a book than in her underwear, and they'd had no children, but she tried to pretend that didn't matter. There were compensations, not the least of which was that he'd always been too busy to pick up on any sign of her occasional external distractions, which had given her the freedom to pursue her own interests in fashionable causes. There were some in the media who mocked, of course. One columnist had described her as 'a woman constantly in pursuit of fashion but never able to catch it'. His entire newspaper chain had been frozen out from its government contacts for three months and the journalist in question was physically thrown off the plane for the next prime-ministerial tour – not that Freddie Danderson had ordered it, simply that those in the System were adept at picking up on what was good for self-preservation. You took on the Danderson family with care. And that was what Dominic Edge, in his role as the new Leader of Her Majesty's Opposition, was about to find out.

Afterwards there were many who said he should have seen it coming, and have prepared a few defences. Perhaps he shouldn't have goaded the Prime Minister so, but in truth there is no hiding-place at the Dispatch Box. And Dom was going to find himself used for target practice, no matter what he said.

The House had returned late in January from the extended Christmas break, and it was the first parliamentary outing for Dom in his new role. Prime Minister's Questions, the weekly occasion when the Prime Minister, more or less reluctantly, is forced to break from his burden of saving the world to answer to the House of Commons. Frequently it becomes a tempestuous time as the leaders of the parties line up against each other like playground bullies. It got to them all, even the biggest of them. Harold Macmillan had been a great actor, yet he had often thrown up before such occasions. Margaret Thatcher, always the commander of her brief, had nevertheless spent many hours in nervous preparation, while Blair, with his studied contempt for all things parliamentary, had tried to emasculate the occasion, reducing it to once a week and insisting that it take place before rather than after a good lunch, so denying the boyoes their opportunity to get themselves properly stirred.

Freddie Danderson adopted a different tactic. He preached. He gave praise unto those who served him and, with the force of a true believer, damned all doubters. In order to back up this high moral tone, Danderson had amassed a dossier on the personal foibles and fumblings of almost everyone in the Commons, even those he couldn't recognise. 'Doesn't matter if I don't know who they are,' he had once grumbled. 'What matters is that they know who the hell I am.' And an embarrassing fact or quotation, hurled like a thunderbolt, would usually have the required effect, reducing the injudicious questioner to a heap of ashes and reminding the entire world precisely who the hell Freddie Danderson was.

And now it was Dom's turn.

To prepare for it he'd spent several nights tossing around the possibilities in his sleep, and three hours beforehand closeted with his advisers, like generals huddled round a map of the battlefield trying to decide where to thrust and when to parry. And they would need some defence. A Prime Minister always has the last word, the last shot. The House was packed for the occasion, the ritual blooding of the new Leader of the Opposition, and an expectant buzz reached Dom as he strode through the doors and into the Chamber. As he emerged from behind the Speaker's chair a loyal roar of approval rose from his own benches, which was almost immediately matched in volume by the jeers of government backbenchers, waving copies of *The Times*. That morning the paper had published an opinion poll. The Government was even further ahead, the beneficiaries of what the editorial called 'a leadership race that, after the excitement had died away, seemed squalid. It lacked only rent-boys. So many contenders betrayed themselves with their own vices that the new leader is indeed fortunate he is not charged with running a house of ill-repute and living off immoral earnings.'

From her seat in the gallery, Ginny winced as the noise burst across the Chamber, like the confluence of two great rivers in flood. This was such a boys' game, so deliberately discourteous, so lacking in rules. She had chosen Dom's shirt and tie and wished him well, but otherwise felt useless. And, as the affair got under way, her sense of unease increased. Dom sat still for a while, biding his time, but Danderson was in ruthless form. The atmosphere was heavy and the scene below reminded her of one from the Roman empire. The two sides of the House resembled a slave galley with the backbenchers bent over their oars, the Speaker seated between them like the fat-bellied drummer marking time, and Danderson in the role of the slave-master, ever alert, glancing at all sides to lash out at those who seemed to flag. A little further along the gallery, she could see the journalists of the press lobby peering over the rail, noses twitching, ready for the smell of blood.

When, at last, Dom got to his feet, the roars broke out once more, buffeting him from all sides. His rise to the leadership had been spectacular, but now he was paying for his lack of experience. He'd never faced anything like this, rarely spoken to anything other than an all but empty House, and the sight that confronted him made him glad of the tot of whisky he'd taken to calm his nerves and quell the judder in his knee. In front of him, he could see nothing but a sea of faces, all contorted, possessed with ill-feeling and mockery. Suddenly he hated his job. He asked a question, but could remember none of what he said. It had been well rehearsed, but only the player's spirit got him through. Then Danderson was on his feet, welcoming him to his new role, suggesting that he should be undeterred by what the pundits and the polls were saying about his chances of success. 'We all serve as best we can,' he said. 'It's simply that some do it better than others.' At which point the government benches erupted in delight.

The plan had been to test the Prime Minister on family issues. It was a strategic strength for Dom, the advisers had decided, and one that the childless Danderson would find difficult to contest. So Dom pressed, not once but three times and, in his anxiety, perhaps too hard. 'Those of us with families understand these problems on an everyday basis,' he snapped, 'and the Prime Minister has had years to pick up these cries for help. Why is he so congenitally deaf?'

Those nearby saw Danderson banging his fist on his thigh, always a sign of impatience and anger. He rose like a god from the seas, his voice quivering with indignation. 'The Right Honourable Gentleman has a very great deal to learn,' he thundered, grasping the side of the Dispatch Box, 'before he comes to this place to lecture me on family values.' He stared at Dom, seated only a few feet away. 'Some would say he has an unadulterated cheek to do so.'

'But Julia couldn't possibly comment,' a wag from below the gangway chipped in, and half the House dissolved into laughter. From her perch above, Ginny saw the back of Dom's neck glowing red.

'I don't doubt that the Right Honourable Gentleman holds family values dear. It's just that he has an extraordinary way of expressing them. Why, practically his first act as Leader of the Opposition' – Danderson glanced down at the notes in his folder in front of him – 'was to write letters to the authorities seeking to excuse his own wife from . . . what was it?' His finger ran theatrically down the page. 'A charge of exceeding the speed limit on the public highway, another charge of using a hand-held mobile phone while driving and . . .' By this point the House was stunned to silence. Danderson looked at the ruffians behind him, urging them to be ready. 'And even a miserable parking ticket.'

They were at Dom, baying like hounds, standing, pointing, jeering, consumed by contempt. Dom sat still, rigid, as though he had been strapped into an electric chair. Behind him, his own benches sat in muffled confusion.

'I don't wish to intrude into his own family arrangements,' Danderson concluded when, at last, the noise had subsided, 'but it seems such a strange set of priorities for anyone who wishes to be a political leader.'

And the damage was done, the journalists scribbling furiously, the tone set. 'Come in long trousers next time,' someone shouted, as Dom left the Chamber. No one on his own side would catch his eye.

Ginny hurried after him but he was already gone, alone, on the long walk back to his offices in Norman Shaw.

He strode purposefully, trying hard to control the urge to run, not looking to either side, and said not a word until he had reached the doors that marked his own territory. That was when he broke into a sprint, straight into his office, slamming the door and screaming repeated curses that made one of the girls in the outer office burst into tears.

Ginny arrived, hotly pursued by Archie, just in time to hear a metal wastebin end its useful life as it slammed into a wall.

By the time they were through the door, Dom was already deep into a glass of whisky. He looked at them, madness in his eyes. 'Archie, they were the tickets Ginny picked up when she was rushing to help Bobby Khan. All I did was write a couple of letters explaining the situation, as any husband would.'

'On House of Commons notepaper?'

'Possibly.'

'Bugger.'

'Does it matter?'

'Yes. Smacks of use of influence.'

'And how the hell did that bastard get to know about it if he's not abusing his influence?' Dom shouted.

'An excellent point,' the Scot replied.

'But, sadly, one that will be lost amidst the laughter,' Dom snapped, finishing the thought for him.

'I'll get to the lobby. Tell them it was Ginny on her mercy flight. See if we can neutralise the story.'

'But it won't be neutralised in there, will it?' Dom muttered bitterly, waving in the general direction of the House of Commons. 'Too late for that.'

Archie had no response. It was true. Danderson had already established his dominance over Dom in a most brutal fashion. The master and the schoolboy not yet in long trousers was an image that would be tough to shake. Without another word, Archie left.

After he had gone, and Ginny was alone with Dom, she crossed to him and took him in her arms. She could sense the tears of frustration that were falling on her blouse.

'He murdered me in there,' he lamented, struggling for control.

'There will be another time.'

'How many times can one man die, for God's sake?' He was losing it.

'A time to get your own back, I meant.'

'But how? How on earth—'

She was shaking him, trying to cast the panic out of him. 'Listen to me. If that moralising bastard wants to take on the Edge family, we're not going to duck it. If that's the type of war he wants to fight, then the Edge family are ready – more than ready – to take on the Dandersons.'

'What do you mean?'

'You deal with Mr Danderson. Leave his wife to me.'

Patrick Creasey made his way through the puddles, passing the uncollected dustbins and abandoned shopping trolleys that marked this quarter of the brave new world. It wasn't the worst example of urban squalor he had seen, but that didn't make him any less ashamed. And how was it, even under the watchful eye of security cameras, that the graffiti artists still reigned supreme? One Minister had recently praised such nocturnal scrawlings as 'culturally and socially integrated twenty-first-century art forms.' Yet somehow, Creasey remembered, this cutting edge of culture was never permitted to extend as far as the walls in Whitehall.

It was the first time he had been to Ajok's home. Normally she would have expected to come to him, at the Admiral Lord Nelson, but he had no heart for forcing her to trail half-way across London through winter showers. He knew she would have walked. She greeted him with nervous, expectant eyes, knowing that this meeting was somehow different. She offered him coffee, which he declined. He wanted no ceremony.

Ajok's apartment was small and neat, with comforting piles of children's clutter. There were few signs of her homeland, little except for a wood carving of a woman with firewood on her head that was hanging on the wall, and a large decorated gourd that sat in the middle of the table. The furniture was sparse, old, and as he settled on the threadbare sofa he couldn't help but guess that most of it was reclaimed from a charity shop, recycled through any number of previous owners.

'In my country, Mr Creasey, these things would be treasures,' she said, reading his mind.

Her simple sincerity made him feel worse. All he had ever wanted to do was help people, people like Ajok, protect them from those with power, yet it had come to this.

'Ajok, there is no easy way for me to be telling you,' he began, 'but the union . . .' He faltered. 'You may have heard that the union has negotiated a new pay deal in Whitehall. Been going on for months, but at last they've had an offer they feel they can recommend to everyone.'

'To everyone who has a job, Mr Creasey.'

He tried to swallow his discomfort but his mouth was as dry as a bone. 'The thing is, Ajok, it's a good offer, rather better than we were expecting . . .' An additional payment to cover the 'exceptional national security implications' of their work, one that wouldn't be available to other workers. 'But they've insisted on one condition, you see.'

'I'm afraid I don't, Mr Creasey.'

'It's that . . . well, they say they must have a clean slate. Insist that the union drops all its backing of outstanding appeals for unfair dismissal. Cases like yours.'

'And how many cases are there like mine, Mr Creasey?'

'That's the damnable thing. I don't know of any apart from yours.'

Could it be that blatant? Using a pay deal to wipe out one little woman who was proving too much of a thorn? Messenger had argued that it was no more than a coincidence, an incidental outcome, and that it would be ridiculous to imperil a pay offer for thousands because of one stubborn immigrant. Yes, he'd used the word 'immigrant'. Yet what was he, Patrick Creasey, if he wasn't the son of an immigrant, a stubborn bloody Irish mule at that, a man who had taught his son that all power was a conspiracy.

'It means, Ajok, that the union will no longer be supporting you.'

'I see,' she whispered, although he was sure she didn't.

'I came here because I wanted you to know how very sorry I am.'

'Thank you.'

Somewhere beneath him an old spring moved, making him feel ever more uncomfortable. He wanted to get out of this place, to walk outside in the rain for hours and hope that it might wash all the dirt off him.

'Perhaps – I can't guarantee it, you understand – but perhaps we could go back and see if they are still willing to offer you a little compensation.'

She sat in her chair, tall, dignified, erect, her hands in her lap. 'That is kind of you, Mr Creasey, but I suspect it is too late for that.'

No, he decided, he had underestimated this woman, perhaps had always underestimated her. She understood things all too well.

'You are a good man, Mr Creasey. I know you have tried, done your best.'

And somehow that made him feel worse.

'But how do you *know* that?' Ginny persisted, showing her doubt as she handed Bobby a glass of wine.

They were sharing an evening at home. Dom was away on a tour of the North-west, leaving them alone once again. Bobby had been reluctant to accept Ginny's invitation to move into the spare room, sensing Dom's reservations, but in the end he had had few options. He had too much other stuff to sort out before he got round to finding somewhere to live on a political hack's wage. He had taken great care to fit in, helping with babysitting, clearing up, acting as chauffeur and car-cleaner, until gradually Dom had thawed. Bobby was always going to be Ginny's friend rather than his, but at least he was unlikely to come home and find them in bed together. Dom owed Ginny so much, and it was a relatively painless form of repayment. If Bobby's presence in their home meant that they lost a little of their privacy, it was nothing to what the new job had done for them. They had all become public chattels.

So much of their life had changed. She couldn't even go shopping without running the risk of some stranger pulling at her sleeve, and when she went to pick up the kids from school there was always a chance she would find a photographer at the gates. Still, it had some benefits. She was able to charge Max double for the columns. Not that money was such a pressing issue, for the moment. Dom's parliamentary salary had more than doubled as Leader of the Opposition, well into six figures, yet that would be the case only so long as he remained in post and there were already those who were muttering that he'd last not a minute longer than it would take to count the votes at the next general election. Even after only a few weeks, there was a queue of those wanting to be the first to kick his corpse.

'Come on, then, let me give your shoulders a rub while I explain it all to you,' Bobby said.

She found a cushion and nestled on the floor in front of him. He really had the best fingers.

They were discussing Mitzi Nicholson, the wife of the Trade and Industry Secretary. Mitzi's name had come up that afternoon, while Ginny sweated in the gym that was part of the prestigious hotel complex carved out of the old County Hall on the South Bank. It was an exclusive and not inexpensive operation, but Ginny had been offered free membership. It was strange how, just as for the first time she might have been able to afford the entrance fee, it was handed to her on a plate. Westminster rules. And although she knew this was yet another part of the largesse she shouldn't rely on, she had accepted, largely because the number of calories being thrust at her in her new role required her to stage some sort of fight back. And many other perks were attached to membership – a superb view across the Thames, coaching under the watchful and none too bashful eye of a stunning Australian personal trainer, envious glances, thighs that throbbed, and the prize that is valued in some quarters beyond all else: gossip. It was while she was warming down on an exercise bike, with the trainer pretending to take a dispassionate view of her quads and calves, that she had heard the latest about Mitzi Nicholson.

Mitzi, it seemed, had been clocked. Being clocked was an occupational hazard in Westminster, where it was almost impossible to conduct any sort of assignation without someone bumping into you, and Mitzi had been observed on more than one occasion in deep, intimate conversation with an exceedingly good-looking younger man. His identity had remained something of a mystery until a friendly waiter revealed that his name was David Gilbert, a lobbyist from Moonraker, a large construction company. So there it was. Mitzi up to mischief.

'But that's nonsense,' Bobby had declared, when Ginny told him. 'It can't be true. It simply cannot be true.'

So Ginny had insisted on an explanation and a massage to rub away the ache in her shoulders.

'When I was recovering in hospital,' he said, 'I had plenty of time to think.' His voice adopted a distant, almost impersonal quality. 'I'd spent the last ten years rushing round trying to pretend I was something I cannot be, and it wasn't working. I knew that if I went on like that, I'd end up doing something very stupid once more, except that next time I might succeed. So I decided to stop all this crawling around in the shadows – after all, what's the point? My father knows . . .'

His fingers dug sharply into her shoulder. It hurt. She bit her lip, didn't complain.

'I'm never going to be an outrageous queen, Ginny, but I am what I am. Gay. A poof. A left-footer. A friend of Dorothy's. Call it what you like. I don't want to get a trumpet and make a great parade of it, but I'm not going to hide it any longer. And as soon as I decided that, it was . . . well, as if I'd taken off some filthy, rancid clothes, and for the first time in my adult life I felt clean. Strange, isn't it? That admitting to being a queer can make you feel clean? But that's how it was. And when you encouraged me to take a holiday over New Year and I went to Verbier – remember? Well, I told you the snow was magnificent. What I didn't tell you is that I went with a group made up entirely of gay guys. Never done anything like that before. Fifteen of us. Took over a chalet and had a ball. Like kids, we were – snowball fights, toboggans, dramas, fallings-out and terrible bitch fights, then all the making up. It worked for me, never felt happier.'

His fingers had relaxed once more, resuming their gentle rhythm on her shoulders.

'Interesting bunch of guys. Mostly Westminster-based. A health-service minister, a couple of MPs, a senior civil servant, an editorial writer on the *Telegraph*, the fellow who owns that bistro in Victoria Street, even a detective from the Palace. Oh, and the vicar from a very high-church parish in Chelsea. Could still smell the incense on him. And it just so happens that David Gilbert was one of them – in fact, he was the principal organiser. Used his corporate expense account to make the whole thing a very jolly occasion.'

'A scam, you mean?'

'Not at all. Mixing perfectly good business with pleasure. Moonraker is one of the biggest government contractors, billions of pounds involved. Needs contacts everywhere. David's job is to open doors. All the better if they happen to be bedroom doors in luxury chalets.'

'So he is . . .' She struggled for the words.

'Part of the gay network in Westminster.'

'I never realised there was one.'

'Then you've a lot to learn.'

'A detective from the Palace, too?'

'Buck House is riddled with them.'

'With detectives?'

'With queens, you idiot. And they don't all wear tiaras.'

'Very funny.'

'It maintains a long naval tradition among the Royal Family.'

'But David Gilbert. Couldn't he be . . . ?'

'AC/DC? Swing both ways?'

'Yes.'

'It's theoretically possible, of course. But, in his case, completely out of the question. You're just going to have to trust me on that one, Ginny.'

'So if he isn't dragging Mitzi Nicholson into the undergrowth, if it isn't a matter of pleasure, it must be . . .'

'Business. Moonraker business.'

'And what sort of business would Mrs Nicholson have with Moonraker?'

'Nothing that isn't connected to Mr Nicholson, that's for sure. Moonraker's made a considerable point of being half-way up the backside of the Secretary of State for Trade and Industry. Metaphorically speaking, of course.'

'Can it be that obvious?'

'Since when has obvious been a problem? This government's been taking care of its friends ever since Bernie Ecclestone barged his way through the door of Downing Street waving a cheque for a million pounds.'

'You don't think Moonraker can be handing across cheques for a million pounds to Mitzi Nicholson, do you?'

'She doesn't strike me as being that expensive.'

'So how much? And for what?'

He had stopped manipulating her shoulders but Ginny hadn't noticed. They were both wrapped up in conjecture.

'I don't suppose David Gilbert would tell you?' she asked hesitantly, testing him.

'No. But an Internet search of what Moonraker's been up to recently might give us some clues. And so might David's partner. He's a hair stylist named Trevor.'

'You're kidding. A hairdresser?'

'Full of sad clichés, we are. And Trevor's stick thin, doesn't take his alcohol very well. Makes him silly.'

'But wouldn't you feel that a – a compromise of loyalties?'

He paused before replying, his voice slower, a trifle sad. 'I'm beginning to discover that working in Westminster is a constant compromise of loyalties. Screw or be screwed. It's the price we pay.'

She sensed that it was another rite of passage for Bobby; there had been so many of them recently.

'Anyway, I need an updated image for my new life,' he continued. 'I think it's time to get myself a haircut. Something a little neater. Cropped.'

'But you've got lovely hair,' she cried, turning to look at him. 'You're a real waste to womanhood, you are.'

'Thank you. But talking of wasted womanhood reminds me. Something I heard from the detective at the Palace. About Lauren Danderson . . .'

January. Incessant rain. Skies like an old grey sweater, all miserable and twisted out of shape. Moments earlier Malith Bulabek, the lodger, had left for work and Ajok was gazing out of the window after him. As he walked away from the block of flats she saw him stop, examine the weather, pull up his collar, then begin his daily trudge towards the bus stop. Her sharp eyes also caught something else. Parked not far down the street was a car with two occupants, both of whom were staring intently after Malith. One seemed to be holding a camera. As his bus arrived, the car pulled out to follow it. Ajok continued to watch until both vehicles had disappeared into the mists of early morning.

Those people had been spying on him.

Then a different thought struck Ajok. Were they, perhaps, spying on her?

'Max, I need to do a deal with you.'

'Come on, Ginny, you already charge me a king's ransom for your column, quite apart from the cost of advertising on your website.'

'Don't be such a grouch. You get good value for your money. Besides, this one won't cost you a bean.'

'Then already I'm suspicious.'

She perched on the corner of his enormous glass desk. 'I've got a story that might do a lot of damage to the Government. Would that bother you?'

'How?'

'You're supposed to be a supporter of Mr Danderson.'

'I'm even keener on my annual bonus.'

'No conflict of interest, then?'

'What's that? Oh, you mean would it embarrass me to pour a bucketload of shit over this lot and still tell my readers to vote for them at the next election? Depends how big the bucket is.'

'Cabinet resignation.'

'Big enough.'

'There's one other problem with the story, Max. I can't prove it.'

'Then it's nothing but gossip.'

'But it's very reliable gossip. And although I can't prove it, I think maybe you can. After all, you've got access to all sorts of things. Telephone records, bank accounts—'

'That would be highly improper – even unethical.'

'Yes. You might even get hauled up before the Press Complaints Commission and have your knuckles rapped.'

'Ouch. So what is it?'

'You men are always in such a rush. Let's talk about the deal. You get the story only on condition that you let Dom raise it in Parliament first.'

'And let every beggar in Fleet Street get their mucky paws on it? No way, Mrs E. That's not how we work.'

'But it's how I work. Dom raises it in the afternoon. You get the full blast the following morning. No one else will have time to catch up. It'll still be your exclusive.'

He considered for the merest fraction of time, then shook his head once more. 'Sorry, Mrs E, couldn't take that risk.'

She sighed and rose from her perch, smoothing out the creases in her dress. 'Oh dear. Then I shall have to find someone who would.'

'Hold it there, Ginny, don't you go playing hardball with me.'

'But isn't that the whole point, Max? For us to discover just how hard your balls are?'

So many impressions. The faintly musky, masculine smell as he squeezed his way past the crowd. The outstretched legs over which he had to clamber. The rustle of expectation, the expressions of good luck. Like a boxer hauling himself into a ring. Dom was back in the pit from which he had climbed, bloodied and bruised, so many times before.

For a Leader of the Opposition, Prime Minister's Questions is not so much a matter of success as of plain survival. Victory is rare, a good battering is far more common, and even on his best days Dom had been able to get away with little more than a split decision. A Prime Minister always throws the final punch, and this gives him a huge advantage. But it also means the stakes are high. He must win those contests, for if he doesn't, if it becomes clear that he cannot control the House, he will soon lose control of the country. That didn't seem to worry Freddie Danderson. Judging by the opinion polls, he was still firmly in charge.

Dom had to force his way into his place on the green leather bench. The House had more than six hundred and fifty members yet had seats for less than four hundred. It is never a comfortable place when crowded; tempers flare like tinder, and all too quickly the mentality of the mob takes hold.

From below the gangway that separated him from his leader, Jack Saunders glowered. He had refused to serve under Dom, and Iain Madden had done so only with reluctance. People said it was no more than a matter of time before one of them made a move against Dom. And there was always Hazel.

As Danderson appeared from behind the Speaker's chair his supporters raised a cry of greeting. In his wake his two parliamentary aides bobbed like Chinese courtiers, and just before he sat down he smiled across the Dispatch Box at Dom. He didn't mean it, of course. For a few minutes, as Danderson began answering questions, Dom reluctantly admired his adversary's style. A nod, a frown, a smile, a sharp thrust here, a dab of approval there, and if ever he got into the slightest trouble he would retreat into his briefing book where he could bash on for Britain with such ferocity that the questioner was left reeling. Pity about the suit, though, and the crumpled shirt collar: he should do better than that, but with a wife like Lauren to take care of him it was a surprise he didn't come dressed like some reincarnated hippie. Danderson preferred statistics to sartorial style, and he hurled them around like weapons.

But now it was time. Dom's moment. He nodded towards the Speaker, his name was called and, accompanied by the chorus of tribal jeers, he stepped into the ring.

'Mr Speaker, thank you.' He looked around him defiantly, which only encouraged the noise on all sides. He took a breath. 'The Prime Minister will, I hope, remember his own words when he first took office. That he expected the highest standards of integrity from his colleagues, that his government was going to be whiter than white.' He glanced at his notes in order to give them the precise date of the announcement, but only for theatrical effect; he had practised the lines for almost an hour beforehand.

'Not like your lot,' a government heckler called. 'Snouts in troughs.'

'I rather think the Prime Minister had his immediate predecessor in mind when he uttered those words,' Dom responded, staring straight at the heckler. 'Dodgy peerages, dodgy loans, dodgy mortgages. They were all at it. Even the previous Prime Minister's wife was at it. If I had, indeed, tried to stand at that particular trough, I'd have got myself trampled in the rush.'

A roar of approval came from behind him; the heckler slipped back into sneering silence.

Dom rubbed the edges of the Dispatch Box, trying to feign calm. 'I'm sorry to have to tell the Prime Minister that I've been given strong circumstantial evidence that one of his most senior Cabinet colleagues has been guilty of serious wrongdoing, may even have been – I hate to use this term but in the circumstances it seems only appropriate – may even have been *corrupt*.'

As the word found its way round the House, all the interruptions stopped. The Speaker leaned forward in alarm. A strange silence fell. This wasn't the banter they expected on a Wednesday afternoon.

'The only thing I'm asking of the Prime Minister is that, when I hand him the evidence, he undertakes to investigate the matter in all seriousness through the appropriate independent authorities. And they must be independent, with their conclusions made public. We want no more of the cover-ups and rigged inquiries of the sort that both he and his predecessor have contrived in the past to sweep such matters under the carpet.' Dom stood at the Dispatch Box a little longer, glancing around as they hung on his every word, expecting more, the names, the details, but he was savouring the moment. Without a further word, he sat down.

Corruption? In the Cabinet? It had been a stunning blow, but the champion was far from done for. He rose to his feet, his eyes red with anger. 'I find the Right Honourable Gentleman's actions abominable,' he thundered. 'To hurl empty allegations in an attempt to smear the Government is surely nothing more than proof of his own lack of standards. He cites circumstantial evidence. Does he mean he has laid his hands on nothing more than cheap gossip? And how, on that basis, can he justify the most serious accusation it's possible to make against a politician?' The Chief Whip turned in his seat to encourage the troops, and now the government benches were in uproar. 'I've always thought there was a good rule for men – *real* men – to follow in such circumstances. Either put up or shut up. I commend it to the Right Honourable Gentleman who, unless he is proven right, will have shown himself to be neither honourable nor a gentleman!'

'Order! Order!' the Speaker cried, struggling forlornly to quell the tide of partisan howling that was sweeping throughout the House.

Dom withstood the storm. He stretched forward across the Dispatch Box, ensuring that Danderson had no doubt that the contempt flowing between them was mutual. 'Why on earth has the Prime Minister suddenly succumbed to this fit of temper? All I've asked him to do is to make sure that the evidence I'm going to give him is properly examined. And why won't he offer me the simple undertakings I ask for? Nothing could be easier for a man with nothing to hide. And, no, I won't discuss the details here,' he spat, at one particularly strident front-bench heckler. 'These charges and the identities of those concerned shouldn't be bandied around recklessly in public. Serious allegations require serious consideration. That's all I'm asking for.'

The Prime Minister was back, jumping forward, pointing, as though he wanted to poke out the other man's eye. 'If all he has to offer is insinuation wrapped in gossip and then boiled in tittle-tattle, I see no reason whatsoever to dignify such nonsense with a reply.' He shoved himself back into his seat. Pandemonium reigned.

Beside him, the Chancellor of the Exchequer looked as though he were having some sort of fit.

Dom rose once more, but in contrast to Danderson's anger his demeanour was almost cat-like, subtle and controlled. He had charge of this moment. His voice had grown soft, compelling the baying hounds to silence if they wanted to hear what was coming next. And they did. The words came slowly, every one picked over with care: 'The Prime Minister deceives himself. I don't ask him to respond to *me*. I ask him to respond to *the people*. Openly. Honestly. And, above all, accurately. This is a matter far too important to leave to the coruscating care of his media minders. Besides, the international ramifications of anything to do with Iraq are far too serious to be reduced to party political banter.'

It took barely a breath for the implications of what he had said to sink into the Prime Minister. Iraq? Where the hell was this one going? He'd become embroiled in a huge row over – what? He didn't know, hadn't even the twinkling of an idea. Danderson was an experienced fighter, knew when the time had come to cling on, to take a rest from the heavy pounding and try to figure out what was coming next. It shouldn't have come to this. He'd been tricked, he needed time to repair his defences.

'Mr Speaker, I've already told the Leader of the Opposition – put up or shut up. If he has anything to offer other than hot air, of course I'll look at it.'

For a final time, Dom got to his feet. 'Mr Speaker, what I have will be with the Prime Minister by close of business today.'

And there the matter was left. Until nine o'clock that evening. Just in time to give a rough outline to the main television news programmes, but too late for the newspapers to make much of it for the following morning. Except the *Record*, of course. Max would still have his exclusive, and in the midst of all the frenzy of speculation mounted by the rest of the media, the value of his prize grew and grew.

★

The bones of it came from Bobby's gay network. After a couple of bottles of Corona sipped through a wedge of lime, Trevor the hairdresser had come through. His partner, David Gilbert, had been diverting most of his hours to building contracts in the British-occupied southern sector of Iraq, something that failed to impress Trevor but had immediately captured Bobby's imagination. The size of the contracts was measured in hundreds of millions, and Moonraker had its hand firmly in the pot. For that purpose, of course, the company required all sorts of permits and approvals from the Department of Trade and Industry, and any measure of inside knowledge helped it keep ahead of the stampeding herd.

It was the women's network that provided the next piece of the jigsaw. Back in the gym, Ginny heard that Mitzi's latest project was the ongoing renovation of a farmhouse in Provence, of which she was apparently very proud. She had even passed round photos.

Once the outlines had been established, the rest was coloured in through the extensive resources of the *Record*. It took a reporter less than two days to establish the location of the farmhouse, the size of the swimming-pool, the cost of the purchase and the rough budget for the conversion – and that it was all registered in Mitzi's maiden name. It took them a little longer, and required considerably more underhand means, to discover that Mitzi, also in her maiden name, appeared as a consultant in Moonraker's corporate records, and that its monies were almost certainly funding the project.

There was nothing directly illegal in any of this: it merely treated the requirements for public disclosure of a Minister's financial interest with the sort of consideration a hungry Viking might have shown a suckling pig. Perhaps Mitzi's husband knew little of it – it wouldn't be the first time that professed ignorance about a spouse's wheelings and dealings had saved a Cabinet Minister's scalp. And none of the *Record*'s burrowing into bank accounts, their delving into private diaries or their raiding of telephone records could prove any connection with the Minister, until the reporter returned once more to the hills of Provence. There, on the wall of a rough-hewn office, she found a kaleidoscope of photographs from all the builder's ongoing projects. In the centre was one of Mitzi's swimming-pool, with Mitzi and her husband standing proudly in its still dry deep end.

The photo made the front page, beneath a headline that screamed: '*Swimming in Sleaze.*'

The Minister, standing wide-eyed with alarm outside his home and defying the sparse flakes of snow that were settling on his thinning hair, still professed ignorance and blamed misunderstanding. He swore he had never divulged confidential information to his mongrel, let alone to Mitzi, not even as pillow talk, and was even reduced to insisting that for several years they had slept in separate beds. He tried to laugh off the accusations as a joke. But by noon he was gone.

It was a famous victory. 'I've done it. I have done it!' Dom exclaimed, still incredulous, watching the tears on live television.

'Don't be silly, darling,' Ginny whispered in his ear. 'We've barely started. This was just a trial run.'

That was also the day Ajok received a letter from her local benefit office. It asked her to attend an interview. About a matter that was 'either fraudulent or in error'. Needed resolving. She phoned, asking what it was all about, but they wouldn't tell her. She didn't worry. She knew she had nothing to hide.

Eleven

PARENTHOOD AND POLITICS. DID they ever mix? Maggie Thatcher had done it, but some said not so well. Too many black marks against her. Westminster took such a heavy toll. The Majors had endured difficulties, and even the Blairs, behind their smokescreen of spin, were supposed to have gone through moments of pure agony. Lauren Danderson had been heard to say she was fortunate not to have children – no hostages. Silly cow. But still . . .

Ben had been quiet, withdrawn, so unlike him, and perhaps Ginny should have picked up on the warning signs sooner but there were so many distractions. Like this evening. A charity dinner, where the great and the glitterati were to be drawn together for the benefit of some fashionable cause but most of all to raise the profile of the organiser. A couple of years of this and there might be a knighthood in it; they'd been handed out for less. Much less.

Ginny had been putting Ben to bed at the same time as she was making her own preparations for the evening. He said he didn't want her to go and she'd explained that she would be there with the Prime Minister's wife, along with many other names he hadn't recognised until she came to someone from Chelsea's midfield. She wouldn't be late, she had lied, promising that he could read his football magazine for a little longer tonight as a treat. And that was when he had burst into tears. She'd spent two days trying to decide what to wear, and now he was sobbing all over her dress, pouring out his misery.

Bullying. At school. Right under the nose of St Xavier. Two bigger boys from his year. It had begun with taunting, inevitably about Dom, but had grown, with all the maliciousness of boys' minds focused on poor Ben. The hidden gym kit, the defaced exercise books, the extortion of the pocket money that was meant to have purchased his missing magazine. As it all tumbled forth her anger grew, but it was nothing in comparison to her shame. This was her fault. When a child is in such pain it's always a mother's fault. She should have known.

'Why haven't you said anything, darling? To me? To one of the teachers?' she asked, and he explained that he couldn't, that he was Dom's son, knew it would be wrong to cause trouble at his new school, and that Father Benedict was always going on about turning the other cheek. And now her own tears were tumbling over her dress, mingling with his.

'Would you like me to go and talk to Father Benedict?'

He shook his head. He rejected even more emphatically her suggestion that Dom should call the school.

'So what would you like to happen, darling?'

'I want to make them stop by myself.'

'And do you know how?'

He nodded. 'Think so.'

And she moaned deep inside when she saw him clench his fists. *You bloody men,* she screamed silently. But the passion was wasted. She couldn't argue with him. She knew what it was like to want more than anything else to get your own back, to harm those who had done their best to harm you. She'd known it from the moment her mother died, and she wouldn't turn hypocrite with her own child.

'So you do just that, young man,' she said, looking straight into his face through her own tear-stung eyes. 'Stand up to them. Don't ever let them bring you down. And we'll keep this our secret, OK, just you and me?'

He nodded thoughtfully, then hugged her. She kissed him, and watched him fall asleep, then Ginny crept out to change her dress.

Ginny hadn't enjoyed the charity dinner. Too many people playing a game of waiting to be recognised, even while they studiously refused to recognise others. Lauren Danderson had been one of the keenest players. It had been suggested by several press photographers that the two women should meet – their paths hadn't crossed before – and be photographed together, but the Prime Minister's wife had made it clear she wouldn't find that appropriate and had made sure she kept her distance.

It didn't help. The press, insistent as always, took separate photographs and stuck them side by side. And Lauren Danderson was right to have been cautious about the comparison. The front page of the *Daily Mail,* labelling its photograph '*First Ladies'*, showed a willowy Ginny, elegant even in her second-best dress, next to a decidedly dumpy Lauren, whose floral outfit appeared to have been stuffed with handfuls of grass.

The images kept a smile on Ginny's face for most of the following morning, so much so that, around lunchtime, when she was shopping and passing near Party Headquarters, she decided to call in on Archie Blackstone. It wasn't mere whimsy: she had to learn to do business with him at some point, to find some way around the Scotsman's reserve, and it seemed like as good a moment as any. Best to beard him in his own lair, make him feel more comfortable. Anyway, she was curious to see how this austere man lived.

The press room was large, open plan, filled with many screens and monitors but, at lunchtime, only a couple of people. Silly, she told herself, he'll be out. But Archie wasn't a social creature: he didn't care much for being a spectator while others swallowed liquid lunches. She discovered him sitting in his office. It had one complete wall of glass to enable him to see what the others were up to, and another wall filled with framed campaign posters and front pages of major political victories. She noticed that Dom didn't feature in any. Just wait, old buddy, just you wait . . . She was also surprised to see that he was bent over a large jigsaw puzzle. The man had hidden depths.

'Sorry, Archie, am I interrupting?'

He looked up, startled, then a little self-conscious. The puzzle was a huge, intricate impression of Edinburgh Castle that, according to the box, consisted of five thousand pieces. 'My way of relaxing. Half an hour a day at lunchtime, if I'm allowed.'

'Should I come back some other time and—'

'Och, no, woman. Come in an' sit yourself down.'

She had noticed that his accent became more marked when he was under pressure, stripped of his Westminster veneer. He rose from the table covered with the jigsaw and went to sit behind his desk. Ginny leaned over the puzzle, studying it. 'Looks very complicated,' she said.

'Takes me away from all this nonsense.'

'Back home.'

'That's Edinburgh!' he snapped dismissively. 'I'm west coast.'

'So . . . why?'

'It's a sort of double whammy. First I get the pleasure of finishing off the puzzle. Then the not inconsiderable satisfaction of smashing Edinburgh to pieces. Call it tribal, if you like, but, most of us are.'

'I've moved around so much of my life, lived in so many different places. Somehow I don't seem to belong anywhere.'

The words were meant to offer an opening, an opportunity to share something, even if it was only a morsel of twisted sentimentality, but he didn't seem keen to pursue the thought. 'So, what can I do for you, Mrs Edge?'

'I was shopping in the area,' she explained.

'For another of those little dresses of yours?' He nodded towards the pile of newspapers on his desk.

She smiled. 'No, just food. You have children, Archie? They seem to grow and grow.'

'And then they go, Mrs Edge. Just turn their backs and leave.' His tone scarcely encouraged further enquiry.

'Archie, I've been thinking.'

He frowned.

'Those photographs this morning . . .'

'You didn't encourage them, did you? Those people are piranhas, they'll end up ripping you apart.' He made it sound almost like an accusation.

'No, not my doing,' she responded, although she rather wished it were. 'My hands are clean.' She was about to suggest that at last he call her Ginny rather than Mrs Edge, but she was more than a little irritated by his attitude. She wasn't going to beg. And they were never likely to be friends. So, on second thoughts, 'Mrs Edge' would do nicely. 'But whether I like it or not, it seems the press are going to carry on comparing the two of us. I can't hide from it. And I don't trust the Downing Street spin machine. Look what the Prime Minister did with my wretched parking ticket.'

'So?'

'So we should get our retaliation in first. I think I can see a few chinks in her armour.'

For the first time, Blackstone seemed to be paying attention.

'I'm a housewife, Archie, she's not. I live among the chaos of kids. I fix their toys, iron their clothes, paint their rooms. I was painting Ben's room last week – the same day that *Hello!* magazine came out with all those photographs of Lauren Danderson in Downing Street. She'd just redecorated the White Drawing Room and was sitting on a sofa in front of the window.'

'I think I recall it.'

'You got any idea how much those curtains cost? Or the rest of the furnishings?'

'I haven't the slightest idea.'

'Of course not. But most women could take a pretty reasonable guess. Downing Street's practically bursting at the seams with designer names, half of them foreign and all of them clearly out of control. She's made the whole place look like an Italian tart's boudoir, and it'll have cost a small fortune. Heavens, I could have found a better use for seventy-five thousand pounds than spending it on drapes.'

'*How* much?' Blackstone spluttered.

'Well, I don't know the exact figure, do I? But we never will until someone asks.'

'So what are you suggesting?'

'I thought you might encourage someone to write about it. Ask how much all those new curtains and cushions and things have cost. Then make a bit of a fuss.'

'Sounds like dirty work.'

'That's why I brought it to you, Archie.'

He nodded slowly. 'The right place.'

'That parking ticket pushed me into the firing line. Not my choosing. And at the next election people are going to vote not simply for a government but for an image. As far as I'm concerned, Lauren Danderson is part of that image.'

'And you . . . ?'

It was her turn to nod at the pile of newspapers. 'So far so good.'

He stretched back in his chair, his hands locked behind his head. 'Sometimes, Mrs Edge, I hate my job. I got into politics to help build a better place for us all to live in. Sounds trivial and pathetic, I know, but that's the truth – or was the truth, at least. Nowadays all I seem to do is to wash dirty underwear.'

'You know, Archie, that sounds very much like my job, too, as a mother.'

He raised an eyebrow, recognising her point, but couldn't summon even the glimmer of a smile. 'It's taxpayers' money, a public issue. Fair game. I'll see what I can do.'

God, he was such a condescending prick. Ginny wanted to scream at the fellow, get some sort of reaction from him, turn him upside-down and shake off all the pathetic chips he carried on his shoulders. Instead she smiled and thanked him for his time. Then she walked out, with a piece of his precious jigsaw clenched tightly in her hand.

★

Ajok walked into the benefit office several minutes before the time set for her interview, but a line of people was waiting at the counter and service was slow. When at last she was able to speak to the receptionist, she gave her name and showed her the letter.

'You're late,' the receptionist said coldly.

'I have been waiting in line.'

'Well, you're going to have to wait some more,' the other woman responded. 'I'll find out if Mr Banerjee can still see you.'

It was a further twenty minutes before Ajok was ushered into a small, airless office with no windows and whose only furniture consisted of a cheap wooden table and four hard chairs. There appeared to be some electrical equipment on the table, and beside it sat a man with greying wavy hair and a complexion almost as dark as her own. He glanced up from the sheaf of papers he was reading. 'My name is Ravindra Banerjee,' he announced. 'You are?'

'My name is Ajok Arob.'

He consulted his notes. 'Yes. You are late. Please sit down, Mrs Arob.' His accent was clipped, precise, still with the whisper of the sub-continent. He took off his glasses to polish them and sighed; Ajok sat with her hands in her lap, waiting.

Banerjee turned to the equipment beside him. She could see now that it was a tape-recorder. 'It is my duty to inform you that we cannot say anything until such time as the recording has started,' he said. He broke the seals on two new tapes and placed them in the twin mouths of the machine, then pressed a button that made a red light gleam. It was all very mysterious to Ajok.

In a ponderous tone he announced the date and the time, then gave both his name and hers. Then he turned to Ajok. 'I am a counter-fraud officer, Mrs Arob. I must warn you that you are being interviewed under caution.' Then he read out the words of the caution, just like the police on television. For the first time, Ajok felt alarmed.

'Do you wish to be represented, Mrs Ajok? By a solicitor?'

'I have nothing to hide.'

'Then will you confirm your name and address for the record, please?'

She did so, and they began to move through a list of questions he had written down on paper, until he reached one about the people living at her address. The room was becoming stuffy.

'We have reason to believe that you are cohabiting with another adult whom you have failed to declare.'

'Then you are mistaken, sir.'

'We shall see about that.' He produced a photograph from his file. 'Do you recognise this man?'

'Yes. That is Malith Bulabek.'

'He lives with you.'

'He is a relative. He is staying with us. But only for a while.'

'For how long?'

'For about four months now, while he finds his own place to live. But it is so hard—'

'He is your partner?'

'No.'

'Then he is a lodger.'

'I suppose so.'

'Then why have you not declared his rental payments to us?'

'Mr Bulabek does not pay me rent. He is from my country, a distant member of my family, and—'

But Banerjee didn't appear interested in the Dinka traditions of hospitality. 'You expect me to believe this man has been living with you for four months and yet pays you nothing?'

'He pays me for food, and his washing.'

'Ah, so you do get an income from him.'

'He pays me only for what he uses.'

Banerjee snorted. 'You say he is a lodger. How many bedrooms are there in your apartment, Mrs Arob?'

'Two.'

'Precisely. So where does Mr Bulabek sleep?'

'In the spare room.'

'But you have two children.'

'Yes. Chol and Mijok. Two boys.'

'And where do you suppose they sleep, then?'

'With me. In my room.'

'They are . . .' he consulted his file '. . . nine and seven years of age. Are you expecting me to believe that your growing children sleep with you while your *guest* sleeps in their room? Doesn't that seem a little unlikely?'

'Sir, where I come from we do not have rooms for this and rooms for that. The whole family sleeps together.'

'But this is England, Mrs Arob. And I think you are not telling the truth. I believe that you are cohabiting with Mr Bulabek and are fraudulently claiming benefits as a single mother.'

'I am telling you the truth, sir.'

More photos. 'We have been watching your home. Seen Mr Bulabek leaving for work every morning. We know where he works, how much he earns, and his income should be taken into account in our calculations. But you have been hiding it from us.'

'No. I have nothing to hide.'

Banerjee leaned forward across the table, staring through his glasses. 'Mrs Arob, under Section 112 of the Social Security Administration Act 1992 it is an offence to fail to declare a change in your circumstances. It is a most serious offence. You could be prosecuted.'

'Mr Bulabek is not my partner,' she responded defiantly. 'He is merely a relative. Why do you need to know about him?'

'Because it is the law!' Banerjee declared, his voice rising in self-righteousness. 'And we take a very dim view of foreigners coming to our country and defrauding our welfare system.'

'But I am not. All I have ever wanted to do is to work for my family.'

'Yet I see you deliberately made yourself unemployed,' he exclaimed in triumph. 'Then you pursued your employer for compensation, a claim which was thrown out by the employment tribunal as being utterly worthless, and almost immediately Mr Bulabek came to live with you. I have to tell you that, rather than representing any desire on your part to work for your living, this looks, *prima facie*, like a cunningly conceived plan to defraud the state and live off false benefit claims, Mrs Arob. What do you have to say to that?'

But Ajok said nothing. A tear rolled down her cheek.

Banerjee thought he spotted weakness in it. He wanted to take advantage, and he shifted from being accuser to consoler. 'Look, many people make mistakes. They think there is an easy living to be made out there, and do not understand how wrong their actions can be. Help us clear this matter up, Mrs Arob. Make a clean breast of what has been going on and I can assure you that we shall be as lenient as we possibly can.'

Still she did not respond.

'No prosecution, no criminal record, no public shame. Wouldn't that be so very much better?'

Silence.

'Think of your children.'

'They are all I do think of, sir.'

He waited, but she said no more. Stubborn black bitch. He sighed again, and clenched his fists so firmly that the knuckles showed white.

'Mrs Arob, the government has made a commitment to crack down on benefit fraud. Zero tolerance. And I have come to the conclusion that you have committed an offence. You leave me no option but to send your papers for further consideration. That might result in you being cautioned, or fined, or even prosecuted.'

'I have done nothing.'

'And, in the meantime, your benefits will be reduced to take into account your new circumstances. There is more. Even if we don't prosecute, you will have to reimburse the benefit monies that you have already improperly claimed.'

'But I have nothing to pay with.'

'Of course you have. You have your legitimate benefit payments. We shall reclaim the overpayments from them before they are paid out to you.'

'But, sir, what shall I live on? How will I feed my children?'

'You seem to be a resourceful woman,' he snapped sarcastically. 'I'm sure you will find some way to manage. You have plenty of passion and time to pursue your former employers through the courts. Perhaps you should devote that energy to finding yourself a proper job.'

'But I ha—'

'You should remember, Mrs Arob, that people like you who try to take on the state do so at their peril.' He closed the file with a sound like a snapping bone. 'Perhaps you should think of that. Next time.'

Father Benedict had telephoned, asking her to call on him at school. He greeted her with a cup of tea, a shining pate and a mournful, serious face. 'I'm sorry to have to bother you, Mrs Edge, but it's a serious matter. Young Ben.'

'No need for apologies, Father. I'm always happy to see you.'

'Not today, I fear. For we must discuss the sorrowful subject of bullying.'

'I am very sorry to hear that.'

'Oh, but so am I, so am I,' he wailed, dunking a biscuit in his tea. 'At St Xavier's we take a most serious view of such matters.'

'Me, too.'

'It was always evident that the passage through our doors of the son of such a prominent political family might not be an easy one,' he wailed in his characteristically theatrical manner, 'but I fear it has become more complicated than ever I had dared think. It pains me deeply to tell you that I'm having to consider suspending young Benjamin.'

'What?' she exclaimed, in alarm.

'Just yesterday two of our boys had to be taken to the sanatorium with cuts and bruises. The injuries weren't particularly alarming, but that is scarcely the point. Both of them said the beating had been inflicted by Benjamin.'

'Have you talked to Ben?'

'I fear he doesn't deny it.'

'But have you *talked* to Ben? Found out the reason?'

'He seemed most uncooperative, I'm afraid.'

'And the two other boys?'

'Said that Benjamin had launched an unprovoked attack. We will not tolerate fisticuffs for any reason in St Xavier's, Mrs Edge.'

'I think I may know something about this, Father. These were bigger boys, were they? Larger than Ben?'

'As it happens, they were.'

'And, without any cause, you suppose that Ben simply had a go at them?'

'Well, it would seem that way.'

'Father Benedict, I think you'll find that those boys have been bullying Ben mercilessly for some time now. Interfering with his possessions and school books, getting him into trouble with teachers and even extorting his pocket money from him. The only reason I haven't complained to you earlier is that Ben begged me not to make a fuss. Said he would sort it out on his own.'

'But he cannot go round beating up his—'

Yet Ginny was at him, interrupting: 'I think what you mean to say is that he cannot go round being bullied without anyone lifting a finger to help him.'

'But I knew nothing of this.'

'It has been going on for some time, yet you knew nothing? Saw nothing? Said nothing?'

'Not a thing!' The monk sounded offended at the suggestion.

'Even though it was taking place right under the nose of the school?'

The headmaster began to bluster: 'But I cannot be expected to know everything.'

'I wonder how that will look in the newspapers.'

'What?'

'You suspend Ben and it will get into the newspapers. Bound to. Won't do a lot of good for the school, or for the staff. Particularly if it became clear that there's a history of extended bullying at St Xavier's.'

'But there has been no such thing!'

'In Ben's case, there would appear to have been precisely that thing.'

'But—'

'And, Father, I must tell you that I have no intention of sitting back and allowing my son to be blamed for things that are the fault of the school.'

'Mrs Edge, I beg you—' He was growing flustered, his cheeks glowing, his biscuit lost without trace beneath the surface of his tea.

'The matter would also have to go before the school's governors, of course. Even lawyers, perhaps. You know how these things are nowadays. More problems for everyone.'

But mostly for him, Father Benedict was beginning to realise.

Yet even as she watched the headmaster's resolve cracking, Ginny knew she would have to take care not to press him too far. She liked the school, so did Ben, and she had no intention of fouling his path by making an enemy of Father Benedict. So, at that point, Ginny burst into tears.

'Oh! Oh!' The monk rushed from behind his desk, burrowing for the handkerchief he kept tucked up his sleeve before waving it in surrender.

'I'm so sorry, Father,' she sobbed, dabbing her cheeks, 'but I know my son. He's been telling me the truth. Perhaps this is all my fault. I should have come to you earlier.'

'But you, of all people, are the most blameless,' he protested.

245

'Little Ben loves this school. I think he sees it rather like his temple. In his mind, I suspect he was doing no more than throwing out the usurers and money-changers.'

'My dear Mrs Edge, please allow me to reassure you,' Father Benedict responded, wringing his hands. 'It seems I may have misconstrued the entire situation. All this talk of newspapers. And governors . . . Oh, my, oh, my.' He patted at his heart as though it had failed on him. 'If you will allow me, I shall call all the boys in and get to the bottom of this matter. The very bottom. The transgressors must be suitably punished. And, bearing in mind what you have said, perhaps an apology from me to Ben might be in order.'

'And . . . no suspension?'

He threw his hands into the air. 'Perish the very thought.'

When she had allowed her tears to dry, he took her arm and walked her to the school gates. He thanked her profusely not only for her visit but also for her understanding. 'We do try so hard to teach them the traditional values at St Xavier's,' he sang.

'That's one of the reasons I was so keen to send the children here, Father,' she replied. 'In fact, I have a website. I might even use that as a theme for my next blog. The enduring strength of traditional values.'

'Splendid! Splendid! Melding the messages of the ancients with the technologies of the Internet age. What a special lady you are, Mrs Edge. Although I'm afraid I shan't see it.' He giggled. 'Haven't quite caught up with websites and all those bloggie things. But it sounds splendid. Absolutely splendid!'

'I'll try not to disappoint you.'

'And as for little Ben . . . Well, I think he's shown considerable strength of character. If only we can persuade him that he should leave the punishment of the money-changers to Our Lord – or, at least, His representatives here at St Xavier's – I predict a very bright future for him. Why, in a couple of years, I could well imagine young Ben as our head boy.'

Ginny smiled all the way home. She was still smiling when she sat down to write the latest epistle for her website, about the dilemmas that all mothers face in guiding their children.

It's all very well telling our children to turn the other cheek. But sometimes that's just plain gooey and wrong. It's a horrid world out there that often isn't kind to signs of weakness and doesn't value good intentions. Sometimes the only cheek our kids should turn is the one that's about to sit down and squash flat those miserable wretches who try to take advantage of them. And that is, perhaps, the most traditional value of all.

★

A scrum of staff stood round Max Morgan's desk, listening attentively while he raised his voice for the benefit of the speakerphone.

'Let's put it this way, Your Honour, just between you and me. Man to man. This young lady suggests she knows just how you like your eggs for breakfast. And she backs this up with photographs of you in a dressing-gown on a balcony overlooking the sea somewhere very hot and very far away. You don't appear to be wearing your judicial wig.'

A strangled cry sprang from the speakerphone.

'She also says you're the nostalgic type. That you enjoy revisiting the places and positions of your childhood.' His lips twisted into a mirthless grin. 'No, not Eton, Your Honour. What she had in mind was your predilection for being – do you mind if I quote from her copy? – buck-naked, breastfed and beaten on your arse by a woman in a nanny's uniform.'

The distant cries grew louder.

'I was just wondering if that's what you meant when you talked about the need for higher standards of integrity in public life. Do you remember? You must do. When you sent down one of my journalists for two months for refusing to reveal her source for those leaked Cabinet documents?'

At the other end the man appeared to be stumbling between a plea for mercy and a question about the possibilities of a deal.

'Well, in normal circumstances I'd always be willing to consider a trade. Giving you back the photographs in exchange for a better story. In your exalted case, Your Honour, that would mean at very least a Cabinet minister or senior member of the Royal Family. But although I thought you were a totally despicable shit for locking up my girl for doing nothing that Downing Street doesn't do on a regular basis, I was very taken by your summing-up in the case. All that moral righteousness. Real wig-trembling stuff. So I think, in your case, I'm going to make an exception. The front page is all yours.'

A string of threats emerged from the loudspeaker.

Max quickly interrupted: 'Well, Your Honour, you'd better get a move on, because we print in . . .' he consulted his wristwatch '. . . three hours. My lawyers are standing by. And, if it helps, they're smirking. Oh, but can I check one fact? You know how the *Record* struggles to get every detail correct. Is it true that you wear maternity tights beneath your judicial gown?'

A very crude curse flew round the room.

'And may I quote you on that, Your Honour?' But already the line had gone dead.

Max sat silently for a while, fingers steepled, as though in a distant and not very pleasing place. 'And let the word go out,' he said softly. 'You screw with the *Record* and you'll have the rest of eternity to regret it.'

A young female journalist came from the other side of the desk and kissed his forehead tenderly. 'Thank you, darling Max.' Tears were glistening on her cheek.

'Enough already,' he protested. 'Back to work. You can't spend your bloody expenses standing in my office.' The tide of bodies in front of him dispersed, revealing Ginny standing at his door. 'You heard all that?'

'Enough to remember never to screw with you, Max.'

'But you are, you are,' he shouted, snapping back into character-istic form. 'What's all this in the sodding *Mirror*?' He scrabbled among the papers on his desk and dragged out a crumpled copy of his rival. Its headline read: 'Curtains For Clumsy Lauren'. 'She's getting roasted for laying out – hell, I can't believe even she could spend so much on bloody curtains! A hundred and twenty grand? A thousand each just for the tiebacks? And you gave the enemy this simpering exclusive interview!'

'I thought it was a rather fine piece.'

'You might as well have taken out a stiletto and stabbed the bloody woman straight in her pelmets. You mugged her. All that bollocks about how you thought it wrong to indulge personal tastes with taxpayers' money. About how when you get to Downing Street you'll remember that it's leasehold not freehold. There to serve, not to squander.'

'Enough clichés, do you think?'

'And then that bit – did those bastards at the *Mirror* think that up? – that the only change you might want to make is to create a nursery room, if you needed it. And perhaps a slightly larger wardrobe. Wicked stuff.'

'Thank you.'

'So why the hell did you give it to the competition?' he demanded, throwing the offending paper into a corner.

'Because they asked for it.' And because, Max, you're not the only editor in town, and you need to remember that.

'I thought we had a special relationship.'

'Of course we do, Max. It's simply not an exclusive one.'

'It's a dog-eat-dog world, Ginny. I don't like it when you climb into someone else's kennel.'

'Just visiting, Max. Anyway, I've brought an even juicier bone for you.'

'My ears are cocked.'

'Lauren Danderson isn't simply in hot water in Downing Street. She's also got a little local difficulty up the road. Up the Mall,

Michael Dobbs

actually, at the Palace. Her republican tendencies getting the better of her manners. Cancelling appointments at the last minute. Turning her back on the Queen. Apparently at Balmoral last autumn she not only insisted on her bedroom being changed but left the dinner table for a cigarette break. I'm told it's been going down in Buck House like a case of cheap gin.'

'Mmm. We keep hearing mutterings, of course, nothing new in that. But you can stand this up?'

'I can give you times, places, even the brand of tobacco. Enough for you to make your own enquiries.'

'How high up the Royal Family do your sources go, Ginny?'

'Really, Max, I'm surprised at you. Expecting a girl to reveal her sources.'

'*Touché.*'

'You know there's a state banquet next week.'

'The President of Bananaland or some other tinpot dictator with an oil pipe running through his plantation.'

'She's been trying to interfere with the place settings. Very fussy about who she has to look at. Throwing a proper hissy fit. Causing all sorts of complications.'

'You serious? Fantastic! Why the hell didn't our royal correspondent get that? Useless bugger should be fired. You sure you don't want to share your source with me?'

No, she had no intention of sharing either Bobby or his Palace detective friend with the likes of Max. 'I'm sure you've got enough pageboys and pauper princesses on your payroll to do all the checking you need, Max.'

'Perhaps give one of them a camera. Grab a picture of Ms Pushy sneaking a quick cigarette,' he enthused, already dreaming up his front page.

'We friends again?'

'Best of.'

'Good.' She turned to leave. 'Oh, there's one other thing, Max. I suppose you'll be going to Lauren for a quote, to get her side of things.'

'Of course.'

'When you do, let her know you got this from me, will you?'

'But that'll mean the biggest cat-fight in Christendom!' he protested.

He thought he saw her smiling as she left the room.

The System took Ajok to yet another building for her appeal. It was on the Victoria Embankment near Blackfriars Bridge where, in earlier centuries, they had stapled criminals so they would be drowned by the rising tide. The employment appeal tribunal was grander than the first place she had been, a proper court, with a large heraldic shield of a lion and unicorn behind the judge's chair, dark curtains, wood panelling and more comfortable seating. There was even a robed usher to give formal order to the proceedings. 'Court rise!' he bellowed. British justice, although the usher's accent appeared to come from somewhere in the Caribbean.

Patrick Creasey had been waiting for her at the entrance, his broad face smiling in greeting, taking her hand, wishing her well, but he wouldn't come inside. He was there only in a private capacity. The union had deserted her, run away with their money, and officially she was on her own. Other things had also changed from the earlier tribunal. She was no longer a claimant but the appellant, and she was not allowed to speak. Her words were delivered for her by Sophie Gaminara, in formal black suit and white blouse, and there were, oh, so many words, often unintelligible, but this time no one took any trouble to make sure she understood them. Lots of discussion about acts and sections, subsections and paragraphs, of treaties, conventions, sources and authorities. As the deliberations continued, Ajok noticed Sophie's hands tightening on the lectern that held her notes. The meniscus on the water jug beside her began very gently to tremble. It reminded Ajok of the fishing-pool in her village, as the thunder clouds gathered, just before it started to pour.

As there had been at the earlier tribunal, there were three middle-aged people sitting to decide her fate; this time one was a woman. Sophie had warned her not to expect too much from them, and she had not deceived. This was neither a place of imagination nor of intellectual risk, but of caution and precedent. Ajok's appeal was to be heard not on the merits of her case but on a point of law, and in essence it was a simple one. Her case, as it was constructed in Sophie's hands, was that the war in Iraq was illegal, had been from its inception and therefore continued to be so. It followed from this premise that the instructions given to Ajok to clean the room were unreasonable and that therefore her dismissal was unfair.

It was a premise that had been tested under different guises many times before, in military courts-martial, through convictions for non-payment of income taxes, and with appeals against sentences for unlawful demonstration. Not once had those who pursued the point succeeded, for some other matter was always interposed, so that no court ever got round to considering the legality of the war on its merits. It turned out that this wasn't a narrow point at all but one that was as broad as civilisation itself, and those sorts of judgements were always the responsibility of somebody else. The problem was passed on, shuffled away, and the three people who sat in judgement that day on Ajok were no different.

They seemed more interested in reminding her that costs might be awarded against any appellant who appeared frivolous. And, no, they didn't want to spend the day considering the circumstances of events that might have happened thousands of miles away in some desert: their brief was to deal with matters that had taken place in the corridors only a little further up the river, in Whitehall. Of course Ajok was entitled to her conscience, but since when did a conscience clean a mucky room? They sat, they listened, their intellects yawned and creaked. This was not a matter for them.

These were people who had their positions in life, good and worthy citizens who knew that rocking the boat might swamp the seats they had toiled so hard to secure in it. They were not the sort to brand their leaders liars.

So they threw out Ajok's appeal.

Iraq. Where so much of it had started and where all roads now led. It was an ancient place, an empire built around the great rivers Tigris and Euphrates, the lands of Mesopotamia, of Babylonia and Assyria, of Sumerians and Semites and Sunnis and Shi'ites and Kurds, a place that had been occupied in turn by Persians and Greeks and Turks, and now the British, beneath the wing of their American allies.

A land of antiquity, of occupation – and of oil. That was why the British kept coming back. They had invaded in the 1920s, in the 1940s, yet again in the 1990s. The first time round an exasperated Winston Churchill had called the place 'an ungrateful volcano' and had forecast that any government would gain popularity by ordering an instant evacuation. But no one had learned. And now they were back once more. Couldn't keep their hands off it. The British didn't like the land, didn't love its people. Most Britons knew little about it and had trouble locating it precisely on a map. But they needed the oil.

It had also become a matter of pride, of self-justification. Many years before, Britain had been mocked by a US leader for having lost an empire and failed to discover a role. When asked to comment on British armed forces another American, a general, had showered them with ironic praise for the excellence of their marching bands. Iraq had been meant to put an end to that. Britain was supposed to be 'a player' once more, but Iraq had proved to be a leap too far. And now, just as Churchill had complained almost ninety years earlier, the time had come to pay the bill.

It was intended to have been a quick 'in and out', a teenage frolic, not a matter that was to dog men into their old age. Mission accomplished, but then mission capsized. Iraq had the persistence of a tapeworm that sapped both the energies and intellects of all those involved, and as the country descended into fratricide, the occupying forces circled their wagons and withdrew into tight, highly fortified areas. The Kurds held the north while the Americans still squatted in the capital, Baghdad, but it had become the capital of nothing but a faded dream. The country was at war with itself, a pit of blood and butchery, and had been that way for years.

The British were based in the south, near some of the important oil installations, under growing pressure, which was why, with the help of the Moonraker corporation, they were building a fortified command centre in Basra, complete with its own water supply, power and waste disposal, heli-pads, even a hospital. It was an island of self-sufficiency in a storm-tossed sea, but even islands may be overwhelmed. So they had been forced to send more troops to guard the citadel and the other vital installations. They weren't combat troops, of course – Parliament had been assured on that point: to admit that they were would be to imply failure, and the British government didn't do failure, so they were described instead as technicians and advisers. Peace-keepers. But there was no peace. So their numbers were increasing, which meant, in simple terms, that more of them were going to die.

Soldiers fight, soldiers die, and if the hostilities in Iraq still gave rise to a trickle of British casualties it scarcely delayed the public in their onward rush to the sports page. The grainy photographs of men in military uniform had become commonplace and no longer excited interest in the media. Iraq wasn't sexy, it wasn't circulation. It was a place very far away about which the British knew little, and would prefer to know even less.

Until the plane crash.

When the Hercules C-130 transport plane was blown out of the sky a few miles outside Basra, it wasn't the first aircraft of its kind to be lost, and it wasn't the first time that everyone on board had been killed, although with thirty-four dead it was the biggest loss of British life in a single incident in the whole of the war. The bodies were returned home, the coffins draped in the Union flag and handled with all the reverence that the British military could muster, even though no one knew for sure whether the scrapings inside the coffins matched the names on the lids. What made this one different, apart from its size, was that most of the victims were women – nurses, doctors and physiotherapists, members of a mixed regular and Territorial Army medical unit. And what made it worse was that, apart from the three-man crew, the rest of the victims had been journalists. Now the media had what they had been denied for so long, a story from Iraq that involved sex and their own acute self-interest. They had something new. This one was big. So big, in fact, that it took over the imagination of the nation that weekend, grabbed it like a terrier and kept shaking it as if it were the last story on earth.

The Downing Street machine, in its well-oiled manner, immediately came up with the usual helping of homilies, a fulsome expression of regret that praised those aboard the plane as heroes and insisted that their loss of life would not be in vain. The Prime Minister himself would be there, representing the nation, when the coffins came back to RAF Brize Norton. No grand public funerals, though, no gathering of the good and the great to pay respects. That would involve too much media focus, set too many precedents. Better not to drag the thing out. Turn up at the airfield, bow the head, appear serious, then let it slip away, like all the others. It had worked before. But Dom didn't see it that way. In fact, he could scarcely see anything at all. In contrast to the carefully brewed plans that emerged from Downing Street, the crisis threw him into a panic of indecision. He hated this war, wanted to wean his party away from it, but too many of its senior members had form on it, had backed it too long and too hard to wriggle out of it without a struggle.

'I can't do it, not now,' he told Ginny, as he peered through the curtains at the camera crews parked outside on the pavement, waiting for a response. 'The whole country's in mourning. It's a national tragedy. I can't start playing party politics when the bodies aren't yet cold.'

'You think it will be easier when they are?'

'No, but . . .'

'You loathe this war, Dom. You've never said a good thing about it and you never will.'

'But there's a time and a place. Best right now to keep my powder dry.'

'An unfortunate metaphor, in the circumstances.'

'So what do you suggest I do?' he snapped in frustration, his indecision making him tetchy as he glanced once more in the direction of the newsmen gathered outside. He couldn't keep them waiting for ever.

'Be honest.'

'But how?'

She studied him as if she were sending him off for his first day at a new school. 'You need your best suit. A white shirt and a sober tie – perhaps the burgundy number from Ede & Ravenscroft I got you for Christmas. This isn't a moment for sweaters and baseball caps. And drag Bobby out of his room. You'll need him.'

'Why, for Heaven's sake?'

'Don't be a muppet, Dom. He's useful colour. A useful creed. Gives you street cred.'

'I thought this was a little more important than simply chasing an image,' he responded, his teeth clenched.

'Now you're being silly. You go upstairs and change while I call Archie.'

'So how's bloody Archie going to help, in God's name?'

'That's precisely the point. We should let God tell us . . .'

A little later, kitted out like a statesman in fresh shirt and furrowed brow, Dom came on to the doorstep to explain to the press pack that he was going to church. Wanted to pray for the families of the dead, to meditate on what had happened. No, not to ask for guidance – there were already too many impostors in this war who claimed divine authority – but to seek inspiration. Then Dom walked to St Xavier's. He was in no rush, and when he got there he spent a good hour inside, mostly on his knees. The press had a fine view through the open door of the church, shafts of solid sunlight pouring through the stained-glass window, like a bridge that stretched all the way to Heaven, giving them some wonderfully atmospheric shots.

It was towards the end of that time that Ginny arrived to be with him. Sat down beside him in the pew, held his hand, talked softly to him for many minutes. Then Archie and Bobby appeared, joined in the exchange, heads bent, talking earnestly, much to the growing interest of the men from the media. When, finally, Dom walked into the daylight outside St Xavier's, his expression was carved in sadness but his eye held a defiant glint for the cameras. Some were carrying it live.

In the doorway of the church, framed by its elegant arch, Dom found stirring words to colour the day. His heart went out to the families, he told them, his thoughts to his duty, his prayers to everyone concerned. 'For me, these latest events mark a turning-point. I never want to have to look another father or mother in the eye and tell them of my regret for the loss of their son – least of all their daughter. Regrets are easy, responsibility weighs more heavily. We have shed enough tears, given enough blood for that faraway land. We have done our duty, and more of it than anyone had a right to expect.' He paused, his voice sombre, his words slow. 'But now it's time to bring our boys and girls home.'

He would say no more: he had colleagues to consult, perhaps some to persuade; it wasn't yet party policy, only his personal preference. Everyone needed time to reflect. But he would ask the Prime Minister to hold a full-scale debate in a few days' time, a request that the Prime Minister was in no position to refuse, not with newspaper headlines screaming about the death of so many angels.

To the millions of viewers who would watch him later that day, he seemed sincere, reflective, inspired. And it matched the mood of the nation. But Dom already knew that. It was all very well seeking divine guidance, but while he had been on his knees, Ginny and Archie had decided to seek a little additional instruction – from the voters. During the previous tempestuous hour, the party's opinion researchers had been running an instant telephone poll. It couldn't hope to be entirely authoritative or analytical, there hadn't been enough time, but by the grace of God and Dr Gallup the message was coming through with celestial clarity. The voters wanted out, more so than ever. And Dominic Edge was the man to give them what they wanted.

Over the next few days he would receive sackfuls of letters from the public. Most were written in praise and gratitude, but more than a few criticised him, denouncing him in evangelical tones for dragging politics and, even worse, a Muslim such as Bobby into the church. Father Benedict was incensed by the criticism. St Xavier's had never been so much in the spotlight, and it had been a long time since he'd had so much fun. The good Father insisted on answering all the letters of condemnation himself. A previous Prime Minister had argued that God had got us into this war, Father Benedict wrote, so it was only meet and proper that we should ask the Almighty to help us find a way out.

Twelve

LAUREN DANDERSON WAS HAVING a miserable day in what had turned out to be the most wretched of weeks. All that fuss about the bloody curtains, then several Scandinavian forests decimated to print more nonsense about her relationship with the Royal Family. Did they never bother to find the facts before they went out and distorted them? It had been wearing but she had kept her nerve, even when the Americans had started questioning whether all this was suitable background music for her proposed lecture tour. She wasn't going to change just for them. But this morning's editions had stretched even the febrile imaginations of the media to snapping point. Not content with allegations that she took home the soap from the Palace toilets, they'd accused her of selling tickets to Buckingham Palace garden parties. Ridiculous! Even she wouldn't stoop that low and, frankly, she had damn few friends who would even want to go. Most of them were like her, from the other side of the tracks, and had no desire to get their hands dirty scrabbling over them. Lauren had never been strong on deference: you don't learn respect being babysat by a television that kept going bling when the shilling in the meter ran out. Her teenage years had been spent as a punk in an age when you could get away with almost anything, as long as at least three people were involved and there were witnesses. But those days had disappeared the moment she set foot in Downing Street.

There was no respite. This evening she was back on dinner duty at the Palace. She'd tried to wriggle out of it, claim a headache and hot flushes, but Freddie hadn't believed her and insisted that she look the enemy in the eye. The headache had been tactical, of course, but the hot flushes . . . Still, she had to go. 'For every rainbow, there's always a little rain,' Freddie had declaimed. And for every curtain, a few loose threads. So she'd climbed into her evening dress, then into the car, but even there she found no salvation. As they drove out of Downing Street, slowing to pass through the heavy iron gates, she saw a woman with the blackest of faces and startling, angry eyes screaming at her. It was difficult to tell what she was saying through armoured windows an inch thick, but it was something about the war being Freddie's war, not her war. She appeared to be very agitated, and she had a remarkable fan-shaped tattoo on her face. Even as Lauren watched, a police-man began to hustle the woman away – she was likely to be arrested, but that was scarcely the point. She might have been a terrorist, might even have had a weapon. The new legislation was supposed to have put an end to all this nonsense, but once again something had gone wrong. Useless bloody police. They had new powers that would have made Mussolini sag in awe, yet still weren't up to the job. Damn it, Downing Street was Lauren's home, and she didn't care for demonstrators camping on her lawn.

A copy of the *Evening Standard* lay on the seat between them, glaring at her. Deep inside, something unpleasant twisted in Lauren and another prickling flush of irritation ran across her skin. Ginny Edge had given an interview about – what else? – the Royal Family, rambling on about her admiration for the Queen. As she read on, the paper began to shake in Lauren's hand. 'Have you seen this bullshit, Freddie?'

'What's that, dear?' he answered distractedly.

'Edge's wife. Going on about how she respects the Queen not simply as a symbol of the state but as an inspiration to all women. Shows that a woman can do practically anything a man can, she says.' Lauren throttled the newspaper in disgust until it was completely lifeless. 'She has a big mouth on her for such an irrelevant little bitch.'

'You're being very harsh.'

'She's been whipping up all this poison about me and the monarchy, you know.'

'Does one whip up poison? I thought . . . cappuccino. Anyway, you may have started a little of it yourself, up at Balmoral,' he admonished.

'But she's leaking it all.'

'You can't prove that.'

'Everyone tells me.'

'"Everyone" told me I'd never become Prime Minister,' he muttered disinterestedly. A phone call came to his rescue.

Lauren remained silent and more than a little sullen as they drove up the Mall, bedecked with colourful flags hoisted on elaborate poles for the state visit. She tried to cheer herself up by imagining herself with a magical axe, chopping them all to the ground, then moving on to Ginny Edge. True to her punk traditions, Lauren Danderson might have pretended she wasn't affected by the many comparisons that were appearing about herself and that bloody woman, but they were cruel and, in spite of her best intentions and regular reflexology, a coil of bitterness was tightening inside her. It was beginning to hurt terribly, the comment about the Downing Street nursery most of all. It had been little more than a solitary line, but it had had the cutting edge of broken glass. She'd never had children, it had already disfigured her life; now the curse had returned. And she'd come to hate Ginny Edge for it.

Yet there she was. As Lauren entered the crowded Picture Gallery, amid all the gilded splashes of the Canalettos, Rubens and Rembrandts, Ginny came clearly into view, holding court in the middle of a group of elderly and ridiculously overdressed men. Even as Lauren greeted those around her, their eyes met. Ginny smiled, was making her way through the throng towards her, looking so fresh, so youthful, so disgustingly fertile!

'Hello, we've never really had a chance to meet,' Ginny said, holding out her hand.

'No, we haven't.' As Lauren was forced to take the other woman's hand she felt as though something inside her had burst, like a dam.

'I'm so sorry there's all this nonsense in the press about the two of us, Lauren – may I call you Lauren?' Ginny was holding on to the other woman, wouldn't let her go. 'I'm sure you hate it as much as I do.'

'I'm sure you do, Mrs Edge.'

'Ginny. I'm Ginny. Perhaps we should show those miserable men of the press how wrong they are. Have a girls' afternoon out and get to know each other better. Go shopping. Choose a couple of new dresses.'

'I won't be needing that, thank you.'

Ginny bent closer, as though to exchange a confidence. 'But those old shoulder pads of yours look about as comfortable as a set of gynaecological stirrups. Time to get you out of them.' She leaned closer still. 'And don't worry about the curtains. I'll make sure they find a good home.'

Curtains. Kids. Physical contact with a woman she loathed. It was all too much for Lauren. The burst dam was sweeping all before it. She let forth a piercing cry. 'You poisonous bloody bitch!' She wasn't very good at impromptu insult, but at least she was loud – loud enough for many people to hear and with more than sufficient power to reach every front page. 'You Edges are vermin!' she added, to the delight of all headline writers, before fleeing as far as possible from the woman who was tormenting her.

In the game of the two halves, Lauren Danderson had just scored a massive own-goal.

In their commentaries historians tend to rely on the things they can touch and rationalise to explain the actions of the players – dates, statistics, social trends, published manifestos, speeches. They prefer rational argument to emotion and find little room for shades of grey on their spectrum, yet political life is rarely that simple. It's difficult to take into account the impact of raw emotion: the inconsistencies, the jealousies, the changes of mind, the outbursts of overwhelming hubris and even the occasional flash of insanity. A Prime Minister is supposed to hold all the reins in his hands, to know where he's headed, but all too often the reins end up wrapping him in the most almighty knots.

Freddie Danderson wished very much that he had got out of Iraq the day he had become Prime Minister and taken all the cheap popularity that would have brought. But he hadn't. He'd ducked it, had too much else to deal with. Delayed, dithered, kept on declaring that we would stay until the job was finished. Or until we'd run out of troops to send, but he didn't say that, of course. He'd only become Prime Minister by accident, after all the other much more fancied contenders had pulled each other down in their furious scramble up the slippery pole, leaving Freddie Danderson as the one they hated least. His position had been weak, he had needed to bring others with him, so it hadn't been the time to overturn years of established policy and declare Iraq to have been a disastrous bloody cock-up. Instead, he'd gone with the flow. Easiest thing to do. He didn't have the freedom that belongs to a Leader of the Opposition, like Dom Edge, damn him, to make it up as he went along.

Iraq wasn't the only life-or-death decision he'd had to make, of course. There had been so many others: the health service, law and order, pensions, even transport. It was the price of living behind the most famous door in the land. Every tick on the paper or squiggle in the margin meant that someone out there would find their lives rescued, while others would be totally destroyed. He still retained a smile for the cameras on his doorstep, but on occasion, and increasingly, he found it getting to him. Like acid dripping on his emotions. He was waking at five every morning after a fitful night's sleep, wondering how yesterday could have been so difficult and worrying about what struggles the new day would bring. The occasions that used to thrill him, like Prime Minister's Questions, press conferences, even those earth-shaking papers that lurked at the top of his ministerial box, now left him covered with sweat. Yet the decision that preoccupied him above all others, and more than a little to his private shame, was that of the election.

Freddie Danderson had been elected by no one outside the narrow caucus of party zealots, and even then with some reluctance. He wasn't the People's Prime Minister, not yet at least, but the time would come when he had to put himself to the test of a general election. He'd thought about holding a snap poll almost as soon as he'd set foot in Downing Street, to give him real authority, but he'd ducked that decision, too. He might have lost, gone down in history as a footnote, Prime Minister for only a few weeks, the People's Poodle. And the gnawing insecurity about the next election kept growing within him, as it does with all Prime Ministers.

He had much going for him. He was in good shape, enjoyed a healthy lead in the opinion polls, not so large as it had once been, to be sure – Dom Edge was getting better at his job – but enough to see him comfortably home at an election. And although this Iraq thing was a nuisance, it hadn't much affected previous elections. On the other hand, it was going to get worse, no doubt about it. There was no solution in Iraq, so at some point the British would have to cut and run. Not a great way for a Prime Minister to appeal for a new mandate, bowed down in submission, with Dom Edge throwing cabbages from the wings. Better leave it until after the election – which suggested he should get the damned thing over sooner rather than later. Stifle all the muttering that was growing on the backbenches. Stamp his authority on the whole bloody lot of them.

There was another consideration that weighed heavily on him, and which also forced his mind towards an early poll. Lauren. She was taking it all to heart, the incessant pressure, the unfair criticism, their life in a goldfish bowl, and being mightily menopausal didn't help. She'd made a fool of herself at the Palace, which had required grovelling letters of apology, but it hadn't been the first time and was unlikely to be the last. If only she'd had some distractions in her life. If only she'd had children. But that had been his problem, his fault, a stupid disease he'd picked up while doing volunteer work in the Gambia, like so many other young kids. He hadn't even known about it until much later when he discovered he was infertile. Yet, despite it all, she'd stuck with him loyally, through marriage and his career, when other lesser women would have found alternatives. And he repaid the loyalty unquestioningly, even to a fault, and certainly enough to see her through a set of dodgy curtains.

But he had to find some way of taking the pressure off her. And an early election might do just that. Get it over and done with, stop him tossing and turning every night in bed, help him smile for her once more. He loved her, and he owed her. Lauren's difficulties weren't a decisive consideration, not one of those that historians would ever get their teeth into, but it was important. It preyed on his mind, and more so with every day that passed.

Ajok hadn't intended to scream at the Prime Minister's car, and she certainly hadn't intended to get herself into a stand-off with the police. Her life had taken so many unexpected turns.

She'd gone to Whitehall to call on Paddy Creasey in his pub. All her efforts at finding another job had failed; she wondered whether he could help. Perhaps another cleaner's post in Whitehall. But it was getting ever more difficult, he'd explained. Too much cheap labour coming in from places like Poland and Lithuania. Too much competition. And too many questions over her record. Anxious to help, he suggested he might find her a cleaning job at the union's headquarters, but there was no night bus service to that part of town so . . . he was very sorry.

The Admiral Lord Nelson was only a little way from Downing Street. After she had left Paddy Creasey, it had been nothing more than coincidence that she'd been passing just as the Prime

Minister's car was driving out, and no more than a rush of frustration that had caused her to shout. Nothing but a few angry words. Nothing, nothing! Yet an armed policeman grabbed her, wrestled her away and pinned her to a wall. Started shouting at her about something called a Serious Organised Crime Act. Ajok Arob, a criminal! They were the ones who weren't being serious. She asked them to stop manhandling her, she was polite, but thoroughly determined, even when they began to talk roughly to her about the threat of terrorism. She shook her head in disbelief. She knew what terrorism was like; it wasn't like this. What had happened to these brave British people that they should manhandle a woman and threaten her for shouting? Not even a drunken Dinka husband would do such things. They took down the details of her name and address. Warned her. Kept her pinned against the wall until they had finished. Many people, passers-by, were staring at her. This was indeed a strange land. But, in the end, they let her go.

A few days later she was preparing the evening meal and waiting for the children to return from school when she heard a knock at her door. Two men. They weren't wearing uniform but introduced themselves as police. She didn't catch their names. She invited them in and offered them tea, which they declined. Wouldn't even take off their ski-jackets. It wasn't a social visit, they explained; they didn't even bother to sit down. Instead they wandered round the room, almost as if they were taking charge of it, filling up her small home.

'Mrs Arob,' the first policeman started, 'you're becoming a bit of a problem, aren't you?'

'I hope not. I haven't done anything wrong.'

'You just attacked the Prime Minister.'

'I shouted at the Prime Minister's car. I didn't know it was against the law to shout at the Prime Minister. They do that all the time in Parliament.'

'But that's their job, Mrs Arob, not yours.'

'I don't have a job,' she said bitterly.

'Yes, we know. Causing all sorts of trouble, you are.' He scratched at his short-cropped hair.

'And fiddling your benefits,' the other man, leaner and taller than the first, jumped in, breaking off from his examination of the tiny kitchen area.

'That's not true,' she protested. She didn't know these men, didn't like them, but they seemed to know too much about her and she began to be a little afraid. She held a cushion to her, squeezing it for comfort.

'That's what they all say, Mrs Arob, even as they drag them down to the cells. We know what you did. And just because we haven't decided to prosecute doesn't mean we won't change our mind.'

'You see, Mrs Arob,' Stubble Head joined in again, 'we don't much like your sort. Coming to this country and taking advantage of us. Grabbing everything we offer and throwing it back in our face.' He was looking at a photograph of the boys that hung on the wall, peering at it closely, frowning.

'But I—'

'We've given you everything. A job. A roof over your head. Schooling for the boys, Chol and little Mijok.' He recounted their names as he held the photograph in his gloved hand, running a finger across their faces. 'They've been getting on so well at school. Pity if that was to get all messed up.'

'Why should it be?'

'No reason, not if you behave yourself. But carry on causing difficulties for everyone and there's no telling where it might stop. The council won't be very happy to hear that one of their tenants has been busy racking up a criminal record. They take a very dim view of troublemakers. Like to get rid of them.' He sucked at his teeth; there was a prominent gap in the middle. 'Then what would your boys do?'

'I am not a troublemaker,' she said softly, but insistently.

'What? Screaming in public at the Prime Minister. Taking the government to court. That's troublemaking if ever I saw it.'

'I only want my job back,' Ajok said.

'Strangest way of getting a job back I ever did see,' he said, scratching away at his head once more.

'You know, Mrs Arob,' Lean Man interjected. 'You're here in this country as a guest. A refugee. You came here saying you were fleeing from trouble, yet all you've done since you arrived is to make more of it.'

'Not a clever thing to do,' his partner added, shaking his head.

'You carry on like this and someone's going to decide to look at your status as a refugee. See whether you've broken too many rules. Decide whether you should be sent back.'

'They couldn't!'

Stubble Head smiled, cruelly.

'I have nothing to go back to,' she said in a whisper.

'Right. They tell me it's tough in Sudan. Getting tougher every day. Particularly for kids.'

She felt she was about to cry; instead she squeezed the cushion so hard that her nails dug into the flesh of her arm. Lean Man had disappeared to the bedrooms; she no longer had the strength to object. He came out of Malith's room, his face expressing a measure of surprise, and nodding towards his partner.

'Look, Mrs Arob, we've come here for a friendly visit. No need to get upset. But a word of advice. You're getting yourself into deep water – far deeper than perhaps you realise. Don't. You and the kids want to go on living here. That's fine by us. So long as you stay out of trouble. Might even be able to get some of your benefits restored – looks like there could even have been a bit of a mix-up over the bedrooms and the lodger. So, what do you say?'

'I would like you to leave.'

'You go on being unfriendly, Mrs Arob, and you'll prove to everyone that you're nothing but a politically motivated bloody nuisance. Pardon my language.'

'I am what you have made me.'

'Very unfriendly, wouldn't you say so?'

'No doubt about it,' Lean Man replied.

'Do I have the right to ask you to leave?' Ajok asked.

'You want us to leave? Well, let me tell you, there are plenty in this country as want you to leave, too, Mrs Arob. Remember that.' As Stubble Head spoke, the photograph of the boys fell from his hands and smashed on the floor. 'Oh dear. Clumsy of me. Would you like me to clear the mess up?'

'Leave. Just leave.'

When they did so, she began to tremble, as she had that day on the riverbank after the Baggarans had left. She was shaking so badly that she had considerable difficulty in clearing up the broken glass from the floor. In her village, women were possessions, something to be bought and sold, sometimes for many head of cattle. A man who had many daughters could become rich. But that was the point: in Dinka society women had real value. Yet these two men had treated her as though she were utterly worthless.

Later that evening, after the boys had gone to bed and Malith was watching television, she sat down at the table, pulled a page from Chol's lined exercise book and, with great care and in the format she had been taught at ESOL, she wrote a letter. It was the first she had ever written entirely by herself. Her handwriting was rudimentary and her grammar left something to be desired, but she was persistent. In her letter she insisted that she was not a troublemaker and that she had never wished to cause offence. She asked only that she be given back her job so that she could take proper care of her children. She wrote it out in her neatest hand, reread the whole thing twice, then posted it to Mr Alfred Danderson at Downing Street.

When it arrived, it was opened by a clerk in the basement. As soon as he had seen the makeshift writing-paper and unsteady hand, he put it, unread, on to the pile marked 'Nutters'.

Ajok's letter never received a reply.

★

Freddie Danderson looked out through the mullioned windows of the bedroom. Dawn was still nothing more than a hint of smudged grey on the Buckinghamshire horizon. Five o'-bloody-clock. He wouldn't get back to sleep, never did. The bed was uncomfortable, they wouldn't use it again, but that wasn't why he couldn't sleep, of course.

He and Lauren had taken to sleeping in many different rooms at Chequers, the Prime Minister's country retreat. They had tried the elegant state bedroom, with its over-carved four-poster, then moved on to the more modest room that had been used during the war by Winston Churchill. They had even hauled themselves up the spiral stairs to the Prison Room in the eaves where Lady Mary Grey had been incarcerated by the Tudor Queen Bess. They hadn't enjoyed that experience. The ceiling was low, stifling, and the whole room little more than twelve feet square. They hadn't lasted two nights in the Prison Room; poor Lady Mary had been imprisoned there for two years. At least they had let her live, and not put her to the axe, as they did her sister. And this weekend the Dandersons were sleeping in the bed that had once been used by Molotov, Stalin's bloody-handed Foreign Minister. He'd kept a revolver under his pillow and assumed that all butlers were poisoners. Mistrust came naturally to most who laid their heads here.

Danderson rolled over in search of a little comfort, his mind snagging on all the possibilities for surprise that the day might bring. Above all else, it kept turning to Iraq, for ever Iraq, but for once he thought he could see a way ahead, a chink of light through the dust-clouds and bilious black smoke that constantly obscured the problem. This bed had also been slept in by Richard Nixon, who'd had his own little local difficulty in a place called Vietnam. The American President's example might prove a useful yardstick. Nixon had been strong, kicked crap out of the enemy, yet just before the election he had found a suitable opportunity to talk of the end of the war. 'Peace with honour' was the phrase he'd used.

He'd won in a landslide – the election, of course, not the war, which had ended in disaster several years later, but by then it didn't matter. So, maybe a good example to follow. A few well-chosen words, a hint of compromise, a successful election, a British withdrawal, with bands playing and flags flying, followed by . . . whatever. Nixon had even got himself nominated for a Nobel Peace Prize for his efforts – or was that Henry Kissinger, his secretary of state? No, it was Kissinger. Typical. There was always some bastard lurking around, waiting to steal your glory.

Beside him, Lauren stirred, rubbed her eyes. 'So early?' she whispered. Her face peered from the pillow like over-dusted pastry.

'Thinking about the debate,' he replied.

'Worrying, you mean.'

'Not half as much as Dominic Edge, I'll be bound.'

'Is it that important?'

'Our first time, head to head, in a debate. I've got to be able to reduce him to dogmeat.'

'You will, darling.' She struggled as she tried to prop herself up on her pillows. There was still no sign of true daylight.

'There's trouble on the backbenches.'

'You've dealt with it in the past.'

'Well, you can always appeal to their ambition, and if not that, then to their shame. You know, those awkward little things, like the lover they forgot to mention to the wife, a bank account that slipped their mind when they last filled out a tax return, or the son tucked away under a false name in some expensive rehab clinic. There's always some way of getting through to their better nature. It's just that, as time goes by, it gets more difficult.'

'Are we in trouble, then?' she asked anxiously.

He shook his head. 'It's nothing. At least, nothing compared with what young Master Edge is facing . . .'

Ginny stretched, opened an eye, found Dom staring at her, already awake.

'It's like I remember the first time I got on a motorbike and opened the throttle,' he said. 'Scared the crap out of myself. Took off in a cloud of dust and gravel, totally out of control, no idea where I was headed or how to stop the bloody thing.'

'How did you finish?'

'In a heap.'

'But then you didn't have me.'

'Or private health insurance.'

'OK. So why the gloom?'

'Hazel. And Jack Saunders.'

'The viper and the lamb.'

'They still carry clout, even from the backbenches. And the whisper is they're going to oppose the new policy. Say it smacks of appeasement and disloyalty.'

'You never break chains by being loyal to the past.'

'Even so, my first major policy shout and I've got senior party members threatening to cut the legs from under me. Instead of a brave new start it could be a disaster. A total bloody disaster, Ginny. Make us look like playschool rather than a serious political party and reduce me to the status of the classroom dunce.'

'You'd think they'd be used to losing.'

He propped himself up in bed and poured a splash of water into the glass that had held his whisky the night before. 'But they've never accepted me as leader. Neither do quite a few others. Hazel and Jack still want the job. They'd like to turn me into St Sebastian, my body hung on some tree, riddled with arrows.'

It was her turn to emerge from beneath the duvet. 'Then they should have a care. You know, I'm always telling the children not to play with sharp objects. It's so easy to end up doing themselves harm . . .'

The clock in the downstairs hallway was striking half past five. Danderson could hear some of the staff creeping around, beginning their preparations for what was going to be a long day at

Chequers. Twenty people for lunch, another hundred and fifty for afternoon drinks. Nowhere to hide, not even here in the bedroom, as Lauren nestled encouragingly up against him. Instinctively he reached for the contents of a box open at the side of the bed, and sighed a deep sigh of duty.

'We have our own problems with the debate, of course,' he muttered distractedly. 'And the biggest bastard of all is that damned fool Dickie Burr. Planning to make an exhibition of himself, according to the Chief Whip. Talking about refusing to support us. He's always been unsound.'

'It's only because you sacked him for cowardice.'

'Not cowardice exactly. He just had a different view from me about how to handle the terrorist threat. Can't have that in a home secretary. He had to go.'

'Weak. I've always thought the man was thoroughly useless.'

Danderson smiled wryly at her dogged loyalty. She hadn't always thought that about Dickie Burr. There had been a time when they and the Burrs had been on holiday together, close friends – close *political* friends. *Amicus fugit,* or whatever they said. 'No need to worry about Dickie,' he responded, half a mind on the paper in his hand. 'I think we have the measure of him. Seems he's been playing truant from school.'

'What's her name?'

'Angie. His secretary.'

'Why are men such pathetic clichés?'

'Apparently it's serious.'

'I thought it was nothing but air-kissing and a wilted willy in his case. Is he going to leave his wife?'

'I've no idea. Perhaps he hasn't, either. But I have this abiding suspicion that life may start to turn on him. It would be a tremendous pity, of course, if he were to find himself too preoccupied on the domestic front to make much of an impact in the debate. But, somehow, we'd deal with the disappointment.'

'You're not going to . . . ?'

'Love and war, love and war, my dear. Sadly, there are always casualties . . .'

Dom had disappeared downstairs for a few minutes, returning with two mugs of tea, still trailing a dark cloud of depression.

'At least I make a pretty good butler.'

'You bring me a biscuit?'

'No.'

'Better stick to becoming Prime Minister, then.'

'Let me get through the debate first.'

'Don't be such a misery-guts. You know, some old-timer once told me that the secret was always to go into the Chamber with a grenade in your pocket and be ready to pull the pin. Just in case.'

'The element of surprise.'

'Mmm.'

'Not so easy when you're in Opposition.'

'Oh, I don't know,' she murmured, rising once more from beneath the folds of the duvet. This time she was naked, her skin shining, catching the lamplight, her nightdress cast off in some distant corner. Her eyes sparkled with mischief. 'Got any grenades in your pocket?'

He almost spilled the tea.

'You're a patient in need of cheering up, if ever I saw one,' she said, taking his arm. 'Come on. Before the kids wake up . . .'

'Need to find a way of focusing their minds,' Freddie Danderson was saying. 'Put the wind up them a bit.' He was still distracted by the debate, not focusing on the papers in his hands.

'I'd threaten to kick out the lot of them.'

'You know, Lauren, I think you may be right. Nothing better to focus the mind of a befuddled backbencher than the prospect of an imminent hanging.'

'Whose?'

'Preferably their own. If I make it clear that I won't tolerate them screwing around, that I'd call an early election rather than let them spend the next year whingeing away and cutting us down to the level of the Opposition, it might make all the difference.'

'It would raise the stakes.'

'For sure.'

'And make you look so very strong,' she said, stroking his arm.

'Bound to be a few stray sheep who won't find their way back into the fold, but . . .'

'It's a dangerous world out there. For sheep.'

'Very.'

'I think you're brilliant, darling,' she said devotedly, cuddling closer.

'And so wretchedly busy.' He rustled his papers back to life. 'Duty calls, damn it. England expects.'

It was a problem as old as ambition itself. When Harold Macmillan had been asked what he most feared, he replied disarmingly, 'Events, dear boy. Events.' It was a little chip of foresight on his part. Events were soon to do for that elder statesman, as they were to do for so many others. No matter how wise, how experienced or how able, there was always the unexpected that sneaked through the back window of Number Ten and kicked every Prime Minister in the crotch. It would be Freddie Danderson's turn some time. Only question was when.

He simmered with frustration when he heard that Richard Burr had announced, in a short, dignified statement, that he and his wife were separating. Sad. Tragic. But not uncommon. Not a cause for public guilt. But a cause for intense irritation in Downing Street, since it screwed up the plans to splash his affair in the press a day before the debate and thereby reduce his credibility to compost. They'd wanted photographs of him sneaking out of his lover's apartment to feed the parking meter, trying to hide his all-too-familiar features behind thick scarves and black sacks of rubbish, or perhaps to catch him as a ghostly face peering through the window of a place that wasn't his home, followed by the usual tight-lipped lies of explanation, but it wasn't to be. A plan unravelled, a sinner saved. Still, with a little luck, Dickie Burr would be too busy with lawyers and removal men to have time for the debate.

The preparations for the debate were meticulous. It was a three-line whip, of course, which meant that everyone who still had a detectable pulse was expected to attend. The Downing Street machine set up friendly commentators to pour columns of liquid manure from a great height upon Dom for playing party politics with the security of the nation, while others were encouraged to rake around the rumours of dissent and division within his ranks. Meanwhile, far more helpful reports of progress started filtering back from the journalists embedded with British forces in the citadel of Basra, although since those journalists were unable to travel outside it they were unable to verify the accuracy of the reports; they simply had to take the British authorities at their word. And almost every day the Prime Minister was seen in the company of members of the armed forces. The day before the debate he was even spotted in combat fatigues, complete with helmet and goggles, driving a tank across Salisbury Plain. Tacky, of course, but so effective. He wanted everyone to know: he was the friend of the British Tommy. It was a battlefield on which the inexperienced Dom couldn't compete.

There was another battlefield on which Dom was outclassed. All parties are coalitions, and some creak more loudly than others. A Prime Minister has patronage and many persuasive powers with which to bring round reluctant supporters, like the promise of a job – a real job, ministerial, with a chauffeur-driven car and red boxes that, at the end of every month, were stuffed with a large salary cheque. And if he couldn't promise such rewards to everyone at the moment, the Chief Whip and his band of warriors were able to imply, and in some cases to promise, that fulfilment was not far away. They were told that Ministers would come to their constituencies, bringing in their wake press coverage, public funds and perhaps even a new relief road. All it would take was a little loyalty. Not everyone could be bought off, of course, but it was a damn sight more than Dom could do. The jobs he had to offer came with no car, little kudos, and no salary, nothing more than the promise of another few years lashed to the mast as they sailed together through the storm. Loyalty in Opposition is based sometimes on nothing more substantial than blind faith; it's a commodity that isn't tradable and is often found to be highly flammable.

So, despite the scars that Iraq had inflicted upon his government, Freddie Danderson was content when the day of the debate arrived. All seemed ready. Speech honed and retyped. Supporters dosed with useful interventions. A few of the pack selected to howl at Dom as soon as he came within range. Downing Street could do no more, but no more was necessary. Hell, Freddie Danderson was looking forward to it.

He stood on the doorstep of Number Ten hand in hand with Lauren, looking up to wave at the pigeons on the upper windowsills of the Foreign Office in order to give his chin the right profile for the cameras. He climbed into his car and left Downing Street with only little time to spare. He wanted to make a dramatic entrance into the Commons, which would be packed to capacity, appearing from behind the Speaker's chair to the cheers of his supporters. It would get things off to a positive start. But as the car swept through the heavy metal gates that kept him secure from the public, his world turned to chaos.

A woman stepped forward from the crowd, evading the barriers and the outstretched hands of a policeman until she was standing directly in front of the Prime Minister's car. His driver swore, jumped on the brakes, sending Danderson, his wife and all his papers tumbling to the floor. But a three-ton car built with the defensive power of a tank takes some stopping, and in spite of the driver's efforts it grazed the woman, who was sent sprawling across the bonnet. The following car, filled with officials, was less fortunate. It smashed into the rear of the Prime Minister's vehicle, sending glass splintering across the roadway and its own bonnet springing up into the air. Steam hissed from a fractured radiator.

Lauren was the first of the passengers to recover her wits. As she heaved herself back into her seat she saw a familiar face staring at her through the windscreen. 'That bloody woman!' she screamed, pointing accusingly at Ajok.

The scene deteriorated rapidly, leaving fragments embedded in people's memories. Special Branch and armed diplomatic-protection officers swarming everywhere, shouting at the crowd gathered by the gates to get back, pushing at them, brandishing weapons. Pistols. Sub-machine guns. Many sightseers fled, screaming, while others stood their ground and photographed everything around them: the Dandersons being dragged from the car, then immediately pushed back as their security escort changed its mind about whether they would be safer in or out; Ajok pinned to the bonnet by an overwhelming force of men, grabbing at her to see whether she was armed; then Ajok being swept away, pinioned to the pavement, men shouting at her that they were from SO-16 and she was under arrest. More confusion as the damage to his vehicle, was inspected. The Prime Minister now out of his vehicle, in heated argument with his personal protection officer, insisting that he would continue on foot, shouting that he had a debate to attend.

By this time Ajok had been thrown into the back of a police van that, with its sirens blaring and radio crackling, was storming through the back streets of Whitehall. She was bruised from her encounters with both bonnet and bodyguards, but otherwise physically unhurt; she was a Dinka, it would take more than a few knocks to stop her. Yet she was confused. She'd never expected to cause such disorder. She tried to explain: all she had wanted to do was deliver a letter. The Prime Minister hadn't answered her first one, so she had carefully copied it out once again and decided to hand it to him as he passed. It couldn't be her fault that they had been driving so fast. Yet even as she tried to make all this clear they screamed at her, held her head down in her lap, very uncomfortable, as they took her she knew not where.

Inside the House, the air of expectation was gradually changing to one of unease. Where was the Prime Minister? The cast was assembled, squeezed into their seats and squatting in the aisles, the scribes in the press gallery sucking pens in anticipation, the public gallery behind the security screen filled to uncomfortable capacity, while the Chamber's digital clocks ticked remorselessly on, and on, and on, until it was past the time appointed for the debate to start. Where the hell *was* the Prime Minister? The Speaker was stooping to whisper urgently to his clerks, his cheeks flushed in disquiet. A government backbencher rose, almost physically wrestled to his feet by a government whip, and stumbled over his words as he embarked upon an entirely spurious point of order designed for no other purpose than to waste time. The Speaker dismissed him but he was replaced by yet another, and another, until the Chief Whip himself rose to his feet. 'On a point of order, Mr Speaker, I beg to move that the House now sits in private.'

He stood in his place, his features set rigid in shame, as his request was hit by a tidal wave of jeering from the Opposition benches. Sitting in private was a parliamentary device to exclude members of the public from proceedings, but it required a vote of the whole House, and that would take time, ten or fifteen minutes, during which the mystery of the missing Prime Minister might yet resolve itself. A deliberate tactic designed to let the clock slip by, even if it was also to carry the Chief Whip's credibility away with it.

Yet, at last, he was there. Uncertain applause rippled through the ranks of government supporters as the Prime Minister appeared in the Chamber, brushing the hair back from his eyes, feeling the dampness on his forehead. He was breathing heavily, over-excited, his belt feeling tight, not the way he had wanted to begin. But he must. The Chief Whip mumbled an apology as he withdrew his request, the Speaker called for order, and slowly the House shed its irritation and settled down to its business.

The Prime Minister began with a brief explanation and an apology. 'But it is the only apology I feel I need to make to the House this afternoon.' Then the years of experience came bubbling to the surface. He had learned to control his nerve, live off the fear, even thrive on it during the years he had spent in this place. When he'd started his career one old-hand had drawn him aside and told him, 'Take nothing for granted and take everything you can, before others steal it from you.' He'd thought it crass, then. All Prime Ministers live on borrowed time, but while it was their time they would sell their soul to stretch it, even just a little. They seemed to lack the ability to recognise when the moment had come to depart the scene gracefully, but grace never sat comfortably beside a Prime Minister under pressure.

And now it was Freddie Danderson's turn. He reminded the gathered Members of their commitment, of their duty, of their promises to others and their responsibility to the international community. He said that the issue wasn't simply about Iraq but the type of world they wanted to live in and would hand on to the next generation. It wasn't a new challenge, he reminded them. With theatrical emphasis he pointed round the Chamber to the painted coats of arms incorporated into the oak panelling, one for every Member of Parliament who had died on active service during two world wars. 'Those men, those Members, they knew their duty. They didn't shirk from it and they did not die in vain. There were voices in those dark days who called for appeasement, suggesting it was not our war, that we should avert our gaze and hide away. But we did not. While much of the rest of the world descended into darkness, we kept the light of freedom burning bright, here in this place, in our beloved Westminster. We did not fail them then. And we shall not fail them today.'

He gazed round him, his elbow propped on the Dispatch Box.

His eye fell, one by one, on those he knew to be unreliable, the potential troublemakers.

'I regard our work in Iraq as an act of faith. It is not something we can allow a few callow minds on the Opposition Front Bench to misuse for narrow party advantage,' he said, dismissing them with contempt. But his mouth was dry. He licked his lips; they felt cracked. His voice was suddenly brittle, but that didn't matter. It served only to add emphasis. 'This House must decide, clearly and unambiguously, whether it will continue to honour the solemn commitments it has given to the rest of the world.' A pause, which he sustained, until he was certain he had their total attention. 'Otherwise we must ask the people to decide. That's how democracy works. That's how freedom is sustained. Through the will of the people. And that is all we ask in Iraq.'

It was a warning. The sheep around him were being told that, if they didn't answer his call to return to the pen, they would be cast out, on their own, into the electoral darkness with all the perils that that awaited them there. It wasn't something he'd scripted or even widely discussed, but it had been churning in his mind and refused to go away. He was on edge, his shirt felt as if it had been glued to his body; perhaps it was the car accident, or simply Fate whispering in his ear, but he wanted to get things settled, once and for all.

The language in which he had threatened might be a little ponderous, even obscure, but they all knew what he'd meant. He was challenging them, drawing a line in the sand. Folly if they were to cross it. He sat down to a comforting roar of approval from his own side of the House. It hadn't been a great speech but it had been a good one, and good enough, given that it had started in chaos. As he felt the taps of congratulation on his shoulder, Danderson looked up to see the bent heads of scribes in the press gallery and the beaming face of the ever-loyal Lauren. He returned the smile. It was her speech, too.

Then it was Dom's turn.

★

'Time. Take your time,' Ginny had told him. 'Don't be in a wretched hurry. First play with them a little, get them in the mood.'

'Mr Speaker, I'm surprised to hear the Prime Minister was delayed by a car crash. I thought his preferred mode of transport nowadays was a tank.'

Gentle laughter rippled through the House; even some on the government front bench joined in.

'He looked very fetching in his tank. It produced some pretty pictures. That's always the case when presentation takes over from serious policy, when image squeezes out serious analysis. But, then, the Prime Minister is a man who is never knowingly undersold, never knowingly understated.'

Ouch. He hadn't played with them for very long before trying to take them by force.

'I'm grateful to the Right Honourable Gentleman for coming before us today, at long last, even if a little late, to restate his principles. It's been almost a year since he came to this place to discuss the situation in Iraq. I hear rumours that he doesn't care for the House of Commons, but I discount them.' He waved down the growls of disagreement with this conclusion that had started to erupt from his own side. 'No, I believe the reason he hasn't been here is because he has nothing new to say. As he's just told us, his principles remain the same. We've heard them all before. He clings to them with the ferocity of a drunk clinging to a lamp-post. As we all know from experience, he's the sort of leader who will grab at anything in search of support.'

The gentle mirth of his opening remarks was turning to an onslaught upon his rival. This was personal. It was bound to get messy. 'I remember when he became Prime Minister. He promised us – the House will remember this, I'm sure – that he would change the face of Iraq for ever. And he has kept his promise – oh, how he has kept his promise. But instead of becoming a beacon of democracy throughout the region, it has become a bloodbath. An

Iraq of fratricide, of despair, of desperation, without water, without power, without hope.' His words rattled through them like machine-gun fire. 'How sick the inhabitants of Baghdad and Basra must be of hearing about the Prime Minister's principles. If only they could exchange his principles for something useful. Instead, while he clings to his principles; they cling to the very margins of life, surrounded by death squads and suicide bombers, wondering what the new day will bring, and whether their loved ones will live to see nightfall.'

Shouts of protest swirled along the government benches, orchestrated by the Chief Whip.

'Oh, look at him.' Dom pointed an accusing finger at the Chief Whip. 'He resorts to his usual tactic of trying to shout others down. Little wonder that he tried to keep the public from hearing this debate. He should hang his head in shame.'

Now it was the turn of the Opposition benches to boil in indignation.

'So let the Prime Minister talk to us about his principles,' Dom continued, 'but while he considers them, let the rest of us consider why the only part of Iraq in which we retain troops is the part with the oil. Some countries have been partitioned along their rivers or mountain ranges or lines of latitude. We have effectively partitioned Iraq along lines filled with oil. It isn't a principled policy. It's nothing but a pipeline policy.'

It was a soundbite that was destined to make every newscast. Too late, Government supporters tried to drown it, battling with the Speaker as he struggled to retain order, but Dom thought he could see more than a few on the Government backbenches who were refusing to join in the outpouring of partisan wrath. Instead, some seemed to be writhing in discomfort. It was time to pile on the pressure.

'The Chief Whip wishes to stifle debate. It's part of the Government's policy not just in Iraq but in this country, too. A war that was meant to save us from terrorism has, instead, even in this mother of Parliaments, left us cowering behind concrete barriers and bomb detectors, with every move recorded on government cameras, and every phone call and email made available to government eavesdroppers. There was an age when this country was the land of the free, when you could think what you liked, and say what you thought. Sadly, that age is but a glorious memory. Mr Speaker, this has become a debate not simply about Iraq but also about the sort of society we have in our own country. Under this Prime Minister it has changed, and for the worse. He poses in his tank as a friend of the British soldier, but the Prime Minister has brought about a situation in which we have become inured to the steady drip of British casualties in Iraq, where the reports of the death of this British soldier or that British technician is buried deep on an inside page or not reported at all. We all know it's true. How many bother even to read the names of the dead any more? How many, instead, pass quickly over the grainy photograph of a young face in military uniform, thinking we have seen that face, or a face very much like it, a hundred times before? It is the Prime Minister's war. It is his doing. It has taken the loss of thirty-four nurses and doctors and others to bring him to the House today. We all know that. Otherwise, with any lower number of casualties, it would have been dismissed as merely another bad day at the office.'

Danderson had jumped up to the Dispatch Box, red marks of fury on his cheeks, demanding the right of reply, but Dom was shaking his head, refusing to let him back. 'I think not, I think not. We've already heard too much of the principles of the Right Honourable Gentleman. He sounds like an old Leninist, trying to drive history forward at the point of a bayonet. We've heard it all before. We don't need more of it now.' And Dom charged on, standing at the Dispatch Box, leaning on it, pounding it with his fist, laying his palms upon it as if it were an altar. And all the time savaging the reputation of Freddie Danderson. When, at last, it came time for him to wind up, he looked directly across the Chamber to his opponent seated no more than a few feet away, close enough to see the anger gleaming in his eye and the loathing stretched across his lips. Dom knew he had made an enemy of this man; there would always be bad blood between them.

'The Prime Minister helped begin this war in the name of democracy. Yet at every turn he has interfered with the Iraqis' own choices. He declares this candidate to be unacceptable, that Minister must be .ignored and yet another local security chief should be excluded from his office. Divide and rule, just like the imperialists of old. Except this time the natives aren't armed with bows and arrows.' Dom bowed his head, gathering his final thoughts. When he raised his eyes once more, his words were softer, expressed more in sorrow than anger. 'Enough is enough. Time to leave them alone to sort out their problems by themselves, because it is beyond hope that we can do it for them. The Prime Minister says that failure is not an option – how often have we heard that phrase fall from his lips? Yet he is right. Failure is not simply an option, it has become a ferocious reality. We have stayed too long, meddled too much, seen too many hopes wither in the desert wind, and we have buried too many of our brave British sons and daughters. The time has come for us to depart from Iraq. And if he hasn't the courage and the fortitude to bring that about, then it is time for him to depart, too, the final casualty of this misbegotten adventure.'

It had been savage, and hurtful. Rarely in the games that are played in the Commons does one leader attack another with such unremitting ferocity. But Freddie Danderson was confident: he knew it wouldn't change the outcome. The Opposition was a rabble, their internal divisions driven far deeper than any within the ranks of government troops. It would be fine. Pity about Burr, though. He was rising to his feet, about to make a damned nuisance of himself. If only they'd had the bit of luck that would have enabled them to reveal to every tabloid reader in the country what a fumbling idiot the man was. But luck was like the summer weather, unpredictable, could blow any which way. Burr was now repeating all the noises he'd made in private when he was Home Secretary. He would linger behind after Cabinet meetings like a bad smell, sharing his doubts, wringing his hands when someone should have been wringing his bloody neck. Except that on those occasions he'd been cautious, measuring out his criticism with care; now there was no need for restraint. His words didn't have the personal edge that Dom had used, but they were biting none the less.

'As a result of the frenzy brought about by our occupation of Iraq, we have made ourselves a target for intimidation,' he told them. 'In its desperate attempt to justify what it has done, to exaggerate the threat it faced, the Government has begun to see enemies lurking round every corner. It has made enemies of its own people. Arrested them on nothing more than suspicion, imprisoned them without trial, the keys thrown away. We, like the enemy, have adopted the tactics of terror. When we began the war we talked about hearts and minds, but instead we use bars and brutality, the language of Guantánamo Bay. We no longer trust our own.'

A backbencher sprang to his feet, determined to interrupt this dirge. 'But wasn't he Home Secretary when so many of these measures were enacted?'

'Of course I was,' Burr replied. 'That was why I resigned. For a while I thought there was merit in following the Prime Minister. I soon found that I could sleep more soundly by following my conscience.'

Yet he was only one, an isolated voice of no real consequence. The Government Whips had done their work. But, unbeknown to Danderson, so had others.

Bobby had arrived home the previous Sunday evening to find Dom, Ginny and Archie sitting round the kitchen table, like the triumvirs of ancient Rome, anxiously pricking the names of those who might swing the debate. He had grown accustomed to spending most of his weekends away, returning with exhausted eyes, from where Dom didn't care to know and Ginny didn't dare ask. Bobby was entitled to his privacy. But now he came bearing stories of the Robin Hood in the King's Road, a pub where on a Sunday morning many of the capital's gay and merry men would gather, wearing their trademark scarves and heavy leather belts to indicate what or whom they were into. They shared their sexuality but that was all; on those occasions most other things – race, religion, income, occupation – were irrelevant. Sometimes you didn't bother asking too many questions, yet there were also occasions when you met the most fascinating people, and you talked. Bobby had met a driver – not just any driver but one from the ministerial car pool, a man who, among his many other charming physical attributes, was all ears. Drivers were the invisible men of Whitehall, ignored by the important people who sat in the back seat and would insist on conducting sensitive conversations on their mobile phones. That was how the driver had heard of the plan to drag Richard Burr's private life into the spotlight. He was an older gay, a bit of a bear, the type who didn't care for all this 'outing', no matter who was on the receiving end, and after a couple of beers he had told Bobby of what was afoot.

Later that evening, when he joined the others at the kitchen table, Bobby hadn't felt the need to share details of all the discoveries he had made during his long afternoon in the Robin Hood, but he did offer them the tantalising information of what Downing Street was planning to do for Burr – it hadn't been difficult to figure out why. So, while the others sat around and Ginny made more coffee, Dom had telephoned Richard Burr to warn him, and the plans of the mischief-makers were undone. Pity about the wife, of course. Another casualty of war. But there had already been so many.

Freddie Danderson knew nothing of this. He sat on his green leather bench, his sweat-soaked shirt cold and clammy beneath his jacket, soaking up the insults, content in the knowledge that storm winds blow in all directions. And the storm he was awaiting with very special enthusiasm was named Hazel Basham . . .

They all knew Hazel – well, she insisted on it. Pushy, ambitious, chippy, a woman who had refused to serve in Dom's Shadow Cabinet not because of any shame she felt at her financial shenanigans but because she believed that she was so much better than him. She was a warrior, not a performing dog who turned somersaults to order – and she certainly had no intention of doing so for Dominic Edge. At least, not until Ginny had walked into her parliamentary office the previous day.

'Hello, Virginia,' Hazel said, not bothering to look up from her desk. 'You'll have to forgive me, I'm very busy. Working on my speech for the debate. What can I do for you? You said on the phone that it was urgent. Not come to beg me to support your husband, have you? That would be too embarrassing for us both.'

'No, nothing like that, Hazel. There's just something I wanted to share with you. Girl to girl.'

Without further explanation she had crossed to the cabinet in the corner of the office, on which stood a television and video-recorder. She inserted a tape. It was the one from the camera that had looked down the corridor in the conference hotel, showing both date and time. It also showed Hazel standing outside her bedroom door with her advertising friend, touching, giggling, glancing furtively in every direction before planting a most passionate kiss on his lips. They were like teenagers. It also showed her fumbling for her door key, dropping it, him bending down to retrieve it and Hazel groping him in a manner that, in other circumstances, might have passed for a medical examination. The tape then cut to a moment, several hours later, when the man re-emerged cautiously into the corridor, scratched his crotch in triumph, and went on his way.

'As I said, Hazel, girl to girl. I thought you should know about it.'

'What? And try to blackmail me?'

'Why on earth should I do that? If that's what we'd wanted, we'd have used it during the leadership contest.'

'So what do you want?'

'Nothing at all. The tape has been hanging around in the back of our safe ever since it was handed to us after the conference. We have no need of it. I think you should take it.'

Hazel's brow furrowed in suspicion.

'It's yours,' Ginny emphasised.

A muted 'thank you' slipped out.

'Dom's got a very high opinion of your abilities, Hazel. You're a fighter. You saw off all the nonsense about the care home. And he's not in much of a position to be a moraliser about other people's sleeping habits. He wants you back in the front line.'

'That's . . . very generous of him.' The words came in the form of a throat-searing croak. Her features suggested she was being throttled, as if the last of the oxygen sustaining her life was ebbing away.

Now, as the Prime Minister watched her from the other side of the Chamber, Hazel appeared to have recovered every bit of her vigour. She wasn't tall, but how she dominated those around her. Even the way she stood appeared menacing. And she hurled words like mortar shells into every corner of the Chamber, yet they were not aimed at random. Every one had a purpose, to cut off Freddie Danderson's means of retreat.

'I'm not suggesting that the Prime Minister is a habitual liar, I would never say that,' she told them, 'but when it comes to representing the state of affairs in Iraq, he does have a habit of distributing the truth a little unevenly . . .'

Danderson winced. This wasn't what he had expected, not at all.

'He wears his principles like a donkey jacket, designed to cover up his failures,' she went on. 'His policy is a race between excuse and catastrophe. It's a race he has already lost. I know it's difficult for a proud man to admit that he's got something so terribly wrong, but if he can imagine weapons of mass destruction in the desert, surely it's not beyond him to find in his heart the power to acknowledge that, despite his own best intentions – and those of many on this side of the House – the time has come to change course. To grasp the nettle. To get out of Iraq.'

Bugger. The bloody woman had turned and run, dragging with her any chance of the Opposition splitting on the issue. Saunders, the other potential high-profile rebel, wouldn't have the balls for it, not on his own. Still, the sight of a united Opposition would encourage any doubters on his own side to climb back on board. The House of Commons was a primitive place, split along tribal lines, and Danderson knew he would still be fine.

Although Hazel hadn't quite finished. Now she was insisting that he show the courage and fortitude he demanded of others in Iraq. The bitch! It was a disgrace, she was saying, that the House had been forced to wait so long for a proper opportunity to debate these serious issues. What did he insist on hiding? Why did he so consistently run from the questions, refuse to rise to his responsibilities?

Danderson pulled himself wearily to his feet to intervene. 'The Honourable Lady seems to have lost control of herself. She knows full well that I have always been happy to debate these serious issues, as I am any others, anytime, anyplace, anywhere. I believe she owes me an apology.'

'Oh, come now, methinks the Prime Minister doth protest too much,' she retorted, mocking. 'Anytime, anyplace, anywhere – so long as it's not in this House and anywhere near the Opposition.' She was taunting him, while he shook his head, growing steadily more furious. 'We know he has nothing but contempt for this place. Why, the only reason he's here today is because he's been dragged here by disaster.'

'The Honourable Lady is being as offensive as she is ridiculous,' Danderson snapped. 'Nothing I can say will satisfy her. This exchange is pointless.' He dismissed her with a sneer.

But Hazel was like a terrier with a rat, shaking it for all she was worth, continuing to torment him. Danderson refused to intervene again; instead he sat trying to maintain his dignity, his temples flushed with resentment, his damp shirt clinging like a straitjacket, but there were many others on his side happy to take up his cause. They weren't going to let a bloody woman get the better of them. 'Anytime, anyplace, anywhere,' they shouted, returning her taunts, the words echoing round the Chamber like the heckling in a playground. The Speaker was calling for order, struggling to restore some sense of gravity to the proceedings.

Suddenly Dom was on his feet, asking Hazel if she would give way.

'Mr Speaker, we have listened to the Prime Minister, and perhaps it is appropriate on such an important occasion simply to take him at his word.'

The Speaker was nodding in appreciation as the noise from the Government benches began to subside.

'I thank the Prime Minister for his assurances that he is willing to discuss these issues openly with us,' Dom continued, 'and I will be happy to take up his offer on the occasion of the next election. I look forward to debating with him in public at that time. But for the moment, Mr Speaker, and with your approval, I believe we should return to the business of today, and the most serious issue of Iraq.'

Inside, Danderson screamed, and moaned, writhing like a chopped worm, even as he nodded in apparent approval. He'd been a complete bloody idiot. Got himself bushwhacked. Given Dom the perfect opportunity to challenge him to a head-to-head contest at the next election, and in a manner that the Prime Minister would find almost impossible to refuse. A leaders' debate. A prospect raised at the start of every election campaign, and just as quickly put to the sword. They might have these things in the United States, in Germany, in Italy, indeed in most other countries, but so bloody what? Sod Johnnie Foreigner. It hadn't happened here, not in Britain, for the simple reason that the man in front had no interest in getting himself tangled up in an unpredictable wrestling match that he might just end up losing. The story of these debates in other countries was littered with accidents, and Dom had no desire to be one of them. Yet now he had allowed himself to be goaded, by a ridiculous woman, and he'd let his conceit run off with his sense. Anytime, anyplace, anywhere, he had vowed, and now it would be at the next election and in front of about twenty million voters. They were going to make history, he and Edge, with the first leaders' debate ever staged in Britain. It was a disaster. Dom, the challenger, would be the only one with anything to gain, and now there was nothing the Prime Minister could do about it.

Danderson's torment hadn't finished. He still had to get through the day, but it was drawing to its end. That worthless excuse for a man, Ken Boston, was winding up for the Opposition in his new role as Shadow Defence Spokesman, raising his voice, rocking back and forth on the balls of his feet at the Dispatch Box, trying to ride the rising tide of barracking that always marked the end of a debate as Members drifted back after dinner. Danderson had sat in on almost all of it, breaking only for a shower and a change of shirt, then a brief dinner that he had found unappetising and had left him with indigestion. Nerves, perhaps. He wanted to be here, in the Chamber, to show them how important this was, how much it meant to him. The Chief Whip had assured him they would be fine, there would be less than a handful of abstentions on the Government side, Burr and a couple of others; the rest of the troublemakers weren't in the mood, not tonight, at least. But the headmaster's presence in the playground would help make sure.

All politicians drag baggage behind them, and none was dragging more baggage at this moment than Fergus Tennant. A

Scot, early fifties, smoker, drinker and Heart of Midlothian supporter. He had also long held doubts about the Government's policy in Iraq, but he was a Cabinet Minister, the Secretary of State at the grandly named Department for Environment, Food and Rural Affairs, so he tried to keep his doubts to himself. No big deal. A few principles sacrificed on the altar of ambition. Politics was a team game; you couldn't expect to score every goal yourself. Yet a new factor had just come into the game, kicked on to the pitch by Archie Blackstone.

Blackstone had tracked him down in his parliamentary office. They knew each other of old, had been members of the same university union thirty years earlier in Glasgow. Had even been drinking partners, for a while. And now Blackstone was back, bearing a bottle of whisky.

'What the hell do you want?' Tennant demanded, more in surprise than hostility.

'Shut up and listen,' Archie replied, placing the bottle on the desk between them. He nodded towards a scuffed policeman's helmet that stood on a cabinet in the corner, a souvenir of the poll-tax riots. 'Those were the days, eh? Both young, both rebels.'

'You here to reminisce?'

'No. Nothing so pleasant, Fergus. I'm here to tell you about your wife.'

Polly Tennant had a problem. A gambling problem. In fact, she was a compulsive gambler, but she could admit this neither to herself nor to anyone else. It was only an amusement, a gentle distraction, mostly on the Internet. Yet when you keep losing, something's got to give. She'd started cadging money from her friends, other political wives, women who met up with each other in the gym. As they had cycled and stretched away, glowing with self-righteousness, she had outlined a little scheme that she said would make them a killing: buying up green-field sites that were soon to be approved for development. Not too many, of course, didn't want to be greedy, but a few acres that would rocket in price when the Government announced the next phase of its housing scheme. It was a bit of fun, really, and there was almost no risk, not when your husband was in charge of the department about to switch on the green light. Oh, yes, and just the tiniest bit naughty, but not really wicked since they were only talking about pin-money, a couple of thousand pounds, perhaps. Just a few girlfriends together.

But it was all going wrong. The money had gone straight to feed Polly's habit, and she was running out of excuses. There wasn't much the other girls could do about it: there was no one to whom they could complain, not the police and certainly not their husbands. So they complained among themselves, bitterly, in the quieter corners of the gym. That was where Ginny had first stumbled across it, in the changing rooms, while the hair-dryers were blasting away and Polly's friends were trying to make themselves heard. Ginny had unravelled the rest of it by eavesdropping over lunch in the salad bar. Eight of them had fallen into the honey-pot, all up for two, three and, in a couple of cases, as much as four thousand pounds. All of this Archie explained quietly to Polly's husband.

'So, old chum, you're going to lose your job.'

The Minister's face set rigid. 'I knew nothing about it, you have my word on that. I'll make sure they all get their money back.'

'Too late.'

'But it's not my fault, damn you,' he protested. 'I've done everything I can. Cut up her credit cards, told the bank. She promised me she'd stopped.' He banged the table defiantly. 'She's sick. Needs help.'

'Even so, you're for the chopping-block. My masters will insist. So will the *Sun*. As soon as they find out. As soon as we tell them.'

'You bastard!'

'Come on, Fergus, you know the way the game's played. You'd do the same.'

Tennant's eyes were rolling in despair. 'Please . . .'

'You can't carry on as a Minister, not with your wife trying to chisel a margin out of every decision you make.' Archie's tone was hard, offering no crumb of comfort. This was dirty work, which was why they'd sent him. Tennant's head was buried in his hands. Archie shoved the bottle across the desk towards him. He was desperate to get rid of it: his own hands were shaking. It had been several years and half a lifetime since he'd been so close to that much whisky. He wasn't finding this easy, either.

'You do get one choice, though, Fergus.'

The head came up, the eyes straining with tears.

'The timing,' Archie continued. 'We haven't given it to the tabloids yet – and we won't. If you resign first.'

'I don't understand.'

Archie poured for him, but didn't take any for himself. 'Don't vote for the Government this evening. Abstain. Say it's time for a change.'

'But if I did that I'd have to resign!'

'Haven't you been listening? You're going to have to do that anyway. But how much better to get out with your head held high, as a man of principle, than find yourself kicked out for being a bloody fool. Hell, give it a year or so, and a new leader, you'll be back at the trough once more. But one way or the other, for the moment, you're walking with the dead.'

His old friend drank. 'You want me to betray Freddie Danderson.'

'Don't give me the loyalty crap, Fergus. Soon as he gets a whiff of what's been going on, Freddie Danderson'll be turning on you like you were pissing on his flowerbed.'

Silence. Pain. Confusion. And also, it had to be acknowledged, the grinding of a conscience. After all, Tennant did so hate this Iraq thing. The Minister sat covering his eyes, cowering from the oak-panelled walls that seemed to be closing in on him. A portrait of the Duke of Wellington was staring down at him, the eyes accusing.

Archie had done all he could. He felt physically sick. He was sweating, tasting the whisky in the air, feeling his mind playing tricks on him. Time to go, to let the other man stew. 'It's the best offer you'll be getting,' he reminded his old friend, on his way out of the door.

Tennant sat alone in his office, all afternoon and into the evening, until the bottle was finished. He was drunk but not incapable when he walked into the Chamber, dragging his confusion and his conscience behind him. He sat silently as the final speeches were made, right up to the moment when the Speaker called for order and the division bells rang. All around him they rose to begin their processions through the voting lobbies. But Tennant remained seated.

'Come on, Fergus,' a colleague encouraged, tapping him on the shoulder.

But still he remained seated. Slowly, stubbornly, he shook his head.

Others gathered round him. 'Chrissake, Fergie, you'll miss the vote,' one said.

'You got a problem?' a Whip enquired.

'The bastard's drunk,' said another. And soon he was at the centre of a small mob, variously encouraging, abusing, prodding, trying to take his arm and force him to his feet. But still he refused.

Tennant had now become the centre of attention in a Chamber crowded to its capacity. All eyes were on him. One Whip had grabbed his tie.

Meanwhile Ken Boston was pushing his way towards the Speaker's chair, raising his voice, insisting that he be heard. 'On a point of order, Mr Speaker.'

'We're in the middle of a division.'

'But that's the point. Look. The government Whips are trying to use physical intimidation to force Members to vote. This is an outrage. I know this Government has a habit of tearing up the rules whenever it suits them, but surely we must still preserve this House as a hallowed place for individual conscience. You, as the Speaker, are the guardian of our liberties. Can I call on you to insist that they stop? Look at them. They're no better than thugs!'

A roar of approval greeted his request. And so they were forced to stop. Fergus Tennant didn't vote for the Government. And neither did quite a number of others, not just Richard Burr but many of those who harboured doubts. If a Minister could sit this one out, so could they.

So everything that Freddie Danderson had tried to achieve that day was left in tatters. More than forty of his own supporters abstained, Burr and several others voting with the Opposition. In the end, tantalisingly, the vote was tied. The House was in uproar.

It is the convention on these occasions that, when a vote is tied, the Speaker uses his casting vote to endorse the motion before the House, in effect decreeing they should play extra time, which in this case meant voting for the Government. Danderson had survived but he could find no comfort in it. It had been a day of disasters from the moment that bloody woman had run in front of his car. Now he felt as if he'd been walking through a sauna. The fresh shirt was clinging to his back and it would be only minutes before ripples of sweat and anxiety were pouring down his face. He had to make a decision, and very quickly. He could ignore what had happened, hope tomorrow would prove a better day, but he knew that once the dogs had escaped the kennel they were notoriously difficult to round up. Like an over-confident idiot, he had threatened that he would take his case to the people if they refused to fall into line, and now his bluff had been called. If he wriggled out of such a commitment they would mock him, show no mercy, and he had seen too many Prime Ministers brought low by the drip, drip, drip of constant derision. On the other side, he was still in his prime, had a healthy lead in the opinion polls, and there was one superb way of putting this day of nonsense behind him. Call that election. Summon the executioner. He'd have to do it at some point, and perhaps better now, from a position of strength, than in a few months after the dogs had been running wild.

All these things tumbled through his mind as he sat in his place, and as he looked up, into the Opposition benches, he could see nothing but a raging sea of faces, snarling, jeering, mocking, their lips curled in derision. It is difficult for a man to endure ridicule without responding, particularly a proud man, as he was, and as he sat there he wanted nothing more than to wipe the sneers from their faces. He was desperate to show them that he still controlled the game. And then he saw Dominic Edge. He wasn't joining in the general baiting, he was simply staring, and smiling. 'Anytime, anyplace, anywhere,' he was mouthing. Punk.

Suddenly Danderson was on his feet, wanting to hurl them all off a cliff, knowing he was the better man and determined to prove it.

'Mr Speaker, the House has been unable to come to a clear decision. It is in a state of confusion and I suspect that, left to its own devices, it might remain so. That's never a healthy prospect. In the circumstances, therefore, I believe it proper that we should call upon others to make up our minds for us.' Ha, that had them listening! They were quiet now, hanging on his every word. And the ridiculous smirk had vanished from Edge's face, replaced by a look of the most intense concentration. 'It is my intention to seek an audience with Her Majesty in order to ask her gracious permission for a dissolution of Parliament. An election, Mr Speaker. I intend to take our case to the people. Let them decide!'

They had taken her to Charing Cross police station, less than a mile from Downing Street. It reminded Ajok of the times after the floods when they would round up the cattle to drive them on to new grazing, with everyone milling around, everything verging on chaos. They took her fingerprints, her photograph, swabbed her mouth for a DNA sample. At Downing Street, as they were pinning her to the pavement, they had told her they were arresting her for a breach of the peace, but now they talked about more serious charges. Criminal damage. Even assault, if it turned out that anyone in the cars had been injured. And this had been no accident: she had been there before, causing trouble. So, a troublemaker, perhaps even a terrorist. Then they insulted her, asking her if she was ill, or had ever tried to harm herself, or if she could read. After that a woman policeman took her to a room and did disgraceful things to her. It was very much like Khartoum.

It wasn't until they had taken her to a cell and slammed the door that she had any time to collect her thoughts, and to grow afraid. The words they had mentioned when they cautioned her were so similar to the ones that Mr Banerjee had used. He had falsely accused her, cut her benefits, reduced her to misery. What would they do to her now?

In a while they took her to an interview room, very much like Mr Banerjee's but larger, with another tape-recording machine. They asked her if she wanted a solicitor, then asked what she thought she was doing outside Downing Street.

'All I want is my job back.'

'Not going to get it with a criminal record, are you?' one said.

'I am not a criminal, sir.'

There was much coming and going from the interview room, calls made to check her identity and her address, other calls to the Immigration Service to see whether she had leave to stay. The computer had her listed for suspected benefit fraud and also mentioned her sacking from the Ministry of Defence. With every step, she was getting caught up in a net of suspicion.

She asked how long it would be before she could leave.

'What? Let you go back to Downing Street?' muttered one of her interrogators.

'No, to my two children.'

'You have children?'

'Yes, sir.'

And their mood changed. Kids meant getting tangled up with Social Services, tripping over even more paperwork, and despite their earlier suspicions, there wasn't the slightest sniff of the terrorist about her. She wasn't drunk or on drugs, she wasn't possessed by demons. The worst they seemed to have on her was that she was exceptionally determined, and that wasn't enough to make the best case in the world. Yet she kept coming up on their computer. A refugee. One with a grudge against the Government. A probable benefit fraudster. A protester. A troublemaker. There was much muttering, both in and outside the interview room, as they tried to decide what they should do.

The decision was the formal responsibility of the custody sergeant. He was a man of experience, not computers, and knew when a decision had disaster woven all through it. So he took it to another old hand, his superintendent.

'Paper trail suggests she might be a real problem,' the sergeant said.

'And your instinct?'

The sergeant shook his head. 'Sometimes these computers are no better than chamber pots. 'Cept you can empty a chamber pot, tip it out of the window. Once crap gets into the computer, though, it's the devil's own work to shift.'

'There's something else,' the superintendent said. 'Downing Street's been on the phone, and more than once. Apparently Mrs Danderson says this is our fault. So far as she's concerned the suspect is a serial offender and we should have stopped her before it all got out of hand. She's insisting that we throw the book at her. Creating merry hell, she is. Wants her charged with assault, unlawful demonstration, casting dark looks at the Prime Minister's wife, the lot.'

'Does she, now?' The sergeant scratched his chin. 'That's a pity. Stirs up the old chamber pot a bit, does that. So what might your advice be, sir?'

The superintendent leaned back in his chair, as though to distance himself from the formality of any issue left on his desk. 'How long you been in the force, Harry?'

'You know darned well. We started together, you and me. 'Cept you've always been better at bowing and scraping.'

The superintendent chuckled. 'And just remind me, Harry, why you and I joined.'

'So long ago I've all but forgotten.'

'Try. Stretch your memory.'

'Well, seems to me it was some nonsense about being on the side of the good guys. And the gals,' he added, as an afterthought.

'Then it seems to *me* you should know what to do.'

The sergeant turned to leave, but looked back again. 'Kicking up a real fuss, is she, the PM's missus?'

'A stinker.'

The sergeant nodded thoughtfully, then went on his way. When he arrived back in the charge room, there were expectant young faces. The sergeant reckoned he'd lost a couple of inches in height during all the years he'd been in the police service, so he stood on the balls of his feet, maximum height, as he gave them their instructions. 'Release her,' he instructed. 'Police bail. To come back in two weeks.'

'But, Sarge . . .'

'You heard me. And find a car to take her back to her kids. We've had her here more than long enough.'

'A car? You serious, Sarge?'

'If anybody asks, it's so that we can make sure she goes straight home. God help us all if she tries to go back by way of Downing Street.'

In bed, exhausted, listening to the house creak through the night, yet neither of them capable of sleep.

'Penny for them?' Dom asked.

'Cost you more than that.'

'OK, an afternoon of rampant and unrestrained sex. When next we have an afternoon.'

'It's a deal.'

'Then . . . ?'

'I was thinking of another man.'

'Who?'

'Fergus Tennant.'

'Why him?'

'We destroyed him.'

'And?'

'He didn't deserve it, Dom.'

'Rules of the game.'

'Your game, perhaps, but . . . he didn't deserve it.'

'But his wife was—'

'Precisely. His wife. Not his fault. Not his fault any more than . . .' Any more than Julia had been my fault, she was thinking.

'Guilt by association.'

'I understand that,' she whispered. The words came soaked with regret. For the first time, she had destroyed someone who bore no trace of guilt.

'Happens all the time in politics. Every reshuffle. Every time you close a red box.'

'It's like Ben being picked on in the playground because he's your son.'

'Well, we've gone too far now. Can't turn back.'

'I know. Can't turn back. Even if we wanted to . . .'

Part Three

Thirteen

THE ELECTION. AN EXERCISE in aspiration and utter exhaustion. Day after day, north, south, east, and places they will never remember as anything other than a blur, they ply their trade. It's at these moments that we expect to see our leaders at their best, yet what we see by the end is often little more than a living corpse, propped up on a diet of adrenaline, prescription drugs and ambition. They ride the tiger, knowing that at any moment they might fall and be devoured. Yet they pursue it because it is the most important moment of their lives. They have sacrificed so much to get to this point. Their journey has already cost them money, emotion, their friends, their youth, more than a few points of principle and, in some cases, a wife or two along the way. An election is like the period of Purgatory, dangling between Paradise and Damnation, with the outcome left in the hands of fools.

Wives have no formal role in this process. They are supposed to shine like the evening star, at a distance, and to take no more than a decorative role, apart from dispensing antibiotics and rationing the alcohol. They follow dutifully, a few paces behind, for the most part lost in the crowd, being photographed, jostled, jeered, occasionally spat at, and generally ignored unless, of course, they should yawn at the wrong moment or show any sign of cellulite, in which case they will find themselves on every newscast. The wife is an optional extra during elections. Unless your name is Ginny Edge.

Dom was still only a half-formed product, his personality as yet not well established in the country, his undoubted oratorical brilliance shot through with glistening threads of insecurity. In truth, the election had come as a huge surprise, he wasn't yet ready for it, and behind the broad and expensively polished smile it was sometimes possible to hear a restrained gurgle of terror. Yet, while he lacked Freddie Danderson's experience, he had other advantages, most notably Ginny and the children. In a game of images, that was one trick the Dandersons couldn't play. Youth, beauty, fecundity. So Archie and the rest of the communications team were keen to show off this advantage with shots of Dom playing with his kids, washing his car with them, even cooking them Sunday lunch on that first weekend, with Ginny in the background directing his every move.

In the battle to be the most dutiful husband, Freddie Danderson tried to retaliate by inviting a hundred or so of the world's press to witness him making Lauren a cup of tea, as if he did this all the time. But the image was rather spoiled when, in front of all those lenses and microphones, he turned to her in distraction to enquire where she kept the teapot.

There were perils in wait for Dom, too. During that first week of the campaign, while on a gumboot trip to East Anglia, he was photographed cuddling a lamb – not a calf, there were some who still remembered that ploy – in an attempt to suggest regeneration and some spiritual link to the rural cosmos. To keep the snappers content he had to hold the thing for what seemed like an eternity, and while he smiled and the beast struggled, Dom racked his brain to remember what had been said in the manifesto about animal cruelty. For days after the photograph had appeared on the front pages, the farmer who owned the lamb had received telephone calls from the press enquiring about its health. Then, one sad day, it was discovered dead. Foul play was widely suspected, but never proven, in spite of the *Mirror* offering many thousands of pounds for the privilege of conducting a public autopsy. The dead lamb got far more coverage than ever it had when it was alive, leaving Dom in a fit of rage.

Jemma, after whom the lamb had been named, was inconsolable. Ginny dried the tears.

And there was bloody Julia again, resurfacing from whichever pit she had been buried in to write an election column for the *News of the World*. 'I've seen the party leaders at close quarters,' she wrote, 'and, in Dom Edge's case, perhaps too close quarters. That may not make me the most objective observer, but so what? It has showered me with insights. And what a lot of insights I'll have to offer you over the next few weeks!' She proceeded to analyse the dress sense of the party leaders. 'I can't tell you whether Freddie Danderson wears Y-fronts or boxers, but I can tell you – and you heard it here first! – that Dom Edge wears *South Park* underpants. Yuk! What a turn-off! Let's hope his politics don't turn out to be pants, too!' It was a complete fabrication, of course, but impossible to contradict without risking ridicule. There was an edge of menace in what she was doing, a threat of things to come.

Another small item of news attracted Ginny's attention, tucked away in the *Independent* in the quixotic manner of that paper. A report that an appeal had been lodged in the High Court by a Mrs Ajok Arob in a case of unfair dismissal, based on the questionable legality of the war in Iraq. It was a matter that had been brought before other courts but which had never been properly tested, no matter how people had tried, the cases always ending up being sidetracked, decided on other grounds. The discussion of the legality of the war was like a cloth infected with leprosy, always to be passed on for others to deal with. But it seemed that this particular practice wasn't confined to the courts: Mrs Arob had taken her case directly to the Prime Minister and had caused all that fuss before the debate. Therefore an admirable woman, in Ginny's eyes. And something else caught her eye, a quote from the barrister, Sophie Gaminara, that Mrs Arob wasn't a political activist of any sort. It seemed that the only thing she had ever wanted to do was to protect her children.

At the time she read this snippet, Ginny was travelling in one of the fleet of small helicopters whisking Dom and his accompanying entourage to the West Country from Battersea heliport. The views as they flew over Wiltshire were spectacular, the noise appalling. Bobby sat beside her, cramped, not enjoying the experience gripping the edge of his seat. She had to shout to make herself understood. 'Bobby, find out about this woman,' she said, tapping the newspaper article. 'See if she's genuine. She might be helpful.'

'In what way?'

'If she hates Freddie Danderson as much as I do, we're bound to make good friends, don't you think?'

Bobby didn't think much at all. He grasped the newspaper as though it were his lifeline to a better world, one in which his stomach knew its place and his head would stop spinning with every turn of the rotor-blades.

'You feeling all right?' she asked.

'No.'

'Don't like flying?'

'Think I've got a bug. Caught it from the kids,' he said accusingly. As if to confirm the point, he suddenly went stiff. Then he threw up into the newspaper.

'Don't worry,' Ginny replied, determined to be cheerful. 'It's only a twenty-four-hour thing. You'll be fine in the morning. Oh, look, there's Stonehenge,' she cried, pointing out of the window. 'Isn't this fun?'

'I feel like a victim,' he complained, wiping the sweat from his brow.

'In this show, we're all victims,' she replied.

By the end of the day, the gods had taken unto themselves other hostages. Dom was also looking worse for wear. It wasn't just a bug – not that bug, at least, because it was still with him the following day and the day after that. Nerves, tension, adrenaline, lack of sleep, being thrown around every day as if he were on a bombing run over Hamburg. It was all taking its toll. And it showed. A lacklustre performance at a major rally, a laboured press conference, his loss of temper with aides that filtered out as reports of division within the camp. He had a temperature of a hundred and one, but you don't make excuses, not when you're going for broke, because people will think you're not up to the job. Meanwhile that old sod Danderson just kept smiling.

Elections are a mixture of chaos and chance. Slowly, day by day, Dom was losing his chance.

Then it all got worse. It was Tina's fault. The flame of betrayal still burned bright within her. She let it be known that Jack thought the election was turning to disaster, and that it was Dom's fault. Not up to the task of leadership. Jack couldn't say so directly, of course, not in the middle of a campaign, so he responded to the questions from the media with a sucked-lemon smile and words that suggested he was a thousand per cent behind his leader – words so extravagant that everyone instantly concluded they were ironic. And Jack wasn't the only one with doubts, so Tina told them all breathlessly. When these reports were piled upon the rumours that Dom was wilting under the pressure, it was bound to throw the preparations off course.

It didn't take the Prime Minister long to play one of those tricks that it is only possible for prime ministers to play. It took advantage of the fact that the President of the United States was on an official visit to Germany. Long planned, no surprise. In Berlin, standing in sunlight on the steps of the Bundestag, he had praised the Germans and their capital city for their historic role in withstanding the terror of Communism and in liberating Eastern Europe. While those with longer memories might have recalled the part Germany had played in enslaving half of Europe in the first place, that wasn't the message of the moment. The President had come to grasp hands with his friends – friends whose more recent past might yet prove an inspiration to other less fortunate parts of the world. Iraq wasn't mentioned, but even the deafest of the dull knew what he meant. Salvation from the ashes.

Then he flew to Paris. Almost a repeat performance, even though the French had always been bitter opponents of his policy in Iraq. But no talk of dissent, not this time. Instead, another speech about enduring friendship, hands across the water, all that sort of stuff. Liberty, equality, fraternity, principles that had always been a beacon of hope to oppressed peoples, he told them, from a spot only a beggar's spit from where the tumbrels and guillotine had done their bloody business. Not a whisper of Iraq anywhere, and nothing about cheese-eating surrender monkeys, or any of the other putrid denunciations of the French that had dripped from American pens in the past. Instead, the two presidents sat on an ornately carved sofa and held hands.

Then the surprise. An announcement that he was flying to Britain for what the communiqué called 'a substantive update'. It hadn't been on his schedule, and he wouldn't be spending long there, only a few hours, but enough time to give Danderson all the photo opportunities he could desire. It was tantamount to direct interference in the election campaign, but the Americans had no qualms about that. Florida, Illinois, London, what was the difference? Elections everywhere required a little fixing. And the President didn't care for what he'd heard about the new man on the block, Dominic Edge. The President knew who his friends were, Freddie Danderson was one of them, and he wanted the world to know that it paid to be friends with the US of A. He denied he was meddling, of course, it was simply a chance to catch up with his old friend Freddie, and that he had nothing against Mr Edge, saying, with studied ambiguity, that he had heard he was an excellent Leader of the Opposition. One day, in fact, he would very much like to meet him, although he ducked the offer to suggest that he supported Dom a thousand per cent.

President and Prime Minister were shown easy in each other's company, two statesmen who represented one of the strongest alliances in the world, joining hands in solidarity to throttle the life out of Dom's campaign. He couldn't possibly compete. And Julia was at it once more, declaring that she had been pressured to stop writing – 'Too many people seem to be enjoying my column for the politicians' taste,' she declared, 'but I'm not the sort of girl who goes down lightly!' In fact, the only person to have raised any objection was Max Morgan, in the tentative hope that his exclusive contract for her recollections about her affair might prevent her, or at least inhibit her, in writing observations for another paper, but while the lawyers haggled, Julia scribbled on and Dom inevitably got splashed by the mud. His temperature rose another degree. Ginny ordered him to bed.

He was woken from a fitful sleep as the latest batch of opinion polls landed on his lap, showing that the lead with which Danderson had started the campaign had increased. Dom stayed in bed for another day. The newspapers speculated that his illness was terminal, politically at least.

It was late. Ginny came quietly into Archie's office. It was crowded with a jumble of advertising proofs, suggestions for new posters that were propped on tables and ledges in such a haphazard manner they gave the impression of having been abandoned. Archie was staring into space, feet propped on the desk, smoking, the blue ribbon winding its way up to the ceiling.

'Didn't know you indulged,' she said.

He looked round, surprised. 'Only during elections,' he muttered.

'Elections like this, you mean.'

He swung his feet down and turned to face her. 'Could be worse.'

Although he still hadn't invited her, she sat in a chair close beside him, trying to narrow the distance that always seemed to stretch between them. 'What will happen if it does get worse?'

He studied her for a moment, trying to peer into her eyes, to see whether she truly wanted honesty, and how much of that rare elixir she could take. But he didn't understand her, had never had much luck in understanding women, so he did what he always did and said what was in his mind. 'The election came too soon. We needed more time to get Dom established, to help him sort out priorities. Danderson's a shrewd old dog. Knew what he was doing.'

'Can we win?'

'Anything's possible.'

'But, in your experience, is it likely? I need to know, Archie.'

'We don't have any experience of a leaders' debate. We've got that to come. It might be the upset we've been looking for.'

'But?'

'I wouldn't bet your mortgage on it.'

'We already have . . .'

'Then I'm sorry for you.'

'It's a bitter game, politics.'

'Always.'

She examined her outstretched hands, as though hoping a solution might fall into them straight out of the heavens. Her words came slowly, picking their way along a path of fire. 'What will happen if we lose?'

'To Dom, you mean?' He drew deep on his cigarette. 'Losers aren't lasters. They fall by the wayside – or get pushed. There'll be a struggle. Jack Saunders. Others. They all want their few months of fame.'

'You've seen so many come and go.'

'Doesn't get any easier.'

'What's the good news?'

He chuckled, but without mirth. 'If we win, we'll all be heroes.'

'Do you believe in miracles, Archie?'

'No.'

'Neither do I.'

Dom would be simply another Leader of the Opposition. A name remembered for failure, and only by a few. A shadow passed over her soul and something inside Ginny died. Not her innocence, it was already too late for that, but she had held on to a naïve optimism that it might one day return. Now even that was gone, too. She had stepped out on to the pathway that leads away from honest ambition and allows no return. With every part of her she hated this world of ruthless advancement that threatened to rip apart her family, but now she had become part of it, sucked in, a player in the most pitiless of games. And she was about to lose.

Yet failure wasn't acceptable to Ginny Edge. If Fate and Fortune weren't to save her, she would have to find another way. She would have to save herself.

Bobby started his enquiries with one of the Special Branch officers. An armed protection team had been posted for duty with Dom during the course of the campaign, and they quickly made themselves at home – too much so for Ginny. The presence of uniformed police outside the front door and armed men in the kitchen had, at first, greatly upset her. She felt as if her home had been invaded and her family was under direct threat, but she relented when she realised how engrossed Ben had become with it all. He almost burst with excitement the first time an officer slipped off his jacket to reveal his gun. From that moment he changed his entire focus on life, deciding he wanted to join Special Branch rather than pursue his most recent passion for becoming a forensic pathologist. Producing bodies rather than coping with them was much more fun, he explained.

At the start of the campaign Ginny had struggled to cope with the guilt of being forced to choose between Dom and the children, knowing they both needed her, but Ben and Jemma had quickly come to treat the whole thing as an adventure, being saluted by a policeman every time they left for school, seeing their parents on television whenever they returned. They had to deal with a series of strange makeshift nannies whose tea-time cooking was erratic, and sometimes Ginny didn't see them from one day to the next, but they slept secure and content in the childish certainty that their father was about to win the greatest game of his life. Any number of opinion polls failed to persuade them otherwise.

When Bobby took his questions about Ajok to one of the Special Branch officers, it was explained to him that it was strictly against regulations to share information from the Police National Database with private citizens, even politicians. But, hell, it was also a hanging offence to sell information to national newspapers and that had never stopped anyone. Anyway, as Bobby explained to Frank, the sergeant, the information was for Ginny, and Frank liked Ginny. He liked Bobby, too. So he coughed.

'Depends on your point of view,' he said to Bobby, as they made two mugs of tea in the kitchen. 'You go by what's in the database and she's about as dangerous as bloody bin Laden. Fraud, conspiracy, politically motivated attacks on the Prime Minister. It's endless. She's even bringing legal action trying to get the Iraq thing declared illegal – imagine what would happen if that ever succeeded. Chaos. So turn on the computer, tap in her name, and you'll find red flags waving like it's May Day in Moscow. They've really got it in for her.'

'Who? Who's got it in for her?'

Frank's head sank. 'Doesn't have to by anyone, not any more. Just the way things are. She doesn't fit in. Take on the System and you're a marked man. Or woman. It's like taking on the Cybermen. Relentless.'

'You don't sound too happy about it.'

'Happiness is not past of my job description,' Frank replied, pouring three teaspoons of sugar into his mug.

'So what is she really like?'

'Dunno. On the one hand she's a threat to national security. On the other she's nothing more than a single mum trying to do her best for her kids. Not a thing proved against her, not yet at least. It's all suspicion. But once it's on the computer, it's gum on your shoes. Follows you everywhere.'

'So?'

Frank sipped his tea. 'Shouldn't be telling you this – any of it – and not this in particular. Just between the two of us, eh?'

Bobby nodded.

'Lauren Danderson's got her fingerprints all over this one. Taken a deep dislike to Mrs Arob, she has. Made a real fuss about how we should throw the book at her.'

'Does that make a difference?'

'Shouldn't. Shouldn't make the slightest difference, not at all. But . . . That's on the computer, too. Another black mark. A bleedin' huge black mark when it comes out of Downing Street. And Mrs Arob's got so many of them.'

Bobby nodded thoughtfully. 'Thanks, Frank. I owe you.'

'Sure. Any time. Well, within reason, of course. So long as it's just between you and me.'

'Trust me.' Bobby smiled.

'Anyway, once this election thing's over, how about you and me going out for a drink? I'd like that.'

Bobby's smile grew. 'I'd like that, too.'

When at last Dom clambered from his sick bed, refreshed but not entirely recovered, he found still further distractions. Waiting for him was a gaggle of advisers, pollsters and fellow politicians who clamoured to offer him advice, much of it conflicting, about how he should relaunch his campaign. To Dom's ears, every word sounded like an attack on his leadership. They discussed alternatives from a new tax policy to a visit to Colin Penrith's graveside, until they reflected on the headlines that such a visit would produce. The Dead. The Dying . . . It was a sign of desperation when Dom ordered a new advertising campaign. He had no specific instruction for its message – that was what they paid the advertising agency for – but he wanted it quick. Energy. Action. It's what politicians do when they run out of ideas.

He was in his headquarters office working on his next speech when he heard a knock on the door. It was Mark Fitzmaurice, the party's treasurer, an elderly, bewhiskered man who had made an earlier career in the Royal Navy. He stood with his feet apart, as though bracing himself on a rolling deck.

'Sorry to bother you, Dom. Need a word.'

'I'm very busy, Mark . . .'

'It can't wait. This additional advertising campaign you want. Can't be done, I'm afraid. Not enough money in the kitty if we want to have anything left for the last couple of weeks.'

'Can't you raise some more?'

The other man sighed. 'It's been a difficult few days. They're not exactly clamouring at the door to sign cheques. And you, of all people, know just how much it's cost to kick off the campaign, keep things on the road.'

'You must have something in reserve.'

'I've only got what we get. Which isn't enough.'

'Then borrow it.'

'I'm not going to bankrupt the party, Dom. There's no guarantee we'd be able to repay any large loans after the election.'

What he meant, of course, was that there would be no money if they lost. If they won, well, the possibilities were endless, but Mark Fitzmaurice was a shrewd man who had sailed many seas and seen many ships founder. Clearly he wasn't banking on sunshine and favourable winds.

Dom stared at him, exasperated, angry, his grip tightening on his pen, about to condemn the other man for his pusillanimity and defiance, when the pen snapped. Two pieces that flew across the room. Useless. It seemed to be a metaphor for his entire campaign. Something inside him snapped, too. When the words came at last, his voice was hoarse, fractured, 'How do I do this, Mark?'

'You do your best, Dom. That's the only advice I can give.'

Dom seemed to deflate. He lowered his eyes to his half-finished speech, studying it with an air of hopelessness, as if it were his own death warrant. Fitzmaurice stepped forward, took a pen from his own pocket and placed it on the table in front of Dom, then quietly left the room.

Courage. Confusion. Overworked policies and preposterous confrontations. Elections are built on many foundations, but the enduring ingredient is the most sordid of all. Money. Dom hadn't enough of it while, just across town, Freddie Danderson was about to get a whole lot more.

Funds for political parties are raised by a team of treasurers, and Aiden Brett was one of the youngest members in the Danderson team. Enthusiastic, ambitious, a stockbroker by training, used to taking care of money and those who had plenty of it. He was not one of the senior treasurers – although he had told his wife it was only a matter of time – so it fell to him to sift through the newcomers who came knocking at the door. Some would be genuine donors, cheques in hand, while others were unambiguous seekers of advantage, and more than a few would prove to be a complete waste of time. Brett's task was to sort the wheat from the chaff, those who were genuinely prosperous from those who were nothing more than posers, then decide how best to extract the maximum amount of money from them. It was never an easy task, made all the more difficult by the scandals of recent years. Honours had been sold too cheaply, too blatantly, without subtlety or even much attempt at subterfuge, and it had landed them all in the muck. They had to be damned careful.

So Brett was cautious about the man sitting opposite him in the tearoom at the Savoy. Rupak Patel was a stranger, someone who had telephoned and been most insistent. 'I wish to help you,' Patel had said, in an English accent that seemed to mingle the back-streets of Bombay with the industrial estates of Birmingham. So they had agreed to meet.

'I have a very large spice-supply business, Mr Brett,' Patel had explained from his seat on an ample sofa, as the waiter poured leaf Darjeeling through a silver strainer. 'It has prospered under your government, and so have I,' he continued, laying a hand on his ample stomach and smiling. 'I wish to show my gratitude.'

'How, Mr Patel?'

'By helping make sure you win the election.'

'In what way?'

'By supporting you financially as well as with my vote.'

'You are . . .' Brett was about to say 'English', but grasped at other words in time to avoid offence '. . . a registered voter?'

'Oh, yes. I was born in India but I came to this country almost twenty years ago.'

'That's excellent. Essential, actually. You have to be on the register in order to make a gift. Unless you wanted to make a corporate donation, in which case . . .'

'No. I wish this to be an entirely personal matter.' Patel had a remarkable neck that seemed to be made of rubber, and his head moved from side to side as he spoke, swaying like wheat in the wind.

'So – if I may ask – why not make your donation through your local party, in your constituency?'

'Oh, I already have, but only a relatively small amount, which I gave anonymously. I had in mind a rather larger donation for Mr Danderson. But I don't wish simply to sign a cheque, Mr Brett. I would like to know what my donation might be used for,' Patel continued, slurping his tea.

The young treasurer tried his own cup, but it was still far too hot. Instead he studied the embossed name card the man had pushed across at him. How high to pitch it? What might he be worth – and not just to the party but to himself? There were rewards in store for those treasurers who performed, he had been told, and although it would be unusual for a party treasurer below the age of forty to end up in the Lords, Brett lacked nothing in ambition. They'd given him the minor donors, the short end of the stick, while the senior treasurers prowled around with the fat cats. Yet the new restrictions and regulations about funding had scared away many of the bigger beasts, made them retreat into the shadows, dragging their chequebooks with them. Perhaps this new face had a little more to prove.

'I know that all parties end up after the elections very deep in debt,' Patel continued, in the lilting cadence of the subcontinent. 'I would not care for any donation I made to be thrown into a black hole. I would like to be associated with something specific. I would like to feel' – he spread his hands wide – 'some sense of ownership.'

'Well, Mr Patel, there are things such as election broadcasts. Cost a pretty penny to make, I can assure you. And the poster campaigns you see around the country take up even more of our budget.'

'How much, may I ask? For an election broadcast, let us say.'

'They can cost up to fifty thousand each. Sometimes more.'

The Indian's head was shaking once more, and Brett's heart sank. Another time-waster.

'I am sorry, Mr Brett, but that will not do.'

'Pity.'

'You see, I was thinking of making a donation substantially larger than that sum.'

Brett lowered his voice, the words squeezing with difficulty past his lips. 'How – much – larger?'

Patel shrugged his shoulders and spread his hands wide, very wide.

Brett's eyes cast nervously around the crowded tearoom, searching for eavesdroppers. 'I'm not sure this is the right place, Mr Patel. May I suggest we continue this in private? In my office?'

Ajok paused as she stood on the steps of Charing Cross police station, looking out at the bustling street before she rejoined her familiar world. The sky above her head was a soft creamy blue and the gentle breeze picked up little whirling funnels of dust. A good day to be outside, away from the soul-stifling interview room with its panic buttons and dead air and recording machines that she had just left.

She had reported back to the station, as she had been instructed to do, but they had done little other than to tell her to come back again in another two weeks. Hadn't got all their paperwork together. Someone had come to the conclusion that they ought to get a statement from Mrs Danderson, but she was busy and, in any event, not proving very co-operative. Other things on her mind. The election campaign. It made everyone's task more trying. The police had no enthusiasm for pursuing political protesters during the course of an election: if they started on that, where would they stop? They'd have to lock up half the country. They tried to turn a blind eye whenever they could, keep out of it, but Lauren Danderson was proving difficult in all sorts of ways. So, wait until the campaign was over, let the dust settle, see what happened then.

The custody sergeant had looked at her with a very serious expression on his face. 'Mrs Arob, do yourself and us a favour – a very *great* favour,' he emphasised, in his world-weary voice, running a finger round his sticky collar. 'Whatever else you do – please – stay away from Downing Street. Too many other people trying to kick their way in right now. You'll only get trampled in the rush.'

'It is an unhappy place for me,' Ajok replied. 'Unhappy memories. I will not go back there.'

The custody sergeant had sighed in relief, then told her she could leave. Yet now, as she stood outside on the steps, blinking in the reflection of sunlight that came off the windows on the far side of the street, someone was calling to her: 'Mrs Arob? Are you Mrs Arob, by any chance?' A young man was drawing closer to her. 'My name is Bobby Khan. Sorry to disturb you, but I wonder if we might have a word?'

Ginny arrived at Ajok's home late the following afternoon with Bobby in tow. The weather had changed: rain was spattering the pavements and choking the gutters, creating great ponds of cigarette butts and sweet-wrappers. In the world of her dreams she would one day be ferried everywhere by a patient driver with a

Special Branch escort; this afternoon she had driven around for ten minutes before she had found a parking meter, then walked the rest of the way, playing hopscotch with the puddles.

The two boys, Chol and Mijok, wrestled with each other as they fought to be the first to answer the knock on the door, but their faces fell in uncertainty when they saw two strangers. Mijok wiped the remains of his tea from his lips. Fried beans. The smell still crept from the kitchen. With all of them in the same room, the apartment seemed extraordinarily crowded. Schoolbooks and bags had spilled from the table and flowed across the floor. It reminded Ginny of her student days, when in their final year Dom had moved almost permanently into her bedroom and they had spent the months before graduation tripping over books and suitcases and little piles of clothes, but always in the end tumbling on to the bed. So much discovery, so much passion, she remembered wistfully, so long ago.

'Thank you for agreeing to see me, Mrs Arob,' Ginny said, sitting in one of the threadbare chairs. The boys retreated to the table as Ajok poured coffee into three mugs. They were all of different patterns, and Ajok's own had a large chip in its lip.

'You are welcome,' Ajok replied. Ginny noticed how graceful her movements were, and how sad her eyes. Ginny knew she was intruding into someone else's world; she sensed that Ajok wasn't comfortable with her being there, and that only politeness had made her agree to the visit. Or maybe it was simply that she was a poor black immigrant and felt she had no place to refuse a request from a white woman. Even the thought of such things made Ginny blush, and her sense of discomfort increased.

'It's a little difficult to explain why I'm here, Mrs Arob,' she began, and sipped the hot coffee. 'I read about your difficulties, and your family. I'm not sure but . . . somehow we seem to have a lot in common.'

'Really?'

'Our children. Their ages. Our shared difficulties with Mrs

Danderson. The fact that we have both found ourselves dragged into the game of politics whether we like it or not.'

'I see.' Ajok's eyes were direct, her tone cautious.

'I much admire you, Mrs Arob. I would like to help, if I can.'

'In what way?'

'I'm not entirely certain. Advice. Support. Just being here for you. Letting you know you're not alone. I think that matters at times like this.'

Ajok offered no reply. She sat gazing across her mug, cradled in her hands.

'I've brought something for the boys,' Ginny said anxiously. She reached into her bag and hauled out an Action Man and a football annual. 'I hope you don't mind.'

From the other side of the room, Chol and Mijok squirmed in their seats with anticipation, but neither moved, waiting for their mother to speak.

'That is very kind of you,' Ajok said softly, and the two boys cried out in excitement as they rushed to get their presents. They both bowed formally in thanks, their faces lit by huge beams of happiness.

'I have a son about their age. I wish his manners were as good.'

'I am sorry, Mrs Edge, but I have nothing in return for your son . . .'

'No! It's me who should be apologising.' A purple shadow of alarm crossed Ginny's face. 'I didn't mean to embarrass you. I had no intention . . . Mrs Arob, all I wanted was a few minutes with you, I expect nothing more. You've already been more than kind to welcome us into your home. All I want is to try to help.'

'So, Mrs Edge, you are someone else who wishes to help me.'

'Someone else?'

Ajok let forth a sigh, a sound of weariness that came from deep within. 'There have been so many people who started off by saying they would help. My supervisor at work. Mr Messenger from the trade union. The local benefits office. Even my own lawyer, Miss

Gaminara – a nice lady, but . . . In reality, they all wish to help themselves. And it is because of them that I am here.'

Ginny bit her lip, a little ashamed. 'Perhaps there's something of that in my being here, too. I apologise. But why don't we help each other?'

'How can I help someone like you?'

'Your case against the Government. It's very interesting. In fact, it could become very important. For us both. As you may know, the war is an issue close to my husband's heart. And then there's your difficulty with the car and Mrs Danderson. Frankly, anything that involves Lauren Danderson also involves me. We're on the same side, you and I.'

'You mean we both hate Baggarans.'

'Beg pardon?'

Ajok shook her head, but for the first time she allowed herself the trace of a sad smile. 'All I ever wanted was my cleaning job.'

'Perhaps I can do something about that, too, if my husband wins the election.'

'If your husband wins the election, all sorts of miracles might happen.'

Miracles. That word again. For a moment Ginny wondered whether the other woman was mocking her, but Ajok was too honest for the flippant games other people played. Anyway, she was right. If Dom won, all sorts of wonderful, magical things might take place.

'Tell me about your own children, Mrs Edge,' Ajok suggested.

'Only if you tell me about Baggarans.'

And while Bobby played with the boys, the two women talked, and drew closer.

'Greetings, Mr Patel. Good to see you again!' Brett extended his hand as he strode across his office.

Patel smiled. As they shook hands, Brett saw his guest in a new light – the Rolex that peered from beneath his cuff, the careful cut of his suit, the slim Louis Vuitton briefcase that he carried, the restrained silk tie. Only the roughness of his hands spoke of the self-made man who had made his millions out of packaging cumin and curry. Rupak Patel had checked out. Not that his local party had been of any use, but that was little more than a skeleton organisation and the woman to whom Brett had spoken seemed to have trouble identifying the party's candidate, let alone being able to cast light on any local business personalities. But he was on the electoral register, of that there was no doubt. And Patel's company was every bit as successful as the man had claimed. Operated in many countries. Excellent credit rating. According to Google, it had wobbled a few years previously when his brother had left the business to set up in competition, but the company had survived and prospered. Patel had devoted himself to his business, had a reputation as a workaholic and no record of industrial indiscretions, social misfortunes or even speeding tickets. Hadn't even made time for a wife and kids. A company man, and mostly his own company, it seemed.

They exchanged small-talk, but Brett was anxious to get on with matters.

'Your donation couldn't come at a better time, Mr Patel,' he explained. 'We've got so many new regulations about party financing. In all honesty, it's made our task doubly difficult. Your help is a blessing at this stage of the campaign. Yes, a blessing. And we will, of course, find some very suitable way of showing our gratitude.'

'In what manner?'

A gentle yet significant pause. 'What manner would you like?'

The two men stared at each other in a moment of intense mutual examination before the visitor reached for his briefcase. He snapped it open, and turned it to face Brett. It was stuffed with fifty-pound notes. Brett gasped.

'A first contribution, another to follow. It will total half a million pounds, Mr Brett. How much gratitude would that buy?'

'A very significant amount.'

Patel laughed very loudly. 'Then perhaps it is an excellent thing that I do not want very much at all,' he said. 'I have read of your other donors. Lordships and peerages and all those silly things. But what would I do with the House of Lords? I don't even have sufficient time to spend in my own house, let alone anyone else's.' The laughter was sustained; Brett found himself unable to join in.

'You want . . . nothing?' The words were soaked in incredulity.

'Nothing, Mr Brett.'

'Nothing? At all?'

'Oh, I have a couple of relatives whom I may wish to bring over to this country to help in my business, and I would like to make sure their passage here is a smooth one, but I believe you wouldn't even have to bend your regulations for that to happen, let alone break them.'

Ah, passports, Brett said to himself. Bit of a history on that front but, with care, could be arranged yet again.

'And I would like, one day, perhaps, please, to have tea with Mr Danderson.' The rubberised neck was working once more, lending a submissive tone to all his words. 'I admire him so much. It would be an honour. He has helped to make my life so very rewarding. I wish only to repay a little of the good fortune that has come my way.'

Tea? Brett screamed inside. You want *tea*? For five hundred thou' you can sleep with his bloody wife . . . 'And? And, Mr Patel? What else?' Brett pressed, wanting to make a full mental note of any conditions.

The head was gyrating wildly. 'Well, the only other thing I can think of is . . .'

'Yes? Yes?'

'If ever a volcano were to erupt in the English Channel and form a new island, it would be comforting if it could be named after my dear mother. But apart from that, there is absolutely nothing.' And he began to laugh again, teasing. This time, Brett joined in. But his mind was in overdrive. Half a million pounds. A couple of passports. A pot of tea. There had to be a catch. Their eyes met, and Patel saw the glimmering flecks of suspicion.

'Nothing. Absolutely nothing,' he repeated. 'Apart from the fact that, as a good friend of the Prime Minister's and as a proud Englishman, I would expect his help with those very recidivist bastards who run the rest of Europe. There are ridiculous men and women in Brussels who try to block my products at every turn. I have spent a fortune – many, many times what is in the briefcase – to ensure that my products are the best available. I take pride in that fact. That they are the best – the very best, Mr Brett. I, Rupak Patel, put my name to nothing but the finest quality. I am known for it wherever I have been. The very finest!' His cheeks were puffed with indignation. 'Yet still there are those in Brussels who think it right to block my work. First they say there are health considerations. Then they say I employ sweated labour. All lies – lies, Mr Brett! What they mean is that my products are so good they threaten to put workers in their own country out of business. But that is what free trade is all about, Mr Brett. They take over our banks and our car industry, yet they cannot stand the idea that we British might take over their curry houses!' Patel paused to allow his emotion to dissipate. He checked his tie, tugged at his cuffs. 'Forgive me, my dear Mr Brett, but they have acted so unfairly. All I ask is that the Prime Minister considers my case, looks at the disgraceful behaviour. And after he has considered it, perhaps he might write a few letters. Go in to bat for me, simply to ensure that there is a level wicket. That is all I ask. And to do that not because of my gift, but because Mr Danderson is the British Prime Minister.'

Brett felt relief flooding through him. At last he understood. Patel was just like the rest. Wanted a favour. A few doors opening, a helping hand that would make this half-million pounds look like small change. He smiled. Relaxed. No problem. The man didn't even want a peerage; it meant there would be one more peerage to spare after all this was over, one that he might be able to claim. Money had become so tight, the party was aching for fighting funds, and he, Aiden Brett, was riding to the rescue. Their gratitude would be boundless, he would make sure of that. Suddenly, he felt as if he had been reborn, his life about to start afresh. He would remember this moment for the rest of his life. Brett leaned across to touch the briefcase, move it a few inches closer.

'Let me assure you, Mr Patel, that the Prime Minister knows his duty very well. He doesn't need a donation to be reminded of it. But generosity such as yours would touch him deeply. And we're the sort of people who take care of our friends.'

'Your words come as a great comfort to me, Mr Brett.'

Brett sat back in his chair, rejoicing, feeling the brush of ermine at his collar. 'Might I suggest something a little stronger than tea to celebrate? A glass of champagne, perhaps, for friendship, while we complete the necessary paperwork?'

'Forgive me, Mr Brett, but I am a Muslim. It is forbidden.'

Brett cursed himself. 'I'm so sorry, I—'

'No offence taken, I assure you. But tell me, please, what is the paperwork you mention?'

'Nothing more than the details of your gift for the necessary statutory declaration.'

'Declaration?'

'Nowadays all gifts of this size have to be declared to the Electoral Commission.'

'And will be made public?'

'Most certainly.'

'I had not realised.'

'I'm afraid it's a suspicious world. We have to jump through all sorts of hoops. It's meant to stop people buying peerages, that sort of nonsense.'

'But I do not want a peerage.'

'Even so, the law insists that we register your donation with the Commission.'

Brett felt the temperature in the room drop several degrees. He shivered.

The other man's face was twisted in an expression of misery. 'I do not want publicity. I have seen what that does to others. My dignity is important to me, Mr Brett. I do not want my name and the good reputation of my business dragged around behind the media.'

'I'm sure it won't come to that.'

'But it already has.'

There was no denying his point. The list of proud businessmen who had come knocking at the door of Downing Street waving their chequebooks, only to be turned into media casualties, was endless. Danderson's predecessor had pleaded with the press to trust him on this, but nobody had. Danderson couldn't afford to be dragged down like that.

'Is there no way that I can help you without publicity?' Patel asked.

'I'm afraid not. The law's an ass, I know, but . . .'

He choked as he watched Patel lean forward to slide the briefcase back towards him. His new life was over before it had even begun. 'Mr Patel, please, there must be something . . .'

Patel shook his head endlessly in sorrow. 'I am so sorry, Mr Brett.'

'I'd hoped we could be such good friends.'

Patel paused. 'Then in friendship, Mr Brett, let me tell you why I insist on privacy.' He squeezed the tip of his nose in a gesture of hesitation. 'I am not married, you see. I live with another man. I hope that doesn't offend you?'

'Of course not.'

'But in Islam that is a most appalling sin. My reputation within my community, among the people with whom I work and trade, would be ruined if ever they were to know. It is the way of our world. So I do not wish to see the media camped outside my gates, nor become the butt of cruel jokes.'

He flicked the locks shut on the briefcase; to Brett the noise sounded like the slamming of the door to his dreams.

'Can I not . . . ?'

But Patel was rising, still shaking his head, briefcase in hand. He was half-way to the door, treading on Brett's hopes with every step, when he paused. 'How much could I give, Mr Brett, without my name being made public?'

'Up to five thousand pounds.'

'So very little? For such a great need?'

'The law!' Brett snapped. There was no disguising his exasperation and sense of hurt. 'It assumes a man is guilty because he's rich. They starve democracy. They'll kill it off in the end.'

Patel stood in the middle of the office, his head lowered in thought. 'How many people give such small donations?'

'Literally thousands. Sometimes we get letters with a five-pound note stuck in it, sometimes a few coins from a pensioner's weekly allowance. This morning I got an envelope with an old wedding ring in it. Came from the finger of a party supporter who had just died. His widow asked us to put it to good use.'

'Then perhaps . . .'

'What is it, Mr Patel?'

'Perhaps there is a way. Take a hundred of such people, even a thousand if you wish, as many as you want. I could add a little to each of their donations, keep them well below the limit. You would have your money. I would have my privacy.'

'But . . .'

'There is no law against me giving money to strangers, is there?'

'None that I know of.'

'You send them letters of thanks. Don't mention the amount. They are happy. The law is happy. Then you and I may be happy, also.'

A long silence, pregnant with decision.

'Mr Brett, I am a great believer in privacy. Only you and I need ever know.'

'Mr Patel, would you mind if I opened a bottle of champagne regardless? I feel in very great need of a drink . . .'

★

Morgan picked up his direct line.

'Max, talk to me. As a friend,' the voice said.

'I'll try, Ginny. Always make an exception for you.'

'Whose side will the *Record* come down on?'

'No one's. Not until after the debate. It's like the shoot-out at the OK Corral. The entire country'll be watching, could be the biggest telly audience in years. Not often you see grown men lining up in front of cameras to blow each other's brains out. So the only decent thing for us to do is to wait and see if there are any survivors. No point in jumping the gun, so to speak.'

'So there's a chance?'

'For Dom? Not a hope in hell.'

'But you said you're waiting for the debate . . .'

'Me and the rest of Fleet Street. But it's only to show how decent and reasonable we are. Face it, Ginny, the latest polls put the government more than eight points ahead.'

'Pollsters get it wrong sometimes.'

'Sure they do.'

'But not that wrong.'

'The only thing that's going to stop Danderson now is if he's caught shagging his own granny. And she's under contract to the *Mirror*.'

There was a deep silence at the other end of the line.

'It's not that they dislike Dom, you've got to understand that, Ginny. It's just that they don't know him very well,' the editor continued, trying belatedly to soften the blow. 'And they don't yet hate Danderson enough to take a risk on the unknown. Maybe next time round, for sure. But . . .'

'Go on.'

'I hear the bookies are about to stop taking bets on this one. For what it's worth, Ginny, you'll still have a column with the *Record*, if you want it. You've got what it takes, girl.'

'I don't want to be a newspaper columnist, Max. I want to be the wife of the Prime Minister.'

He sighed. 'You might just have to wait on that one.'

'No chance of changing your mind? Not even in exchange for my body?'

'Oh, hell, yes. For that I'd do anything I could, you know that all too well. But I'd be shagging you under false pretences. It's not my call, you see. It's the proprietor's. And there's still too much he wants to squeeze out of Danderson.'

He heard what he thought was a sob. 'You asked me as a friend, Ginny. And I've been a better friend than ever I thought I was capable of being.'

The line went dead.

Fourteen

RUPAK PATEL PUSHED THE soft-leather briefcase across the table, throwing its catches as he did so. 'The last tranche of the money, Mr Brett.'

'Please, call me Aiden. I feel like we're old friends.'

'That would be my very great pleasure.'

'I can't find the right words to tell you how grateful we are, Rupak.'

'There is no need.'

'Oh, but there is.' He picked up a telephone beside him and punched a button. 'Hi, there, this is Aiden Brett. The PM wanted to know as soon as Mr Rupak Patel was here. Would you tell him that I have passed on his thanks to Mr Patel and made arrangements for that private meeting we discussed?'

Across the table, the businessman's eyes grew wide with appreciation.

'Thanks so much,' Brett concluded, replacing the phone. 'It's all set up, Rupak, at a time that suits you and as soon as possible after the election. It would be even sooner, of course, but preparation for this leaders' debate is taking up so much of Freddie's time.'

'I fully understand.'

What he didn't understand was that the phone call had been made not to Danderson's office but to Brett's own secretary. The words were merely for show, tinsel, to make Patel feel good, as though it was Christmas. He'd get his meeting, but all in good time. Meanwhile, no harm in letting him feel he was right up at the top of the tree alongside the fairy.

'And I want to show you this,' Brett continued, with excitement, stretching to retrieve a piece of artwork that was lying face down on the table. 'This is what we want to do with your money, if you approve. A national poster campaign in the final week. Our very last word to the electorate. The crowning thought. All made possible by your support.'

The artwork was simple, showing the face of a smiling Danderson above a caption that read: *It's Getting Better All the Time.*

'It's from an old Beatles' song. You know the Beatles? We're planning to play it everywhere. Get the whole country dancing in the streets. Use it as a theme for everything we do in the last few days. It's what Freddie's planning to talk about at his final rally. All this is super-confidential stuff, of course, just between the two of us, but I hope you like it.'

'Very much indeed.' The businessman was rocking with approval.

'Sold, then!' Brett wanted to hug himself in congratulation. It was the third time in a couple of days that he'd sold the poster campaign to a donor. They were all so much happier in the belief that they were paying for something specific rather than digging out the party's overdraft. 'There is just one question, if I may, Rupak?'

'Anything.'

The treasurer wriggled in his seat. 'Please don't take offence but . . . why cash? Frankly, it's a little unusual nowadays for such a generous donation to arrive in this form.' Indeed, it was more than unusual: it was exceptional. Smacked of the old days, before everyone had taken fright and decided that peerages should be bought over the counter rather than off the back of a lorry. His masters in the Treasurer's Department had given him a real grilling over it – nothing but jealousy, of course, and a collective covering of arses, but they'd insisted he come up with an answer.

'Oh, it is very simple, Aiden,' the other man responded, waggling his head. 'You see, my company supplies products to tens of thousands of Indian restaurants and corner shops all over the country. John o'Groats to Land's End. Did you know that nowadays curry is eaten more often than roast beef or egg and chips? I am indeed a very fortunate man. But these restaurants and small businesses are mostly family-run concens. They prefer to do business in the traditional Indian way. In cash. So I am forced to handle a very large amount of it. But if you look at my company's accounts you will see that half a million pounds is only a very small part of the total. And, also – this is very important – if you look at my company's accounts, you will see that they are in impeccable order.'

That was true enough. Brett had already checked. He relaxed. The ermine was his. 'Rupak, I hope you understand I wasn't in any way suggesting—'

'I understand the need for caution, Aiden. It is no more than I would do in your position. Sadly, we live in suspicious times. It is why I always insist on playing with a very straight bat.'

'I hope we're going to see much more of you, Rupak. On a social level. To show how deeply we feel about what you've done for us. In fact, I'd like to invite you on the Prime Minister's behalf to the victory ball on election night. You'll be one of our very special guests. A chance to meet Freddie face to face, before we arrange that more intimate meeting.'

And once again Patel's head was shaking in that curiously rubber-necked way. 'It would be such an honour, Aiden, but, alas, I fear I cannot. I must leave on a business trip tomorrow, for India, and I regret that I shall not be back in time. I very much hope that the Prime Minister will understand. That he will not think me in any way rude.'

'Such a pity. But we'll redouble our efforts to get the two of you together just as soon as we can.'

And Patel was beaming.

Brett felt perspiration trickling on his brow. Perhaps it was the proximity of the money, or the excitement of what it meant for him. He'd already spent idle moments playing with handles for his peerage. Lord Brett of Barking, maybe? White Hart Lane, even? His cup would soon be running over, with his own coat of arms engraved on it. He stretched for the briefcase. 'I'd better lock this away, if you don't mind, Rupak. Can't leave such generous sums lying around.'

The Indian nodded in acquiescence as, with what amounted almost to reverence, Brett took charge of the case. 'If you'll excuse me, just for a moment.' He disappeared into another room.

Which meant he had no chance to observe what took place as soon as the door was closed. His guest rose, crossed the room to the treasurer's desk, took several sheets of his headed notepaper and placed them with great care in his jacket pocket.

The bath was like a cocoon, an all-embracing womb, a world of comfort and introspection where she could be alone with herself. From the other side of the door came the gentle sound of Dom's restless sleep; he was exhausted, still suffering from that bug. She examined her body, the toes, pink knees, nipples that protruded above the water line, a sanctuary that Dom had somehow defiled through his dalliance with Julia. It was also a body she had offered to Max, not in earnest, of course, but none the less . . . Would she? Ever? Like so many others?

Alice Keppel had used her body, offered it around on an exceptionally generous basis to help her husband's career and harvest their fortune. Been the court mistress of Edward VII, yet was still a devoted and much-loved wife. When she had died, in 1947 at the generous age of seventy-eight, her husband had quickly followed her to the grave, succumbing to what many thought was a broken heart. Although no broken heart is ever quite that simple. How had he managed, through all her affairs, to maintain his devotion? What of fidelity, of virtue? Yet when it came down to virtue, Ginny mused, how would she match up to Alice Keppel? Oh, splendidly – if remarkably unexcitingly – in the sexual stakes, but virtue, she had discovered, was a mobile feast that seemed to move almost as soon as you sat down at the table.

What were the limits of love? She had condemned Dom, yet would she revile Mrs Keppel, a woman who, in many eyes, what she had done first and foremost for the protection of her family? Ginny was no longer sure: she had grown less certain of many things. She had changed. Had done things she would never previously have countenanced, to protect her family. And Alice had had more fun, of that she was certain. Ginny and Dom hadn't had sex in more than a month. She was beginning to feel hollow and lonely. With her fingertips she wiped the moisture from around her eyes, and allowed her hand to trace the line of her chin and neck, to slip so slowly over her nipples and down her soapy body until it came to rest between her legs. Slowly, she spread them in the warm bathwater. She could hear the rattling sound of Dom snoring, declaring his exhaustion. Gently, as though with a feather, she touched herself. She hadn't done it in so long. And she continued. Her legs began to stretch, her chin came up, the water turned to ripples as she lost herself, pushing aside all the haunting doubts and reaching out for something no one could take from her. She had discovered that ambitions and desires – lusts, for want of a better term – came in many different forms, and Alice Keppel's had been the most simple of these, perhaps far from the worst, while Ginny's life became ever more complicated and confused. In her mind she saw Alice with her prince; the image got mixed up with Dom with his tart, and even Max Morgan got in there somewhere, until her body went rigid as all the restless uncertainties tried to force their way out of her at the same time. Her back arched. A strangled cry slipped from her lips. Tears streamed down her face. And slowly her body subsided back into the bath.

Still Dom slept.

When, at last, the waters were still once more, Ginny washed her face and asked herself what the bloody hell she was about. What had all this meant? Was it weakness? An expression of despair?

Acceptance, perhaps, that everything was lost, ruined, that she was on her own? The bathwater had gone cold before she thought she knew the answer. It was all about Alice, really, who had done what she needed to do, but on the terms handed to her by others. By men. As women had always done. But that wasn't good enough for Ginny. She didn't have to spread her legs like Alice, least of all like Julia. She had reached down deep within herself and found her own answers. She was in control. What Ginny Edge had to do, she would do on her own terms.

As always.

The debate. A magical moment. One of those turning points in history. For the media it had long been like the Holy Grail, pursued over so many years, but only now had they succeeded in cornering their quarry. Inevitably, it had become the focal point of the election campaign. The entire country was waiting. The analysis had been endless, with pundits parading all the theorems and stratagems – and capacity for cock-ups – leaning on distant memories of Kennedy and Nixon and other excruciating moments that had been filled with sweaty jowls, rubbery faces and haunted eyes. It wasn't a forum for the faint-hearted. The parties had brought in all types of consultants, domestic and foreign, from speech coaches to makeup experts, even specialists in the vernacular. No chances were being taken. The election was not to be lost for want of a powdered smile or well-dusted simile. Meanwhile, the leaders themselves built all other aspects of their campaign round the date. It also made the commentators uncharacteristically cautious: few were willing to give a definitive verdict on the competing merits of the two men until it had taken place and blood had been spilled. The debate was guaranteed the largest television audience for a political programme in British history. Eight o'clock in the evening, exactly one week before polling.

And that morning Dom woke up with a temperature of a hundred and two.

'I can't. I simply can't,' he whispered, in a voice ground to gravel by the infection. 'But I must.'

To delay was impossible: the television schedules would never allow for it. And to cancel was unthinkable – he might as well concede the election. So he had to continue.

The doctor muttered darkly in the traditional murky language of the medical world about mycoplasma and the dangers of ignoring these warning signs. He cautioned Dom about the risk of developing pneumonia, but his patient was insistent. Risk was part of the game. If Margaret Thatcher could get through an election campaign in agony from her ageing teeth, he could surely get through one evening with a bit of a temperature. So the doctor gave him erythromycin for the infection, syrup for the tortured throat and aspirin for the temperature. He also gave him a stern warning that he should take complete rest for the remaining twelve hours before it all began.

'Will he be OK?' enquired Archie as the doctor descended the stairs.

'I'm a doctor, not a maker of miracles,' the medical man had replied, as he left.

So they retreated to the kitchen. Seated round the table, with Dom tucked away upstairs, Archie's team set about devising a media strategy to cope with the circumstances – only trouble was, in their hearts they knew that nothing would cope. It was a little like Custer pretending that the dustcloud on the horizon was nothing more than the arrival of the chuck wagon. Nevertheless, they tried. Archie asked for suggestions. There were none. They sat with lowered heads, waiting for someone else to find the courage to speak and declare it a disaster, But Archie had other ideas. He called them useless tossers, then announced that they would let the world know of Dom's incapacity, praise his courage in continuing, and pray for the sympathy vote.

Ginny turned from studying the instructions on the medicines the doctor had left. She snorted in derision. 'You can't be serious.'

'It's more than just Dom's reputation and career on the line here,' Archie responded, too caustically. They were all exhausted.

You want to gamble your future on the tenderness of the British tabloids?'

The Scot stared into his cup of cold coffee. 'Well, it's an idea. Not a great one, I grant, but we've got to do something. Do nothing and it'll be about as comforting as bending over to pick up the soap in the showers at Eton.'

'Normally I'd bow to your far more considerable experience, Archie, but not this time. I'm the wife. I'm pulling rank.'

'So what's your suggestion, then?'

'We wait. And we see. Dom's already looking better. Who knows what this evening might bring?'

Since Dom was confined to bed with access allowed only to his doctor and his wife, it was a point that Archie could scarcely contest. And, either way, they were going to get screwed. He conceded with a scowl.

She spent the next hour in the garden with Bobby. No one disturbed them. They were like ancient mariners, sailing to the edge of their flat world, about to drop into the depths of the unknown, and no one wanted to distract them, let alone to climb on board. It was the voyage of the damned. Archie and his team left without saying goodbye.

Not everyone was useless. That evening the woman they had retained to supervise Dom's makeup earned every penny of her fee. By the time he arrived at the television studios on the South Bank, forty-five minutes before the start of the debate, the feverish complexion that had given him the look of an aspiring alcoholic had been wiped away, the sweating temples tamed – for the moment, at least – and the bruising beneath the eyes all but totally erased. Only the redness that clung to the rims and the cough that kept scouring the insides of his lungs gave any hint of how much he was suffering. Yet they all knew the subterfuge wouldn't last. It was only a matter of time before, like the Wicked Witch of the West, Dom melted away.

The two sides gathered in separate rooms of the complex. There was no need to meet beforehand: all the details had been agreed long ago – timings, format, where and when they would sit or stand, who would ask the questions, in what order they would answer them, how many invited guests, how many members of the public. They had tossed a coin to decide on which side, left or right, the leaders would stand, and tossed again for first choice on the colour of tie. Yet out of the blue – or was it red? – there was an issue. It had been agreed that the wives should sit on stage, in the background, supportive, nothing too obvious or distracting, yet suddenly Ginny was asking about the children: Jemma and Ben were here, she wanted them beside her, they had as much right to be part of this moment as anyone.

A thin shrill of terror ran through the executive producer responsible for the arrangements. He swayed from one leg to the other, wringing his hands. This was the biggest moment of his life, planned down to the last second, the whole thing endlessly rehearsed. He had even taken advice from the man who had been responsible for the seating arrangements at the latest Middle East peace conference. Yet, in spite of all his preparations, not for one moment had he underestimated the capacity for things, even at this late hour, to get comprehensively fouled up. Carefully and, he hoped, with an air of confidence he explained to Ginny that the inclusion of children was not part of the concordat, but he agreed to take the matter to the other side.

In the part of the studios set aside for the Dandersons, he explained what Ginny was seeking. Immediately Lauren objected. Refused even to consider the matter. It would give the Edges a visual advantage, emphasising family, children, all that sort of emotional rubbish. The producer said he understood, agreeing that the presence of children might offer some sort of inchoate advantage – until, at least, they began to fidget and yawn, stick fingers up their noses and look stupefyingly bored. All of that was inevitable, in his opinion, long before the two hours were over.

At which point Lauren's unconditional opposition cracked. She sucked the tip of her thumb as little bits of her resolution flaked away. That bitch Ginny Edge was trying to cause trouble, but perhaps only for herself. The idea was, after all, worth consideration. It depended on precisely where the children might sit.

And so it was that, thirty minutes before airtime, Ginny and Lauren emerged from their respective corners, accompanied by media advisers and television executives, to examine the proposed chair placements. The two women nodded to each other, did not shake hands, and crept to the side of the set.

And it was there, as she gazed out over the audience who had by now settled themselves in their seats, that Lauren saw Ajok. Sitting in the front row. No mistaking the tall Dinka and those angry-looking tattoos on her forehead. For a moment Lauren turned to stone. This wasn't coincidence: it was clearly a conspiracy. Dirty tricks. A disaster in the making. The woman had already attacked Freddie twice, and now she was planning to do it again, in front of the entire country. How the hell had she got in anyway? And if she had smuggled herself in, it was for a purpose. Might she be armed? This could so easily turn to catastrophe. Images of sobbing people bending over a stricken Bobby Kennedy flooded into her mind and, for a moment, her heart stopped. Then she turned on her heel and ran – literally ran – until she had found the head of Freddie's Special Branch protection unit.

'That bloody woman's out there. How could you allow it? Get rid of her!'

'Er, which woman is that, Mrs Danderson?'

'That immigrant who caused the car crash and who should have been locked away by now, if you'd been doing your job properly.'

'I see.'

'But apparently you don't see. That's the trouble. So I've had to do your job for you. She's out there in the front row.' Lauren was breathing heavily, struggling with her emotions as she jabbed her crimson-painted finger in the direction of the stage. 'She shouldn't be in the country, let alone in the building. I'm not letting Freddie move an inch until you give me your personal assurance that she's out of here and on her way.'

Her finger was now poking sharply into the officer's chest. She was clearly struggling to contain her emotions, and although he had had more than enough of this woman trying to translate her personal prejudices into the law of the land, he had to admit she had a point. The presence of a demonstrator in the front row wasn't in the rules of engagement. Yet, as he quickly ascertained from his radio link, the woman had committed no proven offence. Hadn't even been charged with anything yet. But still . . .

The officer made a rapid decision. It was his task to protect the Prime Minister, not to throw out a troublesome guest from what was legally little more than a private party. It was a matter best settled discreetly. So he had a word with the producer, who summoned the head of studio security. Together all three peered from behind the set and identified Ajok in the front row.

'That woman,' the Special Branch officer instructed. 'Get rid of her.'

The head of security sniffed. He could handle this. He was used to sterner stuff, like breaking through picket lines or ejecting animal-rights protesters from the newsroom. One solitary woman wasn't going to be any trouble. But he was conscious of the occasion's sensitivity. 'I'll turn down the house lights,' he said, 'so no one'll see.'

And that was what he did. He appeared in front of Ajok, with two of his most formidable colleagues, and explained that she was on private property and that the television company reserved the right to refuse admission. He insisted that she leave. They tried to follow the advice of the Prime Minister's protection officer and do all this tactfully, even politely, but those were not the foremost of their gifts and, anyway, she refused. One of the security men leaned forward to place a hand on her arm and tried to pull her up, but he hadn't reckoned on the innate resilience of a Dinka tribeswoman used to wrestling with cows. Now the man sitting next to her had joined in, another dark face, voicing objections – it was Bobby – reaching across, trying to push the restraining hand away from Ajok.

And soon the scene turned to bedlam. Shouts, cries, sounds of a scuffle, with every raised arm, twisted elbow and bent head silhouetted against the glow of the stage. The cameras captured it all. Who threw the first fist was difficult to tell, even with the repeated replays that later made every news bulletin, but the images of chaos were captivating. They eventually involved eight security men and many, many minutes of chaos as Bobby was pushed over the back of his seat, restrained, pinned down, sat upon, immobilised and finally removed, resisting every inch of the way. They got rid of Ajok, too, but she had to be carried and dragged, for she refused to walk. And by the time some semblance of calm had been restored it was too late. Not only had the hour appointed for the beginning of the debate long since passed but Dom Edge was out of the building and on his way home.

Even as Dom was climbing into his car and preparing to flee, Archie was issuing a statement. At the personal instruction of the Prime Minister's wife, two of the Opposition's guests had been forcibly and brutally removed from the audience, he claimed. It was a blatant and characteristic abuse of power. Faced by such thuggery, there had been no point in continuing. It was a tragedy for the people, a tragedy for democracy, and entirely the fault of the Danderson family. Dom was said to be sickened with disgust.

It was meant to have been a historic moment and, in many ways, it was. Most debates are remembered, if at all, for their dullness, yet without even taking place, this one had transformed itself into one of those magical moments that would live in the collective memory of everyone who saw it. The debate was dead, but its echoes would linger, leaving the producer and his reputation drowning in flat champagne as he sat on an empty, darkened stage.

★

'You again?'

The custody sergeant cursed beneath his breath as he saw Ajok being brought in. 'What you been up to this time?'

'The usual, Sergeant.'

'Don't tell me – not the Prime Minister again?'

She nodded.

'I thought I told you to keep away from him.'

'You told me to keep away from Downing Street. I have done exactly as you asked.'

'But—' He was about to deliver a ferocious rebuke when the door to the custody room burst open and, in a trice, the place was heaving with bodies. Uniforms, civilians, a doctor. And a young Asian with a bloodied face.

'Get these people out of here!' the sergeant ordered, then looked up to find himself confronted by two faces he recognised. One was Ginny Edge. The other was a man he regarded as one of the best criminal lawyers in the business, who was claiming to represent both Ajok and the man with the bloodied face. He was also demanding to know why Lauren Danderson and her thugs hadn't been brought here.

The sergeant ran his fingers through his thinning hair. A sigh escaped from his clenched lips, a pitiful sound. It was, he decided, going to be a long evening.

Much later, as Ajok and the lawyer disappeared quietly out of a rear entrance, Ginny emerged on to the steps of Charing Cross police station. Bobby was beside her. His lip was swollen, a cheek cut and one eye was all but closed. A heaving scrum of journalists confronted them. Floodlights had been erected on the other side of the street; television vans with satellite dishes and huge, towering aerials were parked a little way off. For a while, as they stood there, the noise from the press pack was almost overwhelming. Camera shutters snapped and flashguns exploded with the frenzy of a firing squad, until the mob grew silent to hear what Ginny and her friend had to say.

'I have done nothing,' Bobby said slowly, his words coming with difficulty through his swollen lips, 'except try to defend the honour of an innocent woman.'

'Why did you get involved?' one of the pressmen shouted.

'I am a Muslim. It is my duty.' He dried up, blinking his one open eye as the flash guns fired once more.

'Have they charged you?'

Bobby shook his head. 'No. Not yet, at least. I don't think they will. I have committed no offence. It's those others who I believe will be charged.'

'Which others?'

'The security men who set upon me. And perhaps Mrs Danderson, who I believe gave them their orders.'

More furious clicking of shutters.

'But they say you started it,' came the cry.

With grave difficulty, Bobby managed a smile. 'Go to those other men. Examine their faces. Compare them with mine. Then decide for yourselves who started it.'

Ginny held up her hand to stifle the rest of the questions that were pouring forth. 'You'll be getting official statements from my husband. But for my part, all I want to say is this.' She glanced around her, in command of her stage. 'Bobby Khan is a friend of mine. So is Mrs Arob. It was I who invited them to this evening's debate because they both had a direct personal interest in its outcome. I understand that Mr Danderson's staff are trying to paint Mrs Arob as some sort of troublemaker. In truth, she is a victim of a government that has become so paranoid it will allow neither opposition nor debate. You saw that this evening. It tries, quite literally, to stamp it out.'

'They say she might have had a weapon.'

Ginny shook her head. 'She wasn't armed even with a pamphlet, let alone anything more offensive. All she had was her handbag. Yet

Mr and Mrs Danderson decreed that she should be picked up and dragged out. Terrified of a woman with a handbag. Well, I have a handbag, too. So perhaps the Dandersons should have me arrested. Who knows? Perhaps they will.'

'You saying this country's run like a dictatorship, Ginny?'

She put a protective arm round Bobby's shoulders, and pointed to his wounds. 'Take a good look. Then you decide. Goodnight.'

She sprang smartly down the steps, two uniformed policemen helping force a path to her waiting car. Bobby held the door, then climbed in after her.

'Thank you,' she whispered.

'*Eeinth ka jawab pathar.*'

'What's that?'

'It means the answer to a rock is a stone. Force must be met with force. But how on earth did you know, Ginny? How did you know they would come for us?'

'I know Lauren. That was enough. Know your enemies, Bobby,' she muttered. 'Get to know them better than yourself. But don't climb into their skin.' In the peppering light of the flashguns her face seemed gaunt, the eyes almost bitter.

They said no more until they had left the pursuing *paparazzi* far behind. Suddenly she shook herself, physically, as though casting off demons, then turned to him, squeezing his hand. 'I owe you, Bobby.'

'Nothing more than friendship.'

Once more they sat in silence as the brightly lit streets slipped by.

'You know,' she said, after a few minutes, 'that was my first time in a live interview.'

'It was my first time, too, playing Butch Cassidy.'

'Does it hurt very much?'

Bobby ran a tongue round his gum, still tasting blood. 'Funny thing is, I rather enjoyed it.'

He was happy, proud, then fumbling to answer his mobile

phone, punching a button, but as he listened to the voice at the other end, his face seemed to fall apart in pain. '*Amma* – Mother?' he gasped, 'Is that you?'

And Ginny could see the reflection of the street-lights in the tears that began creeping down his cheeks.

The clash of opinions that erupted across the country was un-precedented. Danderson's advisers struggled to counter the accusations being put round by Archie and others with suggestions that the whole thing had been premeditated and the fist fight deliberately instigated to give Dom an excuse for ducking out of the debate. But Danderson and his men were always running behind. Images proved far more powerful than explanations, and the images were all being weighed on the Opposition side. Viewers were voters: they saw two families at war, and it confused them.

The confusion favoured no one but Dom. He had been many points behind but now – well, nobody knew. The electorate was caught in the crossfire, and as they ducked the pollsters rushed to find fresh judgement, only to retire scratching their heads. The row was like a finely cut diamond: the deeper they looked into it, the more reflections they saw. Glimpses of paranoia and abuse of power, freedom and civil liberties, of big brother and a single mother, of racism, national security and bullying – and, since a Muslim was involved, there were also undercurrents of terrorism and religious freedom. Yet, riding to the relief of the tabloids, there was also the vital matter of sex. As the entire nation was able to see, in the cool air of the police-station steps, Ginny's eyes had been bright, her cheeks flushed and her nipples considerably more prominent. There was no mistaking the point, and not even the *Financial Times* bothered to airbrush them out. This was a woman on fire. What a girl. Across the breakfast tables of Britain, she made the Dandersons look extraordinarily dull.

It was as the family was preparing to go to church on Sunday morning that Ginny answered a knock at the door. Dom was upstairs, still poring over the newspapers, his sense of well-being restored not only by antibiotics but also through the lack of certainty displayed by so many of the editorials. This election was no longer as clear-cut as it once had been. He had a chance. And even Julia's column made much less painful reading than he had feared. She had threatened fire and brimstone but there was no new revelation, no painful rehashing of private moments, merely the opinion that 'There was no way Dom Edge ran away from that debate. He has the gift of the gab. I was always bemused at how easily he charmed me on to his sofa. He was never lost for words, and he would never be scared of crossing swords with Freddie Danderson. Politics are all about power and passion, and I can tell you that Dom Edge has both in abundance.' He allowed himself a restrained smile, then put the paper carefully to one side. No point in leaving it lying around in the bedroom.

Meanwhile, the children were slowly getting themselves ready, complaining as always at being dragged off to church. 'There'll be photographers,' Ginny shouted, from the kitchen where she was preparing breakfast. 'Make sure you put on the clean clothes I left out for you last night.' It might have been any other Sunday, except that it was the last of an election campaign. And someone was knocking at the door. She opened it to discover an elderly man on her doorstep, perhaps around seventy, with a walking-stick and . . .

'Hello, Ginia.'

That name. Only one man had ever called her that.

'Daddy?'

It was early but there was already a gathering of photographers and sightseers behind the police barriers on the other side of the street. Too many prying eyes. She hurried her father inside.

'What . . . ? How did you . . . ?'

'You're not so difficult to find. Never have been. I've always known.' The voice was frail, full of dust; he had changed so much.

'What do you . . . ?' She was breathless, winded, having trouble finishing her thoughts.

'Want?' He stood erect, leaning heavily on his stick. So much older than she remembered, but it had been – what? Fifteen years since last she had screamed at him and stormed out of his life? He coughed, lightly, but it made him wince. He swayed a little. 'I'm sorry, I'm not very well.'

She didn't invite him further in, or ask him to sit. They stood in the hallway, staring, his eyes rheumy, hers filled with confusion.

'What do I want?' He sighed. 'So many things, Ginia. To turn the clock back. Way, way back. But we can't. So I've come to try to say sorry.' He held his chin up, still on parade, but now there were folds of skin beneath it. He was wearing his old regimental tie, and his trousers were neatly pressed, but she saw that the hems were threadbare. Everything about him was old. There was a dull milkiness in his eye, like cooling wax as the flame gutters and the candle grows cold. He truly wasn't well.

'Apologies? Forgiveness?' she snapped. 'Isn't it a little late for that?'

'Never too late.'

'So why now?'

'Many reasons. Time isn't always on an old man's side. But mostly right now because of all the battles you've been going through.'

'They've never been your battles.'

'Doesn't stop me thinking about you. And in a way they are my battles, too. The press have been trying to track me down. I've stayed well away from them, but they're a persistent lot. Thought I should find out what you wanted me to do.'

'You're asking *me* what you should do?' She made no effort to hide her incredulity.

'I've watched you all these years, Ginia. Never stopped. Graduation, job, marriage, motherhood. Now all this. Makes a very thick scrapbook, I can tell you. And you've barely started.'

'So what has this got to do with you?'

'Never tried to interfere, had no right. But I am your father. I thought, perhaps, before it's too late, that you might need me – no, *need* is the wrong word. You don't need me, of course. Never have done.'

Oh, how little you know, she thought.

'But I wanted you to understand how proud I am of you, no matter what happens on Thursday. And how very much I have always loved you.' The words seemed to take something out of him; he leaned more heavily on his cane. 'I know how much we hurt you, your mother and me.'

'No. Only you.'

'Then I apologise. Accept the full blame. But you're a grown woman now, you must know there was another side of the story, things that you didn't always see.'

'I doubt it.'

He passed his tongue across cracked lips. 'She was ill. A long time. Mental problems. Depression.' A pause while he searched her eyes. 'It wasn't her first suicide attempt, you know. We tried to keep it all from you.'

Ginny stiffened, leaned against the wall, in pain. It kicked her like a horse.

'I know I wasn't always a good father or husband. I couldn't cope. I tried but . . . Those things weren't so well understood back then. And we were in the military. Stiff upper lip and all that. There was no help. I wish I had had someone like you.'

'You did have me, for God's sake.'

'I meant your column. You wrote something about depression a couple of months ago. I thought it very good.' His lips quivered. 'And you're right. We had you. We thought children might help – help your mother. But it only made things more difficult.' He could see the horror that had flooded into her eyes. 'That's why you were the only one. I'd always wanted more but . . .' He lowered his head, trying to hide his eyes. 'I fought hard. Fought hard for us all, as hard as I could, in my own way. The only way I knew how. And when your mother first tried to kill herself . . . I felt so angry, so alone. It was as if she was trying to take away from me the most valuable thing I had ever had, apart from you. Can you understand that feeling?'

Oh, how she understood. But somehow her own pain seemed insignificant now. It made her feel shame.

'I lashed out. At you. At your mother. Even though I loved you both so very much. I was angry for such a long time.'

He coughed again. Evidently it hurt. He was sick, perhaps very sick. Was that why he had come? Absolution?

'I was always a fighter, Ginia. You are, too. I saw that again on television the other night. But I think I was never very good at it. You're better than I ever was.'

From upstairs came the noise of the children arguing. His eyes wandered in search of the sound, no longer trying to hide his tears. 'So very proud of you,' he said softly.

'Are you trying to blame Mummy?'

'At the time, yes. Not any more.' He could see the hostility in her eyes, knew he had to go further. 'There were other men, Ginia. It was all part of the depression. They took advantage of her, and I couldn't deal with it. But these things happen in a marriage. You have to try, to carry on. I can talk to you about it now. I think you understand.' His hands were trembling on the top of his cane. 'I hope you can forgive me.'

She had never felt more frail. Her anger with this man had been one of the driving forces in her life, spurring her on, sweeping aside her reservations and sanctioning her anger with others. And now he had asked for her forgiveness, was telling her she had it wrong – had always had it wrong.

'I have little left in this world, Ginia, not even my pride. That all went a long time ago. The only thing that matters to me is you and your family. Please, let me share them. Let me try to be the father I never was, and the grandfather I've never had the chance to be.'

The early-morning sun that peered through the fanlight above the door seemed to sway and grow faint as her mind flooded with memories. Of pained faces, of raised voices, of missed birthdays and temporary homes, of cast-off schools and abandoned friends, of packing her life into a suitcase and trying to dig a hole in the garden to bury her tears, of things she thought she had understood, but hadn't. Yet now, perhaps, she did, and for the very first time. She had never wished for anything more than to bring her mother back to life. Her mother was a saint, her guardian angel. Now that love was tainted. As, she had discovered, all love was tainted.

He stood in the hallway, waiting. The children were still fighting upstairs, Dom was telling them to shut up and get ready. He was moving around, calling her name. They were about to come down. And for the very first time Ginny realised that, even more than her mother's love, she had always craved the affection of her father, the piece of her life that had always been missing and had left such a horrendous hole. Now it was here, in her hallway, the answer to all her pain. All she had to do was to reach out, touch it, and it would be hers.

Yet that was from a life she had left behind. Washed away down the gutters of Westminster. It was too late. She couldn't turn back.

'Get out. Go now. Don't ever come back.'

His aged, cracked lips quivered as though they were trying to formulate some appeal, but then they stilled. He stood for a moment, got his balance, turned like an old soldier on parade and, with the help of his stick, tapped his way out of her world.

'Who was that?' Dom asked, bounding down the stairs as the front door closed.

'I'm not sure,' she murmured. 'Wrong address. Wrong life.'

Fifteen

I T WAS ON SUNDAY afternoon that rumours of a scandal began to slither their way around London. At such a moment, four days before the election, with the last rally held and the last poster pasted, the whispers spread like syphilis in a slum. For several hours no one seemed to know the details, and along with the uncertainty came fear. The unknown, the unfathomable, the uncontrollable, all the things that electioneers dread.

The answers came on the front page of Monday's *Record* with a massive headline: '*Dandy's Dirty Money*'. Every detail was served with the subtlety of a cannonball. It seemed that the newspaper had received an anonymous tip-off, made credible partly through the fact that it was printed on official party notepaper. Danderson – the paper personalised the whole thing, tipped it right on to his doorstep – was up to his armpits in a morass of illicit money. Half a million pounds of it. Paid in cash to one of the party's treasurers, Aiden Brett. A secret slush fund, deliberately kept from the eyes of the Electoral Commission to avoid the restrictions on election spending. A blatant attempt to buy the election campaign. The words 'cheat', 'crime' and 'conspiracy' were littered throughout the article, with only enough mention of the terms 'alleged' and 'believed' to satisfy the libel lawyers. And, what was worse, to cover its tracks, the party had dragged thousands of its supporters into the scam. Pensioners, widows, even schoolchildren who had sent in pennies from their pocket money had had their identities stolen, their reputations soiled, their innocence defiled by the big-money bandits behind the scheme.

Aiden Brett had refused to answer any of the questions put to him by the newspaper, although a photograph of him scrambling into his car, eyes wide with terror, like a hunted deer, was printed boldly on the front page. Inside there was a cartoon of Danderson dressed like Al Capone.

At first, Danderson's spokesman issued a flat denial. When contacted by the *Record*, he said the party was confident of the security of its financial procedures. If any inadvertent oversights were brought to light, they would be quickly corrected. It was the automatic, inbuilt response of a political machine. Then someone from the party had contacted Brett and, through his blustering denials, panic set in. While still insisting on its absolute innocence, the party did concede that it had an unusually large amount of cash in its safe. Couldn't say precisely how much, it was still being counted. It took less than an hour to establish that the sums recorded against the names of many small donors had been inflated, and another thirty minutes to suspend Brett from his duties. As it became clear that this was a catastrophe in the making, the party began to imply, through unidentifiable and anonymous sources, that Brett had always been a wayward figure, a bit of a black sheep, a volunteer who had been on the point of losing his responsibilities. *It was all his fault.* The party would be happy to see him dragged away in chains.

By Monday lunchtime, its spokesmen were growing more bullish. Why, hadn't it been this government that introduced all the tough measures on party financing in the first place? And the fact that the matter had been revealed so quickly was testament to the great strengths of its own internal controls. Brett had been forced to try to hide his actions. He hadn't succeeded. Proof that the system was working. In fact, it was almost a triumph.

But it didn't wash. There was too much previous. Too many dodgy deals, too many protestations of innocence, too many peers, too many passports, too many mortgages and simply too many memories of what had gone before. This was a government that had fallen on its knees and begged to be trusted too many times. It had run out of deniability. The only thing left in doubt was how much damage it would heap upon itself as ordinary party members queued to denounce it and cartoonists scrambled to revile it. Meanwhile, the Metropolitan Police announced they were beginning a criminal investigation.

However, one piece of the puzzle was still missing – the identity of the donor. The name of Rupak Patel was bandied about, but quickly dismissed. Mr Patel, the reclusive Asian businessman who ran a hugely profitable international spice business, was a well-known giver to many good causes, but he had been in a Swiss hospital for the past two months undergoing treatment for a very serious illness. No way could he have handed over half a million in cash. So another twist was added to this already sordid tale. To cover their tracks, they had even stolen the identity of a thoroughly decent and desperately sick man. Who would have thought that any political party could stoop so low?

And just how low would they tumble on Thursday?

Almost midnight. Tuesday. They'd spent the last hour driving down from the constituency, where Dom had made his final speech. Not a vast meeting, no great message to deliver, it was too late for that, and Dom had reached a stage beyond exhaustion where he seemed to have left his body behind and was watching himself from a distance, going through the motions. The gathering had been little more than a gesture, intended to show his constituency voters that he hadn't entirely forgotten about them. A lighter police presence than usual, to allow a few moments for mingling, just enough time for Ginny to be spat at by a protester. The young man responsible had been set upon with immense ferocity by two elderly ladies armed with heavy handbags, and the police had taken their time in rescuing him.

Two days to go. Everything done, ticked off the list. Time only to wait.

They climbed wearily from the car as it drew up outside the steps to their home. There were still a few flashbulbs waiting to greet them, blinding them; they waved instinctively as the duty policeman held open the car door while Bobby gathered up the papers and reports that lay strewn across the back seat. No one noticed the figure that emerged from the shadows. Slowly, the outline of Julia's face appeared in the light of the street-lamp.

'What the hell do you want?' Dom snapped, startled, thankful she had her back to the cameras.

'Don't you dare make a scene, not now,' Ginny added.

'A word. Just a word. That's all I want.'

So, not a scene. At least, not straight away. And if there were to be a scene, better it should take place inside, away from all those prying eyes.

As their unexpected visitor climbed the steps, Ginny couldn't help but notice she was a few pounds heavier – several, in fact – than the last time they had met. Notoriety didn't sit well on her, and neither did the hemline. It was strange how easy it had been, beneath the street-light, to mistake her for a tart.

'I wanted to apologise,' Julia said, as soon as the front door was closed, 'for everything.'

'You could have written.'

'I couldn't find the words. Anyway, it wouldn't have meant so much in a letter. It had to be in person. And I wanted to wish you luck.'

So, out of inescapable habit, they drifted to the kitchen and settled round the table as Ginny put the kettle on.

'Your column didn't seem intended to wish me much luck,' Dom said archly.

'Didn't do you any harm,' she bit back, any trace of contrition evaporating. 'They wanted me to put the boot in like . . . like before. Look. I made a huge mistake when I talked to the newspapers last time. They put words in my mouth, exaggerated everything – you know what they're like. Merciless. I'm so very sorry. But that's why they paid me for writing the election column. Wanting to cause trouble. I've had to struggle very hard to keep it so restrained. It could have been so much more . . .' she had intended to say 'sordid', but that would scarcely have helped her cause '. . . *difficult* for you.'

'So why write it at all?' Ginny asked, rattling mugs and wondering why she seemed able to tolerate the presence of this woman in her home without committing violence. A voice inside was screaming at her to reach for a kitchen knife but another part of her, some feral instinct, sensed danger and urged her to bide her time.

'I have to work, Mrs Edge. All I've ever really wanted to do is to help the party, but of course they won't touch me now. So I have to do what I can.'

'Sympathy? You expect sympathy?' Ginny handed Dom a mug of camomile tea and sat down with another. She offered their visitor nothing. Julia was left nervously twisting the over-decorated gold ring she wore on her thumb. She took a deep breath as though she was preparing to launch herself; Ginny noted that her bra was tight, unflattering, pushing her out in front and pinching her at the back. Julia had put on a pound a month, Ginny reckoned; she was young, but time wasn't on her side.

'What I'm hoping for,' Julia said, hurrying on, 'is that we can try to put the past behind us. Not forget what happened, but build on it. Show the world it doesn't matter any more.'

'How?'

'My deal with the newspaper finishes with the election. As of Thursday I have no job. But they want me to continue writing for them. At this point, it's the only job offer I have.'

'So?'

'It would be on condition that I write the sort of column that pokes fun at all politicians and uses everything I know – and everything I've done. It would be an embarrassment for me, but I'm afraid it would inevitably be far, far worse for you.'

'You make it sound like being a prostitute. They pay you and you do whatever they ask,' Dom barked, increasingly angry, but Ginny gripped his arm.

'Let's hear what Julia has to say,' she suggested. Dom looked at his wife in confusion.

And already Julia was fighting back: 'It took two of us to get into that mess, Dom.'

'I didn't feel the need to run off and sell my story for a small fortune to—'

Yet Ginny was squeezing his arm still tighter, cutting right across him. 'Come on, Julia, tell us. What is it you want?'

Julia stared back, the eyes firm, demanding. Gone was the nervous, simpering woman who had been wringing out her repentance only a few moments before. 'I want back into the party. A senior post. So that I can help again. Build myself a reputation for something other than being Dom Edge's former squeeze. Otherwise I'll be left with little choice but to take the media's dirty shilling.'

'Over my dead body,' Dom snapped.

'That's precisely what the media will want. If I can deliver that, the pay will be plenty. And I guess I could.' The words carried a carefully carved edge of menace.

'You . . . you . . .' Dom was still struggling to work up an appropriate insult when Ginny interrupted him yet again.

'What – precisely – do you want? What job?'

'I'm not sure, I . . .'

'Come on, Julia, you haven't come here without working out your game plan.'

'I want to be director of communications. In Downing Street, if that's where you're headed.'

Dom spluttered. He appeared to have lost the power of coherent speech.

'It would be an inspired appointment,' Julia said. 'I've got all the qualifications. I know the media. I know the party. Above all, I know you, Dom. You'll not find anyone else half as effective as me.'

Ginny suspected that Archie might harbour a different opinion, but this wasn't the moment.

'And I'll sign any confidentiality clause you want,' Julia added, continuing with her pitch, 'a guarantee that I won't ever publish diaries or write articles about you without you seeing them first. You'll get full veto rights, be able to cut out anything you find difficult. I'll even backdate it. Cover everything that's happened since we met. Otherwise . . . well, you'll force me to carry on being your tart in the tabloids.'

'This is blackmail!' Dom spat, banging the table.

'It's a sound business proposition. Makes a very great deal of sense.' Dom choked on his astonishment as he realised it was Ginny speaking.

'The only thing standing in its way seems to be your rather overworked sense of male pride,' she continued.

'Oh, it would raise eyebrows, of course, but only for a few minutes,' Julia added. 'There'll be so much else happening in your first few days in Downing Street that people will soon forget to be surprised.'

'And if I don't make it to Downing Street?'

'Then the whole thing becomes meaningless,' Julia said. 'You'll be too busy looking for a job yourself to be able to help me. No one will have much interest in either of us.'

Dom sat hunched, sipping his tea. He was tired, saturated in confusion. This was altogether too much. He couldn't get his mind round it. 'Can we talk about this later?'

'No need,' Ginny said. 'It makes sense – doesn't it, darling?'

Without fully understanding why, Dom nodded. He felt bewildered, bullied. He seemed to have entirely lost the knack of arguing with his wife.

'Thank you,' Julia said softly, and got up, tugging at her dress.

Ginny showed her to the door. At the threshold, Julia turned. 'I never expected you would see the sense of it.'

'We've all changed,' Ginny replied. 'We'll never become friends, you and I, but some things are more important than friendship. I think we've both come to realise that.'

With a small bow of thanks, Julia slipped into the night.

Dom was still in the kitchen, head buried in his hands. When finally he looked up, his eyes were raw with humiliation. 'What the hell was all that about?'

'That was about the walking wounded. Can't you see? Oh, she's tough and ballsy all right, but Julia hates herself, hates her new life of kiss-and-tell. She wants to get back to the point where she can go home to her parents and have Sunday lunch without her father choking on his roast beef. From her point of view, it makes great sense.'

'And from our point of view?'

'Don't be silly, darling, I'm never going to let that bitch back into the kennel.'

'But we've promised her the bloody job!'

'And it's a very important job. One she will need to be vetted for. So the Intelligence Services will dig into her background, her private life, her boyfriends, her ups and – how shall we put it? – her many downs. All that sort of thing. It'll be like excavating Pompeii. They'll find far too much ever to let her near a job like that.'

'How do you know?'

'I know Julia. Got calluses on her knees as well as on her conscience, has that one. So, some very important person in an MI5 raincoat will explain to her that it's completely impossible for her to be offered any post in Downing Street. You will add an expression of your deepest sorrow, and find her some sad but reasonably remunerative little posting in . . .' She grasped for a name. 'Doesn't really matter much where. Brussels. Borneo. Bazookistan.'

'There's no such place.'

'Then we shall make such a place, just for Julia. She'll have no cause for complaint. We'll get rid of her, and have more than enough on her private life to make sure we never hear another peep from her in the press. Anyway, she needs a little time out of the limelight. A few months to get her figure back.'

'What?'

And Ginny was laughing, dancing round the kitchen table with a towel in her hand, hugging him and banging saucepans as she went past. She had made three full circuits before she stopped, shaking, tears streaming from her eyes.

'Can't you see, Dom? Are you so simple that you don't understand what's happened?'

His face melted in confusion.

'There's only one reason why that bloody woman came here tonight, Dom. She thinks we're going to win!' Ginny let forth a cry of joy and continued skipping round the room.

Election Day.

There were others apart from Julia who thought Dom might win, but more, many more, were still sceptics. A week ago Danderson had been ten points ahead. No one had ever lost that much, that fast. The bookies were betting he would still scrape home.

It was almost over. Nothing more to be said. The adrenaline, the urgency, suddenly disappeared, replaced by a sense of expectation tinged with fear. Dom struggled to keep a smile stretched across his face as he toured polling stations in his constituency, expressing thanks to his workers and overdosing on industrial-grade coffee. The hours rolled by in a fog of oblivion until the polls closed. Nothing more to do but wait.

The count in his constituency was to be held in the local town hall. Victorian Gothic, updated in the sixties, horrid. A room with polystyrene ceiling tiles had been set aside to provide a little privacy for Dom and his group – Ginny, Bobby, a secretary, a serious young party pollster hooked into his laptop, and Frank, the Special Branch officer. Everyone else had been left at Headquarters in London. The room was Spartan, the walls decorated with posters imploring them to report benefit cheats. Everything was institutional and sterile, apart from a tray of stale sandwiches. Three large-screen televisions glared at them from different corners. BBC. ITN. Sky. They could choose their own poison. Outside in the hall, the ballot boxes with their cargoes of pearls were being emptied on to the tables ready for the counting to start. Dom's fate was being decided, but for the moment he was irrelevant to proceedings. He switched off his smile. It no longer mattered. In its place, little wrinkles of concern gathered round his eyes.

The exit polls were inconclusive and on all sides deeply discounted. Memories were still fresh of that evening more than fifteen years earlier when, for one tantalising, befreckled hour, Neil Kinnock thought he had won. Best wait for the real thing. And around the country, half a dozen constituencies, wanting their moment of fame, were engaged in a frenzied race to be the first to report. Broadcasters were constantly switching from one town hall to the next. Fragmentary scenes flashed on the screens. Frantic counting. Overheated faces. Scowling agents. Expectations. Bitten nails. Dignitaries. Deflating hopes. Close-ups of the ludicrous costumes being worn by fringe candidates. A final flurry of repairs to the flower arrangement in front of some podium. Then: 'We're off to Sunderland where, I'm told, they switched all the traffic lights to green in order to get the vans with the votes back to the count in record time. It looks as though, by a whisker, they're about to make the first declaration of this election. Fasten your seatbelts, viewers, it's going to be a long night. Even longer for the politicians, of course . . .'

Dom had spent the time pacing relentlessly. 'Sit down, darling,' Ginny instructed. 'This is your moment.' He did as he was told, too tired to resist. And they were off. In the leisure centre in Sunderland the returning officer was already at his microphone, pushing his glasses up the bridge of his nose, blinking owl-like and omniscient in the television lights. Then he began. Names and numbers tumbled forth from his lips, while a voice in the studio translated them in a way that stretched neither the intellect nor the appetite of the viewers. It had been a safe government seat. It remained a government seat, but not as safe as it once had been. Just time for a fleeting glimpse of the face of the victor, glowing with joy, before the cameras switched their attention to Basildon. Similar story. Government seat. Except this time a far larger axe had been taken to the majority.

'What does it mean, Desmond?' Dom asked the pollster.

'Difficult to tell. Need a few more.'

And they came, at first fleetingly, one by one, but then in such a rush that it was impossible to keep track of them all. Soon it became clear that the tide was flowing, and with such force that it was threatening to sweep Freddie Danderson far out to sea. The room became clammy, airless, overheated with expectation. Dom was desperate not to leave, glued to the screens, but his own count was about to be declared, he had to tear himself away. It was like leaving the bed of an insatiable lover in order to feed the parking meter, he later told a colleague.

'Well?' he demanded, his hand on the door.

'I agree with the BBC,' Desmond replied, tense, his face glowing in the lurid reflection of his laptop. 'A very mixed bag. Difficult to see the final result, but the trend is pretty clear.' A final tap of the keys before he looked up. The frown was gone, replaced by a toothy smile. 'I think we're going to win. We're going to bloody well win. Congratulations, Prime Minister!'

Prime Minister. Those most magical words. And at almost the same moment Bobby, who had been bent over his mobile phone, gave a whoop of joy. 'The Home Secretary's gone. Lost her seat! The whole house of cards is tumbling!'

And there it was, coming up on the screens, every one of them, along with the prediction that the Opposition would win the election with a majority of somewhere between five and fifteen. Still desperately small, still only a prediction, but a majority. A miracle. A special moment in a country's history, even more so in that of a man. Ginny walked up to Dom. She put her arms round him, very tenderly, and kissed him. 'Come on, Prime Minister. They're waiting for you out there.'

Dom's majority had increased. Hugely. Yet he felt numb, struggling to ride the wave as he dragged himself through the motions of thanking the returning officer and the local police, before offering a few words for the cameras. He didn't dare claim victory, not yet, not until more results were in. He still couldn't be sure. Then he was rushing from the town hall to pay a fleeting visit to his constituency offices, greeting his supporters, taking care not to get soaked with champagne, shaking hands and scribbling his name on election posters. Words and images whirled in confusion through his mind, blocking out this senses, until he found himself back in the car and on his way down the M1 to London.

Their convoy was made up of four vehicles, headed by a Special Branch Range Rover, then Dom and Ginny, followed by Bobby, Desmond and the secretary, with another Special Branch vehicle bringing up the rear. They listened in almost total silence to the results on the radio, lost in a world of passing lights on a black, anonymous road, feeling strangely out of touch, impotent, expectant, like travellers through space, bound up within their own private thoughts.

As the tyres drummed out their hypnotic rhythm, Ginny's mind wandered, released at last from its duties, almost in freefall, until at last it snagged on something totally unexpected. She realised that out there, lost in the world beyond the darkness, was her father. For some reason that she struggled to explain, she came very close to screaming with pain.

Then Marble Arch. They were back in London. The BBC was still predicting a majority for Dom; it had even grown a little. The voice on the radio was suggesting that by lunchtime the country would have a new Prime Minister. When Dom's mobile rang. It was Downing Street. Wanting to know when he might be near a landline. Mr Danderson wanted to speak to him.

'They called him Mr Danderson, Ginny,' he murmured as he put down the phone. 'Not Prime Minister, just plain Mr Danderson.'

They were speeding down Park Lane, away from Marble Arch, when Ginny noticed that their little convoy had suddenly increased in size. Three more cars had joined them, plus an escort of police motorcyclists that was blocking intersections and allowing them to run red lights, easing them on their way. And above them Ginny thought she could hear the clatter of a helicopter. Things were changing. Their entire world was changing.

Party Headquarters. Awash with people, every one of them trying to outdo the others in expressions of joy. Cheers, tears, balloons, music, more cheers. So many young people. The future. Cameras everywhere. Dom's smile repainted. Then the phone call from Danderson. Congratulations. Concession. 'I wish you good fortune.' He didn't mean it.

No sooner had Dom put down the phone than it rang once more. The Palace. Would it be convenient for Mr Edge to call upon the Queen at eleven thirty? Dom glanced at his watch. That was in less than five hours. He needed a shave, a clean shirt, suitable tie.

'Ginny? Where's Ginny?' he cried.

She was talking to Archie, one of the few in the headquarters building who seemed to have kept his composure. 'Surprised?' she asked.

'Let me put it this way. Five years ago, I gave up drinking. Now I'm giving up gambling. At this rate, I may become a saint.'

'I shouldn't do that, Archie. I don't think we'll be having much need for saints. Not for the next few years.'

Bobby had driven them to the Palace. A special privilege for him, Ginny's idea. The intersections had been blocked once more, the lights all at green. Dom in a dream, and more than a little nervous, fretting about the details of his clothes, his hair, the cut of his collar, even asking Bobby for a second opinion. Perhaps he still hadn't realised that where Ginny went, Bobby would follow.

The wheels crunched on the gravel of the inner courtyard as they drew up. A naval aide saluted, held open the door, was showing Dom up the stairs . . . and suddenly, as she attempted to follow her husband, it was made clear to Ginny that she wasn't to be involved in what happened next. With formidable courtesy, she was ushered into a gilded drawing room where some encrusted duchess was waiting to greet her, as Dom was whisked away, with barely a glance thrown over his shoulder. And there she stayed, making doodles with the duchess, while her life was carved up in another place.

It took only minutes. Dom returned, flushed with satisfaction. He didn't notice Ginny's silent, almost ominous manner until they had climbed back into the car and were driving away along the Mall.

'Why didn't you take me in with you?' she asked.

'I'm afraid you weren't invited.'

'Did you exchange personal secrets or nuclear launch codes with her?'

'Of course not.'

'Then why wasn't I invited?' she demanded again, her voice rising. 'Why didn't you ask for me to come with you, Dom? Do you know what it felt like to be abandoned on the threshold?'

'There are ways of doing these things, Ginny. I don't make the rules.'

'You're the Prime Minister. Of course you make the rules!'

'Get used to it. There are some things I have to do on my own.'

'Such as?'

He was growing exasperated with her defiance. 'I'm the Prime Minister, for goodness' sake. This is my day. Don't rain on my parade.'

'Pull over, Bobby.' Her voice was hard, insistent.

'Don't be silly, darling.'

'Pull over!'

And Bobby did. To the side of the Mall. One security car screeched to a halt ahead, while another crept up slowly behind, the occupants wondering what the hell was going on. As was Dom.

'Ginny, for God's sake. I won the bloody election. Can't we just be happy with that?'

'There's something you ought to know, Dom. You didn't win the election. I did.'

'What?'

'The half-million pounds. Made all the difference, didn't it?'

'Sure . . .'

'I arranged it. With a little help from a distant cousin of Bobby's.'

'You feeling unwell, darling?'

'Never better.'

'So where the hell did you find half a million pounds, then?' He began to chortle in disbelief.

'It was yours. To be precise, it was the party's. I got it from Mark Fitzmaurice, the treasurer. Said you needed it for some very private campaigning.'

'He wouldn't have given you half a million pounds.'

'You seriously underestimate both the gullibility of old men and the way they grow distracted in the presence of younger women.'

'What?'

'I told him you needed the money to keep Julia quiet. Otherwise she was going to blow the campaign apart.'

'Tell me you're not serious. Please.'

'Why do you think you were suddenly so short of money for a poster campaign?'

Outside the car, Frank from Special Branch was peering in agitation through the window. Dom waved him away.

'You bought the election?' Dom whispered, as though fearful passers-by might hear. 'With half a million pounds?'

'Five hundred and fifty thousand, to be precise. Bobby's cousin kept the odd fifty thousand. For his expenses. He's now back in India, disappeared within a tidal wave of humanity. No leads. No paper trail. No one will ever find him.'

'You . . . You really can't . . .'

'Or did you think this sudden extraordinary success of yours was all down to Fate? Your destiny?' Disdain had crept into her voice.

'You *bought* the bloody election?'

'Ironic, isn't it? Everyone thinks Danderson tried to buy it.' She offered a dry smile, confident that he would never again take her for granted. 'Drive on, Bobby. And do cheer up, darling. Someone's trying to take your picture.'

'You gave the enemy half a million quid,' Dom gasped, his face as pale as winter. 'I can't believe it.'

Outside, Frank had been joined by two other officers, all dancing in uncertainty on the pavement. Ginny began to laugh, as though to let them know there was no problem. 'And isn't that the beauty of it, Dom?' she said.

'What is?'

'You not believing it. Don't you see? No one else would ever believe it, either.'

'You seem to have thought of everything.'

'More than you'll ever know,' she said, her humour soaring as she attempted to squeeze life back into his hand. 'Why, I've even got us a new cleaner for Downing Street. Lovely lady. You'll like her. She's from the Sudan. And she can start straight away.' She leaned across to kiss him. So far as the rest of the world was concerned, the Prime Minister and his wife had pulled over for no other reason than to share their private feelings on this most extravagantly emotional of days.

'Ajok, you mean? But isn't she trying to sue the Government? Me?'

'Don't worry, darling. I'll talk her out of that.'

'You can do that?'

'Right now I feel as if I can do almost anything.'

★

Downing Street. Packed with well-wishers. Flags. Cameras. Microphones. Startled pigeons. The lustrous black door.

Dom had made a remarkable recovery. The smile was back, the words flowed. History was made. Later he would remember it all as though it were a dream. That suited him; it enabled him to discount what had gone before, pretend it hadn't happened. Best just to ignore it. After all, he was now the master of the land. Yet, even while he reached for reassurance, he realised it was a lie. As he stood on the steps of Number Ten, with Ginny at his side, the children tugging at his jacket, he knew that he wasn't truly master and particularly not in his new home. Just as he had arrived, one day he would be forced to leave, in tears probably, like all the others. But, as these thoughts tumbled through his mind, he shrugged. Tomorrow was another day, and tomorrow could take care of itself. Today was the only day that mattered, for the moment, and it was his, would always be his.

It was also proving to be Bobby's day, for standing in the crowd was his mother, head covered by a *duppata*, waving furiously, tears in her eyes, and behind her, hesitant, reluctant, his father. 'There are more ways than one of showing you are a good Muslim boy,' she had told him, in her phone call. His father had agreed, with less enthusiasm. Bobby's declaration of pride in his religion on the steps of the police station had gone a long way to healing old wounds, and it didn't do any harm in his father's eyes that Bobby was now standing beside the country's new Prime Minister. There is an old saying that if a son should fall from grace, it is often because his father pushed him. If a son's shame is partly the father's fault, then let him join in the celebration of success, too.

But most of all this was Ginny's day. The day when, at last, she knew that other women would never again snigger about her in a ladies' cloakroom. They might grow to respect her, come to loathe or even fear her, but they would never mock her, not any more.

They smiled and returned the waves of the crowd. Dom leaned

down to whisper in her ear. 'Right this moment, I feel as if I've got everything I ever wished for.'

As a thousand camera bulbs flashed, she stretched up to kiss his cheek. 'Trust me, darling, you've barely started.'

He winced.

Suddenly, in the corner of her eye, she thought she caught sight of an old man with a stiff, military bearing, dressed in a faded suit and with a gleam of rueful pride in his eye. Yet, even as she searched for him, he was gone, lost in the crowd, leaving her to wonder, on this day that was her day, whether her father would still be proud of her, if he knew.

Acknowledgements

Some authors find a book to be a lonely adventure. After all, only one person is required to write, and it devours so much time. Yet the inspiration for a book requires many people, and *First Lady* has had a huge cast of co-conspirators, many of them old friends, and almost as many new, who filled my days with excitement as together we set out on the voyage of discovery that eventually produced this novel.

Perhaps more than anyone, my thanks go to Helen Murshali. Helen works at the Refugee Council and is herself a refugee from the Sudan. Her insights and advice into the life of Ajok Arob were as invaluable as they were humbling. To come through so many painful experiences while retaining both a sense of humour and a positive perspective is a formidable achievement. I owe Helen a great deal, and wish her well.

Ian Patterson shared a huge amount of his own experience with me to help build the background of Ginny and her father, but I am indebted to him for much more than that. He has been a supporter of my books over many years. He has a formidable understanding of the background of those working in our armed forces, along with the mixture of obstacles and opportunities they face in their transition to civilian life. It's what has made him such a success as a specialist headhunter, and a most useful ally.

Michael Dobbs

I always try to raise a little money for a good cause through my books by auctioning the names of one or two of my characters. On this occasion the charity has been Students' Partnership World-wide, which focuses its work on health education in developing countries. My friend Anne Jenkin brought SPW to my attention. Anne is one of the most dynamic women of Westminster who seems to have time for everything and everyone – not a bad template for any First Lady – and with the support of Adam Afriyie and his wonderful wife, Tracy-Jane, we raised a significant sum to help with the work of SPW. You may well have heard of Adam: he's one of the rising stars of the House of Commons, and he and Tracy-Jane were kind enough to bid for two names. They decided to name the characters after their children, so stand up and take a bow, Alfred Danderson Afriyie and Charles Redvers Stanley Malthouse. Somehow I suspect that young Freddie and Charlie will turn out to be the rising stars of a future generation and far outshine their literary namesakes.

Another old friend gave me his name for the book – Ken Boston. I hope he will enjoy dining out on the outrageous character I have invented for him. And so many other friends came to my rescue – Jennie Elias, Chris Poole, Elaine Thomas, Linda McDougall, Julia Hartley-Brewer, Mian and Adiba Zaheen, David Henderson, Tim Mackay, Anne-Marie Perry, Pippa and Anthony Warley, all of whom were willing to help even though their days are packed to the point of fusion with their own commitments. An expression of gratitude in the Acknowledgements is never enough for what they have done for me, but at least it is a start.

In turn, Mian and Adiba introduced me to their great friend, Bakhtiar Liaqat. Bakhti has offered me a wealth of knowledge about the family background of Bobby, and I couldn't have polished the character without him.

374

Others who helped were, at least in the beginning, strangers. I'm always amazed at how charitable people can be when their lives are invaded by someone they have never met, demanding to be told the answers to abstract and sometimes ill-informed questions. There are moments when I must test the patience of a kindergarten teacher, but those I met on this most recent trip were all, without exception, exceptionally tolerant of my foibles and fumblings. So my thanks are offered in abundance to Paul Smith, Victoria Phillips, Robert Wauters, Helen Preece, Michael Reed and Roy Atkinson.

Finally, I never stop wondering how my wife, Rachel, and our four boys, manage to put up with me when I lock myself away to write. *First Lady* is rather longer than most of my books and required even more than the usual amount of endurance on their part. It coincided with major building works at our home. Rachel saw more of the builders than she did of me, yet never ceased to be radiant as she glided serenely through the dust. For me, she is the finest first lady of them all.

Michael Dobbs
Wylye, July 2006
www.michaeldobbs.com